LEGEND OF THE SHADOWS

PART ONE

BOUND BY BLOOD

Alice. E. Johnson

Alice E. Johnson
©AEJohnson 2023
I'm a bookmark. Cut me out and fold me.

Published by Alice E. Johnson, Nottinghamshire, England.
www.aejohnson.online

Content warning! This epic / grimdark fantasy is placed in the adult section of the fantasy genre. Please do not continue if graphic content may disturb you.

Contains sex, violence, and scenes some may find disturbing.

Cover design by ENV Studios & GetCovers.com

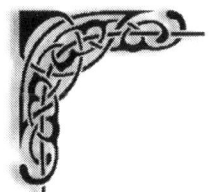

ᚲᚺᚨᛈᛏᛖᚱ ᛟᚾᛖ

1

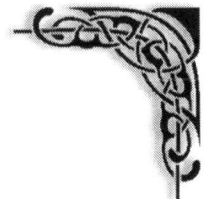

Maude's eyes strayed to the forest in front. A foreboding silence swayed through the branches crowded with dying leaves. Her neat braid of black hair tumbled between the shoulders of her armour. She squinted her maturing eyes forwards. Twitching her nose, she detected the stench of burnt timber, straw, and burning hair. Her slight frame did not carry her armour well.

'It's not far now, sir!' Maude hailed at her commander.

Crisp gravel hurt their ears as the hooves of the horses struck the ground. The birds remained silent as the small company rode quietly towards the carnage.

The commander stared ahead; his eyes wearied. A greying beard and bulging belly saw him struggle of late. Fierce pains hit their heads from the smoke they inhaled.

Coming to a crossroads, Maude could see their destination. Wisps of black and grey embers fluttered down like leaves.

'Farhope,' mumbled the commander. The winter quickened. The long journey all but took his voice. 'It's the later part of his plan. Take the villages. The towns are next.'

'Have we heard from the council?' asked Maude.

'Not since the last turn. Their involvement is limited,' replied the commander.

She shook her head, looking down at the crisp gravel. 'It will displease the king. Knowing the army moves this far north.'

He gave a huff. 'Our attentive king is as informed as his council.'

The air was bitter. She could see the commander's slow blink. A descent into depression seized him.

The weary army entered the battered, fenced village. Sounds of clanking armour echoed as they alighted from their horses. A filthy mass of flesh lay in front of them. Arms, legs, and heads spread in the squalid trodden mud of the village withering beneath them. The summer flies returned for a feast. Dead wolves and horses lined the streets. Chickens and sheep lie slaughtered within their paddocks. Burning homes still blazed. The village stood silent, with only the crackle of flames. Crows and ravens shadowed the search army, feasting on the flesh of the dead.

Maude looked to a crow which ravaged a bodiless head on the ground, tearing the eye from the rotting socket. The ground smouldered. Maude made her way through the village in search of the only thing she wanted to find, hope. Her footsteps squelched. The uncomfortable thought remained with her. 'It had not rained there. It was not water she was treading.'

She entered the only house left standing. A modest thatched cottage in cinders. Bits of wood fell from the blackened frame.

'I hear something!' she shouted. A familiar cry called out to her. She trod over the rubble in the doorway. The roof still smouldered. A strange noise whined from within, the cry of a baby, and oh, what a sound it was.

Maude ventured further, a burnt cradle of hay lie beyond a narrow door. The baby's wail pulled her deeper into the ruins. Crisp, clean linen shrouded the tiny infant. To Maude, it was the most beautiful sign of hope. She gave a look of confusion towards the tiny infant in the dark, smoke-filled room.

'How did you get here?' A beam of light lit the smoke and dust in the room. Outside, the army gathered.

The onlooking army of encumbered men and women gasped as they watched her emerge.

'Commander!' She strode from the ruins, holding the small bundle tight in her arms.

Thundering towards her, the commander barged the onlooking soldiers out of the path. 'Is it alive?' he bellowed.

She lifted the bundle towards him. The smiling face of an infant stared back at him.

'Very, sir,' — she held a confused grin — 'I don't get how, though' — she swung to see the ruined cottage — 'the house collapsed around it. I don't know how it survived.'

'Luck. Perhaps they hid it in the rafters? Either way, we need to get it checked, make sure it's healthy before the camp.' He raised his arm and directed her to the field medic.

The medics would comprise Sharma's from the temples. Thoroughly educated in the craft of nursing and medicine. They, however, had Ulthar, an alchemist of the fae, well versed in the art of medicine. His age spoke of a lifetime of war seen. His retirement proved boring for him.

Long grey eyebrows stretched over his pale blue eyes. His long beard wisped down the front of him. Like an ancient willow tree, his body bent under the burden of knowledge.

Reluctant to present the infant. Maude knew Ulthar's hands were weak. His fingers were like the knuckle of an oak tree.

Ulthar saw Maude approach. 'What's this?' His withering eyes sparked as he observed the infant. 'Take it to the cart. We can inspect it there.'

A wooden cart served as a table. Maude set the infant down. The baby clutched his long grey beard.

'Well done, soldier,' — his smile broadened — 'it's a girl.' Ulthar checked for cuts, bruises, and any form of suffering. The infant was perfect. Looking at the infant's back, he stepped back with a gasp. 'Commander!' His old croaking voice yelled.

Maude felt her stomach twist. Her eyes widened. 'Is something the matter?'

Ulthar's brows drew down, confused he rocked his head. The commander thundered towards them.

'See this,' said Ulthar.

He turned the infant onto her front. On the back of the child, her shoulder bones bulged under her skin. A curious image to observe.

'Is it Torb?' The commander looked at Ulthar, baffled.

Ulthar's eyes remained fixed on the child. 'Torb's are born with wings.' Ulthar nodded and held a look of bewilderment. 'I understand your meaning. It's strange. The skin of this child is fae, you can tell. Her ears have a point to the tip, like mine. I don't understand why she would have those.'

Maude stepped forwards. 'But the child is well?'

With a soft smile, Ulthar looked into the worried eyes of Maude.

'She will live,' said Ulthar, 'we will pass a war camp soon. In the north, close to Bourellis, we can take her there.'

Maude's eyes strayed down to the ground. Her shoulders hunched. The commander spotted.

'It's a fucking baby!' he bellowed. 'Don't be so bloody upset. Do you plan on taking her on the road with you, Maude?'

'No, sir.' Her voice relaxed. 'Apologies. I think I've had too much time on the road.'

'Haven't we all?' he abruptly replied. He came close to her ear. 'Welcome to war.'

She watched her commander storm back towards the carnage of the village.

'I found what I came for!' shouted Maude. The commander twisted. 'Hope. Maybe it's my time to hand in my papers?'

The infant remained in Maude's arms as they journeyed towards the northern camps. Wet snow hissed as it settled on the ground. Winter mocked them. Maude spoke to the child on their journey. Each time she did, the infant lit.

Broken bodies quivered on the battleground. Chaos died as the reality of war hit. Bleeding in what would become their graves, men and women called out for help, salvation, and death.

Turning in the field, Harris Bearwood remained calm. His eyes searched the faces of the dead and dying.

'Return to your station!' his chief yelled at him, anger spit from his mouth.

Harris remained calm. Breathless, and covered with the inners of their enemy. His soot and blood-covered face turned to the chief.

'Where is our commander?' The calm Harris held shook the chief.

'He will return to the castle. Join him there,' replied the chief with a bark.

'Sir, as respectful as I wish to remain, I cannot, and I will not do that, not until we find our commander.'

'You will follow my order' — the chief darted towards him — 'we follow the rules here, and no Xencliff porne, royal or otherwise,' — he looked down at Harris — 'will tell me any different.'

'You seem to mistake me for someone who gives a shit,' replied Harris. He raised his brows. 'Look around you, Saburo,' — Harris lifted his arms, spinning within the carnage of the field — 'you need me more than I will ever need you. Find the commander, or I leave.'

They silently glared at each other. Saburo finally let go of the glare, calling out, 'Our commander! Find the commander.'

'A welcome choice,' said Harris. 'This will remain between us. Oh, and I'm not royal. Something as stunning as this could never come from royal blood. Remember, my mother is the whore of Waron.'

Saburo curled his upper lip. 'You won't be here forever. You'll end up like the rest of them.'

'The rest of who?' asked Harris, spinning to face Saburo.

'The rest of the pond life who believe they can stop an endless war.'

'If this war is endless, and all hope is lost, then why are you here?'

Saburo remained silent. He turned and trampled through the field, standing on the soon-to-be corpses of those alive and dead.

Clinging to life, a moan came from the ruins. Harris stood silently in the field. Closing his eyes, he searched the field by listening. Finally, it reached him, the struggling breath of his commander as he laid on the corpses of the enemy.

Rushing towards him, Harris took a knee. He looked at his commander's hand. Holding a bundle of red flesh.

'It has been a pleasure,' said the commander, congealed blood poured from his mouth. 'Although this is not pleasant.'

'No,' muttered Harris, 'but the battle is ours.'

'Hurrah,' the commander sarcastically replied. A trail of blood dripped from his mouth, landing on his chest where three arrows protruded.

'You can rest now, sir.' Harris furrowed his brows. Unable to look at the face of his commander, he looked at the field instead.

'The Mara will soon arrive.' His lip quivered as he spoke, his eyes were motionless as he glared at the field in front. 'Do one last thing for me. Take the army to Marrion.'

'We take our orders from the council.'

'You must make yourself found, Harris, your brother needs you to.'

'I do not avenge my brother—'

'No, you will avenge our world. Tell them what you have seen here, what you have done, tell my mother,' —he struggled for breath — 'tell her I tried—'

'She knows. But I have a long way to go before I can lead this army, the way you have. Lugus, the world will know your glory. Now, you will rest with the Mara, and I will see you on the bridge.'

'In this life and the next, you will always be my brother,' replied Lugus.

Harris looked at Lugus' hand, still clutching his innards. 'You will not survive this.'

'Then I ask you, my most trusted friend, to pave my way to Fesregoth.'

Harris sighed, knowing what he was asking. 'Do you wish for me to pass on anything else?'

'I fulfilled my life. You know my words better than any,' replied Lugus. He closed his eyes, dropped that which bloodied his hand, and dropped his head back.

Harris stood, standing behind Lugus. He held his head, he whispered, 'In this life and the next.' He quickly twisted his head, snapping his neck.

***

The search army came towards the northern pass. The infant's new home came into sight. On the dull cobbled paths, the stone buildings of the war camps sat uniformed. A misty green woodland to the north sheltered the camp from the wind and harsh weather from the mountains beyond. The crude and often draughty buildings served as a stark reminder of the failing world around them.

'I don't like it here,' mumbled Maude. She trailed along at the back.

The commander twisted. 'It is the best place for her.' He struggled to find compassion. 'Maude, regardless, the child will be better off following her own path. That begins here.'

Maude gazed down. Her stomach twisted. 'I know. I still don't like it here, though.'

'If it makes you feel better, Bourellis is not far north from here. For ten years, I have known you, Maude. All you have searched for is hope.' The commander jumped from his horse; his age showed as his belly pulled him down. 'The puca gather in these woods. That's why hunting's banned this far north. Besides, it isn't your choice.' He took the infant from Maude. Maude's arms flailed forwards.

'One last moment.' A tear welled in her eye.

'If you plan to hand in your papers, find yourself a husband and get your own,' said the commander. His low tone made it hard for the others to hear. 'She does not belong to you, Maude. She belongs to the camp now.'

As the small girl with the deformed back grew, she remained small. Her long locks of wavy blond hair and pale pink skin spelt perfection. Tiny features made for a pretty, yet powerful face. Her flawless eyes were odd. The staff of the camp spoke of the changing girl. Different colours of amber, azure, emerald, and hazel. It enchanted those who noticed. At such a young age, a beauty already shone from her eyes.

For four years, she grew as a secret in the camps. At only four-years-old, she knew the world was cruel, but like any innocent child, she hoped the world would one day prove her wrong.

Spring echoed in the trees. The girl left her bunkhouse early that morning. To collect some small pebbles on the road, pebbles she found interesting. The camp was dull to most, but to her it was bright. It was home. A flittering bird on the path captured her attention. She stood on the path and watched. The morning brought a small rain, puddles filled enough for some sparrows to bathe.

'Good morning,' she greeted. Of course, they did not reply. 'It is a wonderful morning,' she agreed with unspoken words.

Some of the older children noticed her odd behaviour. They would persist in their cruelty. Stood in her tattered clothes, a small pebble startled her, landing beside her.

'That's odd. I didn't call you.' Baffled, she leant down and plucked the stone from the ground. As she stood, a larger stone hit her on the chest. She glanced around the camp; a group of several older boys stared towards her. Unlike the girl, they wore small plimsole shoes. Flour from the mills covered their tattered trousers.

She saw one of the older boys throw a large stone at her. It landed at her feet. She did not flinch as another, much larger rock, hurled through the air towards her. The girl lifted her hand and caught the rock, forcing her arm back.

'Oi! Fucking freak!' shrieked the boy who threw it. He charged towards her.

'I suggest you stop.' Her delicate voice carried her muddled words. A defiant smile appeared on her face.

The boy scowled at her. 'And what are you gonna do?' His eyes turned dark, bullying was not on his mind. Something much darker was. The camps were a place of hardness. He wanted to show her how hard she needed to be.

'I'll break your neck, freak!' Three other boys followed.

The girl glared at him from under her brows. Her chaotic white hair danced in the wind. A storm brewed in her deep green eyes. She lifted her hand towards him. He thundered towards her. She watched as his left arm snapped in two. The bottom of his arm, between his elbow and wrist, flailed in half.

The boy gave a blood-curdling squeal of pain.

Her smile grew in the corner of her mouth as she watched him falter.

'That is what I'm gonna do.' She waved her head.

'I will fucking brain you!' Spit fell from his mouth. His arm flailed, he hurried, trying to hide his agony.

'Not without legs.' A confident smile lit her face.

He fell to the floor and glared at the girl. Terror appeared in his eyes, streaming with tears. He screamed in agony, gawking at his legs. Both showed bone through skin, blood covered the wounds, his tattered trousers covered with splattered blood.

The others watched on as the little girl spun and skipped back towards her bunk house. The boy remained on the damp ground, screaming.

Staff of the camp listened to the boy's story, but they failed to believe him. Until a series of strange events occurred in the camp, always surrounding the strange, Unknown Girl.

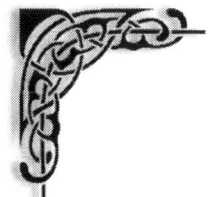

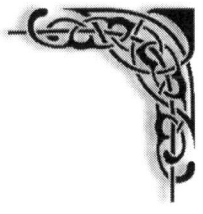

ᚲᚺᚨᛈᛏᛖᚱ ᚦᚹᛟ

2

Nareena strode out onto the cobbled path. Her duty was within the work-mills. Linen, woodwork, and flour were the primary duties in the camp.

The melody of beating anvils punched the air as the older children began their day's work, forging chain-mail, swords, and new delights which would soon adorn the battlefields.

The dust of a dry autumn hung in the air. Pine from the woodland bewildered the senses. Nareena was a no nonsense, heavy-set woman. She saw the children from bunkhouse twelve. They marched down the cobbled path towards the work-mills. A strange rumbling from the bunkhouse at the side distracted her. Bunkhouse thirteen growled beside her.

A popping came from the old wooden door as she peered down. A strange trickle of water appeared. She leant down, her eyes dipped towards it. A torrent of water tore her from her feet. Knocked to the ground, she slid out with a boy beside her. Robb tumbled along the cobbled ground as the strange girl stepped into the doorway.

The girl yelled at him, 'That happens!'

Nareena screamed. She rushed to her feet and hurried towards the girl. Tearing her by her shabby clothes, she marched the small girl to the warden's hut.

The door hurled open, Nareena threw the girl inside. The grey wooden floorboards thudded as the girl fell to the floor. Dust flew from the boards, the bookcases circling wobbled as the tiny child landed.

Sat at his desk, surrounded by chaotic masses of papers, Madoc filtered through his work. He lifted his large brown eyes towards the chaos that invaded his room. He removed his small, rimmed glasses. His aging eyes revealed the lifetime of terror he had seen. His grey brows hurled over his eyes, connoting power. He peered towards the girl with raised brows.

Nareena stood, out of breath, by her side.

'Can I help?' Madoc asked.

'I bloody hope so — ' Nareena grimaced — 'this little shit. She has sent the bunks into chaos! 'tis the second time this turn!'

Madoc stood. 'She's a child, Nareena.'

He moved to the front of his old wooden desk, towering over the young girl. His thick, grey woollen robes hung from him. The girl gazed up at him, her tiny body shuddered.

'What has she done?' Madoc asked.

Nareena pulled on the young girl's tattered clothes, tugging her up to stand.

'What hasn't she done?' she shrieked. 'She is chaos! I can't cope with it. The creature is evil, in the simplest terms.'

'No child is evil,' he growled. He leant down towards the young girl. His brows lifted. 'Perhaps you could explain this to me?'

The girl's eyes flickered.

'The boy, he was being punished.'

Madoc flickered his head. 'Punished for what?'

The girl's eyes widened. She leered at Nareena. She whispered, 'For touching me.'

Madoc's heart sank. 'Touching you?' He narrowed his eyes.

'Like the boy in the woods. He kept kicking me, so I broke his ankle. That stopped him.' The girl scowled with her reply. 'I didn't bring the boar though, that wasn't my fault. Then there was the girl who kept taking my food. I made her plump.' She gave a hearty giggle. She could see a huffing laugh from Madoc. 'But the boy in thirteen, he touched me.' Her voice weakened; her excitement died. 'He has no right to touch me.' Her face became a picture of honest misery.

Madoc's blood boiled, but he remained calm. 'What do you mean?'

'It wasn't the first time.' Her eyes filled with dewy tears. 'The first time someone came in. He stopped. There were other times, but this time, I was alone. I had to get him out. I didn't want him touching me.' Her miserable eyes flickered with a loss of innocence. 'It hurts.'

Madoc tried, with all his might, to hold his anger. 'I need to know. Where did he touch you?' He stooped towards her. 'Point to where it was?'

The girl gazed into his eyes. She pointed at her crotch.

Madoc stood, holding a palm to his mouth as he gaped at Nareena. Rage burned in his eyes. 'You knew of this?'

'Robb,' — She struggled to find her words — 'I have warned him before, many times,' she stammered. 'He can overbear, he's a difficult one.'

'Take him to the workhouse,' growled Madoc. 'Twenty lashes.'

Nareena stepped forwards, shaking her head. She placed a palm on his shoulder, begging him. He rolled his shoulder away from her.

'You knew about this! Take the little bastard or I will!' bellowed Madoc.

Her hands trembled, Nareena rushed from the warden's hut. Her heart pounded in her chest as she searched for Robb. Nareena heard a laugh from inside bunkhouse nine. It was Robb's voice. She made her way to the bunkhouse, where Robb sat on the edge of his bed. Nareena took a deep breath. She gradually opened the creaking door.

'Robb, with me.'

Robb peered up. He still dripped with water. 'It was so strange.' Robb strolled towards Nareena, his eyes widened with excitement. 'She just held up her hands, and that was it.' He saw the plain expression on Nareena's face. His breath became heavy. She did not reply, she did not say a single word. 'What is it?'

Nareena remained silent, bracing the door open with her arm. 'With me, Robb.' Robb stepped towards her. She trod into the bunkhouse, taking a rope hung on the wall at the side. His eyes widened, his smile withered, and died. 'Don't make this any harder. I have my orders. Now take yours.'

'I did nothing!' — tears streamed down his face — 'she needed tellin'. They all need tellin!' At fourteen years old, the camps were a hard place to be. 'Please!'

'Robb, just come with me. If you run, it will be much worse than a tellin' off.' Nareena looked down, her stomach twisted. Lying was not a trait she agreed with. She took the rope and tied his arms. Robb struggled, but her weight overpowered the scrawny boy.

Robb snapped. As the knot tightened, he toiled hard. His eyes turned wild, his muddy brown hair filled with fearful sweat. He attempted to flail his tied arms whilst screaming. 'No!' His voice broke into a terrified squeal.

Nareena said nothing. She dragged him from the bunkhouse. Forcing him across the cobbled streets towards the workhouses.

Robb continued to shriek, 'No! No! I did nothing!' His squealing cry carried through the camp. Children gaped through the windows of the mills and bunkhouses. Anvils ceased working as they dropped tools and stared towards the commotion.

Nareena struggled to drag him across the cobbles. The stones bloodied his trousers as they scraped his legs and knees.

'I have my orders, Robb,' — his squeals disturbed her. — 'You'll be getting twenty. You'll be lucky to live, so I suggest you make it swift.'

Robb was wet with sweat. She yanked him into the work yard. A cross bar at the top of a post showed years of disuse. It was grey and weathered wood. A large man, charged with such duties, peered towards Nareena, who still struggled with Robb. Upon hearing the wailing and hollering. The man raced into the yard.

'He's having twenty,' she ordered. She passed the rope to him. He tied Robb around the post, keeping the skin on his back tight. He left his shirt closed, knowing that the first few lashings would split his clothes.

The caretaker made his way towards his hut at the side of the workhouse. Emerging from the hut, he carried a large whip. Nine ropes hung from a central point of the handle of the rope. They bound six ropes with wire. Three ropes had slight hooks woven into them.

Robb begged. His cries of agony rang throughout the camp as the lashings began. Some children counted. 'One, two, three,' they whispered. Birds fled from the trees. As they came to ten, the wailing ceased. It turned into a dull moan.

Nareena watched on. His scars would heal, but his mind would be eternally broken. If he was lucky enough to get through twenty lashings.

The girl stood quietly in Madoc's hut. Madoc made his way back towards his chair, still outraged.

'Child,' — he observed the girl — 'please sit.' The girl ambled into the chair at his desk. She clambered up and sat. 'What is your name?'

'I don't have one. I've not got one yet.'

Madoc sat back. Pyramiding his fingers to his lips. 'What name would you like?' He opened his hands palm up.

The girl peered towards him. 'I'm not ready for my name yet.'

Her innocence plagued him. 'My dear, you can choose whatever name you wish. All you need to do is say.'

The little girl sat up in her chair. She held a tiny power and spirit. 'Soon, I will be known by many. For now, I am happy being called the Unknown Girl.' Her smile was full and noble. 'One day, I will earn my name.'

He admired the child. Madoc shook his head. 'Then how old are you?'

The girl replied, 'I think I'm five. I was four at the last end, when the trees go yellow. I'll be five.'

Madoc beamed at her innocence.

'Your birth was in the autumn?' The little girl nodded. 'Would you like to spend the day here?'

She held her head low.

'I have some toys in that box,' said Madoc, pointing to a wooden box in the hut's corner. Several books covered the top. The child headed straight for a book. She settled beside the box and read.

Madoc stood, bewildered. 'My dear, where did you learn to read? Lessons do not start until the age of seven.'

The child gazed at Madoc's puzzled face. 'Mother taught me.'

He narrows his eyes. 'Who is your mother?'

'She isn't my mother, she is Mother, that's her name. She visits me in the woods.'

Madoc's eyes drifted around the hut, looking at the woodland outside his window. 'A puca?'

'She is, yes,' — her smile broadened — 'she teaches me many things.'

'The puca do not venture this far south.' He raised his brows. 'Unless for something profoundly important.'

'I like this one,' — she held the book up — 'Malgron. He was a poet, a great commander. The poets can shape this world.'

Madoc nodded and smiled, taking no heed of her strange words. He turned and ambled back to his desk.

Behind his desk was a small door. Beyond the door records of every child in his camp lay stacked on rows upon rows of dusty bookcases. Upon each one, large bound files collected webs and dust. He searched for the child of bunkhouse thirteen.

Sat at his desk. Madoc Peered over the book. He saw the child reading. A sunbeam shone through the narrow window. Scattered dust floated and danced in the beam. There was nothing but a location recorded in her space.

He read, 'Farhope, child discovered alive, assumed to be five-months old. Unharmed, anomaly to the back of the child's shoulder-blades, two protruding swells seem to cause no trouble.'

Again, he peered over the book. He could see the protruding lumps on her back, showing through her ragged clothes. Madoc cleared his throat. She remained absorbed in her book.

'Child?' The girl turned. 'Do you know what happened to your back?'

She gazed at the floor, disheartened by the question. She closed the book and stood. 'They say things about me. They call me names and say my parents hated me,' — she walked towards him — 'I've always been like this.'

Madoc stood and strolled towards her. He towered over her with his hands behind his back. He leant down. 'I think they're wonderful.'

'They are,' she affirmed. 'You don't see it. One day they will be like the torb's. I'll have the power to take the skies from dragons.'

'A dream,' Madoc's laugh grumbled. 'The dragons own the skies with the birds and stars. It's doubtful a fae like you could ever reach them.'

Under the care of Madoc, the trouble abated. Her talent was something she tried to conceal. Madoc noticed many things about the Unknown Girl. Her eyes but also her hair, darkening as the year progressed.

She spent her days roaming in the ancient woodlands. A recent staff member, Dune, became distantly fascinated with the young girl. His mentor, Nareena, stood by him as they watched the girl stray alone into the autumn wood.

‘Keep clear of that one,’ warned Nareena.

‘Why?’ he asked with a sniggering laugh. ‘What has she done?’

Nareena jolted her head, a hard stare of frustration in her eyes glowered at the girl. ‘She don’t work.’ Her tone of irritation grew. ‘Madoc’s little pet. She spends her time in the wood. People say the puca go there. Coming and visiting her,’ — Nareena glared at Dune — ‘the staff avoid her. They say she has powers.’

Dune followed Nareena. She walked back towards the mill-house.

‘What powers?’ Dune asked. The sound of chiming anvils rung around the camps.

Nareena twisted. ‘The kind to get you killed. Now, on with you, I’ll answer no more about the Unknown Girl.’

‘Is that her name?’ Dune asked.

‘I’ll answer no more,’ warned Nareena.

Dune looked back at the small girl, enveloped by the dimness of the misty autumn wood.

‘Mother!’ The Unknown Girl continued rambling through the wood. A rustle in the bush beside her made her turn her head. She held no fear. The late autumn wood was a friend of hers. Others would see mist and fog as frightening, unpredictable. She saw it as magical, beautiful.

‘Who’s there?’

She ambled towards the rustling bush; a few brown leaves moved. ‘Mother?’ She moved the leaves, a black nose and long brown face stared towards her. The face of a four horned deer stood glaring at her. ‘How are you today, deer?’ The deer continued eating the last few bits of green foliage on the bush.

The Unknown Girl continued her day. She did not see Mother that day. Several rabbits, more deer, and many birds gave her company in the wood. She collected stones, leaves, and twigs and left them in a clearing, just inside the treeline. Odd behaviour to most made complete sense to her.

The magnificent city of Cronnin crammed to bursting with trade. Bodies pressed together on the busy market streets. The mighty city stood as an emblem of power and politics. Protected by a towering white marble wall. Only four ways granted access to the city, through four gatehouses. The streets spread like a maze of market stalls and houses. Passing trade trickled through the four gates to the city.

The crooked streets played host to taverns, bakers, butchers, fine jewellers. The hardest sword smiths, and the best horses, all sold on the hectic streets of Cronnin.

Something else haunted the streets there, though. A silent anger mounted. Taxes levied by the council of Cronnin made the people work hard. Those who filled their pockets fast chose death. Fighters were in constant demand during the war.

White walls circled for forty miles around the palace of Cronnin, which stood central to the city. The gargantuan building spelt strength and, to some, greed.

Four buildings reached from the central point. At the end of each, an enormous tower stretched to the sky. Atop each tower flew the emerald stag of Cronnin.

Through the mighty golden doors stood the pillars of power. A step up led into the mighty marble hall. A large fountain in the centre of the hall dominated the magnificent staircase. Split off onto two landings, and a large mezzanine circling. Doors led to the many mighty rooms. Two wooden doors towered over the room to the left. The council of Cronnin met. Elderly robed men made their way into the hall.

A man of power, King Angus Oakwood, paused at the top of the mighty staircase. He caught his hands behind his back. He awaited his council to enter. Fifty years upon the throne took its toll. His face was a picture of youthful age. Eyes of haunting dark blue, set in the lines that a lifetime of worry caused. Heavy shoulders were superfluous to his slender frame. A short blond beard held a few grey hairs. At only sixty-five, he was young, but for a wifeless king, his age concerned his council.

The first door closed; it was Angus's turn to enter. He bounced down the stairs, noting a new member of staff scurrying past him.

He warned, 'Mind your way.'

The woman froze. 'Majesty,' — she gasped, bowing to him — 'I apologise.'

Angus drew a lengthy breath. 'Worry not. I'm assuming you're new. Your name?'

'Maude, sire.' She held her bow towards him.

Angus smiled. 'Well, Maude, lovely to meet you,' he had a bright nature. 'Worry not. I expect a few mistakes. I go in first, then you follow.'

Startled at his grace, Maude gazed into his eyes. It was her first time meeting him. The stories of him being a pompous noble who demanded respect were indeed nothing but stories.

Angus burst into the hall, marching across the echoing grey stone floor.

'Sire,' a disapproving call came from the side of him. He stopped and spun. The man, Ryan, glared down at Angus's side. Ryan was old, a classicist. Long green robes were like that of a temple druid. 'Sire, please.' Ryan glowered at Angus's broad sword. 'You needn't carry them here.'

Angus wore his sword with honour. Black trousers, a red tunic, and green cloak along with long leather boots. He preferred to remain youthful. He was not ready to slip into his role as a tired old king.

'My father taught me very little,' — he pursued his way across the hall — 'one thing he taught is that it's a sword that determines the man. No sword,' — he stopped, looking around the circular auditorium — 'well, I will let you all guess.'

The auditorium circled with wooden benches. In the pit of the political hall stood a single plinth. A small wooden stand set in the centre.

Angus made his way towards the back of the hall. He climbed the dark wooden stairs which dominated the hall. He took his place upon his large wooden throne. It was a shining symbol of Cronnin. The carved throne stood proudly, with all the flora and fauna encountered on Cammbour. The back of the throne created the vast structure. It was a heavy seat for a single man.

The blurred mumbles quietened as a grey-faced councillor took the floor. He shuffled his way to the plinth, bending over as he did. Neat grey hair sat adorn a head filled with spotting wrinkles. His age was ancient, fingers like twigs as he reached towards the stand.

'Gentlemen!' There wasn't a single part age hadn't been unkind to on his living corpse. 'I call this meeting to order.' He had a slow, yet well bread accent. 'Today's order of business. We have several issues besieging the northern camps.'

Maude peered around the door, waiting. Angus noticed her. Holding his hand up, he waved her in. 'The camps in the north?' Angus asked.

Bart replied, 'Issues,' — his battered hands sifted through the papers — 'with the puca and torb.' He glanced around the council hall. 'They are telling us that the camps are showing signs of overcrowding and cruelty.'

As a man with little patience, Angus called out, 'Bart, you're boring me. What is the problem? And can they solve it?'

'Doubtful,' — Bart curled his mouth down — 'the issue isn't with their location; we don't look to have enough of them. Too many children, not enough parents.'

'Fine,' huffed Angus with a lofty tone, 'that's all you needed to say.' Angus stood. His voice filled with power. 'The funds from the camps will remain with them for the next three turns. Send the masons. They roll off enough linen to find the funds. Some additional workspaces as well, the war, Gentlemen, is not settling. We need to be sure we can support our efforts.'

A ringing mumble permeated the silence.

'In the meantime, I will do my best to settle Bushwell and the puca.' The auditorium erupted with discontent; it shook Maude to her core as she leapt up.

'Gentlemen!' — Standing from his throne, Angus made his way towards the stairs — 'Each day we face the same issues, a council hall is not a place of argument, 'tis a place of discussion.' — He walked further down the stairs and to the floor. — 'Until you have calmed, I will not return.' He came to the door. Maude readied herself with another pitcher. 'With me, Maude.'

Grateful he called for her to follow, she hurried behind him. The auditorium erupted.

They passed the corridor to the left and made their way up the vast marble stairs. The thick green carpet stopped any echoes. At the top of the stairs, ancestral kings and queens radiated towards her from the antique canvas. To the left was a long corridor. To the right, a second corridor. They followed the mezzanine to the right and towards the top of the bottom hall. Maude scurried behind Angus. Her hands shook, and legs wobbled. The echoes from the council hall still erupted. They rushed towards the large wooden doors to Angus's chambers.

The guards, statuesque and silent, wore the same neat green tunic. Their long green capes bore the emblem of Cronnin, the white stag. Each wore a sword around their waist and held long wooden spears. The guards parted as Angus and Maude came to the carved wooden door.

Maude stood silently inside his chambers. His quarters were one of the mightiest rooms the palace held. A colossal room stood before her. A large red carpet covered the floor. To the right and left, several towering bookcases stood. Too large to reach from the floor. A mezzanine allowed for bookcases to reach the intricate coffered ceiling. The stench of pipe smoke and parchment filled the air.

Angus lingered by the window. The mighty arched windows stood as high and wide as the room. It was all that stood between him and his metropolis. To the back of the chambers central to the window, his humble wooden desk sat laden with messy papers.

Angus gave a long sigh. He stared from the window.

'It's a shame, Maude.' He twisted to face her. She stood silently by the door. 'My council views this world for its wealth.' He walked towards his desk and rested in his chair.

Maude stood locked on the spot. She held her hands at the front of her, her shoulders stooped forwards. 'It's the way of the world.'

Angus raised his hand. 'Please,' — he invited her in, offering her a seat, — 'how is this world supposed to recover if all that encourages the council are coins?'

'You are melancholy,' she said. Far from shy, this was her king. She would need to tread delicately. She raised her head. 'I was a soldier once, sire.' — As she came to the desk, she sank down into the chair opposite. Her eyes strove to focus. — 'I've never seen battle, but I have seen some of the worst brutalities this world could offer.'

Angus's brow creased as he took notice. He leant forwards, placing his elbows on the desk in front.

'It just takes one,' she said in a soft tone.

Angus held his head up to listen. Her brows gave a sorrowful frown. She stared into Angus's eyes.

'One can change it all. It takes an influential leader to make a good follower. Now, you are the one man to change it, but you are here, behind a desk,' she laughed. 'Arguing with your council. This world needs you.' Her voice became soft, 'If I may speak freely?'

Angus blinked. 'You seem to be fine with that so far. I will not stop you.'

'When I was young, your father frightened me. He intimidated his people,' — she could tell by the drooping of his slight smile she would need to tread lighter. — 'Your father would never bear that change. He used fear to guide his people. You use compassion.'

Angus drew back. 'I admire your honesty, Maude. Many have died for less.'

'I'm just a maid, sire,' she said with a sniggering laugh. 'I know nothing of politics.'

'I like you. I need honesty in the palace. The world has darkened. I need guidance from a soldier who found hope.' He gave a broad smile towards her. He leant forwards. His tone became low and haunting. 'I know who you are, Maude. No one comes through these doors without me knowing who and what they are. You left my army the day you found hope. You left that hope behind.' — Angus leant his elbows on the desk and folded his arms. His voice softened, — 'Why?'

'Wonder,' — her hands loosened, — 'the child had something in her eyes. Destined for greatness. She would not find that with me. It isn't the last I've heard of her. I believe in fate. I believe in the gods. They have not abandoned us. The child will one day wake the gods to listen to the plight of Cammbour.'

'Many of the fae are born gifted. They're vessels for what meagre magic this world holds. Why is she so special?'

'If you were to have met her, you would know she was not just born gifted, she was born as something else.'

Night enveloped Cronnin. The hall became silent. Angus stood in his chambers. His fingers wove together as he remained reclining on his bed. Tensions with Bourellis often tempered on inauspicious. As the night lingered on, Angus came to his decision. The war camps needed a glinting hope, and he wanted to give that hope. The small ally kingdom of Bourellis needed to realise that they were being listened to.

Councillor Ryan stood in the light of the early morning sun within the halls of the council. Councillor Godfrey settled by his side.

'The news is crushing. He repeatedly gallivants and leaves us in turmoil,' blasted Godfrey.

'He believes himself to be a young king,' replied Ryan. His face churned with anger. 'Youth is not what his throne needs. I have spoken to him of an heir for too long now.'

'And even now he cares little for his council, the men who keep this world turning!' Godfrey flung his arms to the empty seats, circling them.

'Not for long, my dear Godfrey,' said Ryan, his elderly brows raised. 'You know who he seeks?'

'The abomination spawn of a tyrant king.'

'Do not let anyone else hear you speak like that.' Warned Ryan. 'Many respect Waron Chen Lu, and Harris Bearwood is no son of his.'

'That's right,' — Godfrey's lips twisted, — 'his mother was nothing but a pity marriage, scraping the filth from the floor.'

'As I warned, do not let others hear you speak like that, whilst most disagree with Bearwood and his tactics, others side with him.'

Angus left the council in tatters. Announcing a visit he would make to the northern camps.

Maude watched the small entourage of the King's guard leave. A small carriage carried their precious king. A view from the courtyard was perfect from his window. Mockery followed their king like an offensive odour.

Sat with his private council, Afie, Angus waved his farewell to the small crowd outside the gates.

'The war worsens,' said Afie, sat in her black lace dress. She wove her hands together on her lap.

Angus's eyes remained on the crowd from his carriage window.

'It does, but improvements are being seen in the west.'

Afie waved her head, her ageing eyes looked from the window.

'You cannot be serious,' — she shook her head. Disappointment covered her curling mouth. — 'He is a berserker. I thought we had discussed this.' Her snapping tone did not rattle Angus.

'We discussed, and I decided against your advice.' He looked back at Afie, who moved her eyes away from his. 'The west has been the worst hit. The moment he joins our army, we win battles. We cannot ignore him, Afie, not now.'

'Bubble, I truly wish you would listen. A man like Harris Bearwood is dangerous. He will see this world in ashes before we win this war.'

'Perhaps, but he is still one of our people, a warrior, bound by blood to protect his brothers and sisters,' said Angus with a prideful tone.

'Harris is not the solution you must seek, Bubble. He's tainted and broken. He will shatter this world before you can restore it. The man is dangerous.'

'He offers me an effective solution to a growing problem. We will see the camps and from there, we will head to Marrion. I can send you back if you like.'

Afie leered at Angus, shaking her head. 'I shall admit, the Commander interests me, The Shadow, a man who has remained notorious yet illusive, but why would he surface now? What has he to gain? Those are the questions you need to ask.'

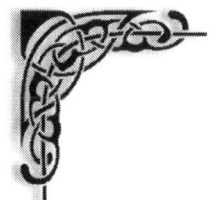

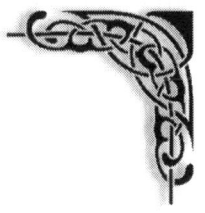

ᚲᚺᚨᛈᛏᛖᚱ ᚦᚺᚱᛖᛖ

3

Dark smoke clogged the air, sent by the chimneys in the bunkhouses. Rich yellow and brown leaves warmed the floor of the forest. The smell of mouldering leaves wafted into the air. Birdsong brought the world to life as they foraged vigorously for winter. The Aenlic moon was ending.

The Unknown Girl woke to a bright autumn dawn. Frost gilded the settled leaves on the ground. The camps were void of the usual sounds of anvils; the mills ceased running. Children lined the streets, disordered. Excitement lit the air.

With her ragged clothes cleaned, the Unknown Girl started her way into the fresh autumn woodland. The crunching leaves brought a smile to her face. She kicked the leaves into the air, lifting her palms to them, drifting around her. A luminous golden glow filled the forest leaves from her hands.

Overgrown brambles on the old cobbled path obstructed her way into the forest. Young saplings sprouted from the path.

Redwoods dominated the canopy. The forest sang with life around her. She came upon a well-trodden clearing. A wide, decayed redwood provided her a seat. She moved closer to see someone had been to her special place in the woodland. She studied an assortment of stones sat on a flattened curve of the fallen tree.

'I didn't leave you here.'

The short grass and sneaking ivy provided the perfect place for her to play. Her exposed feet relaxed among the spongy mosses. The Unknown Girl inspected the stones. The blemishes were her favourite part, wondering, 'What could be inside?'

A four horned deer drifted close to the clearing. Her attention strayed from the stones. A rustling bush to her left stirred her curiosity. She furrowed her small brow, strolling towards it. A soft breeze in the canopy covered the songs of excitement in the camp.

She stepped closer to the bush.

'I see you.'

Two green poplar leaves quivered in the browning bush. The leaves separated. Her smile spread.

'I know it's you.'

The gust in the canopy grew stronger. A woman's voice carried on the breeze. 'Blessed birthday, my Librye.'

The Unknown Girl strode back. 'Thank you, Mother.' She watched as a flash hurried from the bush and settled on the fallen redwood. 'Can I have my name today?'

Mother, as many knew her, had a narrow brown humanoid body, large poplar leaf wings and a pointed acorn head. Her skin was the texture of smooth bark. Mother transformed. A sparrow now stood beside the stones on the log.

'Sit with me, my Librye. A new gift for you.'

She sat on the fallen redwood beside the stones.

'Thank you for my gift. The treasures of this world.'

Mother hopped closer to the Unknown Girl. 'Child, that is not all I have for you.'

The Unknown Girl's face altered, her eyes withered to the floor, a curl to her mouth revealed the terror she felt. 'Worry not, child. I bring to you the gift of dragons.' Mother reached out her wing, touching the wrist of the Unknown Girl. Mother closed her eyes, but the Unknown Girl's eyes altered. All colour dispersed, leaving an empty white shell. Her lip gaped as she gazed at the strange world in front of her.

Where they sat was different. Sat on the side of a hill, the girl looked at the vast field in front. Disorder took over the field and enveloping hills. A mountain in the distance trembled with rage and fury as a white-winged dragon flew close to the ground.

'Do you know what this is?' Mother asked.

The girl shook her head. 'I don't like it here.'

'We are often frightened of our past, for it holds secrets no one must ever learn,' — Mother fluttered to the front of her, focusing the girls' eyes away from the violence of the field — 'many moons have passed since this abomination took place. You are young, my Librye. I do not expect you to understand yet, but this is where your adventure began.'

'My adventure?' She sat back, holding her knees to her chest.

'The story of your people, My Librye. Learning is a gift, one which is offered to a few. Those who are fortunate enough to learn of the marvels of this world must hold it close to their hearts, forever.'

'But what am I learning?'

'You are learning how your ancestors lived and died.' Mother flew to the side, allowing a view towards the field in front. A man lay suffering on the ground, clad in an unusual armour. By his side, the magnificent white dragon rose proudly. As the girl sat, her curiosity spiked, but she did not move.

'What are they doing?' the girl asked.

'They are deceiving, the mightiest beast our skies have ever seen.' An intense light rushed from the figure of the dragon in front. The girl closed her eyes, even then the light stung her eyes. The girl gradually opened her eyes.

'What was that?' the girl asked. She peered at the forest surrounding her. The autumn light through the trees warmed her face, the moss on the ground comforted her feet.

'One day it will all make sense. It is your gift, my Librye. Now, show me your magic,' her voice was a breath of wonder.

The Unknown Girl took a moment to compose herself. Mother was strange, but so was she. Their relationship with nature showed as the girl took the stones. She twirled them in her fingers, feeling each one of them. With her index finger, she touched the top of a stone, a light spark came from her fingertip. The stone smoked, cracking open to expose a bright blue geode.

'Ah! This is one of the rarest. It is vitriol, beautiful, but deadly when handled improperly.'

The Unknown Girl listened to every word Mother spoke. She took another stone, splitting it open. It revealed a vivid pink geode. 'I like this one.' The Unknown Girl gave a wide smile.

'A symbol of love, you're learning fast.' Mother gazed at the blue geode; upset. 'Although, your choices often concern me, Child. You chose that which could destroy before what saves.'

The Unknown Girl was precarious. 'I suppose that sometimes, love and hate are the same thing.'

Mother altered back; the twig-like woman stood before her. 'You seek to be clever with your answers, don't. The answers will come when you desire them.'

The Unknown Girl gazed at the floor. A stiff tone seized her voice. 'Mother, when will I have my name?'

Mother drifted towards her. A thousand years of knowledge rooted in her skin. The world was a part of her. Mother sat beside the Unknown Girl.

'The puca receive names for what they become. When I came into being, I grew, I became Mother. I grew into the carer of all, the nurturing spirit. I am the one they turn to the most.'

'Then what am I?'

Mother's deep eyes softened. Love infused her voice. 'My Librye. I call you Librye. The Librye is the protector, to lead, to follow, through being herself, but the Librye is also a dangerous path to take, a power like yours, it can destroy, and save, but the Librye is something that must learn before it can follow, something that must fail, before it can grow.'

The Unknown Girl tightened her eyes. 'Then my name is Librye?'

Mother rocked her head. 'Not until you are ready for the power of Librye. One day, they will ask you. It's like taking the title of king or queen, chief or commander. It's not something you do until you're ready.'

A pounding drum from the camps sent birds flitting from the trees. They both spun towards the camp. Mother twisted to the Unknown Girl; her eyes were tired, weary.

'There is a celebration,' said Mother.

The girl lowered her head. 'I know. The king is here. The girls were talking about it.'

Mother came close to the Unknown Girl. Her tone was a thin whisper of insistence. 'Then that's where you're needed. You may find your name there.'

A hailing echo crept through the forest from the camp. Delighted shrieks of children rang in the air. The Unknown Girl turned back, indifferent. Echoes faded and died in the towering wood.

'I don't want to be there,' the Unknown Girl whispered. Mother disappeared. The canopy covered Mother; she flew into the grey skies above the imposing forest.

The ancient place spoke to the Unknown Girl. The forest shadows slithered towards her, but she remained. She invited the darkness. A consuming sense of belonging consoled her in the darkness of the mighty forest.

The camp was a dismal place for the King's guard. Angus enjoyed the visits. It provided a welcome break to the tedium of Cronnin. The children squealed with frenzy; the guards remained weary of all, even children. As they came closer to the camp, Angus alighted his carriage. Children thronged around him, and he let them. The guards picked the flailing children away from the carriage. In their droves, they came to get a glance at the king.

Cream coloured soil roads lined the way towards the warden's cabin, which stood alone at the edge of the camp, encompassed by fields. The forest to the north gave Madoc a view of the mighty trees.

Battling through the havoc of the eager and hysterical children. King Angus made his approach to the warden's cabin. Madoc started his way towards him. The steps were now covered with a red silk carpet to mark the occasion.

Madoc received him with his arm extended across his chest. 'A great pleasure to have you here, sire.'

With his arm across his chest, Angus attempted to greet Madoc. 'Yes, yes,' — he rushed his words, struggling through the sea of children, — 'could you call them off?'

Madoc called with an assertion, 'Away with you!'

The children departed. The noble horses drawing his carriage became engulfed by small hands.

'You must be Madoc?' Angus reached him at the end of the path.

Madoc gave a brief bow of his head. 'Yes, sire, please, follow me.' He held his arm out, inviting Angus into his cabin.

Dust no longer covered every surface. His books lined the shelves. His desk was blank of papers. A small inkpot and quill, and a single half burnt-out candle in its stand sat on Madoc's tired, worn-out desk.

Angus stood by the crude window. The dilapidated surroundings had seen better days. Angus glared into the vast shadows in the woods. A haunting darkness veiled flecks of light through the trees.

Madoc looked fatigued; his heart was erratic.

Angus held his head low. 'It's an odd day out there. The rain is holding off, but snow appears to be approaching. In a camp like this, it cannot be easy to keep them all warm?'

Madoc's nerves twisted his stomach. He stepped forwards. 'We have plenty of linen houses.' A nervous laughter held in his voice. 'The north is cold. Unwelcoming in winter, but we have enough to see us through.'

Angus spun. He placed his hands behind his back. 'You wouldn't want more?'

Madoc lifted his eyebrows. 'No, sire.' He joined Angus by the window. They both gazed at the desolation of the unsettled forest. 'It isn't blankets we need, it isn't food, or warmth.' — Angus faced Madoc. — 'It's compassion, sire. Understanding. Someone to show the children that they care. They aren't forgotten.' His grief-stricken voice spoke more than his words.

Angus could see underneath the damaged cobbles, dirty floors, and sloppy clothes the children wore. They cared for the camp.

'Then that is why I'm here. I do, however, need to discuss a new plan. The camps require increasing—'

'How?' Jumped Madoc. 'The camps cannot take any more.' His eyes were gaunt, fatigue ingrained in his aging face.

'Then they'll have to. Children are the future of this world. Changes are coming. You need to be ready.' He turned back to the window, placing his hands on the sill. 'The masons arrive on the next turn. We will build a hundred new bunkhouses. The mills remain for the smaller children. The smiths will also remain. We will add more lessons.

'We need thinkers in this world. A rotation will need to be added. We will also build a training yard,' — turning to face Madoc, Angus raised his brows, — 'I do not intend to tarnish these children's souls further. This world is changing. The war is worsening, and we need warriors.

'The council has proposed a mandatory service. I would sleep better knowing the children here are prepared for such an undertaking.'

Madoc nodded. 'So, the rumours are true. The older children speak of vengeance often. I think that might just work.' A smile grew. He gazed from the window. 'The camps need a focus. These children have had their lives ripped apart.' His voice was soft and forlorn. 'These children are our future. If our future lies with war, then sobeit.'

Watching from the window, Angus squinted towards the forest. 'There's a child in the woods.'

Madoc peered through the window. With a lofty tone, he replied, 'She's fine, sire. She's a remarkable child.' — He stood back and advised Angus. — 'It would be best you avoid that one. She's a different child and can be dangerous.'

A broad smile grew on Angus's face as he twisted. 'Danger invites me. In what way is she dangerous?'

Madoc glanced back through the window. 'I assume your visit isn't just to deliver news of new camps. Who informed you?'

Angus raised his brows. He eased his eyes. 'Dune, one of your staff here has been observing the camps for me. I received a report a while ago from Bourellis. Telling of a boy, beaten half to death.' His eyes roamed towards the child in the forest. The tiny figure was barely distinguishable through the thick brush in the hedge line. 'The Unknown Girl captured his interest. He explained observing various traits from her, certain oddities.'

'Odd is one way of putting it. She is under my care now. The boy you speak of, his punishment, fit his crime —'

'By beating him half to death?' snapped Angus.

'Yes!' Madoc replied, 'the boy deserved more! The girl you see in that forest. He was doing things to her that do not bear mentioning. He got what he earned. Before that, we knew the child was extraordinary. We didn't realise just how special she was.'

He ambled back towards his desk. He spun to the back. A tall shelf at the back of his desk held several books. He took one of the soft green leather-bound books and handed it to Angus.

Angus took the book. His eyes scanned the first few pages. 'What is this?'

Madoc strode towards the window. 'Every event from the Unknown Girl, from the day she arrived at these camps.' He glared from the window. The changeable weather outside chilled him.

Angus asked, 'What's her name?'

Madoc lifted his brow. 'The Unknown Girl. She's not received her name yet. She declines to give one, or to choose one. As I say, she's a strange child.'

Angus stepped from the hut, making his way towards the old forest. The grass was damp under his boots, a cold mist clung in the air, dampening his clothes.

A few flickering glimpses of the girl appeared from inside the mystical forest.

Each step he took rattled with the sound of an army behind him.

'She's a child!' — Angus called as he twisted. Four guards followed him from the hut. — 'I am sure I will be fine; I don't need sitters!'

The men stopped. 'Apologies, sire.' One man stammered, lowering his head.

The Unknown Girl heard the yelling. She twisted to see him wading towards her. A curiosity drove her to the treeline. She watched as the strange tall man approached.

Angus bent under the twisted branches of the forest and made his way towards her. A moment of sheer delight struck him. She was such a tiny child, a pretty face, a glow of innocence radiated from her. Her hair was past her shoulders. The tangled locks of red hair showed it was clear she made some effort with her appearance. She had so little, she still tried a lot.

'Are you the king?' The forest consumed the echoes of her voice.

He replied with a wondrous tone, 'I am.' He battled through the brush and low-lying branches.

'That's nice.' It was not the response he was expecting at all. 'Are you coming to meet Mother?'

A strange thought hit Angus, an awareness of vast potential. His mind galloped.

Angus stopped. 'Who is Mother?'

'She's the puca. She's here somewhere.' The wood was vacant. 'I think she's gone now, but she'll be back tomorrow.'

'Then I can meet her tomorrow. But for now, what's your name?' He narrowed his eyes at the child.

She gazed up towards the king. 'I don't have one. Today is a good day. I may have one soon.'

Angus came close to her. 'May I join you for a walk?'

The Unknown Girl peered at him, bewildered. 'Of course you may. You're the king. You can do anything.'

Angus gave a grumbling laugh. 'Anything within reason.'

The Unknown Girl trudged through the forest, Angus followed by her side. Her tiny feet toiled through the thicket of the old forest floor. The moss-carpeted boulders provided her with some foothold. Her bare feet saddened him. It baffled him she did not flinch at a single stone near her feet. The girl stopped and spun towards him.

'Why did you come here?'

Angus furrowed his eyebrows. 'Why would you ask that?'

The Unknown Girl thought for a moment. 'Because it isn't nice here, and kings always live in nice places. The books in Madoc's hut tell of kingdoms, palaces, riches, and wonders. That isn't what you'll find here.'

Angus raised his brow. He crouched in front of her. 'Perhaps not. Maybe I can make it a nice place.'

'I know, they told me, that you're going to bring the war here.'

Angus stood, startled at her words. Her innocence faded. 'Who told you that?'

'My secrets. They said, one day all elite warriors will be born from camps. One day, this camp will be the camp closest to revenge.' She could see a darkness falling on Angus's face. A look of silent horror captured his eyes. 'It's what the camp needs. The pool of fate has ripples. They all start with you.' His body spiked. His face remained constant. 'They told you though, didn't they, to stay away from me?'

Angus's smile slipped. 'They told me you can be different,' he whispered in a tone of wonder. 'Those are my favourite kinds of people. Tell me, where did you take lessons?'

'Lessons? Mother shows me many things. I like to read the books that Madoc has, but lessons, apologies, I don't know what they are.'

'Soon enough, you'll have lessons. You will learn all the world's marvels.' His promise was worthless. He knew that the lessons he spoke of would teach them how to die and how to kill.

Their trek through the misty forest continued. As they came towards an impenetrable part of the forest, it forced them to move inward. Frosty pine thickened the air. Silence from the king troubled her.

'Do you have children?'

Angus would do anything to change the unpleasant subject of war. 'I don't yet, but one day I would like many children.'

The Unknown Girl halted. 'I think we should go back; it isn't safe this way.'

Angus caught his hands behind his back. He twisted towards her. 'What makes you say that?'

Without a single thought, the girl replied, 'My secrets.' Angus gaped at the girl. 'A pack of wild boar is drifting close to the border of the forest. Last year, they injured a boy. We should turn back.'

The girl's 'secrets' fascinated him. 'How did your secrets tell you this?'

'In my head,' she replied in a lofty tone.

'Very well.' They both turned and headed back towards the camp. The interaction was to get even odder. They came upon the trail in the forest.

The path to the village beyond the wood remained overgrown. Pushing Angus away from the wood, back to the thick branches he clambered through to get into the wood. She watched Angus struggle.

'These were my woods once,' she said, not knowing if he could hear her or not. 'But my secrets are right. It's time to share them.'

Angus emerged from the gloom. He climbed through the low trees. She caught his attention; he noticed the girl stopped near the old, unused path.

Angus watched her lift her tiny hand towards the choked path. The brambles relaxed their grip on the ground. The bindweeds retreated into the darkness of the forest. Dust went flying from the dusty old road below. He heard the loud creaking and cracks of breaking and loosening. A long-cobbled path showed through, stretching into the heart of the forest. Brambles crept back into the ground. The small saplings absorbed back between the cobblestones.

The girl was the most beautiful version of strange he had ever seen.

She skipped back towards him. 'That's better. I keep getting caught by brambles.'

His mind was on fire with questions. He could not leave her in the camp. Anyone could reach her there to abuse or waste her abilities.

'I think today you should receive your name.'

The girl spun. An expression of pure delight stretched across her face. 'I would like that, but I don't know if I'm ready.'

Angus knelt in front of her. His knees thudded to the ground. 'Ready for what?'

'I need to know my purpose.'

'Your purpose is to be the strongest form of you possible. Anyone's purpose is to protect their world, to lead by example, to follow with heart and virtue.' Each word he spoke ignited the Unknown Girl's spirit.

Her eyes lit with pride. 'To lead, to follow, to protect.' It was the answer she had waited long to hear. 'I can be that.' Her lip trembled. 'Then I will be that; I shall be Librye.'

Angus stood. 'I know the name of the ancient ones. They reserve the name of Librye for the Mara.'

'Or those who wish to live by it.'

'Then your name is Librye. Protector of the bridge, and all that is sacred.' Angus could think of a thousand questions for the child. He only wanted the answer to one. 'How would you like to live in a palace, Librye?'

She skipped by his side. 'I would like that. But they wouldn't allow me in a palace.'

'Why wouldn't they?'

Librye stopped skipping. She stood still. 'Because I'm a fucking freak.'

His heart spiked. 'Why would you say that?'

'That's what the other children say. My back isn't right. There's a lot wrong with me. Even Madoc thinks me strange.' Her mouth contorted.

Angus took Librye's hand in his. 'Do not listen to them. Remember, I'm a king. I appreciate nice things. That is why I like you.' His smile grew.

Her voice turned solemn. 'But I am strange. I like it that way, but I don't like my back. Sometimes, it hurts a lot.'

'What is wrong with your back?'

Librye spun; she pulled her tatty cotton dress forwards to show the outline of the bumps on her back. 'A boy once said my dad laid with a torb, and I was a freak. Another said my mum was a porne of the Xencliff taverns, her client was a torb and had me. Either way, they say I was unwanted.'

Angus inspected her back. He decided. They would all know Librye. He could not waste her power in a war camp. A talented mind belonged by his side. At only five, he could mould the girl. The protector, the spirited leader, the loyal follower, whilst remaining herself, Librye.

CHAPTER FOUR

4

Doused in mud, Harris trudged through the centre of the courtyard at castle Marrion. Wails of hardship resounded from the tunnels in the castle's heart, where the viciously wounded would spend their last days.

A temperate rain cascaded on the grounds, raising the stench of blood and filth. Dressed with nothing but loincloths, Sonnin soldiers yanked a chain of men shackled together through the courtyard, towards the dungeons.

Their shattered bodies toiled to walk as the chiefs forced them forwards.

'Wait!' called Harris, tearing towards them.

'Sir, this is all we could find,' said one chief, averting his eyes.

'Twelve men, from an army of thousands.' Harris sneered. 'Line them.' With his order, they turned to face Harris, driven to their knees. 'Twelve of you, from what your master says is the most powerful army in the world, twelve survived,' he taunted, laughing at their sodden faces. 'Get them washed,' his voice calmed. The chiefs looked at each other. 'You will need to look your best before your burial.'

'But, sir, we were told to question and stake,' said one chief as he stepped forwards.

'I am the commander of this camp now,' replied Harris. His mild facade was unnerving. 'One of them will live, the others will receive a proper burial.'

'You show them mercy,' said Saburo, striding towards him with a leg of chicken in his dirt filled hand.

'I show them benevolence.'

'For your Atlanti roots?' teased Saburo.

Harris sarcastically chuckled, before drawing his sword and slashing the chicken from his grip. The leg fell in two.

'My roots are Azorae, but the creatures we fight are distant from the Azorae they once were. A lesson in ignorance, we fight the Atlanti, correct, but the Azorae are peaceful, they are the people our king will one day lead, and today we will show them we have mercy holding the hand of cruelty.'

'And what does that mean?' asked one chief.

Harris casually turned. 'It means that they will give us all they have for a respectable burial.'

The dawn was breaking as Harris looked to the east from the tower of the castle. A crude burial ground was dug. They lined eleven graves. One man stood as a survivor, with a small brown horse. His hands remained shackled, he watched his brothers-in-arms, still alive, in their ultimate resting place. A heavy push of wet dirt covered them, loaded with buckets of water, ensuring they would never get out alive.

'Go from here and tell them all. Tell them what you have seen.' Harris heard the chief say to the prisoner.

'Here!' hailed Harris. 'What is your name?'

The man turned, seeing Harris high upon the tower. 'Gaius!' he called.

'I shall see you another day, Gaius, safe journey!' he called.

'You let one go?' asked the fae commander, having gracefully made his way to the top of the turret.

Harris turned to face him. 'Lister, a pleasure to see you're still alive, as always.' Lister smiled, walking to the side of Harris. 'I let him live, otherwise our victory ends with Cronnin, and Sonnin, of course.' He bowed his head.

'Of course, but freeing our prisoners was not something we agreed,' said Lister, stopping in front of Harris. 'We agreed to wave their rights to information. That was hard enough to persuade Harelda.'

'I understand, but Harelda is a brilliant queen, so I've heard. She will know my reasons, and she would agree.' Harris continued walking. 'The Atlanti hear of our victories and laugh, believing them to be tales, but hearing of the horror from their own warriors, the terror which swept through their army, they will have no alternative but to listen.'

'Many would've returned from war on Atlanti soil. They tell their own tales of Atlanti victory.'

'Well, first, the Atlanti have no land, and second, no they don't, they kill those who are too injured to fight, and those who run, they don't get far. They have a much more savage culture than you think.'

'You speak of them like animals, and yet you are one of them.'

Harris coolly turned to face Lister. 'The next person who remarks I have Atlanti or Azorae blood, I will rip their tongue from their throat, personally, followed by an experimental torture. You may wish to spread the word.'

Lister raised his brows, allowing Harris to walk ahead of him. He would say no more of Harris's lineage, and he pitied those who did.

As the dawn broke, so did the skies above. The ancient forest fell to a frozen vista. Offering nothing but a bitter, windswept, and unwelcoming warning. The snow consumed the enveloping land. Librye drifted to the snow-carpeted path; it provided a simpler way into the forest.

From his slumber, Angus woke. As he emerged from the guest house, he started his way towards the warden's cabin. His footsteps creaked in the fresh snow as he ambled across the cobbled paths.

Madoc stood by the window. A forlorn look covered Madoc's deteriorating face.

Madoc twisted and greeted him with an arm across his chest.

'The winter will be an unpleasant one,' Madoc murmured. 'This close to the Ciele moon often gives us snow, but this will cause some upset.'

Angus stepped into the room. 'Speaking of upset,' he held a low tone, 'the girl, she told me her name.' Madoc twisted, awestricken. 'She told me a few other things.' He stepped towards the window. The cracks in the glass appeared as the deep freeze set in. 'I saw the potential you spoke of.' Angus raised his eyebrows. 'You should've reported it to council.'

Madoc shook his head in mistrust. 'The council would do nothing. Not to sound disrespectful to yourself or the council, the child was safest here.'

'I don't mean the Cronnin council.' Angus's tone became smooth. He gazed from the window, hoping to see Librye. 'I mean the council of Bourellis. The power the child holds is beyond anything I've seen before,' — Angus twisted to Madoc, — 'upon my return from Marrion, I expect to see the child in the palace of Cronnin.'

Madoc swayed his head. 'They will strike me down for this. I shall seek council approval—'

'I'm the king, Madoc!' barked Angus. He gave a cynical expression to Madoc. 'I can defend my actions,' — he glanced from the window, — 'have her in the palace before the Seooer moon. I'll be sending for her myself. By the time she arrives in the palace, I should be returning.'

'This is lunacy, sire. Respectfully, it is unheard of for anyone of nobility to adopt a child of a war camp.'

'Then perhaps if I adopt, it will prompt more people. More will follow by example.' Angus turned towards the door, placing his hand on the knob. 'One of my councillors, before I left, he said too many children, not enough parents. As cruel as it may seem, he was right. It is time we stand for what is right. If there are no children in camps, then they cannot use them as battleground fodder.' He leered over his shoulder at Madoc.

'There will always be a place for the camps.'

'I sincerely hope so, but war is never welcome here, nor anywhere.'

Angus proceeded from the cabin towards the ancient forest. Each step he took resounded a hundred steps. It grated at him. He twisted, the same four guards accompanied him.

'I can't even piss in peace!' he cracked.

The guards stood back. One raised the spirit to speak. 'Apologies, sire, but it is our duty to protect.'

Angus's eyes fixed towards the guard. 'I am your commander! Puca shrouds these woods. Never in the history of Cammbour has a puca harmed anyone. I don't believe they're going to start now. Take the rest of the day to consider your future in the King's guard.'

The men spun and marched back towards the camp. He meandered towards the path. The tiny girl sat on a decayed redwood. She heard him approach.

'If you're here to see Mother, she isn't here.' Her eyes sank.

'I'm here to see you,' — Angus made his approach towards her, — 'I have news for you, Librye.'

She turned to see him entering the clearing. 'Is it about the palace?'

Her tone of confidence astounded Angus. 'How did you know that?'

'My secrets. They told me I need to say goodbye by the end of the next moon.'

'There goes my surprise then.'

'Just remember, we do so much good in this life, but there will always be those who wish to use that good for their own benefit.'

'What do you mean?'

'If more come forwards to take the children as their own, I can show you what could happen?'

Angus stepped forwards. Sitting beside her on the log. He leant down. 'How can you show me?'

'Give me your hand, and I will take you.' She reached out, taking his hand. 'Close your eyes.'

The moment his eyes closed, his heart weakened. Hundreds of children before him, muddied and broken, a simple loin covered their tiny beaten bodies. Their jaws opened as their hollow eyes dawdled on him. Stood in a field of dirt, the children toiled. Back-breaking work lay ahead of them as they turned the soil, planted the crops. A distant laugh from a barrel-bellied man rung through the field. Several men on horseback lashed at the children in the fields. Some moved boulders, others fell to the drudgery, unable to continue.

'I know it may look bad, but the camps keep them safe. It is your duty to do the same.'

'Is nothing sacred anymore?' Angus muttered as he watched the horror in front of him.

'We should cherish life. That is why we protect it. If that means they perish on the battleground, then you know what decision you must make.'

Children lined the road as the carriage and horses rumbled away. Chased from the camp by screaming excitement. Staff members hurled after the children, pulling them back.

Angus sat silently as he stared from the carriage.

'You're troubled,' said Afie.

'It is one way of saying it, awe, shock, horror,' — he leant forwards, breaking his stare, — 'honestly, I do not know what I feel, or if I even can anymore.' He sat back, resting his head on the padding. Afie remained silent, while Angus continued staring from the window.

'The child is unique. Dune told us that,' said Afie. She twisted her eyes, attempting to make eye contact with him.

'I know what he told us, but I do not believe he saw her full strength. The child speaks with the voice of someone else. She is too young to know what she does, and too vulnerable to be left without council or care.'

'And you will provide this?' Afie raised her brows, widening her eyes.

'I will do all I can. We have the resources.'

'She is not a commodity, she is a child. A child who deserves a proper family—'

'Then we shall all give her that,' Angus snapped. He finally peered into Afie's eyes.

'You are a king, Bubble, not that I need to remind you. A king has duties you must not ignore. She cannot take your place, only your child can.' — Afie leant forwards, she eased her tone. — 'I know you care for her, but do not let her presence hinder the future of your kingdom. Many children are born with strange abilities—'

'She is different.'

'I'm sure she is, but how rare cannot influence the success of our kingdom.'

Her secrets helped her. She was merely a child. All needed to be gentle with her. As Librye made her way back that night towards bunkhouse thirteen. An isolation settled in her stomach. Transition struck her, it welcomed her, and she knew what excitement was. The girl would be free from the camps.

The lingering evening affected Librye. She viewed from the window of her small, crooked bed. She stared at the snow. Voices of young girls all around her sounded dull in her moment of contemplation. The cloak of snow sparkled perfectly. An unusual glow over the forest lit the mountain. The moon was the brightest she had ever seen it. A new hope lingered. Her heart thumped hard, knowing she would see the palace of Cronnin.

Drifting towards her bed, a tall girl glanced towards Librye. 'Are you well? You look a little pale.'

'I'm well, Emma. Thank you for asking.' Librye crept to the bottom of the bed. 'And thank you for being kind to me.'

'I'm head girl, of course I'm nice to you. You've done nothing wrong.'

'May I tell you a secret?' Librye's eyes lit.

Emma walked closer, lowering herself onto the bed. 'I can keep a secret.'

'I know who I am. There is a name for me. It's Librye.'

'Well, that is wonderful news.'

'But that isn't all,' she whispered, 'one day, I will be known by all, but please, Emma, be careful, I see a cruel world out there, one I will soon be a part of, and if I'm out there, I can't protect you here.'

Emma rose, giving a cheerful laugh. 'We protect you, Gir… Librye, now, to bed with you.' She lifted Librye, easing her into her blankets. 'Sleep and dream of the world we can make, the world you can make.'

Emma ambled back towards the others, who became quiet.

'Is she alright?' asked one girl.

Emma glanced at Librye, settled in her bed. 'She is fine. She said she has a name now. We are to call her Librye—'

'The Mara of the bridge?' sniggered one girl.

'The Mara of the bridge. If that is the name she prefers, who are we to judge?' said Emma. She looked down her nose towards the others. 'The girl has talent. We've all seen it. All we can hope for is that the world isn't too damaged for a sweet child like her.'

'Rumour says the king is taking her away.'

'Then she will grow among warriors,' said Emma. Her pride silenced them as they slunk into their beds.

CHAPTER FIVE

5

The bleak winter gales died. Rocky terrain turned to beaten rock roads. Scattered pastures remained short in the harsh sun as it blasted down on the land. Life strove to flourish on the borders of Thrasia. The crossing to Marrion would take twenty-five days. The stone and shingle landscape altered, so did their pace and spirits. They left the north and headed southwest. Angry sandstorms churned in the skies, taking days from their already gruelling journey.

The intensity of the orange sun was painful for the riders. They could not wear their cumbersome armour on such journeys, placing them at significant risk. The horses were fast, broad beasts, built for war and speed.

Rolling orange hills of Marrion came into sight. Marrion was a place of agonising war. Chests tightened; their legs weakened. Even the horses could sense the restless moods of their riders as their bodies became shrouded with sweat.

A grey, towering castle stood upon a vast bay on the coast. Its haunting presence stood dark on the bright orange landscape. The cliffs where castle Marrion stood towered over the immense field to the west. The empowering presence rose proudly above the rolling fields below. Which led towards the blue sea of Endrea.

A far cry of sea birds sounded lost as the calls of carrion crows took over.

'Their mission to conquer far out-weighs their intellectual capabilities,' said Angus. He swayed in the rumbling carriage. Small deep circles under his eyes spoke of his burden.

Afie sat opposite Angus. Her hair gathered into a tight bun. Afie wore dark clothing. Her shadow like presence fitted with her title of chief adviser.

'I still think you're being hasty. First the girl and now this,' said Afie.

Angus crumpled up his brow, laughing the comment off. 'Hasty.' He peered from the window of the carriage. The freshly speckled grass pushed through the orange dunes. 'Well, excuse me if I'm trying to impede their assault.'

Afie pressed her crumpling lips together. She too gazed from the window to the approaching barbican of the castle Marrion.

'I know. Harris Bearwood though?'

'What do you know of him?' He coiled back to Afie. His head lifted.

Afie glimpsed back at Angus. She whirled an emerald ring on her finger.

'Born of Xencliff, my knowledge of him is limited. The taverns and Xencliff pornes all talk about him. They call him The Commander.' Her eyes softened and lowered. She gazed at the ring on her finger. 'They say he is a shadow of war. Every tough battle we have, he seems to turn up somehow, and never asks for payment.'

Angus raised his eyebrows. He sat up straight. 'How does he support his travels?'

'We know enough about his family,' explained Afie. She leant down, her elbows rested on her lap. 'His mother, Riah, she married King Waron. We perceive little about his father, Eric Bearwood. He isn't Waron's son,'— she sat up straight, — 'of course, the heir of Waron would be a fresh worry for me. We know that Eric Bearwood was known for his forging skills, also leatherwork. They often favoured him as the champion who would saddle your father's horses.'

Angus sat straight. He gazed from the window as they came onto the barbican of the castle. Shrieks of crows steered them towards the castle courtyard. Guards in the gatehouse ran.

'Your disapproval of the Xencliff king often troubles me,' said Angus. 'We will need their armies. If they include soldiers the likes of Harris Bearwood, this war is as good as won.'

Afie laughed. 'The people are nothing but pornes, philanderers of the most wretched nature. To have Xencliff on our side would mean hardened soldiers. Not the hard we would like.'

Her mocking drove Angus to laugh. 'Therefore, I bring you with me. I always forget just how entertaining you are.'

A large mezzanine surrounded the courtyard; a small stone staircase took them to the keep. Afie elected to head straight up the grey stone stairs. Towards one of the many rooms in the heart of Castle Marrion.

Angus rumbled up the stone stairs. Grey walls echoed an obsolete past. Angus's brisk footsteps pounded across the corridor of the mezzanine. He forced his way towards the master's quarters.

Without considering, Angus exploded through the door. Disturbance took hold of his face. A young beauty stood exposed in the centre of the chamber. The pert young woman gave a loud squeal upon seeing them burst in. She struggled to cover herself.

Shirtless, a young soldier stood behind her. His belt dropped unbuckled, his piercing green eyes scowled towards Angus. Wild black hair framed his face. Slight scars on his skin revealed tales he was not willing to tell. A look of exotic allure flowed from him.

The man Angus was there to meet took the woman's wrap dress and ran towards her to cover her.

'Can I help you?' asked Harris, irritated at the intrusion.

Angus responded satirically, 'I would hope so.' He turned to allow the woman some privacy. She rushed to the bed at the back, throwing her wrap dress around her. 'I presume you're aware this is Castle Marrion. The commander should only use this chamber?' declared

Angus. A desk to Angus's right was immaculate. The walls lined with bookcases, crowded with old leather-bound books.

'I am aware of this! And you are?'

A smile of great satisfaction grew on Angus's face. 'Where is your commander?' He assumed the woman was dressed, so pivoted to face him.

'Dead,' — Harris replied, relaxing his posture, — 'they killed the last one at the end of the turn. Lister, the Sonnin commander, has asked me to replace the commander. Until they sacrifice another.'

Angus's eyebrows furrowed and released. His body lurched towards the young soldier.

'So, Lister must revere you,' said Angus, holding a lofty tone. His arms caught behind his back. 'Are the council informed of this?'

The Commander trudged towards a drink's cabinet beside the bookshelves; he took two glasses.

'Like they give a shit. They know I'm here, but the feckless cretins don't seem to bother with the war anymore. So long as their pockets are full.' He poured the drinks.

Angus flipped his head up, asking, 'And what of Angus?'

Harris lifted his eyebrows and leered at Angus; a smile spread from the edge of his mouth. 'Nice try,' — he nodded with approval, — 'sire, I know who you are. *Why* you're here, I'm yet to work out. My father used to saddle your father's horses. I know who you are.' He held his hand across his chest. 'Harris Bearwood, sire.'

'You've been rather elusive, Harris, difficult to find. Your past is hard to distinguish.' Harris peered up; he handed a glass to Angus. 'Your mother Riah, married to Waron Chen Lu, of Xencliff.' Angus took the glass and drifted towards the desk. The young woman lingered in the shadows. Angus lowered himself into the seat at the back of the desk. 'When your father died. Such a shame, he was a good man. I know you and your brother got taken to the palace of Xencliff. Records on you are scarce.' He leant forwards and placed his glass on the desk, having not taken a single sip. 'Why is that?'

Harris sauntered towards the bed. Picking up his black tunic, he dressed. 'Eric, Eric Bearwood, of Xencliff,' — he walked to the desk, — 'my father, our home, was all taken by the repulsive scum I fight today.'

He sat opposite Angus. 'Odalis and I detested the palace of Xencliff. Nothing but extravagant bullshit to hide the iniquitous, seedy delights of Waron.'

His eyebrows raised. He took a large drink from his glass. 'I learnt a lot from Waron.' His voice mellowed. 'I wasn't made for palace life. When Odalis left, I learnt more. He opted for service with the Cronnin army. I was young, left behind. I was a little shit in the palace. Waron has no male heir. Nine wives and not a single son. He took me under his wing. I never behaved. Never did as mother said. I had enough when my mother set me to work with the pornes, so I travelled.' — He sat straight; his smile widened as he spoke to Angus. — 'I learnt more in the taverns. Xencliff women are,' — he peered at the woman — 'vigorous.' He carried a lifted brow and a vast smile. Harris peered at the glass sat by Angus, still untouched. Harris reached over; he took a sip from Angus's glass. 'It's moonshine, won't kill you. Yet.'

Angus gave a slow bow. 'This is where you became elusive.' He reached for the glass and took a small sip. 'Until you showed up and finished Blodmoor, and Portsmere.' He gave a nod of approval. 'I have heard of you.'

'Then why ask?' Harris perched forwards in his chair.

Angus mirrored Harris, sitting forwards. 'During your travels, I have nothing but blemishes of knowledge. I know all my commanders, but you,' — Angus raised his eyebrows at Harris, — 'you, I am yet to figure out.'

Harris sat back. He relaxed in his chair. He flicked his hands up. 'First, I'm not a commander. Second, I have nothing to tell. I kill the bastards. I don't ask for wage, or title, what's the issue?'

Angus leant back in his chair. 'How do you support your exploits? They do not pay you as a mercenary.'

'The lowest form of scum,' Harris replied. 'Not a single mercenary will ever walk among these ranks. Only good men and women devoted to Cronnin.' Harris tensed. 'During my travels, I earned a title, a nickname.' His smile spread.

The young woman crept further into the chamber.

'We call him The Commander, sire.' Her soothing tone was one of tenderness.

Angus raised his brows. He gave a brief shake of his head. 'You're not a commander,' said Angus.

The woman strode forwards. She moved languidly towards them. Frightened of her king.

'He's our commander, sire. Before he volunteered, Harris was the one protecting the taverns.' She gazed at Harris. 'He was never a porne like me. He was a gentleman. The Atlanti caused issues. Harris always seemed to be there.' Her smile raised towards him. Angus could see the gleam in her eye. A curious bond between her and Harris showed on her youthful face. 'Always when we needed him, always in a dark corner, from the shadows, he would rise.'

Harris sat further back; his chest thrust out. He lifted his brows, placing his fist under his chin to lean, staring at Angus with a confident grin.

Angus's eyes widened. 'Well—' Angus struggled to find his words. He puffed his cheeks. 'I'm lost.' He exhaled.

Harris rolled his eyes; he took a heavy breath. 'I spent my time in the taverns. My father always used to say, to find a fight, find passion. The unstable relationship between him and my mother taught me a lot. Waron loves his spirited women, hence, he married my mother.' He took another drink, waving at the woman to join him. He took her hand and gave a loving kiss on the back. 'You can leave, thank you.'

Turning back to Angus, Harris told him, 'When I left Xencliff, I left to find Odalis. We both despised the place, apart from the obvious exchange of bodily fluids. I hated the place. Long story short, I left, spent a long time in taverns, killing random Atlanti, fucking many, many women. That's where I earned the title of 'Commander.' I found Odalis among the camps of the Narra army.' His eyes drifted to the floor.

'And?' Angus leant further forwards.

Harris lifted his eyes to his armour, which stood proudly on a wooden pole towards the back of the wall beside his desk. Angus swivelled to see it. He stood. Horror took hold of Angus. He felt the strange leather scales on the arm of the armour, a feel of solid velvet.

Angus muttered, 'Lizard skin, so the legends are true.'

Harris took another drink from his glass. This time, he finished it.

'I arrived at the camp. Odalis joined the Narra Army. The dragons of old lit the skies.' Pain was in his voice. His eyes wandered towards the armour. 'I saw Odalis. He could see me riding towards him. I tried to stop him. It was too late. The dragon took him from the ground, plucked him like a defenceless fucking grape, and yanked him in two. It had no heart, no compassion.' — He glared at Angus, who listened. Harris gave a menacing laugh. — 'Can you believe that?'

His eyes drifted towards the desk. He wrapped his arms and rested them on the desk in front. 'I couldn't let it live. It took down half our army. I'm from Xencliff, born of rage. I took the bastard thing with one shot. None of them thought about the eyes.'

Angus ambled back towards the desk. 'Don't make a habit of killing dragons, Harris.' He sat and gaped towards Harris, waiting for him to finish. Harris ran his finger around the rim of his glass.

'What happened after that?' urged Angus.

Harris broke his silence, his eyes fixated on Angus with a curling brow.

'Not long after, I used the scales to fund my time with the army. Dragons do moult; however, the hard scales underneath are stronger, lighter. I used a solution, formed the scales for my armour, and sold the rest.'

Angus shook his head. He sat back. 'Why not just join?'

'Freedom,' — a delicate tone adorned his voice, — 'I choose where I go, what I do, who I do.' He smirked.

'Why did you choose Marrion?'

Harris stood with his glass in hand. He reached for Angus's, but he still had plenty left. He ambled towards the cabinet.

'The Golden war, Lugus gave his last words to me. He helped so many, and now I believe I can do more.' He poured his drink and spun back to face Angus. His brows lifted. 'The Atlanti have stronger forces than you give credit, and they're rising.' He marched towards him and lumped back into the chair. 'Battles are raging, and the kingdom is slow to react. Sonnin and Cronnin's blood is being spilt, yet nothing is being done.' Harris gritted his teeth. He leant back and tried to calm himself. He placed one hand on the desk in front. 'You need me.'

Angus sat back and raised his brow. A consuming curiosity grew. 'An astonishing statement. We have survived without you before. What makes you think we need you now?'

'You barely survived. The army of Rathen increases daily. The Atlanti are greater in numbers than we are, but with my tactics, as much as they are frowned upon, they work. I can end this. All I need are the funds to do it.'

'It's all about wealth, then.'

'I'm a commander in the taverns. I don't need the title, but the wage would be nice.'

Angus could see past the pompous exterior of Harris. His well-groomed appearance was a show of confidence. Every word he said carried pain. He could not hide from the attentive king.

'It would be my pleasure to place you here, as commander of the Narra army,' announced Angus. He stood and sauntered closer to Harris. 'On one condition.'

Harris nodded. 'I'm sure we can compromise.' He leant his arm on the chair and held his chin.

Angus leant on the desk. 'End Marrion.' His voice was soft and looming. 'I have fought hard in the realm of politics, opening a new title. I am going against everything my council has suggested, everything my advisers have told me. When you're through with Marrion, I will give you the title of Chief Commander. I'm impressed with your conduct. To live in shadow, have so many speak of you, and seen by none, it takes cunning.'

Angus rose. He took his glass from the desk. 'Marrion is our fortress, it's a vital trading port with the west. It would please the monsters in Thracian waters to see our vessels diverted.' — Angus strode with his glass towards the drinks cabinet. — 'You're no longer needed at war, once Marrion is over.' With a raised brow, he twisted to face Harris, who sat silently in his chair. 'You will be crucial everywhere. Which means I will second you to Cronnin.'

Harris rose. His eyes softened, leering at Angus. 'Now, my compromise. I don't approve of the council's strategy throughout this war.' He searched Angus's eyes for a response. 'If I accept the position, they leave matters of war to me *entirely*.' His brows lifted.

Angus replied with a deep grumbling voice, 'Deal.'

Angus left, making his way towards one of the larger chambers at the end of the castle mezzanine.

At the top of the eastern ridge, a battle buzzed in the air. Neither side would call a retreat. The battle tore into the night. The courtyard of the castle remained lively throughout the night. Angus could get no sleep. The confusion of war was all he could smell. The rancid stench of battle put many off returning. Festering blood, ordure, sweat, and filth seeped into the pores of the skin. It clung to the heavy velvet drape in his chamber and drifted in on the heated breeze.

He'd had enough. Angus left his chamber to be followed by his guard. Unlike the children's camp, his guards remained close, and he welcomed it.

Slight fire flowers lit the entrance to the Commander's chambers. They were an extravagance often seen in palaces and the homes of the fae. As Angus flung the heavy wooden door open, a cry of passion greeted him.

A woman lay on Harris's bed in the throes of passion, her fingers wove through his long locks of black hair.

Angus hollered as loud as he could, 'Harris!' A different woman stared back at him.

The woman, horrified, gave an ear-splitting scream. She spun and grabbed the silk sheets to cover herself. Harris pulled his head up from pleasuring the young woman. He still wore trousers. He swiped his arm across his mouth, giving an exasperated sigh.

'Apologies, Carrina,' — his eyes rolled, he rose from the bed, — 'you'll have to be done for now.' Harris stood.

'A battle is raging,' Angus began. He did not remain calm. 'And all you seem to care about is getting your cock wet!'

Harris drew back. He raised his eyebrows and threw a heavy sigh. 'In case you didn't notice, my cock is dry. So this is what my life is to become?' He sighed, gazing towards Carrina.

Angus did not take the comment light. He bellowed, 'I don't care what part of your anatomy you plan to moisten! A battle is erupting. You are here, you should be there!'

Harris sauntered to the drinks cabinet. He poured two glasses of moonshine. He handed one to Angus. Angus slammed his glass to the desk. Harris gave a full smile.

'Worry is all you do. I don't sit idle at war. I'm waiting.' His calm exterior cooled the fiery temper of Angus. 'Come. I'll show you.' He drank his moonshine. It was a blast of bitterness which revived him, burning his stomach as it hit his gut.

Harris threw on his black tunic. He took the breastplate and helmet of his lizard skin armour. Threw his harness strap filled with daggers over his shoulders and buckled his swords. He took his green cloak and left.

A storm moved across the castle mezzanine. Stood in the centre of the courtyard was a striking black horse. The black stallion stood proud and still. Adorned with black lizard skin armour, awaiting his orders. Angus's horse, Aridius, did not stand as tall or as impressive.

'On, Svend,' Harris told his horse. Svend started his way through the courtyard to the barbican.

He accompanied Angus to the northern precipice. They watched from the plateau as the butchery of battle roared in front of them. A distant view of the ocean reflected the moon as it bounced in the calm waters. Sounds of clanging swords clattered towards them. The harrowing sound of hailing and yelling turned to a dim commotion. The air was clammy on their skin. An eerie silence enveloped the plateau where they settled. Several large fires blazed in the field, giving light to keep the armies fighting.

'Keep watching.' Harris rested his arms on the back of Svend. The commander took light breaths, relaxing his eyes.

Angus waited. He wanted to see what the young commander had planned. He hoped to see a savage commander. What he saw was barbarous. Harris lifted his arm, making a tight fist. From the back, the mighty blast of a horn echoed towards the battle. The Cronnin army fell back, but that was not the call for retreat.

Again, Harris lifted his arm, his fingertips pointed to the skies. He slammed his arm down. A barrage of arrows flew from the cliff behind them. The black night skies covered the traces of the arrows.

He failed to impress Angus, who remained silent beside him.

'The Castle Marrion isn't just a castle,' explained Harris. His voice carried secrecy; a firm knowledge strengthened his voice. 'They also used it as a way in.'

Angus furrowed his eyebrow. He shuffled his way around on his horse towards Harris.

'A way in? For what?' asked Angus.

'Who?' Harris corrected him with his head held high. 'Marrion was a mining town. It all ceased when the war moved west. The coblyn used the mines as homes for a while, but they are also perfect for something else.'

They dismounted their horses and trudged to the edge of the cliff. Angus peered down. He could see the savagery of his new commander. He heard a surge of water. Angus inspected the cliff. Thousands of mining holes scatted across the face. A golden liquid poured down the cliff. A tumbling waterfall fell into the drudgery. Smoke poured from the holes, but it was not fire he was pouring. It was something much worse. Liquid engulfed the battle ground below. Upon reaching the Atlanti, blood-thickening wails echoed towards them.

Angus stood baffled, seeing them squirming in torturous pain on the ground. A peculiar smell of sharp burning drifted up to meet them.

'What is happening?' Angus gave an astonished glance.

Harris stood calmly. 'The mabeara have supported this. Vitriol oil, masses upon masses, of vitriol.' They peered over the cliff. Harris stood back as the dead smoke floated up on the light breeze. The hollering deafened those on the ground. On the cliff, it was a distant whisper of agony. 'They are the miners of this world; they know where the blue crystals grow.'

Angus remained with a turned down mouth of disgust. Harris reached his hand out, placing it over Angus's chest. Two guards stepped forwards. Harris gave a piercing glower towards them. 'Step back, sire. The smoke will burn your eyes.' The guards stepped back.

'You're playing a dangerous game, Commander.' Angus spun back to his horse. 'A very dangerous game indeed.'

'I know, but if danger will win this, let the games begin.' Harris sneered.

Upon arriving back, Harris followed Angus up the stone stairs. The atmosphere in the castle was forlorn. Many returned with burns. They didn't look at Harris with contempt. They observed him with pride.

Angus silently stepped into Harris's chambers. A putrid churning was in his stomach, a mist of sweat covered his brow. Harris made his way towards the drinks cabinet.

'I don't sit idle. Tomorrow, if the Atlanti call the horn, I will be there,' said Harris.

Angus trundled towards Harris. He snatched the decanter from him, pouring himself a large drink. 'It must end,' he murmured.

Harris lifted his hand to stop Angus from speaking. 'A king must not engage in direct battle. One day, you will lead these people, when they accept you are their true king.'

Angus stood, horrified. 'This is not battle. This is barbaric!'

Harris flung his arm out. 'And what they do isn't? You cannot get involved. One day, you will be the king of these people. It was your commanders who did this, your army, but never your orders! We do this to survive, to win. Praise me when this is all over.' Angus glared into the room. 'It's war they chose. We gave them that.'

Angus relaxed his posture, his shoulders hunched over. 'How many must die before we can just live?

Harris's eyes widened. 'All of us.' His voice became tender. 'We fight for freedom, but freedom isn't free. It's paid for by the blood of our children, and our children's children. Life comes at a cost.' Harris walked towards the desk. He sat in his chair. Angus followed.

'I came here to end this battle. I knew there were few others. Since being here, three battles have begun. Countless villages lie in ruins, and the council believe all is well.'

Angus glared towards Harris. 'Where there is death, life will flourish. Perhaps you are what we need?' His voice trembled, unsure.

Harris sat forwards; he folded his arms onto the desk in front.

'The council does not favour your ability to cause chaos. I favour it, though, and that's all that matters now.' Angus eased back into his chair.

Harris's smile widened. 'At only twenty-eight years old, I have already seen enough war to fill a lifetime. Everywhere I go, I bring chaos.' Harris gave an intimidating glance from under his eyebrows. 'Just make sure the council is ready.'

Angus sat forwards. Harris did not let his look go. 'The council of Cronnin is a challenge. They will leave me be, having a figure of arrogance there every day.'

Harris barked, 'Arrogance? I've earned my arrogance. Not only by ending battles you know of, but by turning Atlanti armies from entire villages. They fear that which they do not understand.' He fell back in his chair, raising his brows. 'I have saved more than it is healthy for you to know. My arrogance has saved many, and if they think me arrogant, let them. I couldn't give a shit.'

'Whilst I would enjoy being regaled by stories of your crusade to become The Commander. I return at dawn. Finish here, return upon my command.'

'As you command, sire.' Harris bowed; his smile continued to flourish. 'I'll see you soon.'

Angus liked his new champion. Harris was honest. He did not hold back on his language towards Angus. Harris dealt with him like he would any who came across his path. He was not one to repress his words.

The roads back to Cronnin were exposed, dotted with crumbling shingle rock. Many of the dwellings stood deserted. Cronnin's plains gave an eerie look into their future. If the war advanced, on an unfavourable path.

'Do you think him worthy?' Afie glared from the window of the carriage.

'He is very worthy. Whether he complies is another question.' Angus took a pipe from his trouser pocket.

Afie threw a frightening glance towards him. 'If you light that, it will be the last thing you do. I'm still unwell. Pipe weed is something I could do without.' Angus placed his pipe back in his trouser pocket. 'I have a doubt, Bubble,' — her voice spilt with a sorrowful tone, — 'the people of Xencliff are thoughtless. They do as they please.' Her eyes strayed towards him. 'Harris Bearwood isn't just born of Xencliff. He is the personification of the place. He is a shining symbol of unmanageable thoughtlessness.'

Angus sat back. He shook his head. 'Why do you scold him?'

'Xencliff are volatile, most of the mercenaries are from Xencliff—'

'He hates mercenaries. I saw the sincerity of hate within him when he spoke of them.'

She rocked her head and blinked. 'Harris is much like Waron. His need for extravagance, showmanship, let's just hope, it's not just a show.' Her deep brown eyes stared towards the worried eyes of Angus.

'I am certain, beyond measure, he is the man for this.' She was his maid once. She was the woman who cradled him when his father died in his arms. Everything about Afie spoke of the mother he always craved. He longed for her to see peace before the otherworld greeted her.

'Remember, Bubble, he is just one man. Can he handle it?'

'He is a large man; I am sure he can.'

'I only hope you are correct in what you are doing. You will learn more about him than you care to know.

Something you may choose to know before this undertaking. Harris Bearwood has Atlanti blood.'

'I know, Afie, but he has proven enough to me.'

'I cannot bear to see you disappointed again, Bubble.'

Her age was not on her side. She served Angus. A man who lived in shadows was the only light that Angus found.

For a full turn, the Cronnin palace was in disharmony. Something was coming to create more conflict with the Cronnin council. Bitter elderly men watched a carriage arrive through the imposing gates. Turrets teemed with guards as the carriage approached the main gate. The courtyard was brimming with the King's Guard as they awaited his arrival. A guard stood at the carriage, the door squeaked open. Librye tiptoed out.

A simple cream dress sat clumsily upon the small girl's frame. Small black slippers now covered her feet. She was not used to wearing shoes. She braided her hair to the back of her. Her eyes filled with awe as she peered at the architecture before her.

She stared towards the colossal palace in front. Her mouth was wide, her eyes lingered on the very top of the palace walls.

'It's so clean,' she whispered to herself. A bright wondrous smile covered her face, showing her bright white teeth.

Councillor Connor stalked forwards from the stone steps to the palace. Scampering forwards hunched over. His grey cloak tripped him.

Connor called out, 'What is this abomination?'

Uproar emanated as the councillors made their way towards the child. The chaos caused her to jump back in fear. Librye lifted her hand.

They held back. A well-known face glared at them. Grendel towered from the carriage, alchemist to Queen Harelda of Sonnin. A tall grey figure and broad shoulders. He was the epitome of the mighty power the ancient alchemists of their world held. A clean grey beard and maddened blue eyes forced the council to stop.

His rich voice greeted them, 'Good morning, Gentlemen.' A smile increased. He stepped onto the gravel of the Cronnin path. Librye softened her arm and dropped it to her side. She sheltered in the shadow of Grendel's dark blue robes.

Connor stepped forwards. Bowing towards him.

'Lord Grendel,' he greeted with a quiver in his voice. 'What draws you here?'

Grendel stepped from the carriage, towering above them all. His unusual size was intimidating. The fae were often smaller than those of mixed blood, but Grendel was not all fae.

Grendel's tone swelled with mystery and charm. 'I deliver a gift.' He leant towards Connor. 'She is far from the abomination you so claim. Hold your words, councillor, else it will force me to place them back in your mouth for you.'

Grendel commenced his way towards the council, Librye followed beside him. Her glimpses towards Grendel reassured her.

'Who is the child?' councillor Adamar asked. His pale face glared down towards Librye. A bald head reflected the light of the sun.

Grendel gazed towards Librye. 'This is Librye.' He raised his arms to his side and held his palms up, announcing, 'She is to live here, with you, as the king's ward.'

'Outrageous!' called councillor Omar. He thrashed his heavy arms in the air while stepping closer. 'He's said nothing of this!'

'Well.' Grendel's mouth pulled down. 'You know now.' Marching towards the steps, Librye followed, remaining in his shadow. The council jostled their way behind him.

The mighty doors opened, Librye gawped up to the towering beauty. Her head spun around. She saw a woman holding a basket of clothes.

Such a modest child caused a tremendous uproar. The council followed Grendel, rushing his way into the council hall.

He spun to Librye, who followed. 'Wait here, little one.' The doors slammed closed. Librye stood, baffled, and overwhelmed by the magnitude of the palace. Silence hit her. She spun in the halls. She could hear nothing but the odd few sounds of rustles from the statuesque guards.

Maude meandered towards the small girl. She placed the basket on the rim of the fountain. Ambling towards the courageous girl, she spun to the side, leaning down.

'My name is Maude. What's your name?'

Librye spun; a captivating smile shrouded her face. Her battered clothes saddened Maude.

'I'm Librye.' She twisted to face Maude. 'I don't know what's happening.' She shook her head and lifted her eyebrows. 'I'm waiting for the king.'

Awe seized Maude. Her linguistic skills were exceptional for a child so young. Maude stood up straight.

'He should arrive soon. He's been in Marrion. I expect he will be back before Seooer. Our king likes to take his time.' Maude strolled towards the fountain. Librye followed. 'Roads are dangerous, but he is safe.'

'I know,' Librye held a very sure tone. Maude furrowed her brow but asked no more. 'He should be home soon. The weather is clear.'

'I take it you'll be staying for a while. I can show you to your chambers if you wish?'

Librye's eyes grew towards Maude. 'I have a room?'

Maude smiled. She led Librye up the stairs. 'There are many rooms in the palace. I can find the perfect one for you.' As they came to the top, she took her towards the east wing. The towering walls in the palace engulfed Librye. Maude took some keys from her pinafore. Librye stepped inside the room as Maude unlocked it.

A shower of blue and green fire-flowers cascaded from the ceiling as she stepped in. Pale green walls surrounded the room. An immense double bed on the right, adorned with silk green sheets. A thin drape cascaded from the window. Where a small round balcony overlooked the gardens and city beyond. To her left, a small washroom, beside it, two towering doors; upon opening the doors, the room was empty.

'I think we'll need to get you some fresh clothes.' Maude remained behind her. The staggering look of joy on Librye's face warmed Maude.

After seeing the kingdom's treasurer, Maude and Librye spent the day in the large city. Quality silk dresses, linen pinafores. Velvet cloaks, woollen jumpers, leather shoes, and boots. All things Librye were not used to. The dirty, itchy rags she wore would become a distant memory. Librye arrived at her new home.

'There she goes again,' said Helen, stood by the door to the king's chambers, she watched Librye skip around the corridors.

'It's such a shame, really,' replied Evan, the guard beside her. 'They take her from a world she hates to one filled with such miserable lies.' He glared at the councillors in the halls below. 'They don't even see she's there.'

Librye squeezed past two of the councillors who stood talking in the hall.

'It's no place for children,' said Helen, stepping to Evan's side. 'But neither are the war camps. Plus, if you heard some of what they have been saying about her, you'd know she's in the perfect place.'

'I only hope you're right, and that they haven't plucked her up as a symbol of hope, only to exhaust and ruin her.'

'Like Harris Bearwood?' Helen sniggered.

'Yes, well, we all know that story.'

Librye skipped through the foyer and towards the galleries at the back. Sitting at a large wooden table, she looked at all the staff members with a wide grin.

'More apples?' Mocked Gethen. 'You'll have them wondering who we're feeding down here.' He placed a bowl in front of her, filled with apples, grapes, oranges, and strawberries.

'I loved your pastry last evening, it was delightful.' She complimented with a full smile.

'That was Rebecca's,' replied Gethen.

'Oh! Where is she?'

'I believe she's outside, skiving. If anything is normal around here,' he replied. Looking out of the door at the back, he could see Rebecca standing with a tall guard on the green grass of the palace grounds. 'Yep, there she is, not working as usual.'

'She likes her secrets, like me,' said Librye.

'Only yours are secrets. Hers is gossip. That's the difference.'

'Ah, back again I see, madam?' said Calven, his dirty boots caused some discomfort in Gethen.

'How are the horses today?' Librye asked.

'They are well. They await the day you can ride them.' He reached over, taking two apples from the bowl. 'One for Rogue and one for Stella.' Calven ruffled her hair before leaving. He quickly turned, taking out a small bunch of sprigs from his pocket. 'Before I forget, your flowers, madam,' he said with a wide smile, presenting them to Librye.

ᚲᚺᚨᛈᛏᛖᚱ ᛊᛁ

6

The Cronnin palace echoed with the blast of slamming doors. The city beyond the gates remained curious about the young Librye.

'They're saying she has a gift,' whispered Elsa, stood on the corner of Little Street with the well-known gallery help, Rebecca.

'She is gifted, that is for certain. I don't know what the people have heard, but I know this. She isn't dangerous, but she is one to watch.'

'Ain't the last we've heard of her, then?'

Rebecca lifted her brows, leaning with her back to the wall of The Little Flour store. 'Well, if Angus has his way, he might even make a wife of her when she comes of age.'

'Ugh.' Elsa glowered at the pavement in front. 'He is old enough to be her grandfather, and he plans this?' Her look of repulsion had many heads turning.

'No, that is just part of the rumour of the palace. I believe she is a tragic symbol of hope. They will educate her in the palace, and manipulate her into believing she can win unity in our lands, only to be crushed like the others.'

'And what of Bearwood?' Elsa's demeanour changed. A look of elation swept her face.

'He still battles in Marrion, but it is doubtful he will return. Marrion is abundant in Atlanti warriors. The battle will be theirs.'

'You sound disturbingly sure,' said Maude, stood at the side of Rebecca.

Rebecca set straight. She hastily twisted to face Maude. 'It is the rumour I hear.'

'A rumour,' said Maude. She caught her hands behind her back and held her head high, staring down her nose at Rebecca. 'Such rumours are enough to see you in the first quarter for treason. Hold your tongue, girl. Or I shall remove it for you.'

Rebecca gave a tense bow to Maude. 'Apologies, I simply repeat that which I have heard.'

Maude shot forwards, forcing Rebecca back. 'You hear poisonous lies, and your forked tongue spreads them. End it now, else I will.'

Rebecca watched Maude start back towards the palace grounds, away from the hectic city streets.

Councillors scurried as speedily as they could through the halls, escaping the strange young guest.

'Why are you wearing those robes?' Librye asked. She pursued Connor through the enormous hall.

'Because I do,' Connor replied, flustered. He slipped away into the council halls, slamming the door behind him.

'How old are you?' she asked Devon, as he drifted towards his room.

'I'm one hundred and ninety-four, not that it's any business of yours,' he derided. Again, a door crashed in her face.

Doors blasted in Librye's face as she awaited Angus's return. Maude followed the young girl as best as she could, but with her duties in the palace taking up much of her time, she grappled to keep a regular eye on her.

Maude scrutinised her every move. Only one councillor observed Librye closely. Kailron, much younger than the other councillors, watched as Librye bound about the hall. The shadows obscured his prying eyes.

‘She interests me,’ he said to Maude. Stood on the edge of the west wing to the councillor’s chambers.

‘I watch her closely, my lord. She is still only a child,’ she sheepishly responded.

‘That she may appear to be.’ His eyes slid to Maude; his darkened eyebrows shadowed his eyes. ‘We all know she is something much greater.’

‘What makes you say that?’ Maude wrapped her hands together in front of her.

He held his head up, watching Librye skip through the hall and up the stairs. He wove to face Maude.

‘Seventy-two, that is how many camps our King has visited in the past few years, never was a child fetched or accepted into his care.’ His head twisted to the side. He glared at Maude. She looked at the ground, unable to look him in the eyes. ‘She must hold something special for him to be so infatuated.’

‘Innocence, perhaps?’ Maude replied, still staring at the ground.

‘Innocence, like all the others?’

Maude looked up. His lingering eyes unsettled her, but she held a brave tone. ‘He sees something in her, law supports his decision. The council should, too.’

‘Indeed, it must, but only for the good of this kingdom.’

‘If I were a simple woman, I would suspect a hint of fear in your tone.’ She swung around to face him, gaining power from his words. ‘She is but a child. There is nothing to fear.’

’Perhaps,’ he gradually answered. Kailron turned and gently strayed down the hall towards his chambers.

The autumn dawn welcomed a gathering of starlings in the woods. The trees stood stark, ready for the winter sleep. Ambling towards the main hall, Maude carried a basket of clothes down the stairs. She watched Librye sat on the edge of the fountain. Her bored hand whirled the surface of the water. As Maude came halfway down the stairs, an odd blue glow came from the water Librye was moving. Maude stared, mouth gaping.

Librye peered up to see Maude stood. Her smile stretched upon seeing Maude.

'How are you today?' asked Librye. Her joyful voice echoed around the large hall.

'I'm wonderful, thank you, Librye.' She drifted down the stairs, placing the basket on the edge of the fountain. 'What do you have planned for today?'

Librye peered up. She gazed towards the stairs. The gardens called to her.

Librye murmured, 'I want to go outside.'

Maude leant down towards Librye. 'Then go. Make sure you stay close to the palace as the skies darken. I'll call you for dinner when it's ready.'

Librye leapt up and headed towards the gardens. 'Gentlemen.' She uncoiled, looking at the guards. 'Maude has given me permission.'

One guard peered around the large wooden doorway into the palace hall. Maude gave a single nod.

'If you need us, just shout.'

Librye bound from the patio towards the long gravel path. Rose bushes lined the path, leading towards a low round fountain and pond at the end. The guards meandered along the walls on their patrol.

At the back of the gardens, a woodland led towards the wild meadows. As she entered the wild meadow, she saw rows of kennels. The dire remained hushed in their slumber. Even further still was a second span of woodland before reaching the palace wall. A trickling stream ran by the side of the wall into a drainage tunnel.

Librye sat beside the stream, watching the small autumn leaves travel by. A starling fluttered from a great oak tree at the side of her. The ground was bitter, but she sat still. Her green silk shoes slid onto the bank of the stream. She saw the bird bathing.

'I'm just as lucky to live here too,' she whispered to the bird. It gave no mind to the girl and continued bathing.

Her day of exploring was almost complete. Librye arrived back at the kennels.

'Good afternoon,' she said to the wolves as she strode past. The often-volatile wolves appeared inquisitive about the young girl. Their usual pacing paused as they came close to the bars. Librye trod from the path. She plodded through the short grass towards them. The kennel host started his approach to the front.

Librye reached her hand through the bars.

'Stop!' He tried to run towards her, but his portly belly would not allow for enough speed.

A curious look in her eyes slowed the host. Her mouth gaped. She continued to reach towards one wolf. A mink-coloured wolf bared his teeth towards her. His shining ice-blue eyes glared at the tiny Librye. She reached out her hand to the wolf. The host strove towards her. As he arrived at her side, the wolf surged against the heavy iron bars towards the kennel host. The host jumped back, petrified of the wolf's unusual behaviour. The heavy-set guard gawped at Librye. Her hand remained through the bars. The snarling giant jumped down and placed his heavy giant head against her hand. She shushed the placid beast.

The kennel host pointed, stunned. 'How? How are you doing that?' he stammered.

Librye broke her eye contact with the beast. 'Everyone needs love, that's how.' Her sweet voice evoked the other wolves as they joined the side of the mink wolf.

After her moment of bliss with the dire, Librye skipped back down the lane, watched by the astonished host.

Small temple buildings peppered the woodlands of the gardens. They offered a place to sit and watch, as the palace before her grew her every expectation of life.

'Dinner!' Librye heard a call from the palace. Her day of exploring was through.

'That was the best day. Thank you, Maude,' she said to Maude. Librye's eyes lit, dark circles showed her the day of exploring drained her energy.

Morning broke, silence remained in the palace. Librye remained in her room. Maude gathered the laundry from the upstairs rooms. She twisted and scoured the corridor to Librye's room. Eerie silence troubled her.

She walked back up the few steps. The audacious girl would have woken at the first bird song.

It struck Maude with fear as she stepped inside. She exploded from the door and screamed, 'Call an alchemist!' Hastening back in, she took a sheet from a chest near the bed.

Covered with vivid red blood, Librye laid in her bed. Her back flowed crimson. Maude removed the sheets. She could see the lumps on Librye's back had opened. A sore, oozing raw bone showed, coated with congealed blood.

Pandemonium outside Grendel's chambers roused him. The corridor outside was awash with activity. Peering out, Evan raced towards him.

'The palace alchemist has retired for the turn. Please, there is something wrong with the ward.'

They both rushed through the hall, bursting through the door.

Grendel glanced at the child, his eyes held an expression of fearful rage. His heart fell in his chest.

He roared at Maude, 'What have you done?'

Maude jolted her head. Her panic-stricken hands sought to stem the bleeding. 'Nothing. I found her like this. She was fine last night!' Maude's face turned wet with tears. She shook as she glared towards Grendel.

Grendel softened his tone. 'Keep her warm,' — he gave a slow nod towards Maude, — 'I'm sure she will be fine.' He lowered himself onto the bed. Maude kept the wounds covered. Grendel inspected the damage. 'These have grown from her.' His mumbling voice rumbled through Maude. 'Has she woken yet?'

Maude swayed her head. 'She's solid asleep. I felt there was something.' Her eyes tightened. 'Is she torb?'

Grendel gave a low nod. 'It could very well be. There is nothing I can do here. I can help get her bandaged, but apart from that. This girl needs help beyond the means of the fae. She requires the torbs and puca. I will consult Harelda.'

A gentle winter sun chilled the air in Librye's chamber. Maude called a member of staff from the galleries to make a fire. Her eyes remained powerless to move from Librye's sleeping face. Her flickering eyes told of the horror the girl was seeing in her dreams. She could not wake her. All Maude could do was wait.

As the afternoon faded, Librye's eyes fluttered open. Maude still clasped her hand.

'I'm tired.' Came the complaining voice of Librye. She sat up in her bed. Maude bound forwards. 'Why am I tired, Maude?' Librye's eyes snooped around the room. The sun was already awake long before her. The birds outside sang a dull whisper in the woods.

Maude raised her brows, her hand squeezed Librye's.

She replied in a low whisper, 'Don't worry, if you need to, you can get some more sleep.'

Librye stared at Maude with her brows furrowed. 'My back hurts.' Her mouth sank at the sides; her eyes filled with fright. 'Why does my back hurt?'

Maude shuffled her chair closer to the bed. Librye swivelled to face her.

'My dear, something happened. In the night, your back bled. I didn't know until this morning.'

An unexpected smile grew on Librye's face. Her eyes enlarged, gazing at the ruffled sheets on her bed. 'It's happening.'

Maude furrowed her brow, gawping at Librye. 'What is happening?'

'My secrets.' She stared back at Maude, her eyes widened. 'My secrets said I'll do great things, from the skies.'

Maude sat with her brow in a furrow, shocked by Librye's acceptance. 'I don't know what to say. You're *glad* this has happened?' Her eyes narrowed towards Librye.

Librye eased her smile. Her eyes swirled around the room. 'It hurts, a lot, but they said that with the greatest victory, there will always be pain.'

Maude shook her head in disbelief. Her eyes flickered. 'What are these secrets you speak of?'

'The voices.' Librye gazed into Maude's eyes. Her hair fell to her side, giving a maddened expression to her innocent face. 'My secrets tell me everything I need to know and more.'

'Who are the voices?' Maude pressed Librye.

Librye gave a clear answer. 'They're the gods. They talk to me through the stars.'

Maude's stomach twisted. A strange emptiness consumed her.

'Well, my duties I have today can wait.' Maude tried to reassure Librye, changing the uncomfortable subject. 'I will stay here.'

The whites of Librye's eyes turned pink. Small circles marked her exhaustion. Maude knew Librye was a challenging child. One that would suffer boredom, if not entertained. Whatever was happening to the tiny child, it was not yet over.

'Let's find you something to do.' She rose from her chair with her hands on her hips. 'If you aren't too tired?'

Librye glimpsed at Maude. A mist of sweat sat on her forehead.

'I'm not tired. My body is, but I'm not.'

Maude raised Librye in her arms.

'Where are we going?'

Maude replied, 'A place where your body can rest and your mind can escape.'

She carried Librye towards the mezzanine, and into Angus's chambers. His guards at the side opened the doors.

Librye inspected the magnificent room in front. Her eyes spun around the large ceiling towards the windows at the back, ending with the towering bookcases on either side. Her eyes enlarged in awe. Maude placed her down, still shaky. Librye made her way to the bottom of the stairs towards the right mezzanine.

'I'm sure you'll find a book here.' Maude smiled.

Librye climbed the stairs and marched as far as she could. She came towards the furthest book away. Librye found her favourite place in the mighty palace of Cronnin.

'These are Angus's chambers. I'm sure you're welcome here.' Maude gazed around the vast library of books. A smell of pipe smoke still stuck in the air. 'Although, I don't think there are many for children.' Her sorrowful voice and pout made Librye smile.

'If you haven't noticed,' — Librye held a noble tone, — 'I'm not your ordinary child.' Her darkening hair hung by her side. She climbed to the top of the steps to retrieve the first book.

Maude made her way closer to Librye, to see her odd choice of book. A book on alchemy.

'I take it you've found one?' Maude held her hands to the front of her.

Librye took the book down and peered at Maude. 'I've found the first one.' She held a broad smile. 'I'll start with the first. Thank you, Maude.' She sat on the floor and read the very first book.

Sat in his small guest chambers, Grendel gazed from the window of his balcony. His hands caught behind his back; his eyes gleamed a whisper of wonder. Grendel stepped onto the solid stone balcony, he watched the world outside; the noises of the city dusted the air. The sun on his skin warmed him, but it was uninviting. He strode back into his bitter stone room.

Sat at a small desk, he took some parchment.

'*My dearest Harelda. The child is safe and well. Angus was right. She is a force of extraordinary power. I fear she needs help beyond our means.*

Our King Bushwell will need to be informed of her arrival here, and I look forwards to details when I return.'

Sending the letter via pigeon, Grendel settled, awaiting Angus's return.

Grendel watched Librye as she made her way each morning into Angus's chambers.

A brisk winter moon brought a frost to the city of Cronnin that morning. The afternoon sun battled to thaw the frozen ground, to no avail. As Grendel sat in Angus's chambers. He watched Librye, dumbfounded.

'What are you reading now, little one?' He gazed towards her, huddled on the balcony.

Her eyes peered from the pages of the book. 'It's called Ailment of Alchemy, fascinating, it's about the backlashes of using bad alchemy.'

'Ah,' grunted Grendel. His eyes remained staring towards her. 'Dark magic takes from its user, just as it does its victim. Using magic to take a life. Using magic to create an imbalance awakens the darkness. Something will always restore the balance.' Her need disturbed him. 'At such a young age, you're learning the iniquities of beautiful magic.'

'Magic is so glorious it can boil people from the inside,' mocked Librye.

'There are different magics, little one. The magic you possess is far more than the magic of natural skill.'

A carriage approached the main gate to the palace. The crunching gravel outside stirred the palace guards.

As Angus made his way from his carriage, he bolted through the doors and headed to his chambers. Angus nodded at his council, whom insisted he call a meeting. A vacant smile broadened his face. He continued his path up the stairs. Angus removed his leather gloves. He passed them to one of the staff who followed him. Another took his cloak.

Maude came scurrying down the stairs towards him.

'Sire,' — she gave a languid bow — 'I sorted her room.' She followed him up the stairs. He rushed too much for her. 'However, she has opted to spend her time in your chambers.'

Angus listened and gave a brief nod. His rush to see Librye hastened his pace.

'Is she well?'

Maude panicked. 'She will be,' — the rush was all too much, she raised her voice, — 'sire, please stop!' She stopped at the top of the stairs. Angus froze in his tracks. 'Lord Grendel stayed. It was lucky. Her *ailment*. A few days ago, I couldn't wake her. As I stepped into her room, I came upon a scene of carnage. The issue she's been having is growing.'

Angus furrowed his brow. 'For goodness' sake! Is she well?'

'She is now, but her shoulder-blades, her back, they grew. It pierced her skin. Grendel has it in hand, but I believe he's sent word to Sonnin, to our good queen Harelda.'

Angus nodded. He placed his hand on the door. 'So long as she is well, Maude.' His eyes drifted to the door handle before he stepped in. He stopped at the door and glanced at Maude. 'I will need to speak with you soon, alone. Before dinner, please join me here.' Maude gave a small nod and left towards the galleries.

Angus stepped into his chambers. Grendel sat at Angus's desk. His hand caught his chin and feet rested on the desk. He stared towards the mezzanine.

Grendel spun to see Angus step inside. He lowered his legs from Angus's desk and remained seated in Angus's chair. Angus made his way forwards. His brows raised with a look of incredulity.

'Apologies.' Grendel stood. He edged towards Angus. 'I'm fascinated with your girl. I spent many days with her. I feel suitably educated.'

Angus made his way towards the stairs of the mezzanine.

'I hope she hasn't been causing any issues?'

Grendel drifted closer. His voice swelled with awe. 'Well, during our passage here. The conversation was some of the most interesting I've ever encountered. Her love of nature matches the puca, but she has several other attributes.' Noticing they spoke about her, Librye gave a rapid glance over the mezzanine. 'However, she shows a need for secrets, like the ggelf. She is remarkable.' He joined Angus, making his way up the staircase. 'All children are remarkable, of course, some more than others.'

They made their way to the top mezzanine. Librye sat at the end, surrounded by books. Her dark hair trailed over her shoulders, sat with her legs crossed.

'That's odd.' Angus twisted towards Grendel. Grendel drew his brows down with a lingering question. Angus whispered, 'In the camp, her hair, I'm certain, was auburn?'

Grendel raised his brows. 'There is nothing surprises me with her. She is the turning girl. Her eyes shift every morning, like the days. Her hair could also follow the patterns of the seasons? Like that of a Solnox.' A tone of wonder filled them both.

The shoeless vision he saw in the camps was far separated from the girl who now sat atop his mezzanine.

'She enjoys reading,' said Angus, impressed.

Grendel replied with a lofty tone, 'She's been here for three days reading. She's so far read seventy-eight books. The girl is odd, the most beautiful example of odd I have ever seen.' He swelled with pride, gazing at Librye, still sat clutching her book.

'I told you.' Angus knelt in front of Librye.

Her eyes drifted from the book she was reading. 'She also has perfect hearing and can understand everything you are saying.'

Angus smiled at her. 'How have you been?'

Librye did not smile. She glowered at Angus. 'It doesn't take that long!'

Angus drew back. 'What doesn't?'

'You were in Marrion.' She slammed her book closed. 'You should've been back three nights ago.' She stood, holding the book in her fist, her other hand balled, her shoulders hunched forwards.

'Apologies.' He tried not to laugh at her innocence. 'We got caught up in Roma. The taverns there can be fierce places. It's vital I meet my people, Librye. Now I'm back. I can spend the next few turns with you.' His smile grew.

'And the council, they aren't happy with you or your new commander.'

'Commander? What have you heard?' asked Angus.

'Plenty.'

Grendel stood, baffled.

'I know the secrets of this palace. I grew up here as well,' said Angus, burying his hands in his pockets.

Maude came into the room, hearing what Librye was saying.

'The new commander, in the west, they said he is a berserker. They say he is not worthy of leading an army. They believe he will be dead soon. But they aren't happy with you either.' Librye stood. She took Angus's hand and led him down. 'I think you need to stay home for a while. It will calm the council. Not everything is about rushing.' Her tiny brows raised. Her dress followed her down the steps as she made her way to the bottom.

'I knew you were demanding, Librye, but my heart flutters,' Angus said mockingly. 'I take it you have been trouble for the council.'

'Not trouble, no.' Librye lowered her head. She stopped walking. 'The council has no interest in silly little girls.'

'Is that so?' murmured Angus.

'But they have important work, and so do you. That is why you must remain here.'

The call for dinner rang. Librye looked up at Angus with her eyes wide.

'I shall see you after dinner,' he said with a wide smile. Librye rushed to the galleries in the bottom hall. Maude stepped in further.

'The girl likes her food,' said Maude.

With a grumbling laugh, Angus lifted his head from looking at the vast amounts of papers on his desk. Scrolls spilled onto the floor. Maude stepped towards the desk and picked the scrolls up from the floor.

'I shall leave you to speak,' said Grendel. He took leave, closing the door behind him as he did.

'Please sit, Maude,' his tone was strange. He grew an age following his journey to Marrion.

Maude sank into the chair opposite his desk.

'I'm sure you are aware by now, Librye is the child you found. You found hope, Maude, Librye is without doubt a remarkable child, but as she grows, she will become the force we need.' His voice deepened to a sinister tone; his eyes glassed through Maude. 'We have a new world heading towards us. I have given you the duty to care for Librye, because I know she will need it.'

'She will struggle.' She rang her hands in front of her. 'Librye is not like us.' Her heart beat faster as she glared at him. 'We will need to help her. The fae will need to help her, even the dragons.'

Angus raised his brow. 'I see. Well, I will expand her education. King Bushwell will want to meet her, as well as Harelda.'

'Just remember,' snapped Maude. She rose. She gave Angus the first warning he had ever received from a commoner. 'Librye is just a child. Not a weapon of war, she isn't a fighter. She is a six-year-old, sweet, scared little girl. Keep that in mind.'

Angus widened his eyes, remaining calm.

'If I forget, I'm sure you will remind me.' His smile grew. Angus stood. 'So, for now, let her settle. Her lessons will begin soon.' Angus escorted Maude to the door of his chambers.

***

The battle of Marrion roared on. The castle stood as a fortress, but the Atlanti pressed. For three days they battled, for three days no one would call a retreat. Numbers thinned on both sides.

As the midnight moon graced the skies, Harris readied himself on Svend. He waited with his chiefs Anna, Saburo, Kyla, and Dominic.

He heard a heavy sigh from the side of him as Saburo's impatience showed. Harris twisted to Saburo. A creak of leather from his saddle broke the silence. He glanced to the other chiefs who each waited on their horses. He leered back at Saburo. The seasoned chief had never attempted the commander's position. A large scar which ran down his left cheek spoke of the unsavoury past he held. Long locks of wild grey hair tied at the back. He grew a beard, attempting to hide the pockmarks on his face.

Harris's tone was low, his brows raised. 'Is there a problem?'

Saburo sighed. 'Why are we waiting?'

Harris grew straight on Svend. The warhorse felt Harris move, Svend was restless.

'We are waiting for a better light. We're flanking,' he explained with an irritated tone. 'If we hit them from the west, we will weaken the additional support from the east.' He gave a slow blink towards Saburo before turning away.

'Any news from the north?' called Anna.

Harris twisted with his brows raised. 'Not yet. I know they ambushed the second lot of supplies.' He moved forwards on Svend. The others followed. 'We spent the last lot too fast. They watch the northern passes. The shits will get what's coming to them. I have contacts in Enderton. They say messages are hard to get through, however, time is on our side.' He glared at Saburo, holding a scathing tone. 'Sometimes, patience is what's needed.'

The moon hid behind a storm cloud which drifted from the ocean. A berserker of war, Harris earned his reputation. He favoured swords, daggers, and axes. The flesh of the Atlanti covered every inch of him. Blood soaked the field, mixed with mud and filth. All would need a strong stomach for the stench. Harris's long crimson cape covered the stains of savage spray, his black lizard-skin armour dripped maroon from the Atlanti he butchered.

The hard decision fell upon Titus, the Atlanti commander, to call a retreat.

The last Atlanti hurdled through the field. Dropping as they fled, the poison from the arrows worked into their blood. Horrifying marks appeared on their faces, which turned blue. Strangled by Harris's poison. Harris blended with the twisted steel and broken bodies.

'Harris!' Kyla stood amidst the chaos. He twisted his body to see her stood laughing. She could not contain her laughter, peering at the state of him. She pointed to him, calling, 'We will clear the bathhouse to offer tribute!'

Harris glanced down; all mannerisms of flesh stuck to him. He took his gloved hand, wiping the blood from his saturated sword, he flicked the red liquid away. 'Ah, the bathhouses are where I shine with company, Kyla!'

Harris treaded through the carnage with several of his chiefs from the camps. The remaining Atlanti would find their end at the point of a sword. The medical teams scurried into the field. To take surviving Cronnin and Sonnin soldiers to the camps.

Harris looked at his chief, Anna. He watched her blast her sword through the neck of a surviving Atlanti who wore a blue cape.

'Anna!' he yelled. She stopped to face him. 'We need some alive!'

'Apologies, sir.' Anna pulled her bloodied sword from his neck. She raised her brow, her mouth curled in disgust. Her sword pointed towards the corpse as she replied, 'Not that one though, he called me a cunt.'

Harris gave an approving nod. 'Very well. Make sure we have some left, cunt or not. You can torture them later.'

Harris trampled the grounds, tagging the Atlanti he wanted to keep alive. He placed red bands on their arms.

'You realise they frown upon this? You do not have the right.' Chief Saburo joined the side of Harris.

'I understand your concern. Your age has guided you through many battles, Saburo, but this is one of those moments where your wisdom will tell you to ignore what is in front of you.' Harris continued, ending the suffering of the Atlanti. 'I understand certain loyalties may remain. The commanders of this army they did what they could.'

He kept a low tone. 'My duty here is to stop all of this.' He stood straight and twisted in the field. 'And if I take pleasure in vengeance,' — Harris spun back to Saburo and glared at him, — 'that's my right.'

Saburo drew back. 'I follow the old law, Bearwood. What of their rights?'

Harris pivoted; his eyes widened with rage. 'Where were the rights in Farhope?' he scolded, pointing his sword at the back of him. 'Or Stathen? or Dorm? Why should they have rights to hold knowledge?' — He glanced at the filth of the field. — 'They removed their rights the second they stepped onto this field,' — he blasted his sword across the neck of an Atlanti, — 'the first one of our women they raped.' The head rolled across the floor.

Again, he threw his sword across an Atlanti's neck. His head fell from his shoulders, still attached to the skin.

'The first child they murdered.' Harris came close to Saburo. He warned with his brows low and teeth gritted. 'Do you know how young many of their wives are?' His eyes were bloodshot as he came close to Saburo's face. 'How many children they are required to bear before they even have their bleed?' Harris paused, looking at the disgust on Saburo's twisted face. He looked at his chiefs in the field surrounding. 'Don't make me question your loyalties.'

Harris marched back towards the castle Marrion. A searing pain shot through his body. Harris stumbled to his knees.

'Shit!' A mighty call of pain echoed from him. He spun to see one of the last remaining Atlanti holding onto life. An arrow driven through his kneecap from the back forced it outward. He gritted his teeth in pain, another cry of pain roared from him. The man held him, driving an arrow under his lizard skin armour and into his back. With gritted teeth, the man twisted the arrow in his back, pushing it as deep as his weak hands could.

'You fucking bastard!' Harris screamed. He pushed the man back and fell onto his back, twisting the arrow further. Harris staggered to his feet. He pulled one of his long daggers from the front strap of his armour and took it in hand.

He was relentless as he beat the man's head with the dagger hilt in his fist while screaming, 'Die, die, die!' Pouring blood frothed at his mouth.

The chiefs spun to see the chaos. They ran as fast as they could to help. By the time they arrived Harris had beaten the man, dead.

'Harris, stop!' called Anna, 'Harris!' The chiefs jumped onto Harris, now covered with the man's brains and blood. Harris continued to beat his flattened head. His face was no longer visible.

They dragged him off. Harris calmed, out of breath. For a few seconds, he stood quietly. He wheezed, unable to find his breath. The arrow still protruded from the back of Harris's knee as he whirled and kicked. 'Die!' he yelled.

'Harris, for fuck's sake!' Saburo ran towards him. He took his shoulders, forcing him to calm. Harris pulled his shoulders away. 'Know when your revenge ends.'

Harris coughed and panted. He struggled for air. Pandemonium took over the field.

'I can't stand!' Harris called. The chiefs gathered around to help him back. As his leg hit the floor, he fell.

'That's because you have an arrow in you, Harris.' Anna put his arm around her small neck. His weight was too much to carry. 'You're a bulky bastard, Harris,' she puffed.

Harris gave a wide smile. Blood covered his teeth and mouth. 'You should know.'

'Fuck off, Harris.' She inspected his back to see a trail of blood leading to the floor. The blood was thick and pouring fast. Still struggling to help, she removed his armour. The lizard skin armour was as light as cotton, but harder than steel. Every space on his harnesses and straps held a dagger. Upon pulling his tunic up, Anna could see the damage. Her eyes widened, observing his back, her hands shook.

'Get him on a stretcher!'

'I don't need a stretcher!' Harris struggled for breath. The air he breathed turned solid. Harris fell to his side onto a stretcher. His vision faded; blood poured to the floor as they ran him back. Surrounded by the dead and dying.

The tents often stank of rotten blood, open festering wounds, sweat and fear.

Hours passed, another battle raged on. This time though, Harris's plan was coming together. Arrows arrived from the north, they met the Atlanti with another barrage. A special coating of Harris's own design covered the tips. Even the stray arrows which glanced past their intended targets were deadly. Large war horses pulled in the ballistas to sit atop the plateau of the cliff. They needed Harris back, they needed his vitriol oil, his cunning, and his anger to end the battle of Marrion.

Harris remained weakened in his room. His blood loss was severe. A nurse from the camps, Branwen, was there to care for him. Her hair was a dark-golden blond, which cascaded down her back. Tied with a few small wisps which framed her delicate face. She was a beautiful creature, and pure. Her pinafore clung around her decanter shaped waist. Her ivory skin was as flawless as fresh fallen snow.

She busied herself with dressing the wounds she could. Her delicate, long fingers were perfect for the duty they bound her to.

Harris was yet to wake to discover the damage. Branwen had time on her hands now. She wrote to her mother in Sonnin. To tell her of the fallen commander who she now cared for.

'*His reputation perceives him.*' She wrote. '*They named Harris Bearwood our new commander. He is, without doubt, handsome. However, I have watched many women from the taverns. A carriage is bringing them to satisfy his desires. He has no regard for his life, he has injured many. I cannot tell you about his tactical plans. Many horses have arrived with machines of his own design, hoping this will help end this battle. The air is thick with talk of victory.'* She ended her letter with a warning. *'The commander is dangerous. Please be cautious.'*

She sent the letter by falcon and waited for Harris to wake.

He was handsome to her. Branwen was untouched. A sacred fae. She never considered a man, apart from treating wounds. Harris was different. The wrinkle of his brow appeared like a hidden sadness was dwelling deep within. Tiny scars covered different parts of him. The deepest wound he had was not visible.

To Branwen, Harris was just a soldier. He had seen more than most. His mind was a cesspit of war.

CHAPTER SEVEN

7

A rumbling chaos struck the gate of Rathen Moor. Bloodied, broken, half-dead. Gaius staggered into the city. The blood-sodden horse by his side strode gently through, stricken with flies.

Mouths gaped as he wandered through the small cottage houses which stood in drenched mud. His battered face ignored them. Gawking at his own front door, Gaius strove forwards.

'Gaius!' called a neighbour. Rushing to his side, the man stood in front of him, stopping his slow pace. 'It is no use,' he murmured. Gaius furrowed his brow, his lungs still struggled to fill with air. 'She left. We had word our army had fallen. You didn't write, so she left.'

'Where?' Gaius grumbled.

The man shrugged. 'She could be anywhere. We thought you were dead.'

'I saw death, but even that could not take me.' His head raised. Grasping the rein of his horse, he glanced at those who stared at him.

'Gaius, you must go see him. He can help you.'

Gaius leered at the man, his eyes filled with frigid contempt.

'He cannot help me,' he groaned.

Gaius walked forwards, struggling to his front door. 'He knows where she is!' called the man. Gaius froze. His body twisted, his eyes grew to the imposing tower their city encircled.

Kairne's lavish chambers warmed Gaius. It was the first time he felt warmth since leaving the south. A rippling flame from the fire sent a shiver through Gaius as he glared out of the window towards the city below. He remained still, silent, not even hearing when Kairne stepped in behind him.

'The rumours are true then,' said Kairne.

'Where is my wife?' Gaius burst, his mouth gaped as he turned to face Kairne.

'All in good time,' replied Kairne with a wide grin.

'Please, they said you could help.'

'And I can.' Kairne shifted to a cabinet at the side, taking some glasses. 'First, I must know more about your gruelling journey.' He tightened his eyes as he faced Gaius. 'How did you escape?'

'I didn't,' — breathed Gaius, his mouth still gaping, — 'they allowed my freedom.'

'And under whose command?'

'Harris Bearwood, the traitor,' replied Gaius.

'Ah, not a traitor really, more a lost wanderer,' mocked Kairne. He slid towards the sofa at the end of his bed. Relaxing in front of the fire. 'So, tell me?' he asked with a shrug.

'Where is my wife?' Gaius glared at Kairne; his patience wore thin.

'She is safe, and she will remain safe. Tell me more about Harris?'

'I know little. Rumour says he ended the golden war. When he took over in Marrion, change came and ended half our army. Our commanders were afraid of him.'

'Afraid?' Kairne raised his brows.

'Word in the camps spread, the talk of a man of Atlanti descent taking charge of the Narra army, many of them gave up hope —'

'Did you?' Kairne interrupted.

'Never.'

Kairne flashed his eyes before taking a sip from his glass. He looked at the state of the man in front of him. 'Why did they let you go?'

'So I could tell you what I saw.' His eyes spun.

'And what did you see?'

'I saw plenty,' replied Gaius.

'They were cruel, weren't they?'

'No,' he muttered. 'They beat us, gave us many reasons to hate them, but then, it was Harris who gave them a proper burial. He made them bury us.' Gaius grappled to speak. Fear was something they all had to hide.

'And they let you go?'

'Yes, my lord, they allowed me to go free. They gave me a horse and said I must tell them what I've seen.'

Kairne stared at the fire in front. 'I have been in power, for only two years, and I have worked hard to bring our people from the pits they put us in, my father worked too, until taken by the grave, and this man gains such notoriety, in such a short space of time, with no title, no nobility.' Kairne rose, he wandered towards the window. 'Who does he think he is?' he murmured.

'With all respect, my lord, he is nothing but a glimpse of hope for a hopeless people.'

Kairne smirked as he twisted. 'Your wife is well. She believed you died, having not received word from you.'

'They are stopping letters from Enderton. I tried —'

'I know, don't worry, she is safe and in service.'

'Service?'

'To the false king,' said Kairne with a broad grin.

'Sir please, she is a delicate soul, a woman of pure love —'

'Oh, please,' scoffed Kairne. 'If such a woman existed, I would never have placed her in such peril,' he chortled.

'Peril?'

'She is a brilliant girl. She knows her duty, and you must know yours. You will meet Bearwood again. Until then, I have plenty to keep you occupied while you await the triumphant return of your dear wife.'

A smoke-filled chamber met Angus as he woke. Shuffling from his bedchamber door, he glanced at his desk, overflowing with scrolls. A hard sigh heaved from him as he lumped in his chair. Angus took the first scroll in hand. 'Decree for the death of Hani Flower.' He peered around the room.

At the top of the mezzanine, Librye sat. She had passed the first five bookshelves and was halfway down the sixth. Librye glanced up from her book and down towards Angus.

'I've nearly finished the A's.'

Angus's heart fluttered. 'You should slow down, Heart. Reading can be good for the soul. Too much can warp the mind.' He made his way towards the door.

She held her effervescent smile. 'My mind remains solid and free, only my own.'

The door to his chambers opened. Rebecca stood with a tray. 'Your meal, sire.' She sashayed into the room. Two guards followed, taking their place at the side of his door.

'I appreciate it, Rebecca, but not now. Ask Gethen to send something later.'

'You should eat something,' Librye nagged, standing at the top of the mezzanine.

'I agree, sire. Keeping your strength in the arena of politics is important.'

Angus looked to his side, where a guard stood. 'Help,' he whispered.

'Apologies, sire, but I agree with them.'

Angus slowly blinked, turning from the door. 'Rebecca, leave it on my desk. I shall have it when I return.'

'You're going to the hall, aren't you?' Librye's voice broke as she spoke.

Angus stopped at the door. 'I am. You'rc welcome to listen, if you wish.'

'It's fine. I don't need to know everything.'

She glinted a smile towards him, sitting back with her book as she watched him leave.

He headed towards the lower west wing. A long white corridor guided him to an old wooden door. He stepped through and made his way down a long, unwelcoming, grey stone staircase. Fire flowers lit his way. As he came to the bottom, rows upon rows of towering bookcases met him. Several years of dust collected on the shelves and surrounded the floor. His nose filled with the smell of old paper and ink.

He swung around to his left. 'Poppy!' He continued sauntering towards an old desk at the end of the shelves.

The record keeper, Poppy, called out, 'Sire, please!' She rushed through the winding walls of bookcases towards his voice. 'I've told you before, it is dangerous down here.'

'It's hardly a battle-field, Poppy.' He could hear her scurrying towards him. He glimpsed to the few scrolls on the desk. An old inkwell lay in a puddle of spilt ink. A quill was missing. The desk had a small trinket box with a carving of the Cronnin stag gilded on the top of it.

'No, sire, but the bookcases are weak. The structure isn't great since the flood!' She could see him in the gloom of the palace archives.

Her Cronnin uniform was grey with dust. Her hair knotted back with a feather quill sticking out of the top of her bun.

'Did you find it?' He stirred inside.

Poppy's small stature made it easy for her to manoeuvre through the narrow, dark spaces of the archives.

'I found something.' She made her way towards him. Several scrolls remained tucked into the ribbon around her waist.

Poppy rummaged through the scrolls, pulling one out. 'This is the one.'

'Thank you, Poppy.' He hurried back to the council hall.

'You're welcome, sire,' her voice echoed. 'But please send a guard next time!'

Stopped by the fountain, Angus waited for the hall to fill. With the main hall devoid of councillors, the doors closed.

Angus made his way into the council hall. He stood in the centre, making his way towards the central table. He stepped onto the plinth, removing his green cape, and placing it on the table at the side. Wondrous whispers met him.

'Gentlemen, I intend at no point to raise my voice. Order is all I require. Something of fatal importance has arisen.' The council sat statuesque in their seats. Angus held the scroll up. 'The dragons have long been our allies, but something now binds us. The scroll is from Draco. Dragons are our history, the blood of Cammbour. Many years ago, during the reign of Grenhilda, a dragon wrote this, telling of a creature born from war, a creature which would have ended the atrocities. Before they could act, Grenhilda took action, sending the Atlanti to the depths of Tataria.'

'Your point, sire?' asked Connor, sat impatient on the side.

'My point is this, that creature was a boy, born with an ability to talk to the stars, wield nature in the most unnatural way. His name was Artreus, when he died, as did the Gods. You know yourselves that the Artreans follow him as their guide, they worship him. The child which now resides in this palace, the child under my charge, has such abilities.'

Kailron stood, taking Angus's attention. 'Sir, might I ask, after the incident, a while ago, is the child well?'

'Have you tried asking her?' Angus replied with wide eyes. Kailron sat.

'The dragons claim to be an ally of ours, if only for notoriety, for peace,' called Devon. 'They are, in fact, idle in this world.'

A mumbling room of disapproval met Angus.

'The dragons have reason to not trust us.' Shame filled his voice as Angus spoke. 'We fully understood their reason for going into hiding. The Rathen dragons wanted no part in that. The dragons we speak of are still a part of this world. This war is not theirs, gentlemen.'

'The world is theirs. They should show some concern for their allies,' Kailron lightly suggested.

'My dear councillor.' — Angus turned to face him, — 'I understand you are new and wish to make your mark, but understand your meaning before you speak.'

Kailron rose. 'I do, sire, it was your own father who saw the dragons as a threat.' A searing temper grew from Angus. 'They have harmed none, but your father still needed to cover vital information from them, information which would've stopped so many being slaughtered at the hands of the Atlanti and Rathen dragons.'

'Hold your tongue, councillor,' said Omar, casually taking a seat beside Kailron.

'I would listen to him,' said Angus, pointing at Omar and gritting his teeth.

'It was a massacre,' whispered Kailron.

'We are not here to speak of the past,' Bart stood, breaking the tension. 'I believe our king had something more important to say?'

Angus broke his glare with Kailron. 'I have a script, a single scroll for now. The rest is being found as we speak. It will tell us more about the creature you shunned.'

'And is that all?' asked Bart.

'I will remain as the child's guardian. She is to be cared for by Maude.'

'All of this, over one child,' scoffed Kailron. 'A child that isn't even your own, that cannot take your place, cannot give your orders.' His voice rang through the room.

Disapproval, realisations, the room divided. 'I know my loins cause you some upset.' Angus glanced at the table. He rolled the scroll out and weighed it down. 'This is something I have in hand. I will give my everything to ensure the future of Cronnin. While doing everything possible, to secure Librye's.' He stood straight with his arms behind his back.

Kailron stepped down from the benches towards the steps at the side. His footsteps were silent. He padded towards the centre of the hall.

'We can all agree that she is remarkable. However, she is just a child, one who is without your blood. I understand every child with such ability should have respect, but she is not your child, sire, besides, yesterday you spoke of change coming to the kingdom, Harris Bearwood taking a seat by your side to help lighten your burden, and now you take on more?'

He turned in the hall, peering at the councillors who remained on the benches. 'Gentlemen, our good king is doing everything he can to support this cause, but we must all be wary, if a child will win this war, it may not go in our favour, the war belongs to the Atlanti, just as it does us, whatever that scroll says, I beg of you, read it with impartial eyes.'

'Impartial eyes?' Angus scoffed. He came close to Kailron, disguising his voice. 'Be careful, councillor, your father brought you to the political arena for fear you would be worthless to your family. See me in my chambers.' His voice raised towards the council. 'If you weren't so quick to dismiss her. Then you would already know.' Angus made his way towards his throne.

He sat and waited for councillor Bart to stand. Taking the floor, Bart made his way from his seat.

'As interesting as that is,' he sneered. 'We have important matters to approach.' Bart glared at Angus. 'First, we have approved a new appointment.' His smile was tight. He peered at him. 'We will give Harris Bearwood the title of Chief Commander.' The auditorium filled with disapproving mumbles. 'Although!' His small voice struggled to carry in the hall. 'This has caused some controversy. He will fail or succeed. We have afforded him the chance.' Bart again glared at Angus. 'A wife.'

Angus rolled his head back. 'Why is my council so concerned about my bedroom activity?'

Bart made his way towards him. 'A throne without a king is just a seat.'

Angus shook his head. 'I have already spoken of this; I will listen no more!' His arms flew to the air. 'Librye, she will be my heir.' The auditorium erupted. Angus stood, followed by Bart and Kailron.

Rushing to his chambers, Angus began the day's task of sifting through the papers on his desk. The door opened. Angus raised his head.

'You made it then?' Angus glanced up to see Bart toddling towards him.

'This is all just a joke to you, isn't it?' hissed Bart. Angus placed his quill back into its pot. 'This is a matter of urgency. Librye could not take your place. As endearing as she is, her blood is not yours.'

Librye listened, still sat on the mezzanine.

'Then who would you suggest?' asked Angus.

'I have thought of this. Our relationship with Thrasia could do with a better foundation.' He sat opposite the desk. 'Helena, she is very suitable.'

Angus sat back. He glared towards Bart; his mouth twisted down. 'She is fourteen. That is the most disturbing thing you've ever said.'

'It's only six years,' defended Bart. 'It isn't a lifetime. The union will harden relations, and you will have a young wife.'

'Out!' insisted Angus. He stood to rush Bart to the door. 'I will hear no more of marriage to children!' He pushed Bart into the corridor.

Stood on the landing, Bart replied, 'You will need to do something soon. Age is not on your side. You need a wife!' Heated, he made his way back towards the hall.

Stood in his chambers, Angus remained staring at the door. He glimpsed at the guard. 'A child?' he sneered.

'I agree,' replied the guard. Angus enjoyed conversations with his statue guards. 'But also, you will need an heir.'

With a raised brow and wide eyes, Angus replied, 'I am aware of this, but the matters of women confuse me,' he mocked, making his way back towards the desk. He shouted to the guard, 'Your wife, Becky! Lovely woman. Does she have a sister?'

The guard on the other side laughed. He called to Angus across the long room, 'It's easy, sire. A man of your breeding. If you can't find a suitable wife. There's no hope for the rest of us.'

'A wife isn't what concerns me,' said Angus. 'If you'd have met my mother, you would know. Superior breeding doesn't always bring the best result.'

'What was she like?' Librye held a soft voice.

Angus jumped. He held his hand to his chest. 'She was different.'

Librye made her way to the mezzanine above his desk.

'I have read the soldiers' books, telling of battle. I'm sure that stories of your mother will not frighten me.'

He glanced up. 'She spent most of her time entertaining guards. She suited palace life. Married life she did not.' The guards cringed as they heard Angus speak. 'My father found out, as did the council, the guard ended his days in Offenmoor —'

'The prison isles?'

Angus nodded. He glared into the room. 'My mother had a choice. She chose the easy way out, death. They sent her to the dungeon of the palace. Three days later, her head left her shoulders in the first quarter.' The sadness in his voice distorted his actual feelings. 'It was the last time they used the dungeon.' Angus glimpsed at Librye. 'Anyway, such nasty business isn't what I wish to discuss.'

Librye glared at him. 'You were there, weren't you? You were in the first quarter?'

Angus's eyes misted, his heart felt light, empty. 'I don't wish to speak of it.'

The door to his chambers opened, Kailron stepped inside. 'You wanted to speak with me.' His hissing words saved Angus from the awkward conversation.

'I never thought I would be glad to see you. Sit,' he ordered. Kailron ambled towards the desk, taking a seat opposite. 'I asked you here to make sure you are aware of your appointment.'

'My appointment is simple,' replied Kailron, his scathing tone sent a shiver through Librye, who hid her face behind one of her books. 'As a lord of Enderton, my close connections to Atlanti generals have caused some upset in the council halls.' He leant forwards, his eyes wide. 'I am not on anyone's side, which is why your council has failed in the past. You brought me here to be an impartial voice to all peoples of Cammbour, and now you berate me for doing my duty. I shall admit I do not agree with how the Atlanti have conducted themselves through this war, but your commander has done worse, this will only end if both sides see sense, in a senseless war, I cannot see an easy resolve to this.'

'Thank you for that, but I did not bring you here to question your loyalty. I brought you here to ask about the loyalty of others.'

Kailron furrowed his brow. He remained silent.

'My council was reluctant to have a lord of Enderton here, but some were more than willing to see you in your new role. Three turns have passed. Surely you have something by now?'

'I was not aware my actual duty was to spy on your council. I believed it was to work as impartial eyes, to bring peace to both communities.'

'I am not asking you to spy —'

'Then what?'

'I simply wish to know who of my council has shown interest.'

'I believed you were an intelligent man, and I hope I was right, by placing someone into the council to relay information back to you, it tells me there are many you do not trust, I will not tell you who has shown interest, I respect you far too much for that, all I ask is for the same in return, for you to allow me to work as an impartial agent between both.'

'Your father warned me, may his soul forever rest. He said you were a difficult one to tame, but you could see right and wrong on both sides. Kailron, I apologise if I offended you, but the Atlanti's conduct has caused a lot of distrust. I only hope you realise that.'

'I do, and I accept your apology, just know this, the commander you bring into these walls to end this war, he is as impartial as me, his family are from Crede, his mother's father was their lord, he has closer Atlanti ties than I do, be careful, wolves come in many forms.'

'He prides himself as being from Xencliff, his past has not altered his feelings towards the Atlanti.'

'That you may believe. The Atlanti commanders tell me nothing of their plans, and I tell them nothing of ours.' Kailron lowered his head. 'When I came here, I was naïve, I can admit that, I know my time here will be useless until this war is nearing its end, until then all I can do is hope to guide us, being impartial is hard when a man of such brutal reputation gets invited in to take charge.'

'I sense a certain animosity towards him.'

Kailron glared at the desk.

'Kailron, Harris Bearwood is not his rumour. I believed the same when I met him. He kills, yes. Unfairly. Who is to say? War is war, it is death, destruction. Some would argue Harris's tactic of a quick death spares many from their suffering. These men would die anyway. He simply stems the suffering.'

'You make excuses for a man who tortures, a man who builds his reputation using death —'

'Not true.' Angus raised his brows. 'Harris had a reputation long before he took to the battleground. His reasons are obvious. He needs this war to end. He has the same needs as you.' Angus sat back, folding his arms across his chest. A wide smile grew. 'You will learn to like him, as many do.'

'Yes, but there will always be one who hates, for the sake of hating.' Kailron stood and rushed to the door.

'I don't think he will like this Harris person,' said Librye, remaining with her book.

For days, Branwen observed the commander's slumber. Her eyes gazed towards his chest, watching each breath he took, hoping it would not be the last. She gave him a little water. He would not wake. She dressed his wounds as best she could. Her boredom took her towards his desk.

She cleaned his armour and replaced it on his hooks. Sat at his desk, she reached into his draw; where some small notes sat. She puffed out her cheeks and pondered the area around the desk.

She leant back in his chair. The hot Marrion breeze entered his window. She made her way towards the bed.

'Commander,' she sought to rouse him. 'Harris,' she whispered. His eyes did not flicker. He remained silent in his bed. His body lay twisted to make it easier to dress his wound. He was larger than she thought, a well-fed figure and dauntingly large arms. She placed a pillow behind him to stop him from rolling onto the still protruding arrow.

Branwen made her way to the front of him. He was deep in slumber. Her eyes inspected his chest; she saw his skin filled with scars. A past life tormented him. She reached out and touched a red lumped scar just below his left shoulder. He caught her wrist.

Pools of emerald glared towards her. Her smile lit her angelic face.

'Good morning,' she greeted.

Harris looked uneasy. 'Do I know you? I feel like I know you.' His head was still light from his injuries.

'Harris, you need to let go of my wrist.' He let her wrist go, holding his hand stiff in the air. He blinked around the room, struggling to focus.

'You will feel rather strange, but you need to hold still. An arrow pierced your lung. You need to rest your knee.'

'I'm aware of that.' He tried to sit, calling with pain, 'Why?' he moaned, 'is the arrow still in my back?' He gawped at her, horrified.

Branwen gathered a bowl and some cloths. 'Because it is a barbed arrow. In order to remove it, we have to push it through. Your knee wasn't an issue, but this will be.' Harris relaxed. 'It will go through your lung, but could go through your heart,' she explained.

'Either way, the thing needs removing.' — He glowered at her. — 'Why didn't you do it before?'

Branwen studied Harris, unable to move and vulnerable. She gave a sigh of deep regret. 'Your chances are slim. If we remove the arrow, it is possible you won't live. You are the commander of the Narra army. They gave you five days to wake, and we would've removed it. If you have any orders, you need to give them now.'

Harris stared straight in front. 'If I die, I couldn't give a shit about what happens. Those are my orders.'

Branwen replied, 'Very well, get rested. I'll fetch my team.'

Harris panicked. 'You're leaving me?' He again tried to sit up.

'I will be back. I can't remove it alone,' she laughed.

Harris shouted, 'Wait!' — Branwen stopped at the door. Harris struggled for breath. — 'I don't want them to see.'

Branwen whirled, confused. 'Don't want who to see?'

'Them!' — he flailed his arm up, — 'I've already established that I have no orders. Can you do it, please?'

Branwen stuttered her reply, 'I can't, not alone. I need help.'

'Look,' — he struggled for words, — 'what was your name?'

'Branwen —'

'Branwen,' Harris interrupted, 'I need you to do this, please,' he begged. She let go of the door handle and edged towards him. 'I don't care about dying. I need you to do this, only you. Please, just do it!'

'Alright,' Branwen rushed towards him and tried to calm him. 'But why?'

His eyes widened towards Branwen. 'A commander shows no weakness, and this will make me very weak.' His mouth curled.

Branwen laughed. 'Apologies. Pride is a horrid thing.'

'I'm serious. I have only my pride left, so allow me to keep that. Besides, I'm Xencliff. We don't show pain,' — his eyes glazed over, — 'apparently.'

Branwen thought. She knew where the arrow was. She would need to push the arrow towards his arm to avoid his heart.

'I can't, not without killing you.'

Harris replied, 'Then kill me.' It horrified Branwen he would say such a thing. 'I'm not scared. The last moments of my life were with a beautiful woman. I am more than ready, and I don't fear death.'

His words stirred her. He was not afraid to die, which frightened her. Such a handsome young man should have been looking forwards to his life. Death showed nothing but mercy to him. Branwen stood. She took some towels from a wooden chest at the foot of the bed. Placing them down, she made her way towards the back of him. She placed a bowl of water to the side of her.

Having placed a wooden spoon handle in his mouth, she warned, 'Hold still, you'll need to push against me.'

'I know how it's done,' he mumbled through the spoon. 'Just don't be gentle.' His brows rose. He rolled back over as Branwen drove the arrow forwards. It would not budge. Harris jolted back. She heard a cracking of bone as it made its way through his front ribs. Harris bit the handle as hard as he could, whilst giving a muffled cry. His chest forced out. He clutched the sheets on the bed, wailing. Breathing fast, he tried to remain still. Branwen started shoving as hard as she could. She forced the arrow to the side.

Sweat flowed from his brow. Harris fixated on his chest to see the arrow making its passage out. Blood streamed from the bed and onto the floor. Pooling blood covered Branwen's shoes. Harris carried on, shrieking and wailing in agony. He Struggled to remain still. Giving a mighty roar of agony, he saw the arrowhead under his skin. He took a dagger belted to his right leg and hacked into his flesh. With a mighty cry, Harris grabbed the arrowhead and pulled it. Branwen's hand slid forwards; Harris held the arrow up. She fell into the blood on the floor.

'Water! Or beer, get me something, Branwen!'

She rose from the floor and hurried to the side to fetch some water. Branwen twisted. Harris gave one last groan before he crashed into the bed.

'Harris! Commander!' She shook him, struggling to wake him.

She rubbed his face, trying to open his eyes, his cheeks covered with the blood from her hands. His lips became blue. 'Commander, please,' she sobbed, trying to rouse him. Branwen stood straight, holding her hand to her mouth. 'Oh shit,' she whispered, 'I killed the commander.' Her eyes widened as she stared at his lifeless body.

Harris gave a loud snore. Branwen gave a heavy sigh of relief.

With a large hole in his back and lung, it needed to be dealt with, and fast. She opted for the magic of the fae. Ferns, salt, and several oils. Along with stitching the parts she could reach. Her people's magic would help stop the bleeding and heal the wound. His chances would increase if she were a sharma or alchemist. His chances raised with her being fae.

The night lingered; Harris slept. Branwen remained by his side. Unable to leave him. She knew him for only a few moments. In those moments, he shared more about himself with her than any before. He was not afraid to die.

The heat of the night brought the stench from the battle outside. Branwen stood and closed the window.

'I'm sure we've met before,' murmured Harris as he woke. Elated, Branwen rushed towards the bed. She took a glass of water from the side, helping him to sit up. She held the water to his lips. Instead of drinking, he drolly glared at her.

'My hands work fine.' He took the glass from her.

'Apologies,' — she gave a slight laugh, — 'I'm used to a different fighter.'

'I can imagine. Have I laid with you?'

Branwen stood, disgusted. She continued to clear away the bloodied cushions from the back of him. 'We certainly have not! I've never met you. I've been here for a while. Before this I was in Assanin, and Sonnin, but our paths have never crossed,' she affirmed.

Harris's eyes narrowed. 'Untouched.' A smile grew. He watched her tidy the blood-soaked linen. 'You're Sonnin fae?'

Branwen stopped clearing. Forgiving him for his previous comment. Her arms relaxed by her front.

'I am Sonnin fae,' she replied with pride, 'but where are you from, Commander?'

Harris's eyes widened. 'The shadows, people have said I was born from war,' he held a whimsical tone, 'I could be from anywhere I like.'

Branwen shook her head. Her eyes dropped. 'All this talk of the dark stranger, The Shadow, and The Commander. You were just of lost Xencliff, the taverns alight with your name. But you're just a man, forgotten.'

'You know nothing of my life, Branwen,' he dropped his whimsey.

'I don't *claim* to, but I have sat here for days, wondering who you are?' She sat in a chair beside his bed and leant towards him, holding her hands under her chin as she waited for his reply.

Harris raised his brows. 'I will need to see my chiefs.'

Branwen sat back. She lowered her arms. 'Oh, come on. I saved your life. At least tell me about you.'

'So, you save my life. You're a nurse, that is your job, you do your job, now I must reveal everything about myself.'

'Yes, that is the deal.' Branwen raised her brows. A flirtatious smile from her plump caramel lips drew Harris in.

Harris took a moment; awkwardly, he scratched his chin, his eyes flickered towards her.

'Fine, I'm from a small coastal village. It's on the Xencliff path. My mother and father were both Xencliff, but they didn't partake in the on goings there. When my father died, my mother met Waron. She was beautiful.' His tone changed. Branwen leant forwards. 'The rest, we can save for another day.' His smile died.

Branwen sat back. She crossed her legs and placed her hands on her lap. 'You don't sound Xencliff.'

Harris raised his brows. Impressed, she noticed his accent. It was not the usual harsh overused vowels of the Xencliff tongue.

'I was young when my mother met Waron. I spent a lot of time in the cliffs.'

'A palace? So how did you come to be here?'

Harris gave a satirical glance at Branwen. His brow creased in the centre, his nose wrinkled, he swayed his head from side to side. 'Things happened. I'm here now, and that's all that matters.'

'Very well.' Branwen stood and continued to clear away.

'What of you, Sonnin fae?' He watched her glide through the room.

The floor still had a covering of dried blood. She fetched a pail of warm water and poured it onto the stone floor.

'I'm in my second service.' Harris furrowed his brows. He tilted his head. 'I plan to return soon.'

'I haven't met you before,' he gasped, his eyes shone with delight, 'but I met your mother, Branwen Duirwud.' Branwen held her head up. 'Daughter of Queen Harelda, of

Sonnin. I met her when I travelled through towards Ashdel last summer, I believe.'

She gave a slow head bob. 'Well, then I am pleased to make your acquaintance.'

'This feels strange. I have the next in line to the Sonnin' throne, cleaning my blood from the floor.'

Branwen laughed. 'I am doing my service. I'm not the next in line. That would be my sister. And who better to serve than my mother's champion of war?' Branwen stood by the bed.

'She's spoken of me?'

'Many times,' Branwen rolled her eyes. 'It was the main reason she wanted me in Marrion, so I would meet you.'

Harris gave a perverse smile from the corner of his mouth. 'I like your mother's thinking.'

Branwen snapped, 'Not for that,' — she came closer to him, — 'she has her ways, she knows what she is doing, it's your king I worry about.'

Harris flicked his head. 'Angus? he seems alright, he's a little odd but then who isn't?'

'It's the new girl he has. The child he found in the camps, some concern has arisen over her health. Apart from that, he is yet to have a child. It's all my mother speaks of.'

'He needs a wife first, maybe you? The royals like to keep it tight.'

'That isn't such a bad idea.' Branwen's smile widened. 'Now rest, you've been through an ordeal, we can talk more tomorrow, I'll get something to eat sent in.'

As Branwen left, Harris coughed. 'I've got a problem.' The corner of his mouth pulled up. Branwen raised her brows. 'Can you bring a bucket?' She furrowed her brow. 'I've been here for almost four days. I'm yet to piss.'

Branwen grinned. 'I am a wonderful nurse. I wouldn't allow you to go that long without it.'

'Really?' he blasted.

'Yes,' she said with a nod. 'But I'll have one sent in.'

Branwen discovered the arrogant, forceful berserker of war was nothing but a soldier who tried too hard. Her intrigue with him grew. His blatant disregard for life had her questioning. His life interested her.

The fae quarters in the castle of Marrion were silent that night. Anna took it onto herself to question the Atlanti they had retrieved. The dull dungeons of the castle filled with years of unkempt dust. The orange sands of Marrion covered the floors of the grey stone dungeons. With only one left to question, Anna stood with several of her soldiers.

A dark dungeon filled with pain from a thousand years of war. A large man slumped. His face bleeding and beaten, one eye was closed, the other almost hung from its socket. His cheek bones sunk shattered in his face. Hair covered with dried blood being re-moistened by his sweat. Fear was not a part of him.

Anna paced the room. His smile lingered. Dried blood covered his lips, red blood blackened his teeth.

'So,' — she continued pacing, — 'our question is simple.' She stood in front of him. 'What can you tell me to save your life?'

He laughed, 'I have lived a life fulfilled.'

Anna came closer. 'Not the answer I was looking for,' she replied in a deep tone. 'How many?'

An unexpected moment hit Anna; his closed eye flickered. 'More than you could ever count, bitch.'

She did not react to the comment. 'What do you mean by that?'

The man quivered. Sweat covered his heated brow. The thick dust on the ground swirled. A silent rumble hit the room. Dark shadows began descending on them, moving across the walls. He called in torment, throwing his head forwards and back again. Anna stood back.

'He has risen! He is the next!'

Anna stepped back further. The man's voice echoed both male and female tones. The guards grabbed the ropes which restrained him. He grew from the chair. He stood central to the dungeon and continued to shake. His nose poured with fresh blood. His mouth spat red, he roared in a voice that was not his. 'Be ready for him, fore you lead your people to a place of trembling pain. I am the necromancer!' His voice rumbled through the dark tunnels. His mouth poured with blood, he fell heaped to the ground, dead.

Anna panted with dread. The shadows lifted and sand dropped. She stepped back, glaring at the soldiers. 'Are we clear on this?' she asked them as they stood, still holding the ropes.

The soldiers glanced at the body of the man, they leered at each other, one twisted his eyes towards Anna.

'I'm not telling him,' he insisted.

'No, me neither.'

The other also joined in with, 'Not a chance.'

Anna flailed her arms. 'Fine, me again then!'

'Wait,' said one soldier. He glanced towards her. 'Perhaps it would be best to leave this with Lister? given that Harris is in no fit state at the moment. If he heard that the man we're fighting against possessed the body of a dead man. Claiming he is the necromancer. Well, I just think that could do more harm than good.'

Anna did not like lying to Harris. She knew he was volatile.

'Fine, Lister then.'

'Anna, if what you're telling me is accurate, you need to assure me of something.' Lister's rich voice echoed from the bath in his chambers. He remained behind a stone wall. She remained in his large chambers. 'This stays with us. You tell no one, you warn no one.'

Stood in his chambers, she called to Lister, 'Agreed.' Her voice filled with relief. 'I don't want to be dealing with this right now, so this is yours.'

'And, Anna, that goes for your commander as well.'

Anna nodded, knowing he could not hear her. A silent promise to Lister tore at her, knowing she would have to lie to the man she trusted the most.

A silent breeze fled through the courtyard as Anna returned to her chambers. The silence that night shattered her.

ᚲᚺᚨᛈᛏᛖᚱ ᛖᛁᚷᚺᛏ

8

The skies above Thrasia rumbled. Eerie panic on the ground had sheep sweating, as a striking crimson dragon, the greatest of his kind, Egan, flew with his thunder. The colossal creatures bought a sight they considered lost in their lands.

A mighty voice roared through the skies.

'Await, my return in the valley!' boomed Egan.

'We expect your return before nightfall. These lands are unsafe,' called Kayda. The lilac beast was beautiful to behold.

The air from Egan's wings roared as they sailed through the skies. 'I am sure a thunder of nine can fend off any curious enemy.'

'What have the stars told us?' asked Jara, a huge green dragon. Each scale gilded with bright gold.

Egan circled around, bringing himself to the side of Jara. 'Their silence remains. The king shows excitement with the power the child holds.'

'And you believe this to be true?' called Barron, a smaller blue and orange dragon.

Again, Egan circled in the air to join Barron's side. 'I believe they found something. While Angus's eccentrics often concern us. She was born in Farhope. Even her discovery was strange.'

Sat on her mezzanine, Librye pursued through the books.

Angus sat at his desk, working below her. The sun warmed the smoke left lingering from his morning pipe. Angus stood and made his way towards the window. To the side of the window, he opened a sliding vent. The smell of pine needles and wood smoke floated in on the icy breeze. The warm fire in his chambers grew with the fresh, inviting air.

Librye peered up. 'Is everything alright?'

Angus looked up. His eyes softened towards her. He replied in a blissful tone, 'Everything is perfect. Would you like to join me for a walk?'

Librye stood, slamming her book closed with a frisson.

The gardens brightened as they strode into the slumber of winter. A dusting of snow settled. The fountain sat as a frozen wonder of winter.

'The world looks so new,' said Librye, skipping towards the meadow.

Angus murmured his reply, 'It would be nice if it were so.'

'The council has been busy this turn,' she mentioned.

Angus ambled with his hands behind his back. A thick deerskin warmed him.

'They're busy every turn.'

'You know I've been there; you know my secrets have told me.'

'What part have your secrets told you?'

She replied, 'They want you to get a wife. You once said that one day you'll want lots of children.' She shook her head whilst looking down. 'You can only do that with a wife.'

Angus burst with a laugh. 'You're supposed to be on my side.'

'I am,' Librye replied in a high-pitched tone. 'But I agree with them. You would make a wonderful father.'

'Thank you, Heart.' Angus stopped walking. Wispy clouds journeyed across the sky against the backdrop of icy blue. A soft, chilly breeze hit him. He gazed towards the palace. Upon hearing a familiar deep pounding sound. He crouched in front of her. 'I have a surprise for you.'

Her smile grew. She, too, could hear the strange sound. 'A surprise?'

'Look to the skies, Heart.' Angus stood. He watched as she gazed towards the icy sky. A bluster of wind brushed her thin hair. From the top of the palace, flew a mighty red dragon. The size of the palace made him appear small. Gliding down and making his way towards the tiny Librye, she could see just how magnificent he was. A thrill of hairs stood on end. A twisting in her belly as butterflies took flight.

'Egan!' greeted Angus, making his way towards him.

Egan stood proudly on the path. He adorned the two blunt horns on his head with golden bands. His friendly face warmed Angus. Librye stood, frozen with the rest of the garden.

'Angus,' Egan grumbled. He ambled towards him. 'It has been too long.'

'It certainly has.' Angus spun to introduce Librye.

Her smile was unwavering. 'Good afternoon, you must be Egan?' asked Librye.

His deep blue dragon eyes lit towards the young girl. 'I am. You must be the Unknown Girl?'

Librye shook her head. Her voice was soft, filled with pride. 'They gave me my name. The stars said it would be so.'

'The stars?' asked Egan, 'you speak with them?'

'I must interject,' said Angus. 'Heart, did your secrets tell you of this visit?'

Librye thought, 'No, nothing, but I don't mind, I like surprises. I speak with the stars often, do you?' She looked at Egan.

'As often as I can. So, what is your knowledge of the stars?'

'I've heard the whispers for a while. I hear them at night. The stars are usually my favourite moments in the day. They're so peaceful. I know they hold many of your secrets. I also know why you're here.'

'Oh, and why am I here?'

Librye smiled. She gazed at his scaled face. 'To see me.'

Egan replied in his booming voice, 'I am, but only to learn all I can from you.'

The two strolled towards the wild meadow. Angus stood proudly on the path, watching his prodigy walk with the largest beast their world held, but also the gentlest. Egan's wings brushed the trees as they strolled down the lane. Librye received an enchanting light snow as the flakes fell from the branches. The wolves remained silent as the dragon passed.

'How odd,' said Egan. They passed the kennels. The host was absent.

Librye struggled to take her eyes away from the beautiful beast in front of her. 'What is?'

'The wolves.' Egan stopped on the path and glanced towards them as they relaxed in their beds. 'No pacing, growling, snarling even.'

Librye broke her stare with Egan. She glanced at the wolves. 'That's because they know me. They won't bark or howl, because they are safe. Truly safe.'

His giant brows furrowed as Egan leered towards the wolves. Some raised their heads to watch Librye pass. Others continued to sleep on their hay beds.

'So, the wolves view you as their protector?'

Librye strolled towards the bars. The kennel host peered around the front to see the giant Egan.

'She's an enigma,' said the kennel host waddling towards the front. Egan glanced towards him. 'Dane, sire,' he introduced himself, 'and I know you must be lord Egan, of the Draco stretch.'

The mighty dragon nodded his head towards Dane.

'Well, from the moment Librye met the wolves, she took them.' He pointed towards the wood with his brows raised. 'The moment she steps into the garden, the wolves change. I've never seen it happen in all my years here.' He relaxed his arms to the side of him. He eyed Librye, stroking the wolves from the bars.

Egan stared at the wolves, who paid no attention to him. 'Fascinating.'

Their walk took them to the furthest part of the meadow and back again. The dragons did not care for a cold climate.

'We should head back. I promised to return before nightfall.' Egan gazed at the skies.

Librye strutted at the side of him, dwarfed by him.

'Do you hear your kin?' asked Librye, her deep tone threw Egan. 'You mentioned the stars told you about me. What have they told you?'

'They told me that the Unknown Girl has arrived in Cronnin. That was a while ago. They have been quiet of late.'

Librye stopped walking. Her tiny frame stood frozen on the path. 'Not for me they haven't.'

'My dear, the stars are quiet, it is quite common, the world rages with the anger of men, the stars are silent, to allow them rest.' Egan swirled to see her apple green eyes staring back at him.

Her head was low, she held her hands at the front of her. 'I stopped them.'

Egan narrowed his eyes; a twisted look of fear took over his face.

'I stopped them. I knew you would come, so I needed to show you the ability I have.' Librye lifted her hand towards the skies, a soft breeze ran through the woods. A flutter of snow fell from the canopy. Birds whistled and sang in the woods. Egan lifted his head and gazed at the skies; the stars whispered to him.

Egan glimpsed back at her. The overwhelming whispers flooded his mind, he listened. All whispers about the Unknown Girl.

'The child is Librye,' he heard. 'They fly.' They whispered.

Librye strolled away. Egan struggled to move. The power over the stars was a terrifying power. She blocked all messages and whispers for half a turn. She led the entire race of dragons to believe that the stars fell silent.

'I need to ask you something,' said Librye. She waited for Egan to join her side.

'Anything,' he replied, still dumbfounded.

'What do the stars mean when they say the dragons will fly when the king is found?'

'A question I will struggle to answer,' he breathed his reply.

'I am not all mighty and powerful,' said Librye. Shame caught her voice. 'Can I be truthful?'

'Always.'

'I am so scared,' she said with a quiver in her voice. 'The council looks at me like I'm something to be feared. Angus looks at me like I'm something to be revered. I'm just me. I'm nothing special.'

Egan's grin widened. He lowered his head to just above hers. 'You are the most special creature ever to be born, just like the child that was born before you, and the one before them. Every life, no matter how drole, is remarkable. That is all the stars want you to know. You have nothing to fear, providing you live a good and noble life.'

'What if I'm not destined for that?'

'You speak of destiny as though it is already written. We are the masters of our own fate. We wield the power to choose.'

'And if they chose your fate for you?'

'Then you must take charge of your life. Never let your fate be chosen for you.'

As they reached the path, Angus stood waiting for them.

'Ah,' he sighed. He stepped towards them. 'Finally, you're back. Librye, dinner is ready. Please, leave me and Egan, we need to talk.' He embraced her before she ran down the path and towards the palace.

'Well?' Angus held his hands behind his back. He strutted towards Egan.

'There is little I can say. The dragons will help, all we can, but her power far outweighs ours.' Egan watched Librye. She ran back towards the palace. She gave a bow to the guards before stepping back inside. They too bowed at Librye.

'She is a wonder of nature, and one to keep a close eye on. If she is to lead this world towards the victory it needs, we must protect her.' He gave a stark warning to Angus. 'Protect her as you would your own child. She is only a child. Her innocence is as precious as her life.'

'Do you believe she is one of the Solnox?'

'She is what she is, a child of heart, one that feels fear. Her title or birth rite does not matter. She is frightened.'

Angus nodded. He ambled down the path towards the palace with Egan. 'And what of her secrets?'

Egan shook his head, looking at the floor. 'They are not the stars; her secrets are something else.' Egan stopped; he held his head high. 'A warning I can give,' he held a deep thunder in his voice. 'Do not question her secrets. Let no one question her secrets. A fate worse than death will await those who do.'

Angus raised his brows and walked towards Egan, his hands caught behind his back. 'Believe me when I tell you this, Egan. There is nothing in this world that could ever harm her. While I'm around, that is my promise to you.' Egan softened his eyes towards Angus and bowed his head. 'Now go, tell them what you've seen.'

'One more thing, before I leave.' He twisted his head towards the stars. 'The man from Xencliff, do not listen to his rumours. I have known him long enough to know he is a frightened soul. He begs for death to take him fairly. Fear guides him, just as bravery does.'

'You speak of Harris Bearwood?'

'I speak of a man born to turmoil who found privilege and threw it away for loyalty, a man so twisted in fate, he is hardly a man at all anymore.'

'Egan, is he dangerous?' shook Angus.

Egan turned his head over his shoulder, widening his eyes. 'Oh, very.' A grin caught the left of his mouth before he took off into the skies and disappeared over the Cronnin palace. He flew low over the city, giving the people there one last view of might before he left.

Angus meandered into the kitchen. Staff members bowed in shock at his presence. Librye sat at the table eating her meal while swinging her legs.

Librye asked, 'Well? what did he say?'

'You impressed him.' Angus sat opposite her. The staff remained silently scurrying in the shadows of the kitchen. 'I need to warn you of something, though.' He raised his brows, lowering his head towards her.

Librye lifted her eyes towards him. 'I already know. The Draco dragons, they're different.' A strange solace in her voice sent a shiver through Angus, running up his spine. 'The black dragons of Rathen. They're not on our side.' Her eyes leered at him. Angus sat upright. 'Books tell you a lot.'

Angus raised his brows. 'But the stars will always tell you more.'

Gethen listened to his soft words. 'They were once the dragons of Volnot,' said Gethen.

'A time long passed,' said Angus. 'Egan will listen to all you need to tell him. Just remember, you can always talk to me as well.' He distanced himself from her as he stood. Sauntering from the kitchen, he took an apple from Gethen's bowl on his large workbench as he left.

Hope grew in Marrion. Harris hobbled from his bed, with his knee strapped. He held his chest as he tried to stand.

'You're well on the way to recovery,' said Branwen, returning from the laundry with some sheets.

'I cannot waste my day sat in a bed. Moving is recovering,' replied Harris. He lounged down to watch Branwen work.

'Well, you're up, and that's the important part.'

'Only with thanks to you.' His soft voice fluttered through her. 'I will tell Angus of your heroism, and your mother, if she would meet a rogue like me,' he chuckled.

'You are no rogue to her, Harris, you are a champion.'

'When did she hear of me?'

'She first heard of you when you entered Dorm, the battle there took my brother, my mother paid close attention to the movements there, when a warrior joined, of Xencliff, fresh from battle, he held no rank or title, he had no payment, and he ended the battle, chasing the Atlanti from those lands.' Branwen joined his side, sitting on his bed beside him. 'I remember my mother told her guards to watch him, to ensure he is no mercenary. He is not a rogue. You fascinated her. It was her who found out where you were from, she spoke with your mother a lot, it was then she realised, it was your father who used to saddle my father's horses, from that moment, she believed the fates brought you into this war, because you had the honour of your father, and the strength of your mother.'

'You would love my mother, all women do. She certainly is a woman of power.'

'Then you are your mother's son,' she smiled, standing from the bed.

Fresh from battle. Anna burst into the room. Instead of walking straight in, she spun and faced the door with her hands held at the front of her.

Branwen glanced up.

'It's safe, Anna,' said Harris, holding a grin.

Branwen brought a pitcher of water to Harris's bedside. 'Safe?'

Anna made her way in. 'Our promiscuous commander is often in the most uncompromising positions when we enter.' She stood by Harris's bedside, receiving an unwelcome glare from Harris. 'We've all learnt to enter with care.' Her brows raised towards him.

'I get lonely,' Harris mocked.

Branwen raised her brows. 'It's no excuse.'

'What news, Anna?' Harris's mind was fully awake, but his body failed him. 'If it's bad, then you know what I expect.' He held a wide grin.

Anna sighed, 'Not going to happen.'

'What would you expect, Commander?' Branwen innocently asked.

Harris gave a broad smile and glanced at her innocent face.

'Anna is Xencliff. She left with me, from the tavern there.' He could see the growing question in Branwen's haunting blue eyes. 'Branwen, something we did in Blodmoor, if Anna lost a battle, or didn't perform as expected,' — Harris took a long pause, — 'why am I struggling to say it?' He scowled at Anna.

Anna furrowed her brow and tilted her head towards him. 'No idea,' she replied with a snigger. 'If I fuck up, he gets a suck. Not anymore, though.' She glared at him. 'Not since you know what.'

Branwen drew back. 'I'll ask no more.'

Anna removed her breastplate and dumped it near the desk. 'It's not good. The ground is ours for today. We set the next battle for three days from now. We've retired the field for them to remove their corpses, I have Saburo and Markus watching. It will take us into Saed.' She walked towards his bed. 'You need to heal, fast. We can hold them off, but the vitriol is terrifying to them. It's pushing them further to the coast.'

Harris sat on the side of his bed. 'That was the plan. As long as the threat is there, we need no more of it. We can't rely on supplies. We must now rely on their fear and use it against them.'

Anna wandered towards his desk. She could see the piles of papers.

'Your desk is filling with unread letters, Harris.' She lifted some and held them up to him.

Branwen peered from the darkened corner of the chambers towards Anna.

'While he is healing, work stays on the desk,' said Branwen. 'You are all more than capable of doing his duty. Please, take them.'

Harris gave a saddened look to Anna. 'My leg still won't work, and this one,' — he flicked his head towards Branwen, — 'won't help. Last time I tried, she shouted at me.'

'How the mighty commander has fallen,' laughed Anna. She took some scrolls and threw them on the bed. 'We cannot stop him, Branwen.' Her smile twisted. 'I know you're trying to help; we all appreciate that.' She gave a large, exasperated breath. 'But as much as I hate to say it, we need Harris's mind right now.' Anna swirled in the chambers and gave a disgusted groan. She sauntered back towards the desk. 'I can actually feel your ego growing.'

'Come closer,' Harris widened his smile. 'See what else you can get to grow.'

Anna gave a slow, very unimpressed blink towards Harris. Harris gave a wide grin towards Branwen. 'I told you, I have earned my arrogance.'

Harris read through the scrolls. Anna unravelled her platted hair. Her hair appeared wet, but it was dry, filled with dried blood. Harris reached over his bed and took a drink from the cabinet at the side.

'It's not looking good. The mabeara have mobilised. They're sending them south.' He glanced at Anna, furrowing his brow. 'You look like shit.' Branwen raised her brows towards him disapprovingly. 'What?' he barked. 'She does.'

'Might I suggest?' — Branwen strutted closer to Anna, — 'a relaxing bath, a night to recover?'

Anna peered around Branwen's shoulder. She, too, raised her brows towards him. 'And that, Harris, is how you speak to a lady.'

'I don't need to be told how to speak to women.' Harris's grin widened. Anna left. 'You should know, Anna!' he called to her.

'Piss off, Harris!' she shouted back over her shoulder.

Harris shuffled his legs back into his bed and got back to reading silently. He glanced up as Branwen floated about the room. Tidying the linens, cleaning the sides, and dusting the shelves. His eyes followed her every move. Her hourglass figure was inviting to his eyes.

'If you're going to continue to stare. I can remove the papers from your bed.' Branwen dusted the shelf in front of him.

Harris laughed. 'Apologies, but you are just,' — Harris paused, he gave a look of pure delight, — 'stunning. I mean, look at you, stuck in the camps as well. You should be out there for all the world to see.' He raised his brows. 'At least that way, the Atlanti might *not* want to kill us all.'

Branwen spun; she narrowed her eyes coming close to the bed. Taking the drink from the side, she gave a large sniff. 'Apologies. Thought you might be drunk.'

Harris burst with a laugh. 'I'm being serious. You're really a very attractive woman.' He nodded approvingly with his mouth curled down. 'In Xencliff we call women like you wifeable. Others are just fuckable.'

Branwen shook her head. She sashayed away. After a few moments of further cleaning, she could not hold her questions any longer. Sharply, she twisted.

'I've heard of you, Harris Bearwood.' She drifted towards him. 'What I cannot see, though, is the attraction.'

Harris remained plain faced. Branwen pryingly continued to drift closer to him. He found it overwhelmingly attractive.

'I've heard stories of the commander who never has to pay for a tavern. Any woman would be glad to see him in their bed for the night. But why? I mean, yes, you're handsome, but many are.' She strolled towards her chair near the window. A darkness covered her there. 'What makes you so special?'

Harris sat back in his bed. 'First, I often pay. Second, I am a fucking delight.' He held his head high with a slight sway to his head. A shocked smile covered her face. 'Let's see, if you can guess, what makes me so good at what I do?' His grin widened.

She was pure, she was clean. 'You're insufferable, immoral. You think you're a charmer.' She sat forwards from the shadow. 'You make these women think they need you. You make them feel better about what they do,' she guessed.

Harris gave an audible laugh. His lofty tone told her she was wrong. 'Ludicrous, utter bollocks.' He gave a flirtatious grin. 'By "them" I assume you speak of tavern pornes, and by the way, there is no shame in what they do. They deliver pleasure to this world. The only bit of pleasure Cammbour has left resides in the taverns. As drenched in spit and debauchery as they may be. If you really wish to know what makes me so good at what I do.' His voice lowered and softened. 'I may just have to show you, then you'll understand.'

Branwen flew her head back and laughed. 'I'm untouched. You really think I would choose you as my first?'

He whispered, deeply, 'You are curious. You've sat there for days, watching, wondering,' — he drawled the word, 'wanting. You want to know what all those women feel? You want to know what I do. Mostly, you want to know what I would do to get *you* in my bed.'

'As an untouched, I would never do such a thing. My chastity is my service to the gods.'

'The gods!' laughed Harris. 'Since when did they make an appearance? And since when did they care about who's fucking who?'

Branwen was solemn. 'Do not give up on them. They have not given up on you.' She could see something in Harris, which only drew her closer to him. 'You may feel that now, but you're alive.'

Harris shook his head. He sat up and gave a scornful look. 'Exactly.'

Branwen stood. She sauntered towards him. 'Who hurt you, Harris?'

'The world hurt me, just as it hurts everyone. I don't charm women. I don't act like I deserve to bed every one of them. That makes me unique.'

Branwen took a chair from the side of the bed. She placed it beside his bed. Sat quietly, she listened with a chastened look.

'I lost everything, but the only thing they couldn't take was me. I am who I am, because I remain the same arrogant, splendid arsehole I've always been. My father has good looks and my mother is passionate. It makes for a volatile mix, granted, but I will never deceive someone for my own passionate gain.' He glanced at Branwen. Her parted lips attracted him. 'My mother sent me to the taverns, hoping I could work as a porne. The best taught me and I became better. I protect people, Branwen, simply by remaining the man I am.'

'You really are just you. I think I'm impressed.'

'Better still, you must be bored.' He pointed to a cabinet close to his desk. 'In there, there's a small checks game, if you're up for a quickie?'

'Very well,' she stood, collecting the box. She lowered herself onto the chair. 'So, tell me more about the real you, not The Commander, but Xencliff Harris.'

Harris gave a quick flicker of his eyes towards her; his smile grew. He began the game. 'I lost my father to the murk, or the black. It was at the same time an army was passing through. They took our farm. My father died in the flames. My mother escaped with me and my brother.' His voice was honest, but he was still holding back.

'Apologies. It's a horrid thing to hear.'

'Well, before that he was a man of many trades,' — he beamed when speaking of his father, — 'he was a leatherworker, blacksmith, cook, one of the best. His way with words was powerful. I learnt from the best because he could twist anyone into thinking he was the best.'

Branwen glimpsed to the board, checks, a game of tactics, she could see she was clearly winning. 'And your mother?' Her eyes remained fixed on the board, but Harris, his eyes remained fixed on Branwen.

His tone lowered, the enthusiasm was gone. 'I loved her dearly. She did everything right. She was a force, still is.'

'You mean love?' She finally broke her gaze with the board. Giving a quick glance towards him, her lips parted with concentration.

Harris nodded. 'I did, you know, of Riah Chen Lu.'

Branwen gave a low nod. 'I have heard her passion many times from the mouth of my mother. She has a way with words.'

'My mother met him following my father's death. My brother and I were young. She needed to make a choice. When Odalis was old enough to join the war he left, I had nine years in the cliffs of the Xencliff palace. The place was pleasing enough, but I didn't want that life.'

'Palace life can be hard,' Branwen sympathetically uttered.

Harris shook his head. 'No, that was the simple part. The hard part was being me, in a place where you had to be someone else. I wanted pleasant conversation, but they just wanted pleasing. I learnt a lot from them, but never spoke much.' His constant attitude of truthfulness drew Branwen closer to him. 'I didn't care for the violence in taverns. The constant flowing of bodily fluids.'

He gave a loud sigh. 'Until I left, then I realise it changed me. I enjoy passion and pleasing. My mother is who I take after. I'm sure you've heard she is like a lit fire, with hot oil poured on. All I wanted was a bit of conversation, just being myself.' Harris gave a slow blink. 'That keeps them coming back.'

He reached for his check. 'One thing that always shocks people. They call me dangerous, even though I have risked my life for thousands.' His eyes remained fixed on her soft, pale skin. 'I respect people, I respect women, I am a protector. That is why your mother chose me.' As quick as the game started, Harris placed his last check down. 'I win.'

'That's not fair,' argued Branwen. 'Your story distracted me. I demand a rematch.'

Harris set the board again. 'Distraction is a friend of any commander.' He enjoyed her company, but he also enjoyed the conversation. The smell of her sweet lavender and vanilla hand rub reminded him of nothing. It would forever remind him of the caring nurse, who, despite everything, saved his life and his pride.

He watched her each day; she would have most of her duties finished within an hour. Tenderly dressing his wounds was his favourite. Taking breakfast and dining together was his second favourite. Where it not for Branwen, he would have succumbed to boredom long ago.

The pleasant conversation as the days drifted on kept him grounded. Sitting and sifting through letters of war. Branwen took the time to listen to all he said.

A light mist cast a shadow over the mountains in the north. A raging fire warmed Gaius's new chambers. He stared at the fire, his lips parted as he watched the flames.

'I have a visitor joining us today,' said Kairne as he entered. The strange relationship between them thickened the air. Kairne wavered, his spirit crumbled. 'I wished to see a favourable future in my lifetime. Perhaps my heir will bring me such. My father, my mother, they were wrong. All I wish for is a fair fight, to see our world in balance, where the fae will leave us alone to live.' Gaius glanced at Kairne. Uninterested in his words. 'Did you plan to have children with your wife?'

'Aye,' murmured Gaius. 'Her father passed her to me. He knew I was a dedicated soldier. When she was a child, a horse caught her belly in a brawl. An alchemist told her she would never bear children. Her father saw me as a comfort to her, someone who wouldn't live long enough to consider a family. She was more comfort to me than anything. She even spoke of taking in a child with no family to raise as our own.'

'You will see her again, Gaius. Her duty is vital in this world.'

'I understand that, my lord.'

'She is the reason you breathe.' Kairne sat beside him on the small sofa. The fire warmed them. 'My father would tell me love was a fae concept, something they made up to make them feel superior. Then I met Isradella, a beautiful flower, someone who would strengthen our kingdom, give me an heir, and love me.' He twisted to face Gaius. 'Love is real, and that is something the fae cannot take from us. She will return to you, because she loves you.'

'If only that were true, but we don't know what peril she faces, what atrocities she sees.'

'I know enough about Cronnin to know she is safe, providing her identity is hidden.'

A young soldier stepped into the room, breaking the conversation. 'Sir, a woman has arrived from Arktos.'

Kairne's dark eyes brightened. 'Isradella?'

'It could be, sir. I have guided her to the second tower to keep her in comfort.'

'I appreciate it,' said Kairne. As he stood to leave, Gaius held his robe, stopping him.

'Love her, please.' He took a deep breath, refusing to allow any emotion out.

'We are Atlanti, of the Azorae, but we are still men, men who love. Our ancestors told us to show no fear, shed no tears. Perhaps this is where our fae enemies have tainted us.'

'I am not tainted. I have just had enough.'

'Haven't we all.' Kairne slowly left the room. Gaius remained glaring at the fire in front.

The evening was clear in Cronnin; the palace was alive with talk from the galleries. Gethen was still cleaning the oven from the evening's feast.

'Takes about a quart turn, getting from Draco. It's difficult for the dragons now.' His undercooks continued to prepare for the morning's breakfast. 'Whatever that girl brings, it's going to take the world by storm.'

'Still, the council are talking.' Emma cleared the plates from the middle table. 'I heard Connor saying that she's being sent to Bourellis.' She gave a low nod.

Gethen furrowed his brow. 'Why Bourellis?'

'Because that is where the child will be better off, with her own kind. She ain't going to learn nothing ere,' Emma sneered.

'Well, she's almost finished the shelves of the king's library.' Maude sauntered into the galleries. She stood straight and held her hands to the front of her.

Emma gave an awkward look. 'She's a clever little one.'

'Yes, she is.' Maude felt the atmosphere change. 'Bourellis won't help, though. I have heard that Angus is trying his best to get it stopped. It isn't the council's place to tell the girl where she will go. She's Angus's ward. It's up to him.'

'So, the council are pushing for this?' Gethen stopped scrubbing and twisted to Maude.

Maude gave a quick nod. 'They are. I've been told not to say anything.' Maude whispered, 'But Librye is having private tuition from the dragons. As you know, she has been with Egan. The thunder is waiting for him. They still refuse to join the war.'

'It would be over in a turn if they did.' Gethen held a disapproving tone.

'I agree.' Maude gave a heavy sigh. 'Hopefully, the scroll that Angus found could provide some answers.'

'Perhaps,' replied Emma, 'but these are tough times. We need to be looking out for each other, especially children.'

The night-time gardens were pleasing that night. A light snow settled. Librye spent the entire day with the wolves. Angus had long ago retired to his room.

'The hour is late,' warned Dane. He stepped from the side of the kennels.

Looking up, Librye begged, 'Please can I stay? I don't feel tired.'

Dane laughed; her tired-looking eyes told him different. 'I heard you talking to Egan about the stars. Perhaps you could spend the rest of the night talking to those?' He gazed up to see the speckled skies above.

Librye's smile grew. She stood from the side of the wolves who appeared giant beside her. 'That is a wonderful idea.'

Dane followed her back, making sure she was safe. The moment he could clearly see the guards by the door, he stopped, allowing her to go alone. Librye stopped at the fountain and sat. She gazed up at the tiny, glittering stars. Peace flooded her mind. Whispers surrounded her. From the side of her she heard the whisper of her name being called, 'Librye.'

She closed her eyes, her head pointed to the stars. 'I'm here,' she thought in her mind, sending her whisper back.

'It was a pleasure meeting you today,' said the whisper of Egan. 'I hope to see you again soon.'

'Tomorrow? I will wait for you in the gardens.'

She heard a rumbling laugh from Egan. 'We must return. My thunder has had a long journey; they need us in Draco.'

Librye felt a sinking pain, deep in the pit of her stomach. 'Please don't go.'

'I will see you when the world is ready for the dragons' return, my Librye.'

'The world is ready for you now,' she begged.

'The world is not yet ready,' his whisper was regretful. 'Our lands will one day unite,' his whispers became dull. 'Listen to the stars. Become the writer of destiny.' The stars silenced. Librye opened her eyes and ambled to the porch. Maude stood on the porch waving to her.

A crisp winter morning awaited Angus as he woke. He made his way towards his chambers. Librye beat him there.

'Good morning,' greeted Librye, sat on the stairs to the mezzanine. She had started on the bottom bookcases.

With a deep baritone voice, Angus replied, 'Good morning, Heart.'

'The pigeon carrier has just left,' Librye stood. She watched as Angus pushed the messages to one side. 'No!'

Angus glimpsed up. His brow drew in.

Librye ran as fast as possible towards his desk. She frantically searched his desk. 'This one.'

Angus stood bemused. He took the scroll. 'What is this?'

Librye took a step back. 'It's bad news, but it's news you need to know.' She took another step back, and another. 'Open it.'

Slowly, Angus took the ring from the scroll and unrolled it. A small piece of battered paper delivered the worst news possible. His eyes contorted to a look of defeat as he read the note. His smile withered and died. This was no longer a good morning.

'Damn,' he whispered. His hands shook, his face turned red. 'Damn!'

Librye stood back. Angus saw her jump. 'Apologies, Heart.'

'I have suffered a slight setback. Worry not. I am being cared for. Yet I feel this may set Marrion back a few turns. The injuries could have ended me. I fight on.'

Harris remained in his bed, irritated. He limped into his chambers, awaiting his reply from Angus. The battle continued around him.

Stood upon the plateau, Harris watched as the battle raged. Flaming boulders pounded the Atlanti army below, followed by mighty tree trunks.

'Reload!' Those loading had brows covered with sweat.

'Please, sir, just a few moments.' Panted one soldier working with the others to lift the enormous trunks.

Harris pounded towards them. He pointed towards the field. 'Where is their break?' — he roared at them, — 'no, you can rest when you're dead, now load!'

He heard a distinct sigh. 'They aren't even touching any of them,' grumbled one of them.

Harris leered at him with a furrowed brow. 'I do not intend the poles to injure,' he replied, walking towards them. He pointed to the field. 'Take a moment and inspect your work.'

Three of the four soldiers marched towards the edge. They searched the field to see the poles protruding from the ground. Impaled Atlanti horses struggled to get through. The ground was virtually impenetrable. Forcing them to attack from the west, diminishing their entire force. 'Now, they aren't there to injure, they are there to hinder.' The battle would again belong to Cronnin.

CHAPTER NINE

9

Nestled deep in the second tower of Rathen, a beauty awoke. Crimson red lips framed by swaying curls of deep mahogany hair. Haunting brown eyes stared towards the face of her sleeping lover. Kairne respectfully slept on a long sofa beside the dim fire in the room.

Isradella stood from the bed, her flowing gown graced the stone floor and carpet as she walked towards him. A small blanket covered him.

She knelt beside him, taking his hand from under the covers. His eyes flickered. Looking at the face of his young bride.

'Good morning, my love,' she muttered to him. His smile widened, small lines and circles around his eyes showed. 'This world is taking from you.' Reaching up, she stroked his face as his eyes opened more. 'We will take from them as well. Our union begins today. With that, this world will be forced to see the Azorae people and their plight.'

'The Azorae do not struggle as the Atlanti struggle,' he replied. Shuffling up to sit, he kept hold of her delicate hand. Rubbing his fatigued face with the other. 'You are inexperienced, therefore, I can excuse your ignorance.'

'We met for a moment, when my world collided with yours.' Her eyes flickered down. 'Tell me, what is the difference between Azorae and Atlanti?'

He rubbed his eyes, peering at her with contemplation. 'It is an answer which sees much debate. It does not depend on where you are from, but on your ideas.' Her brows furrowed in confusion. 'My father was of fighting blood, but that is not the only thing which divides us.

'Many years ago, there was the island of Crede, where their ruler took Atlanti values and traditions, and destroyed them, by introducing the traditions of the fae. Those are the Azorae. He was ultimately outcast, with a few followers.

'The Azorae were not accepted by the Atlanti, and the fae and faeman wouldn't take them either, so they drifted, until they settled along the borders of Enderton and Amerius. I do not fight for the Azorae. I fight for my people.'

'Then the Azorae are your enemy too?'

He sniggered at her innocence. 'You are lucky you're pretty. They are neither friend nor foe, they bear no threat to us. The Azorae are nothing, tavern owners who welcome everyone into their bars, farmers who let anyone cross their land.'

'So, they are neutral?'

'You could say that, but I prefer to see them as nothing. They abandoned their people who died for their freedom. They are nothing but deserters. When we win this war, they will expect the world. I will give them nothing but the freedom they craved.'

'And you have seen war?'

Shocked at her question, he sat upright. 'I have seen enough,' his tone snapped. 'What the faemen do is barbaric. They will never allow the Atlanti to live in peace.'

She raised herself onto her knees. 'But with our union, the land of Arktos will be ours. My mother does not have long for this world.'

He leant towards her, taking both her hands in his. 'She has longer than you realise. Remember, I am the necromancer. I see death, and where death lurks. Your mother is not close, her mind is no longer her own.'

He stood, throwing the blanket to the side.

'I warned her, the precious material within the mountains of Arktos has its uses, but ingesting them can lead to insanity. She was simply lucky she sent you away to grow, otherwise, you would be insane like the rest of them.'

'My mother is not insane!' Isradella stood, taking a firm stance. 'She is a stable leader.'

Kairne coiled to face her, drifting towards her. He bound her face in his hand, inspecting her eyes.

'If you do not see your mother's actions as insane, perhaps it is too late for you as well,' he sniggered. 'Your own father saw his end upon a pyre he built for himself. Hold your tongue, I am a fair and equal ruler, but brutality is what the Atlanti are famed for. I do not fear using punishment on my wife when her words escape her.'

Isradella watched as Kairne left the room. The inexperienced sixteen-year-old bride shook, but her naïve mind settled. She had never known normality, accepting her older husband's words as the truth would keep her safe.

Sonnin stood as a stark contrast to Cronnin. A place of mystery and wonder, of magic and life, a place of the fae. Old dust paths wound through deep, ancient forests. Stretching far into a mountain range. Nestled in the heart of the ancient and mystifying forest stood a tree as old as time. A slow mist crept along the vine paths. Surrounded by a high golden fence. To the front, a towering gate stood.

The tree was not ordinary; it did not look ordinary. Twisted oak branches curled towards the sky. The old bark of the tree appeared thick and swollen with age. Prowling roots along the ground created a path to the tree. The leaves sat still, adorned with shining gold. It was the only tree that winter's cold clawing fingers had not touched.

The mid-afternoon sun graced the woodlands of Sonnin. The heavy frost melted as it glistened on the ground. Pine needles lined the old wood. The frozen ferns on the ground remained still. A feeling of peaceful hush swirled in the air that day. The dry dirt paths remained empty. The golden sun woke the world.

A call resounded through the trees. Towards the east of the city, a man came sprinting through the streets of Sonnin.

Bernard, the pigeon keeper flailed a note in his hand. He waddled as fast as his legs could carry him. Brown, dusty tunic and trousers sprayed a mist as he ran from his old tree. The soles of his shoes flapped behind him.

'Open the gate!' he yelled at the guards resting beside the old palace tree. Bernard hustled towards the guards. Without pause, the gates broke open.

He made his approach, coming to the palace door. Coiling patterns swirled within a door on the trunk of the tree. A glorious light formed as the guard touched the handle in the centre of the door.

'This way, Bernard,' said the guard as he entered.

Bernard straightened his greasy hair with his dirt filled hands. A smell lingered with the old man, not a foul odour, an earthy scent of nature. The guard kept his distance. A long, winding staircase met him as he entered. Making his way down, he came towards the long passage.

Magic played a huge part in the lives of the fae. The palace tree was a centre for all things magical. Bernard's eyes searched the familiar walls. As they reached the end, they stepped into the gargantuan room. Silver sconces lit the marble floors.

To the centre, a large round plinth held a great, gilded throne. Above the plinth, an intensely large chandelier hung. In all her greatness upon her throne, his queen and commander sat silently.

A bitterness in her eyes was built from a lifetime of loss. A perfect blush sat on her soft skin.

Bernard instantly took a knee. He averted his eyes. The cold marble floor chilled his crumbling bones.

'I have news, Majesty,' his words shook from his mouth.

Slowly, she rose. Her plum dress flowed around her, clasping to her perfect hourglass figure. She glided towards him. Her pigeon keeper was a calm man. Such an important note was to be collected by her. It was a great honour for the lowly Bernard. He remained trembling on the floor. Her long fingers took the note from his hand, caressing his fingers as they did, sending an icy shiver through him.

As she read the note, she froze.

'Thank you, Bernard, that will be all.' A bleak look remained on her face, continuing back towards her throne.

'He's fallen,' murmured Bernard.

In an instant, her face altered. Darkness fell in the hall. She twisted to Bernard. 'You must learn to keep your words to yourself. Else you will lie with your elders.' Bernard stood. His hands shaking, a cold sweat misted his brow.

Her haunting, dark blue eyes glared towards him. 'That, Bernard, is all.' Her deep, ghostly voice echoed through the halls of the palace. Bernard left, and Harelda remained dazed.

The queen composed herself. Looking at one of her guards. The guard broke formation. Marching towards her. He took a knee.

She roamed towards him. 'We send a second army to Marrion.' She stepped from her plinth. 'Anything they encounter on the way, kill it.'

The guard stood and bowed. 'Sonnin Third are well on their way, a few issues have held them back. I shall send another.'

Harelda hurried towards her chambers. Her scribe, Borvo, followed behind her. Even writing letters was beneath her.

Sat at his desk, Harris continued to work. His knee was improving fast, although he was still short of breath. His eyes remained locked on the papers in front of him.

'This is the longest I've spent with the same woman,' he said with a broad smile.

Branwen gathered a basket from the side of the door. She gracefully sashayed past his desk. Harris admired her figure.

'It must be awful for you.' Her manner was cynical.

Harris cheerfully replied, 'I rather enjoy it.' He lifted his head. 'It's what I imagine marriage to be like.' Giving a wide grin, he ogled Branwen. 'What are your plans, marriage, I mean?'

'My mother had enough of us to allow me to keep my options open.' Her amorous manner only fed Harris. 'I suppose my mother will be the one to decide. Of course, it will be some overbearing lord or promised king, perhaps a councillor's son.'

Harris took a bite of his sweetbread, a delicious bread baked with hardened sugar. 'How about Xencliff?'

'You are not of Xencliff royalty or nobility.' Branwen lowered her eyes.

'Close enough,' he murmured.

She took his clothes from the basket and placed them in the wardrobe on the back wall. 'Besides, Xencliff is not vital to Sonnin. I believe that Thrasia, or Elmoor, would suit better.'

'Elmoor?' he barked in laughter. 'A mabeara,' he sniggered. 'I can't see it. You're a woman, Branwen. You need a man, not a builder, architect, or artist. They use bears as their strength, that's it. In all honesty, you'd be better off sticking with Cronnin.' He peered towards Branwen; her perfect skin shone in the Marrion sun. 'But until then, you're free,' he celebrated with a full smile.

Branwen spun from the wardrobe. 'I am not free,' she laughed. 'I am untouched, and I am not tempted. I never have been.'

'So, what lord would you choose, then?' asked Harris. Branwen glanced at Harris. Her mouth gaped. 'In fact, I've told you quite a lot about me, Bran. I think it's time you told me a small bit about you.' Harris placed his quill down. He stared at Branwen, intrigued.

'There is very little I can tell,' an amorous laughter flowed from her.

'Tell me about your family. What about your sisters, brothers?'

'My father, Taranis, died of the black, like your father. So, I know what it's like. It also took my sisters, Epona and Macha.' She placed the basket at the side and filled it with washing. 'As you probably know, they killed Angus in Blodmoor. I believe it was shortly before you arrived there.' Her eyes lit towards Harris, knowing he had ended the battle which took her brother warmed her. 'We lost Lugus during the golden war in Dorm.'

Harris shuddered. A vision of Lugus came to the surface. His loyal friend and commander. His words led him to Marrion. And Harris's hands took the life of Lugus. Harris wondered, what would Branwen think of him, if only she knew?

Branwen went on, a solemn expression pasted on her face. 'Bacchus is in Bourellis. He is young, so he won't be home for a while.' Her eyes strayed towards him; she could see the intrigue in his eyes. 'Sirrona dedicated her service to the temples in Assanin. Olwen, Sulis and Brighid have dedicated their service in Tyrone to the Mara.' Her neck stretched with pride. 'Camulos and Ogma, who knows, those two do as they please, when they please. They're archers, so they could be here for all I know. Finally, there is me, and Xania, she is someone even you wouldn't mess with. Xania is to take my mother's place when the time comes. She is well practiced in the art of bullshit.'

Harris widened his eyes. 'Did your parents do anything but fuck?'

'They weren't that bad, Harris.'

'Twelve children? come on, that's impressive even by the commander's standards.'

'What about you?' She leered at him from the corner of her eye. 'Do you have any children?'

'Hey! I'll hear none of that, and no, I bloody don't. Children are not my speciality. I used to be one, can't stand the little shits.'

Flicking through the papers on his desk, Harris sat back. He leant further back in his chair, stretching his arms above his head. He flinched back down, holding his chest and pinching his eyes.

'This is depressing,' he sighed.

Branwen saw him flinch. 'You need more time to heal.' She ambled towards him. 'I know you feel as though time is not on your side, but you need to make it.' She saw him watch from the window on many days and nights as the battle roared below him. He grew restless. 'What is it you're doing?' she asked, seeing the papers on his desk.

Harris leered at her. 'I'm doing the job of my chiefs. While I'm here, I might as well do all I can. Each night, upon the return from the field, we must call the count. We check how many are no longer with us. I then need to ensure that the council of Cronnin knows how many we have lost.'

Branwen shook her head. She walked towards him. 'This is all what I should learn,' she said with contrite. 'I am nearly finished with my service here. When I return, I will need to know everything about running a palace. I've lost two brothers and two sisters. With the world as tattered as it is, it's risky to Xania. She is next in line, but if anything happens to her, it falls on me eventually.' She took a chair and sat opposite. 'What better person to learn from than The Commander?'

'You want to know about battles?'

His manner of doubt stirred her. She had a lofty tone, leaning forwards with her elbows on her lap. 'I need to know. I do not wish to appear ill-informed to my people.'

Harris shook his head. 'What is it you need to know?'

'I have spent my entire time in those camps. Not once have I spoken to a commander or chief about war. They don't want to hear about it.' She leant forwards.

Her lavender and vanilla scent filled Harris's nose. He saw how pert her breasts were; his eyes forced him to look. He was trying to pay attention to what she was saying, but his nature distracted him.

'I speak of their families, their homes, why they must try to carry on, why they must fight to live.'

'I can teach you all I can, but battle isn't always a set of rules. Each day I'm sent a new letter from the Atlanti commander, with their terms, to end this.'

Harris took a small parchment from the side of his desk. 'Here,' — he passed it to her. The strange lettering and writing confused her. — 'This is his note of today. It is written in Runen script. It would serve you well to learn.'

She held the paper flat to the desk. Harris pointed at the parchment.

'This is a warning. He is asking for an extra two days before battle, but that is only so they can increase their numbers. I have refused. We resume battle tomorrow morning. If they refuse, we give different terms. Here,' — he pointed to another part, — 'he is telling us to leave, and they will leave as well. This is what we call bollocks.'

Branwen sat back and laughed. 'Surely they don't think us that stupid?'

'Sadly, they do, and often we are.' His voice was soft, his eyes remained fixed on hers. 'While there are rules in battle, it does not mean we always follow them. Every day, a thousand are sent. If we have over five-hundred return, that is a victory. If we have less, that is a tragedy.' He took the paper and placed it back in his desk draw. 'Since I began my campaign here, we haven't dropped below eight.' He was not arrogant at all; simple pride was all he showed.

'I just deal with numbers, the books in Tyrone, they deal with the names.'

'I've seen the books of Tyrone.' Branwen's eyes filled with a sorrow Harris instantly wanted to end. 'I was just a child when I first went there.' Her eyes wandered towards the wooden desk. The desk appeared overused. Many commanders had used the same space. Her finger wandered towards a small bit of raised wood.

'You can watch the spell work, the names, appearing from the pages,' — she shuffled in her chair, — 'when I was young, it was a book each turn being filled. Today, they fill a book every day, ten thousand names to each book, all deaths of war.'

Harris glimpsed to the wood she fiddled with. He reached over and held her hands still. A jolt of warmth ran through her blood.

'I don't like the idea that those out there are numbers, but they are. This is the reality.' Harris let her hand slip from his; he sat back in his chair. He stretched back with his hands on the back of his head.

'Every commander has different tactics; fear is my biggest.'

He pulled her into his world. A world he very much controlled.

'I want to learn, Harris, but in order for me to do that, I feel like I need to see it.'

Immediately, he bolted forwards and dropped his arms. Setting them on the desk. 'That will never happen. If you think I will ever allow you onto the field, you're more insane than me, and that is impossible.'

'I just think that if I could experience it for myself, *see it* for myself —'

'No,' Harris snapped. He raised his brows. 'I will never allow it.'

Branwen sat back in shock. 'Why? Even just to the cliff.'

Harris tried to distance himself. 'You're not a fighter, Branwen. The cliffs are as fatal as the ground. Someone has ambushed me there.' Harris leant forwards. He gave a distant look at the desk.

'The Atlanti are creatures. They prey on pretty things like you, Bran. They would use you. Cut you deeper than the thickest sword. They take everything from you before taking your life.' He broke his glare and glanced at Branwen. Warmth occupied his eyes. 'I would never take you through that.'

'I won't ask again,' she assured. Her brows pinched in the middle. 'I need to learn, though.'

Harris replied, 'And I will gladly teach you.' His voice broke. 'From here, I can teach you everything you need to know, about war, about tactics, politics.' He glanced at his desk and up towards her from under his brow. 'Pleasing a husband.' His smile grew from the edge of his lip.

Branwen laughed at his fervid mood. 'I'm sure I can do that on my own.'

Getting back to work, the hot chamber dimmed as night swept the land. Silence fell in the castle of Marrion. The scratching from Harris's quill was the only sound. Branwen's silent footsteps did not even wake the dust on the floor.

Branwen walked across the balcony, away from the commander's chambers. Anna walked towards her. A sword remained at her side but she was free from her armour.

'Evening,' greeted Anna.

'It is pleasant, no rattle of metal in the distance,' replied Branwen.

'I feel you've had enough of this place?'

'Just about, but it has its perks,' Branwen grinned.

'Perks? Like the perk of a dictatorial gobshite,' chuckled Anna.

'He isn't that bad.'

'He is, though,' Anna clearly replied. 'I love that man with every inch of my soul, the only man I would readily give my life to protect, but he is a gobshite.'

Branwen grinned. She looked back at the brown door to his chambers. 'Careful, he might hear you.'

'Oh, I'm counting on it,' chuckled Anna as she made her way past Branwen and into Harris's chambers.

A fleeting grin met Branwen's face. A guilty happiness unsettled her stomach as she crossed the yard towards the chambers of Lister on the other side of the castle. Met with several bows from wandering warriors, Branwen bid a good evening back to them.

'It's been quiet of late,' said Lister, stood in the centre of his chambers, wrapped in a silver robe, his hair fell platted between his shoulders.

'It isn't a bad thing,' replied Branwen.

'I like noise from the chambers of the commander,' mumbled Lister. He slowly glided towards her. Branwen stood rigid. 'I haven't seen a single cart delivering a woman to his door in a while.'

'They are not cattle. He is recovering,' replied Branwen. She was not stupid. She could see the question lingering over his head like a grey cloud.

'The man was pierced by an arrow to the chest, his knee was shattered. It has been only a few days and you expect him to perform for a woman?'

'You clearly don't know Harris Bearwood,' replied Lister with a relaxed brow.

'Perhaps not, but if you believe the absence of women in his chamber has anything to do with me, I can assure you you're wrong. I have no desire for Harris Bearwood, beyond being his nurse and a friend.'

Lister threw his head back, an anguished expression seized his face. 'Friend!' he bellowed, turning away from her. 'That's where they all go wrong.' He twisted, catching her shoulders with both hands. 'Harris is my most trusted ally,' his voice hushed to a whisper. 'You are his nurse, not his friend. As gracious as your mother is, she would not forgive any indiscretions with Harris Bearwood.'

Her lips parted. 'Why are you whispering?'

Lister stood straight, dropping his hands from her shoulders.

'Do you know of his lineage?'

Branwen shook her head, looking at the floor. 'His mother, married to Waron Chen Lu, his father who died many years ago, that is all.'

Lister grew a grin to the side of his left cheek. 'His mother, who married Waron Chen Lu, whose father was Tirius Crede —'

'His grandfather is Atlanti?'

'Azorae, and his father's mother Brianna Rushworth, a woman of merrow blood.'

Her eyes widened as she gasped and whispered, 'He has merrow blood? No wonder all the women.' Her brows suggestively raised.

Lister slowly bobbed his head. 'And the hearing. The man knows more than you realise.'

Contemplation hit her. A moment of trust filled her. 'He has not harmed me in any way. He flirts as many do, but he respects my wishes. I trust him, Lister, and I have been warned away from his company enough times. He is a man you placed in a position of trust, and I trust him, too. Regardless of his history, he has shown more loyalty than most. Good evening.' She turned with her shoulders straight, her head high, and left.

Branwen returned to her chambers beside Harris's. Before entering, she made her way into Harris's room. He remained at his desk. Anna had left.

'You need your rest,' she nagged.

'I'll rest when I'm dead.' His eyes did not leave the sheets on his desk. 'How was your chat with Lister?'

'I never told you I was with Lister?'

'No, but your whispers did.' He placed his quill down. 'You are right, we have fun here, and I would never take it beyond that. I appreciate you making that clear to Lister.'

'He has more than a war to think of. My mother places my chastity in his hands,' — she twirled, 'ensuring I keep it intact, that is.'

Harris laughed. 'I will do nothing to destroy that. I know it is important for you. But now you know more about my past, my history —'

'And my opinion of you has not changed. You are still a good friend to me.'

'Friend,' Harris grinned, a childlike flutter hit his stomach. 'It isn't often I have friends who last. I would like to keep you.'

'And I you.' She gave a warm smile. In that moment, she could've sworn she saw a tear in his lonely eye. 'Well, I've almost finished my duties, but tomorrow they will need me in the tents.'

'It will be a crushing day without you,' Harris tried to mock. Truth seeped from his words.

Silence spun in the chambers as they both busied themselves.

A grumble came from Harris's desk. 'How?'

Stepping from the shadows, having cleaned some shelves, Branwen asked, 'Pardon?'

Harris lifted his head; he placed his quill down into its pot. He gave a look of curiosity.

'Earlier, you said you knew how you would please a husband.' His brow furrowed. A cool breeze drifted in through the window, brushing Branwen's long blue dress. Confused, she stepped closer to him.

He raised his brows, his mouth curled at the side. 'I'm just curious. As an untouched, you need to understand that perfection in pleasing, it takes practice.'

Branwen stepped closer; her voice was hard to hear. 'I will find my way.' Her eyes shone with fear. His company provided a warm embrace. She wanted to enjoy it, but she appreciated how dangerous that could become for her.

Harris gave a low, grumbling laugh. 'What are you afraid of?' — he shook his head, adding, — 'I'm not here to bed you, Bran. I have far too much work to do.'

'Work? last turn you were willing to die, not afraid of death at all.'

'Last turn was a lifetime away. Each day is no gift nor blessing. It is torture.'

'You speak like this often, yet you take pleasure in life as well. If death were to grace you, would you not miss life?'

'Who knows?' He shrugged. 'We do not know what awaits us on the bridge, or beyond, perhaps a world of comfort? Where you would feel welcome.'

'I am welcome in all worlds. The field beyond the bridge should not be your concern. Harris, you are still young. I know you fight in a world tainted by isolation, but beauty lies in this world too.'

'I know. I'm speaking with one,' he promptly interjected.

She glanced at him from under her brow. 'I love this world, the world you fight to protect. I only wish you could see the value of what you protect.'

'I see her,' — his voice grew, — 'you want to know why I do what I do, you are right here, I see the beauty in this world, but our worlds are different. Where you see trees and grass as a beauty to be protected, I see people, young and old, I see that as deserving of protection.'

'And now I know why my mother chose you,' said Branwen with a wide smile. 'But I see you are still trying to charm me. It will not work.'

'You caught me,' he sniggered. 'Well, let's be honest, if your mother knew of my flirting, within the turn, I would suffer a fate worse than death.'

Branwen nodded. 'This is true.' She sashayed towards his desk and lowered herself onto the chair opposite. 'I'm afraid of many things. I'm not afraid of love, but I just want to make my choice on this.' The soft amber glow from the candles on his desk lit her face. The fire flowers in the chambers enchanted the atmosphere.

'I have lived a life of being told what I can and cannot do. They sent me here, they sent me to Assanin, they sent me to Elmoor. I have chosen nothing. Until I came here. I want to keep my choice.'

'I respect that, but, if ever you change your mind.' He softly offered, 'You know where to find me. I make a wonderful teacher.' — He sat straight in his chair. — 'Although, I would prefer to become a better friend.'

Silence saturated the room. He gazed into her eyes. The deep pools of blue carried honesty, trust, and innocence. At twenty-eight, Harris had seen a lot in his young life. Branwen was only twenty-one. Her innocence and naivety were obvious to him.

'Harris? I know it's for more than just pleasure. What is it? As a friend, I fear you may be lonely.'

Shaking his head and ending his stare, he blinked, peering around the room. He was uncomfortable. She hit a nerve. 'I have many reasons, Bran.' He pleaded as he stood. 'Stay innocent.'

Hobbling into the room, he took a large leather-bound book from the shelf behind him. It thudded as it struck his desk.

'I'm just interested.' Branwen's vast innocence stirred fear in Harris. He would not kick her from his bed, but he knew what he would face if she took it too far.

'Interest, it will get you into trouble,' he warned. He sat back at his desk, looking directly towards the book.

Branwen smiled, sitting back. Her sumptuous caramel lips pouted. She gazed at him.

'I might like trouble.'

'I wouldn't recommend it,' Harris warned. 'Besides, I can't tell you.' He sat back in his chair; gradually he leant forwards. He lightly murmured, 'I would have to show you.'

She shook her head and sat back, breaking the amorous manner.

As the night lingered, Branwen was ready to retire to her room.

'I will be here in the afternoon for lessons.' Branwen tidied the last few bits away.

Harris stood beside his wardrobe. He removed his tunic. His battered and torn body showed the scars from a career of turmoil.

'Which lessons?'

'Oh, come on, Harris,' Branwen gave a cursory laugh. 'I think we have established that this will be strictly professional.'

Unbuckling his belt, Harris gave his last chance to Branwen. 'Just think about what I've offered, and remember, I can teach you,' — his voice became tender, — 'and keep you pure.'

Branwen furrowed her brow. She would have asked what he meant, but before she could speak, a loud knock at the door startled her. Branwen spun to the door.

'I'll thank you to get that,' said Harris.

Branwen strolled to the heavy wooden door; a clunk of wood sounded as she opened it. On the other side, peering in, was a young woman. Her pale skin gleamed in the light from Harris's chambers. Her slim frame was nothing like Branwen's. She was slim, appearing tiny compared to Branwen. Her long curls of red hair tumbled down her back. Wearing a violet sheer dress. Branwen averted her eyes from the woman's nipples showing through the flowing fabric.

Branwen stepped back, inviting her in. 'I think it's for you, Harris.' She shyly glanced back at the small woman. 'I'm just leaving.'

Harris saw Branwen's wavering smile.

'Oh.' The small woman gazed into Branwen's dark blue eyes. Her voice was a striking delight. 'What a shame.' Her lingering stare into Branwen's eyes set her on edge. The pornes did not care for the sexuality of their clientele.

Branwen stepped from the room. Keeping the door ajar. She watched to see the woman run towards Harris. Branwen sneaked around the door. Slowly, she closed it. She saw Harris's passionate embrace with the woman. He gave a glance at the door.

A burning jealousy hit her. She had never known that pain before. She wanted to be that woman, to feel his touch, but she wanted to remain untouched.

The palace of Cronnin rumbled in chaos. The small white stones on the road crunched as the king left with his guard. His carriage rode through the gates. With a council left on the steps to the palace, utterly bewildered, Librye stood in Angus's chambers.

She peered out of the window and watched him leave. The second she saw the carriage pass through the gate, emptiness hit her. Maude knelt by her side with an arm around her shoulder.

Librye's eyes remained fixed on the disappearing carriage.

'My secrets are quiet. Even the stars aren't whispering. How long will he be gone for?' Librye looked at Maude.

Maude had no answer for her. She glanced at the books in the chambers.

'I'm sure, by the time you finish the bottom, he will be on his way back. By the time you reach the other side, he will be here.' Her soft motherly voice helped Librye.

Maude was her family now, and Angus. The staff in the galleries. Even the council were her disapproving uncles who she enjoyed annoying. For now, a family member would be missing. As Angus rode towards Marrion.

That night brought loneliness for Librye. She had spoken to the stars that night, only to hear distant whispers of the king's journey. It depressed her. Lying in her bed, she gazed at the concave ceiling. Her eyes followed the swirls of the ceiling until finally she was deep in slumber.

'Librye!' called Maude. 'Wake up.' She stood at the side of her bed. Librye flittered her eyes, waking. 'It's gone breakfast time. Oh, sweetheart,' she sighed. The look of pain on Maude's face told Librye all she needed to know.

'I'm not tired this time,' assured Librye. She looked to the back of her, where her sheets were still wet with blood.

Librye opted to spend the rest of the day in the palace. The winter was retiring. Tiny buds on the trees in the gardens arrived. The mornings felt colder, but brighter. Dieredh was fast approaching. Librye's interest strayed more towards the palace. The secret tunnels and abandoned towers offered her a place to play; a place to explore.

The west wing was where most of the council rooms were. The corridor of each of the bottom wings led towards a tower at the end. Librye explored almost all of them. The south tower housed the bells, used to mark festivals, feasts and celebrations. They used the north tower to house the King's Guard. The west tower was the pigeon keeper's loft.

She was still to explore the east tower.

Breakfast began in the galleries the next morning. The staff were busy preparing for the day. Librye sat silently at the centre table, listening to any gossip which was always rife in the kitchen. With her meal eaten, she jumped from her chair and joyfully made her way towards the door.

'Where you off to today, my lady?' Gethen asked as he kneaded his bread dough.

Librye twisted. She smiled at Gethen with her head held high. 'I'm exploring.'

'You be careful,' urged Katryna. She wandered past with a bowl of potatoes. 'If the council were to see you exploring the walls, they'd have you locked in.'

Librye's smile grew. 'They don't frighten me.'

Hopping from the galleries, Librye made her way towards the east tower. 'Strange girl,' mentioned Gethen. 'Lovable, but strange.'

The lengthy green carpet in the east wing guided her towards the large brown wooden door at the end. Pictures of kings and queens long passed lined the corridor. The doors to the guest chambers were silent. Noises from the council halls did not reach her there. The silence overwhelmed her.

The large brown door towered above her. Her tiny hand reached for the large brass doorknob. Slowly, she twisted it. The door clunked open. Stepping inside, it appeared completely abandoned. A large room with dusty wooden floors, old timbers stood against the walls. The room was awash with spiderwebs and dust. To the centre of the room was a wide, towering staircase reaching to the top of the tower. The splintered wood was unfinished.

Climbing the large timber staircase. She kept looking at the wide-open space at the top. She reached the top of the stairs, a large room awaited her. Again, it appeared abandoned. Large oriel windows surrounded the room. Each one was void of any glass or shelter from the elements. As a result, nature reclaimed the tower. Small weeds and grasses grew between the floorboards. Making her way to the window, her footsteps tapped on the old brown floorboards.

'Why would they abandon it?' She wondered, strolling to the window. The people appeared like ants; she could no longer see the palace courtyard. The furthest her eye could see was to the edge of the eastern gate. She could see the watch towers either side of the gates and distanced along the city wall.

She explored every part of the tower. The only furniture she could find was a large desk at the back. Pushed against the wall, a wide chair, gilded gold and covered with a green plush back and seat. The dust aged the chair to a dull green and dark golden colour. Piles of wooden floorboards covered the desk. A pile of sconces was in the room's corner. A large golden chandelier sat discarded beside the window.

Librye explored as much as she could of the empty room. The window would serve as a perfect place to talk to the stars. The room served its purpose.

Librye, satisfied with her findings, left towards the stairs. As she did, she heard a whisper from the room. She swirled to see a breeze travelling through the centre. A whirl of wind brought some leaves from outside before making its way back out of the window. Her secrets spoke to her.

She made her way to the wall at the side of the stairs. Her fingertips searched the stone wall. The shape of a door revealed itself. Another hidden passageway unveiled.

Making her way in. The dark and uninviting secret room was small. Years of built-up dirt surrounded her. A long, narrow staircase led to a small corridor. She ventured further. The ceiling became low; the walk was narrow.

Librye sat in a small crevice, tucked neatly in the rafters above the council hall. Chaos was in the hall that day. Ryan, Kailron, Gurrand and Kean tried their best to establish order, but it did not work. The hate of Angus's travels lit the air. Speech of betrayal rang in the voices of the council.

'We must stop him!'

'His need to travel is threatening this war!' called another. 'If he does not stop, then we will lose Marrion!' A rumble of approval met his call. Librye sat for hours and listened to the loathsome council.

A call of a bell rang in the council's hall. Some of them remained sat on the back benches. She could hear their whispers, but could not hear their words.

As one of them stood, she heard a faint whisper. 'Soon, this will all be over. A throne without an heir is just a seat. The council will resume control,' said the councillor. Her body prickled with cold shivers.

'Beasts,' she whispered.

Each book she read spoke of the Atlanti as though they were animals. It spoke of the fae and faemen as innocent keepers of peace. Her open-mindedness searched to find positive in all. With a council grasped by greed and betrayal. She struggled to understand who was at fault.

'Balance,' she muttered to herself, ambling back through the corridors. 'This is all about balance. It must be right and wrong.'

She looked at her hands, filled with grey dust from the wood at the sides. Old plaster which crumbled from the walls covered her dress. As she stood behind the door to the tower, her purpose slowly became clear.

'Perhaps I am the balance?'

An overcast sky hid the hissing waves of a furious ocean. Harris stood upon the cliff. A stern sea breeze soured his skin. The moon was high but half, and buried with cloud. A rainstorm rumbled in the west.

'We have gained ground,' called Anna. The wind took her breath from her lungs as she pulled a thick skin around her shoulders.

'Hardly ground, Anna,' huffed Harris, his angry brow troubled her. She knew his moods, and this was not a good one. His long black hair brandished in the merciless gale. 'I won't always be here to figure your shit out. Call them to arm a second army. We lack archers on the ridge and consider some fires. They're battling under a hidden moon.'

'Straight away, sir,' Anna rushed off, knowing her actions had not been enough to satisfy her commander.

'You!' He pointed to an accompanying soldier. 'Any word on the ballist—' he stopped, his head raised. Narrowing his eyes, he looked to the west, where mighty waves blasted the old cliff.

'High tide,' muttered Harris. His eyes narrowed to a close as he drifted closer towards the edge.

'Sir?' called the soldier.

Harris held his hand out for him to quiet.

'Call the archers!' he yelled. Soldiers scurried. Harris scoured the back of him. 'Saburo!' He spotted him. 'Call for Lister, ships in the northwest. If they reach the cliff dock, we are done here.' Panic in Harris's eyes moved him to a rush. Taking his horse, Saburo hurried down the hill.

'Sir, I see no ships,' said the soldier, stepping towards the cliff edge.

'Not yet, but I hear them on the wind.'

'How?'

Harris suspended his hand for him to quiet. 'There is a song on the gale, a song of death,' — he turned away from the cliff. — 'We have less than an hour and the cliffs will be teeming with fresh blood.'

Mere moments passed like endless nights. Harris waited, hearing the auspicious waves beating the side of ships. Harris's blood ran cold.

'Sir, I see nothing!' called a soldier who ran towards him from the north.

'Not yet, you don't.' He turned in the field, his chest tightened. 'Where is Lister!' he yelled.

'I can confirm, sir, there are no ships!' argued the soldier.

'If Harris says ships approach, then ships do indeed approach,' said Lister, hurrying his black steed towards them. 'Where are we needed?' Lister's eyes begged Harris to guide them.

'A decent army, the strongest you have along the west coast. Archers to the north might light their ships enough to slow them down and warn of the approach.' Harris looked at the doubtful soldier. 'For your insubordination, it will be your duty to load and carry the pitch.' He drifted back to Lister, holding his chest as he gazed off to the west.

'No, Harris,' Lister grumbled. 'I know what you plan, but please, we need you alive. For once, trust that we can do this without your need to pick up a blade. We can do this.'

'I have no doubt,' Harris blinked in his reply. 'But sitting idle is not what I do.'

'Then you will be dead before the dawn, Harris. Go back, take your rest, and live to fight another day.'

'I shall await your return.' Harris stood deflated on the cliff, watching as a thousand or more rushed towards the shore. From the north, a beacon travelled through the air, flitting sparks grew on the heavy vessels as they sneaked through the water. Harris was right, but of course he was. He was the commander, a man of Atlanti heritage, and merrow blood.

ᚲᚺᚨᛈᛏᛖᚱ ᚦᛖᚾ

10

Gaius remained glum. Sat at his dense oak table, reflections of memories enveloped him. A crushing depression gripped him. He had not eaten properly in over a turn. All concerns remained with her. The tender radiance of her skin. Her cackling giggles. Her need to leave the front door open for passing guests. He knew her better than himself. She completed him.

Startled by a rapping at his door. Gaius rose from the oak table, his footsteps pounded the ground as he walked across the room, dodging the low beams as he did.

A smart, well-groomed soldier stood at his door. 'Our lord Kairne has asked for your company in the first tower, sir.'

'Does he serve me my orders?' asked Gaius, stepping into the foggy morning.

'Not yet, sir.' The soldier strode by Gaius's side. 'Although if my gossips serve me right, I believe he has a task for you which may have your mind reeling.'

'And what is that supposed to mean?'

'You'll see. My name is Daniel, sir. I believe we will work closely together on this.'

'And what is this?'

'I will let Kairne explain, but from what I hear, we have a new ally, and with that comes a certain amount of integration into our camps. I believe that is where we will be placed.'

'A new ally?' scoffed Gaius. 'For hundreds of years, our ranks have gone undefended. The Mae Apha family has ensured we remain pure. Why now?'

'I will let Kairne explain.' Daniel strolled off ahead. A tidy uniform, never scathed by a sword had Gaius wary of him. Daniel had never seen the ruin of the war. His clothes were clean, his hair perfectly trimmed, not a single scar sat on his perfect skin. He was a snake to Gaius. He trusted beaten and battered men, war-torn and imperfect, not men of silken skin.

The chamber was quiet, a calm day outside made for a day of silence inside.

'I am pleased you could both join me,' said Kairne as he stepped towards his desk. With her head down, Isradella stood with her hands at the front of her, scolded for being improperly dressed that day. Kairne stood proudly beside her. He sought to kiss her cheek, but she withdrew. 'You'll get used to it.' He held his arms out. 'Gentlemen, I trust you have acquainted yourselves?'

'Yes, sir,' said Daniel. 'We all know the remarkable tale of "he who survived death."'

'It is far from remarkable,' said Gaius, noting Daniel's tone of sarcasm.

'You survived, that's all that matters.'

Kairne continued, 'Good, then you'll be pleased to know —'

'Could I ask something?' Gaius cut off Kairne, which was not taken well. Isradella raised her head, wondering what Kairne would do with such insubordination.

'Of course,' replied Kairne, holding back his small man's rage.

'Daniel mentioned the integration of an ally. Who are they?'

'Well, if I could finish, I will explain all.' Kairne scowled at Gaius. 'For many years, the Atlanti have been undefended and undefeated. We are relentless. There is another. They may take some convincing to join us, but I have ways to make them comply.'

'So, they have not yet said they will join us?' asked Gaius.

'Trust me, they will.' Kairne's confidence was rattling.

'But how do you know?' asked Gaius.

Irritated, Kairne slowly stepped towards him. Gaius towered over him, but he still felt insignificant.

'My dear, Gaius, the gods chose my family, our blood, to be bound to death, to know all there is to know, to feel the loss in this world, but it also means we know mans biggest fears.' Kairne turned back towards his desk. 'There is a creature who dreads death just like man does, but their fear,' — he stopped, staring at Isradella, who stood in his way. She stepped back. — 'Their fear comes from something much deeper. The coblyn have been outcasts for many years, just like we have. It is time we join our forces, integrate them into our army, and together take our lawful place as rulers of Cammbour.'

'The coblyn?' Gaius tightened his eyes. Daniel sharply thudded Gaius in his side, hoping he would stop, but he did not.

'The abomination of a creature which digs up our graves, and consumes the flesh of the dead, the creature so despicable there is a ban on looking at them in the north? You expect our people to hold their judgment and accept them into our ranks?' he spat.

'I expect my people to follow the word of their great leader, and I have chosen you to make certain that happens.'

'I can't,' said Gaius with a breathless gasp.

'You forget your place, Gaius. One letter, one word is all it takes, and your wife will be sure to never return.'

Gaius twisted his eyes to Kairne, an outraged look pasted on his face. 'Why?'

'You survived the man death cannot touch, his fear of death, it does not exist, I cannot see him, or feel him. Many say they are not afraid to die, but many lie. He has no fear of death, not a single scrape.'

'Harris?' asked Gaius. 'This is all about a piss ant commander, so he's not scared to die, and?'

'You don't understand. No one has ever returned from Marrion. Why did he let you go?'

'To tell my story.'

'There is always more with Harris Bearwood.'

'Harris didn't choose me. A random soldier chose me. It could've been any of us who survived.'

'No, fate intervened. Perhaps it was not Harris who chose you, but someone did. Someone smiled upon you that day, and now, they will smile upon you again. You both head to the Morigar mountains in the morning. I will instruct you when you've thought.'

They left the icy room together. The hall was empty. 'You were silent,' said Gaius. 'Do you support this?'

'Of course I do. He may sound insane, but he has a point. He is still a necromancer. His business is death, life, and all that in between. I am not one to argue.'

'You follow through blind loyalty?'

'Do you not?' Daniel stopped walking and turned to face Gaius. He, too, was significantly smaller than Gaius.

'I follow through respect. His father earned his title, Kairne also, but I fear his plan will lose support from those who have been on the wrong side of the coblyn.'

'Acceptance, it is not something we find in plenty. Let's just hope Kairne proposes another plan, in case this one does not work.'

Branwen stared towards the grey stone ceiling of her bed chambers. The medical camp turned out to be a welcome break from Harris. Listening to the silence in the room, her jealous rage calmed. Her window was open. A dim sound of clanking armour drifted in. Smoke and filth drifted in on the breeze.

A dusting of sweat graced her brow. It was a sultry night in Marrion. Drifting from the bed, she made her way towards the window. Her stomach fluttered, empty. Her thick, long cotton nightgown flowed across the warm stone floor. The gloom was dimly lit by the bright moon outside. She hoped to hear a sound from Harris's chambers, but nothing. She could hear nothing.

A faint knock at Branwen's door made her turn from the window. She straightened her hair with her hands.

'Come in,' she lightly called.

Anna strode in with a solemn look of sympathy on her face. 'I've not seen you all day,' said Anna.

Branwen released her shoulders, the confident stance she had died. 'I was busy in medical, we are short since losing Grisha.'

'Well, we missed you around here.' Anna drifted in, knowing that feeling, the departed guilt, the seething rage, and animalistic want.

'I highly doubt it,' said Branwen, lowering her brow.

'It gets easier,' said Anna, unexpectedly.

'Apologies. I'm not sure what you mean.'

'You're convincing no one,' Anna said with a full smile. 'I know how you feel. I see how you look at him, and how he looks at you, but you aren't the first, and you won't be the last.'

'What happened between you?' asked Branwen.

'A story. It's in the past, and I won't speak of it. I love him, Branwen. I would give my life for him, but his terms, the way he draws you in, when I'm with him I feel important, I feel like he sees me, but I realised long ago, he doesn't do that to bed you, he does it because he respects people, and that is the most attractive quality a man can have.'

Branwen huffed as she sat on the edge of her bed. 'I'm just bloody furious.'

'It'll pass,' said Anna with a smug grin. 'Harris grew in a palace, all the extravagance one could ever need, but he grew as a creature in the corner, banished to the shadows. He was never important, never listened to. Harris sees people as important. He knows what it is like to be looked down on, but he also knows from the simplest of minds comes the most beautiful of thoughts. It's why he listens to all.'

'I know, and that's what has me so absorbed. I don't have any right to be angry with him. He's a free man. What right do I have?'

'You don't,' Anna rested beside Branwen. She laughed, 'But you want to, you want to have that right, you can't do it, Bran, he is your commander, you are a nurse, here in service to your people, until you take your place as a promised queen.'

'I know that.' She let out a heavy sigh. 'But I'm furious with him.'

The two sat close together, laughing at the ridiculous notion. 'I completely understand, but it gets easier.'

'What did you do to make it easier?' asked Branwen.

'I didn't, he did. Harris has a way of pushing people away, a fear, that the moment someone gets too close, he's going to lose them.'

Harris sat at his desk, his eyes raised from his papers, listening to the conversation next door. The thick stone walls sat as thin as satin sheets for his skilled hearing.

'So, he believes it was to protect you?' asked Branwen.

'Harris knows he's loved. His problem is he doesn't like himself, or love himself. Only the gods know what goes on in his head. I believe he's scared, not of failing, or death, but he has a fear, that all of this is for nothing.'

'I know he doesn't believe the gods care.'

'It's more than that. I can't go into detail, but Harris lost more than most. He saw more than most, so go easy on him, be his friend. That's all he really wants.'

Branwen leant towards Anna, she whispered, 'But what if I want more?'

Anna pulled her head away, staring into Branwen's eyes. She shook her head. Uttering the word no. 'If you care about Harris, you wouldn't. You are the daughter of Harelda Duirwud. She would see him hanged for touching a single hair on your head.'

The blistering sun beat down on the fields in Marrion. A battle roared since dawn. Harris enjoyed being hailed as an able commander, a selfless lover, and a formidable fighter.

Readying herself for the day, Branwen stood by a floor-length mirror in the room's corner, exposed. Judging herself, she did not know if she was pleasing to a man's eye. Many men tried to tempt her, but she would refuse them all. Harris was unique. He had not tried to trick her. His seduction was clear and honest.

Branwen dressed. She chose a long, red fae gown. Silk and satin were the choice of the fae. Hemmed with golden trim, her dress would have cost more than most of the soldier's armour. Slowly, Branwen opened the door to Harris's room. The sun belted through his chambers. The air was stale and warm. Dust sprayed across the air as it danced in the rays.

Making her way inside, she called for him, 'Harris!' A silent room lay before her.

Getting to work, Branwen cleared his room. The sheets of the bed were in a terrible state. Sprawled across the floor, clothes flung carelessly across the room.

The afternoon lingered. Branwen emerged from his chambers with a bundle of laundry to take to the galleries. The courtyard outside was bustling with the comings and goings of soldiers. Making her way down the stone stairs overlooking the courtyard. Branwen searched for someone familiar to her.

She eventually spotted Kyla as she made her way back from battle. Tearing across the courtyard, calling for arms.

'At them! Move now!'

Branwen hurried down the stairs. Dropping the basket, she pushed past the chaos of the soldiers.

'Kyla!' She waved, struggling to get her attention. 'Kyla!'

Branwen tried to get to her. Kyla was a young chief, one of the youngest. A well-built figure made her a fierce fighter. They considered her as pretty, but she was far too daunting to receive any seductive passes.

'Branwen!' She drove past the soldiers as they made their way towards the castle gate. 'What are you doing out?' She knew Branwen's title kept her well behind the battle lines. As she reached Branwen, she could see the concern on Branwen's face. 'What's happened?'

Branwen's eyes flickered through the camp. Her mouth curved down. 'Have you seen Harris?'

Kyla's mouth twisted with disapproval. 'Not you as well?' Her shoulders and posture slumped. 'Oh, Branwen, no.'

Branwen shook her head. She gained focus. 'No,' she shrilled. 'I just want to know where he is. His knee is still bad. He can barely breathe properly.' Branwen could see Kyla's growing unease. 'What is it?'

Kyla looked towards the balcony. 'I'm afraid, he's on the field. We need him out there. We're falling short.'

Branwen's faced contorted into anger and hate. 'Sword.' Kyla furrowed her brow. Branwen blinked. 'Kyla, give me your sword. I'm a Sonnin fae. They tutored me in the fields.'

Kyla shook her head. 'You'll need more than a sword. No, Branwen, if your mother found me out, I would be dead within a day.'

'You are fae, and I am your promised queen. You either do this with me or without. Make the right choice, Kyla.'

Kyla shook her head. 'As my promised queen, I will protect you, even if it is from yourself. My answer stands.'

The smell of rancid blood saturated the air. Mangled metal and arrows protruded from the drudgery. Anguished squeals from horses were deafening. The hailing soldiers wildly tried to make sense of the turmoil. A chiming of metal clogged the air. Soldiers' mutilated remains lie in the red-hot mud, calling, crying, and dying. The dead lie in the chaos of battle. Nothing made sense, apart from the cries of Harris.

Always at the front was the commander. Always with a plan more brutal than the last. Slicing, gashing, and relentlessly thrusting his blade into the approaching enemy. He was reckless in battle. His own life mattered for nothing.

The disarray of battle rang on. Harris heard the thud of a drum. Standing on the back of his loyal horse, Svend, his balance was remarkable. He glared at the plateau. He could see the distant outline of an army stood along the side.

Harris roared, 'Let's see how hot the bastards like it!' He twisted into the army behind him. 'Light them up!' The army kept calling to the back, carrying his words. The Sonnin and Cronnin army moved back towards the camps.

From the plateau came a deafening rumble, followed by a petrifying crackle. Harris called his army to, 'Fall back!'

Desperately, they ran. Dead horses and soldiers lie in the mangled remains of the battleground. Among them, those barely clinging to life. Harris carelessly rode over them. Sitting back down onto Svend, he stopped him and circled.

A beauty of battle was before him. Blue dust glistened in the blazing hot Marrion sun. Drifting through the air, it made its way down from the cliff, towards the Atlanti. Who had begun their celebration too soon. As the blue mist reached them, it clung to their clothes. Blazing arrows fell from the cliff plateau.

A thundering wall of flames rushed through the army. The heat was blinding. Taking every life the blue mist touched. The wall of flames reached closer towards Harris. Something was off. Looking at the erupting flames as they hurled towards him. He saw an outline. A soldier stood, fully clad in shining silver armour.

'Run!' he yelled.

The soldier stared towards the flames in front, wanting to run but frozen to the spot.

Harris panicked; he had seen enough die that day. He pulled hard on Svend's reins. Desperately, Svend raced towards the soldier stood alone in the turbulent field. The flames tore towards them, but so did Svend. Grinding to a halt by the side of the soldier.

'Get on!' Harris yelled. The soldier held out her hand. Harris violently swung her onto the back of Svend. The flames roared across the field towards them. Svend ran as fast as he could. The shrieks of those left in the field as the fires caught them plagued them both as they made their way back to camp.

Riding towards the barbican, Harris's face reddened, his eyes widened, and teeth gritted. The guards at the gatehouse ran towards the courtyard. They could sense his rage.

Svend slowed, but Harris twisted and threw the soldier from behind him. She thudded to the ground. A clatter of armour rang as she rested on the soil. Jumping down, Harris made his way towards the cowering soldier.

'What in the almighty name of fucks was that?' he hollered at her. She covered her face with her arm. 'You nearly had us both killed!' The soldier remained petrified on the floor. 'Answer me!' He lifted her visor to expose her face. An instant look of dismay seized his face. 'Bran?'

Shaking in terror, Branwen remained on the ground. 'Apologies,' she sobbed. She shook her head. 'I meant no harm,' she cried.

A crowd flocked. They gaped at Branwen, trembling on the ground. Harris spun to see the gathering crowd.

'About your business!' He helped Branwen stand. His forehead creased. 'You look ridiculous. Why were you out there?'

Still sobbing, Branwen could not look at Harris. 'I didn't know where you were. You shouldn't be out there, Harris.' She strove to catch her breath. Harris held her close. She wept in his arms. 'I didn't know what to do.' He removed her helmet, throwing it to the ground. 'I didn't know what else to do.'

Harris wrapped her head in his arms, holding her shaking body.

Suspicions and rumours surrounded the camp.

Branwen sat on his bed. She calmed. Tear tracts ran through the black soot on her cheeks. She removed the heavy armour. Harris paced the room. Still shrouded in the violence of battle.

'What were you thinking? What possessed you to do such a thing?'

Ashamed, Branwen hung her head. 'I don't know. I thought I could go out there and tell you to get back. Your body isn't healed yet. I realise now my plan was not that great to begin with.'

Harris stopped pacing. With his hands on his hips, he leant towards her. 'You can't be serious?' he scoffed. 'You. You came onto a battlefield.' He continued to pace. 'An active battlefield filled with death, terror, blood, death! Just to have a go at me?' Branwen held a pinched grin. With his hand on his forehead, Harris pivoted. 'It really is like being fucking married.'

Branwen smiled at his wit. 'Like I said, apologies.' She removed the last plate of armour, her breastplate. Underneath, she wore a small cotton tunic and black trousers.

Harris raised his brow towards her. 'And what would they do? The outer shell is nothing if the inner is not protected.'

'Kyla is much broader than I am. Her chains didn't fit,' said Branwen. 'I wasn't intending on fighting, just finding you and bringing you back.'

'Kyla?' he leered at Branwen from under his brow. 'She put you up to this?' His eyes tightened.

Branwen shook her head. 'She did nothing wrong. She was just doing as I asked, as I commanded.'

'You pulled rank?' He scowled at her. 'You have no rank here, Branwen. If something were to happen. How stupid can you be?'

'I did, but I never meant to harm anyone —'

Before Harris could reply, Anna surged through the door. Seeing Branwen in such a compromising position, she twisted. 'For fuck's sake, Harris!' she barked. 'Not her as well?'

'No, Anna,' Harris snapped. 'Branwen thought it a good idea to join us at battle today,' he satirically mocked.

Anna spun. 'Branwen, I would strongly suggest you take the day.' She glanced at Branwen stood sheepishly in the room. Anna stared back at Harris. A grin came from the edge of her lip. 'Harris is about to get a formal bollocking from your commander.'

'Lister?' Harris asked. 'Oh! that's great,' — he threw his arm into the air, — 'that is just fucking wonderful.' Branwen stood silent. Harris left the room. She could hear him muttering manically as he marched across the mezzanine. Anna followed Harris, trying her best not to laugh. Branwen stood, ashamed.

Atlanti blood still covered his lizard skin armour. He passed the courtyard, where he saw Svend being taken into the stables under the arches of the castle. He saw a blackening to his tail. 'It's burnt Svend's arse,' he grumbled.

'At least it's just his arse. Surely it's not that bad?'

Furious, Harris continued. He and Anna made their way up the stairs.

Harris sharply twisted. 'He asked for me, Anna, save yourself, clean up, we battle again in the morning.'

Anna stood, bewildered. 'Can I just listen?'

'Off you fuck!' he rumbled with wide eyes.

He walked towards the chambers of Lister. The fae were nimble in battle. Harris provided warriors and fighters, but the fae were the archers. The sprightly and dexterous dancers of death. Their fighting skills were formidable, and Lister was one of the finest commanders they had.

Knocking on the door to Lister's chambers, Harris had a fair idea of what was in store for him. The door opened; a small fae woman peered towards him.

'Commander,' she greeted; she had a broad smile on her large pouting lips. She gave a curtsy before opening the door. Harris tightly smiled at her.

Stepping inside, the room was much grander than his. The boiling air cooled in the chambers. Lister stood in the centre of the room. He, too, was fresh from battle, but his armour was clean. His station had been upon the plateau, perfectly placed there by Harris.

Lister whirled as Harris entered. 'Harris,' he joyfully greeted. His smile grew, strutting towards him. Lister threw an arm around Harris. It was not the type of greeting Harris was expecting. Lister gripped him by his shoulders.

'I'm glad you came.' He held out his hand, offering Harris a seat at his desk.

Harris gradually sat, confused, waiting for Lister to join him. 'Why am I here?'

Lister removed the breastplate of his armour. He sat opposite. His eyes strayed towards Harris's lizard skin armour. Even Lister only had polished steel armour. They saved lizard skin for kings, queens, and those who were rich beyond their means.

'Branwen.' Lister leant back in his chair and glanced at Harris. 'What was she thinking?' Lister shook his head.

Harris gave a long sigh of disapproval. His eyes rolled. 'I don't know.' He relaxed. 'She wanted to have a go at me, I suppose.' He gave a cynical look towards Lister.

Lister shivered his head; unconvinced. 'That's all? To shout at you?'

Harris did not want games. A warm bath and early night invited him. His voice was deep and stern. 'I know what you're thinking.' His casual attitude spoke of the truth. 'When I got injured, Branwen seemed to have it stuck in her head that I would need her to tell me what to do at all times. When she worked out, I was on the field, she tried to follow. She believes I'm not yet ready for battle.' His eyes became weary as he spoke.

Lister stood. He crept towards Harris and leant on the desk. 'I know you, Harris.' His smile was menacing. 'You're a philanderer. Branwen is one of the few untouched.' Lister stood. He ambled to the back of Harris's chair. 'Tell me she remains that way.'

Harris stood; he did not appreciate Lister's attitude towards him. He gritted his teeth. 'If she is no longer intact.' He leered down at Lister. 'Don't blame me, I haven't touched a hair on her head.' Harris stepped to the side.

'Very well,' Lister deepened his tone, 'our queen will want to thank you. You saved her daughter from her own foolishness.'

Lister walked towards a cabinet at the side of his desk. He poured two drinks. Harris could sense the change in attitude. Immediately, he relaxed.

'Foolishness is one way of putting it,' scorned Harris.

'Well done today, by the way.' Lister spun and handed a glass to Harris. He didn't know what was in the glass but drank it. 'Your tactics are something we could use more in Sonnin. Though you had me worried there for a moment.' Harris sat, confused. Lister could tell. 'I thought you'd fucked Branwen,' he laughed.

Harris sat and drank. The sweet water was not what he was expecting. He preferred something harsher. 'I would never take chastity from anyone. Besides, I know the stories of your "good queen."' He widened his eyes towards Lister. 'I rather like my balls where they are.' A sardonic smile formed.

'She isn't that bad.'

Unconvinced, Harris replied, 'If I did anything to Branwen. Harelda would have me strung from the highest limb of her tree. With nothing but my bollocks to support me.' His brows grew towards Lister, who could not argue.

Lister raised his brows. His mouth curled down, he gave a curt bow in agreement with Harris.

Librye's obsession with the east tower grew. She enjoyed her days spent in solitude among the dry dusty boards of the hidden room. Listening to the council spit hate.

Opening the curtain in Librye's bedchambers, Maude opened a window to let some air in. She missed the smell of the fresh spring flowers as they bloomed. The trees showed more traces of blossom.

'Where you off to today, then?' asked Maude.

Librye was pale, drained, and despondent. 'I think I'll stay here, just for today.'

Maude curled her brow. Stepping towards the bed, she felt her head. 'You're not fevering.' She stood upright. 'Perhaps a day to relax would help. I'll have something sent from the galleries.'

'You'll have Gethen worried,' said Rebecca, sauntering into the room with a glass of water.

'Gethen knows,' said Librye. 'What news do you have, Rebecca?'

Maude leered at Rebecca, the palace gossip.

'Oh, plenty. I hear that Angus reached the common shore this morning, and soon enough he will be on his way home.'

'How would you know that?' asked Maude.

Rebecca squinted. She hurried to Maude's side. Whispering, 'I don't know that. Is it so bad to make a child happy?'

Maude glanced over her shoulder, where Librye sat, trying to listen. 'No, it isn't.'

'Truth be told, I do not know where he is or if he's even coming home. Marrion is dangerous. All I know is that he never should've left. It's selfish if you ask me.'

'While I do agree, no one is asking you, Rebecca.'

Rebecca turned to face Librye. 'No trip to the tower today, then?'

'Ugh! So that's where you've been disappearing to, then?'

'I like it there. It's peaceful.'

'Peaceful it may be,' said Rebecca, 'but it isn't the safest place to be, when your Appa. I mean, Angus gets home. We can ask if you would be better suited to have the tower as your own.'

'I'd like that,' said Librye, 'but I believe it's made for another.'

'And what does that mean?' asked Rebecca.

'Never you mind, Librye has secrets just as we all do, and she's seen the plans in Angus's chambers. The tower is to be remodelled for the use of our new second in command.'

'Oh?' asked Rebecca.

'Harris Bearwood, some real secrets for you to dig into there, Rebecca.'

'I look forwards to it,' replied Rebecca with a grin.

A warm bath and early night were yet to be had by Harris. Still sat at his desk, checking the numbers. The battle ended well in their favour. His note from the Atlanti commander was ill written. He could sense their panic. Harris refused his note, hoping that the next battle would see the Atlanti finished.

Sat silently at his desk, the courtyard to the castle was ringing with the sounds of festivity. The galleries teemed with soldiers for most of the evening. Even though her footsteps were silent, he could hear Branwen coming. He could hear the cotton ruffling of her gown as she came towards his door. He heard her lift her arm, ready to knock.

'Come in, Bran,' he called to her.

The door groaned open. Sheepishly, she stepped inside. He stood and strutted towards her. Holding her shoulders, he tightly smiled.

'Never follow me, Bran,' he begged. 'I don't want you in my world. You're not meant for the world I know.'

Branwen stood silent, stiff. 'I want to know.' Her eyes softened, she was calm and reserved. Harris's brows pulled down slightly as his lips parted. She was trying to tease him. 'I want to know,' she repeated, pressing her body into his.

Harris stepped back. 'No, you don't.' Shaking his head, he clarified. 'I can't, Bran. You don't want that, you think you do, but you don't.'

'All my life, from the moment I was born, people have told me what I want, what to do, how to act, and I'm done. I want this, Harris, I want to know.'

Harris paused, letting her shoulders go he turned. He blinked heavily, fighting his urge. 'You think you do, Bran, but none of it was real. How to keep a husband happy, keep his balls empty and his belly full, that's it.'

'I won't know that unless you show me.'

'Stop, Branwen!' he pleaded. Harris twisted to face her. 'You don't understand. You're fae, taught to frown upon people like me, told that Xencliff are all pornes, nothing more.'

'I was never taught that, besides, any views I had on Xencliff were changed.' She stepped closer, holding her hand to his face. 'By you.'

Harris looked down, his face placed in her delicate hand. 'I can't do this, Bran. I care about you far too much.'

Branwen laughed, dropping her hand as she stepped back. 'That is the most ridiculous thing you've ever said. If you cared, you would take my feelings into consideration. I went on that field chasing something I never felt before—'

Harris quickly lifted his hand, covering her lips with his finger. 'Not another word.' His eyes widened, frightened.

'What are you so afraid of?' she asked, curling her lip.

Harris took a deep breath. It was rare he would refuse such advances. 'You really want to know?' His eyes narrowed.

She replied with a whisper, 'Yes.' Branwen leant to kiss him. Harris leant back. Her frustration grew.

'Please sit.' He moved away from her. Making his way behind the desk, cowering. 'I need to explain something to you.' His deep voice only fuelled her passion more. She took his instruction and sat.

'You are one of few. In Xencliff, the untouched are the sacred,' he explained. He spoke quick. His hands shook. Branwen saw his hands. She thought it was sweet he would show such concern.

He sat opposite her. 'In Xencliff, women are sacred, but in Sonnin, Cronnin, they are just women. The man you choose to be your husband, he must worship you. I simply want you to understand you have to set a standard, good enough will never be enough, in bed and out.' She watched his lips. Every word he said drew her closer. 'I gained my name in the taverns. I am just Xencliff, that's all. There is nothing special about me.'

Branwen sat back. Her flirting stopped. 'I don't believe you. I did something idiotic today, and that made me wonder, why, why would I do something like that? Harris, I have grown a passion.'

He shook his head. 'I have a different passion for you, Bran. I have never had a friend who would risk so much. I have soldiers, chiefs, commanders. Even Anna is trained for battle, but you aren't. I don't want to lose you,' he pleaded. Branwen stood, letting her arms droop by her side. Harris, too, stood. 'This has not been easy,' he begged her. 'Branwen, please, I would give everything up now, just so I could call you my friend.'

His pouring of emotion triggered her. 'I struggle to believe that, but if that is how you wish for this to be, then fine,' she softly agreed.

It was hard for Harris, so extremely hard, since the day he had seen her. In her angelic form, he thought of that very act. Writhing passion was all he wanted to give her. The respect he had for her reached far beyond friendship. He did not understand what he was feeling. It was new to Harris. It unnerved him, and The Commander feared nothing.

Thoughts of Branwen and her offer to accept disturbed his bath and early night. Branwen was the daughter of a queen. Destined to marry someone of superior breeding. Her chastity was sacred. Harris was only a commander. The son of a queen, but with no right to any throne. He needed Branwen as his friend.

The hot Marrion morning brought battle. Branwen remained in Harris's chamber; it would be the most arduous battle so far. Little did she know, it would also be one of the longest. She left his chambers to look from the mezzanine towards the courtyard. A few left towards the field. She promised herself she would not leave.

Wandering back into his chambers, her work was done. The room was perfect. She tidied all she could; she cleaned all she could. There was nothing left for her to do, only wait.

As the afternoon became night; she heard a faint sound in the courtyard. Darting from Harris's desk where she sat for hours; she opened the door. Harris finally returned. He glanced at the mezzanine to see her.

'To arms!' he yelled. The reserve army moved. Soldiers poured from the castle towards the field. Harris frantically moved them along.

Harris ran towards the stairs and thumped his way up. His limp had almost gone.

'Inside,' he insisted. He pushed Branwen's back. Rushing into his chambers. The door slammed closed. He panted while gazing at Branwen from under his sweat covered brow. 'I may be gone for some time.'

Branwen panicked. Her voice was a shudder of apprehension. 'What's happening out there?'

'Their numbers have grown.' Branwen roamed towards the bed, close to the wall. 'Branwen, I need something from you. Send word to your mother. She needs to send the third. I believe they may be on the way, but we need to be sure. We are not far finished here.' He whispered with excitement. 'A matter of days.'

'I will send word. Just stay safe,' she begged.

'One more thing.' Harris removed a glove. He did not calm. He glanced at Branwen. 'You wanted to know,' he breathed. His hand struck out and held her delicate neck. Holding her under her jaw. Fear filled her eyes. He pushed her back into the wall. Releasing his grip, he gave an intense kiss to her soft caramel lips. A lifetime passed in seconds as she embraced him. His warm hand, soft lips and firm grip gave her a feeling she needed. Her chastity was no longer an option. Harris released his grip. 'That should keep me going.' He ran from the room. Branwen stood speechless. A burning passion coursed through her breathless body.

The night gave way to morning. She heard nothing from the courtyard. Those returning were taken straight to the medical camps. She could not see the field from his chambers and did not want to venture onto the high turrets.

Branwen stayed in Harris's chambers, but mostly in his arms. Sleeping in his bed, clinging to one of his tunics. Her lust lingered into obsession. The smell of him remained on his pillow and sheets. A scent of clean sweat, soap and tea tree oil clasped to the sheets where he last slept. It was the scent of him.

The second day of conflict hit. A rattle of armour woke Branwen as she slept in Harris's bed. She stood and ran to the mezzanine overlooking the courtyard.

'A lot,' she heard Kyla say, speeding through the centre of the courtyard with Dominic and Anna. 'Numbers are holding.' Her voice quickened as they stopped by the entrance to the dungeon.

'And the third?' asked Dominic, his gruff voice was hard to hear through his helmet and visor. 'Did he even ask?'

Anna stepped forwards and glimpsed up towards the mezzanine. 'Branwen!' Branwen peered over the mezzanine to see the three of them stood. 'Did you send it?'

Branwen nodded. 'Sent by falcon,' she clarified, 'is Harris —'

'He's fine!' Anna called, before Branwen could even ask. She laughed, turning to the others. 'Although after this, every woman in the kingdom will need to avoid him for a while.'

The king's carriage made its way through the dune roads towards the distant Marrion.

'He has talent,' Angus asserted. 'You've seen his figures yourself.'

The disapproval from Afie was still clear. 'For over a hundred years, I have sat by your family's side. You are the only one of disobedience,' she sneered. 'If he is as able as you say, let him return when Marrion is safe.' She delicately placed her hands on the lap of her lace dress.

Angus glared at her. 'Disobedience,' he sniggered. 'My family has never obeyed. My father needed a wife, so he chose the worst one possible.' His eyes shot from the window. The patches of long grass dwindled. 'He went against everything you said.'

'Your mother was a different story, and now she's dead, so no longer my burden.'

'Burden?' barked Angus. 'I never considered myself a burden.'

Afie nodded. 'One of the worst.' Angus sniggered, as did Afie. 'And now you've mentioned it.'

Angus's brows raised, he glared at Afie, warning, 'Don't do it.'

Afie held her head high. Her delicate voice filled with certainty. 'I have to. If Kailron, Ryan, or that bloody irritating shit, Connor says another word to me. We will reopen the dungeons.' Angus felt her annoyance. 'You need to think of your kingdom. Your time on the road, it must end. As your chief adviser, I must tell you. Pay more heed to the girl you saved. Librye is sweet. You must find a wife.'

Her persistence would not fade. 'It would be a mother for Librye.'

Rolling his eyes, Angus wanted to reply, but could not find the words. Cammbour was a place of acceptance. Royalty, however, was over-looked. 'I will find one soon.' Gazing from the window, Angus wanted to argue. He feared he would not make a good husband or father. He knew he could be a great king, and with his champion in the palace with him, the world could again be at peace.

Harris did not care who he slaughtered. He did not care who stood in his path. There was a critical key to Harris's success. His anger fuelled him. His passion guided him, and his past kept him going forwards.

'Forwards!' Harris called. Blood puddled on the dry ground. The harsh climate forced a bloody sweat from them all. The season of rain was far in the future, but Harris soaked the ground with the Atlanti's blood.

Another Commander would feel the wrath of Kairne, but Kairne learnt. Barrus, the Atlanti commander, slammed his helmet on the desk in his tent. It slammed from the desk and to the floor; the racket made his chiefs jump. Several of his chiefs surrounded him.

'Whoever brings me the head of Harris Bearwood gets their own fucking army!' he roared.

'Sir, we did all we could. The next army arrives tomorrow,' his chief assured.

Wide eyed, his maddening dark eyes glared towards his chief. 'We need them now!' He slammed his fists on the desk. 'We nearly had them!' Spit tumbled from his enraged mouth.

The carriage swept into darkness. A walking pace began as the guards dismounted to relieve their horses.

'What was his stance on Xencliff?' asked Afie.

Angus leered at Afie. He opened his mouth to speak but closed it again and looked out of the window.

'You haven't even asked him.'

'He is not on good terms with his mother or Waron,' Angus replied.

'No one really is, but surely their own son —'

'He is not Waron's son, and Riah hardly speaks of him. The cliff is closed to Harris Bearwood.'

'As a mother, I hardly see that being true. Given the chance, Riah would welcome him home.'

'I doubt it. She has refused to speak with me about him. The tone of her letters is hard to decipher when she is born such a bitter woman.'

'Have faith, you are the one who defended Harris so readily. Don't stop now. He is our only hope for unity with Xencliff.'

'They are not our enemies,' said Angus.

'They are not our allies either, and from where we stand, if you are not an ally, you are an enemy,' Afie replied.

'Well, that just isn't true. Don't be so dramatic.'

His eyes lingered on the road outside. Moonlight graced the top of the scattered trees.

'I miss this world, Afie. The travelling dancers, the show and sparkle of the old ways.'

'The world has changed, Bubble, but now it is time to change it back. We cannot do that in a world where the Atlanti exist.'

CHAPTER ELEVEN

11

Exhausted, broken, and bleeding. The battleground finally belonged to Cronnin and Sonnin. Forces from the east were advancing. The Sonnin third marched towards the fortified defences of Marrion.

The clamour of clattering armour headed towards the barbican. A hollow victory reverberated through the moans of shattered men and women. An excessive atmosphere of grief enveloped the returning wounded.

A broad, black stallion drifted with them into the barbican, Svend. His rider was not with him. Branwen hung over the mezzanine. A smell of batch stew drifted up from the galleries.

One after another, they spilled through the courtyard. Down towards the bathhouses. Hundreds survived, but not without their wounds.

Branwen watched as Svend wandered, alone, into the courtyard. Orange dust coated his majestic black body. His lizard skin armour had taken a battering, his hind was oozing. Branwen rushed towards the beast, stopping him. Caressing the side of his neck, his large brown eyes flashed at Branwen. The horse had seen so much. Sadness bled from Svend. The war-beast made a soft snit from his nose before one of the stable keeps took him.

She glanced from the courtyard towards the gate. Stepping forwards, she could see no one on the barbican. The setting sun cast an orange hue in the skies. Branwen stood and lingered on the end of the stone bridge. Dwarfed by the grand castle barbican. The circling crows blotted the skies.

'You'll catch your death out here,' said Lister as he strolled towards her.

'It isn't cold,' replied Branwen, turning to greet him. A painful looking dent across the front of his armour spoke of the brutality he had suffered that day. 'Is Harris returning?'

'He will. He has a duty on the field.' Lister stepped forwards, releasing his arms to his side. He glanced down. 'You really shouldn't be so concerned about him, my lady.'

'I am not your lady,' she abruptly replied. 'Here I am just Branwen, and my concern is for good reasons.'

'Those reasons have me troubled.' He gave an awkward squint to the darkening skies. 'Branwen, you cannot be so infatuated with Harris Bearwood, your mother —'

'My mother is my concern,' snapped Branwen. 'To you, I may be just a nurse. My duty reaches beyond that which you claim to know. Your duty is to end this battle, and on to the next.'

'I am aware of my work, Branwen, but yours is to aide in the recovery of broken soldiers. Harris is not your burden.'

Branwen raised her head, looking down at the tall Lister. 'My burden is whatever my mother says it is.'

'Your mother?' He tightened his eyes.

'As I say, my duty here is something I am fully aware of. Your duty is war, not me.'

'She has sent you to watch Harris?'

'She has her ways. This war has taken enough. She needs to be sure it is worth carrying on.'

'Surely she does not speak of a truce?'

Branwen slowly blinked, looking towards the horizon. The dull hush of the tumbling waves gave the only stillness that place held. 'My mother is duty-bound to protect her people. If that means a truce, then she must consider her options.'

'If she believes that Kairne Mae Apha would approve such a thing, she must be drinking from the vessels of Arktos.'

'She is not insane. She simply must consider the toll this war is taking.'

'As it has for over fifty years —'

'Battles were sparse. They were rare fifty years ago. The war began with the death of my father, and that is something she must consider, Lister. You must understand. For five years we have battled —'

'But our people have suffered for longer.' Lister stepped towards her. 'Branwen, what your mother must understand is that her people led this war. Those who had their crops ruined, their houses burnt, barbaric rampage from the Atlanti caused this, not the death of a very respected king. We chose this, and we still do.'

Branwen lowered her head, looking at the ground. 'I shall pass your sentiment to her.'

'And until then, you must break yourself away from Harris.'

'I chose my path, Lister, just as you choose yours.'

Lister bowed and left. Branwen waited for his shadow to disappear through the turrets before she made her way back.

The night cooled the battleground. Dying fires smouldered. The bloodied corpses would clear. Stood amongst the silent chaos, Harris inspected his damage. Low moans from survivors weighed on him. He walked towards a low groan coming from the ground by a small mound.

'Please!' breathed a large man as he held his hands up to Harris.

Harris gawked at the Atlanti soldier, crushed and broken. He suspended his hand in a gesture of calm. 'I'll let them on. Hold on, soldier, you fought well.' Harris turned to Anna, who wandered behind him. 'Off!' he called.

Anna didn't question. She saw the struggling soldier, but she knew. The battle had broken many, but the war slowly destroyed them all.

'Thank you,' the man struggled through an exhausted breath.

'Don't,' chuckled Harris. 'You have nothing to thank me for.' He looked at the cliffs, scarred from the vitriol. The waves in the distance mocking a harmonious hush. He turned back to the soldier on the ground. 'When this is over, go home, hug your wife and children, and just be grateful they exist.'

The man wildly nodded as he watched Harris trample through the decay of battle.

A cooler night hit. A lighter mood broke in the castle. As they sat at the long benches in the dining halls, the castle filled with laughter and cheer.

Branwen joined the celebration. 'It's the first time I've heard them all laugh together,' she commented, stood beside Dominic.

Dominic grinned at her. He spun to face Branwen. His clothes were finally clean. It was the first time she had seen them all without their armour. His fine tunic relaxed around him. His slim frame showed that not all soldiers were built like Harris.

'It's the charm of Harris,' said Dominic.

He pointed to a small man, sat at the end of the table. Branwen could just make him out in the dimly lit and energetic room. The man wore a padding to his face. Blood oozed into the dressing, which showed a large gash. He made merry with his fellow fighters.

'Him there. He wouldn't be here, were it not for Harris.' Dominic took a drink from his tankard. A tender expression captured his eyes. A smile of indebted pride filled his cracked voice.

'In fact, half of this lot wouldn't be here.' Branwen peered around the vast amount of soldiers in the dining halls. 'Many call him a cruel berserker.' — He strolled with Branwen. They made their way to one of the large tables set out for the banquet. — 'But Harris is more than that. The other commanders would see you dead in an instant. Harris, he takes care of us. His obsession with being better than any, it seems to have served him.'

'Strange, so many of you think so highly of him, but where is he?' she asked, turning into the hall.

'Where he always is, working.'

'He should be here.'

Alone in his chambers, Harris's work was not over yet. The door to his chambers opened. Slowly, Branwen stepped inside. He did not lift his head from the papers.

Her tone was soft and troubled. She whispered, 'Apologies, Harris.'

His eyes lifted from the paper; his body remained solid. 'For what?'

Branwen sat at his desk. Gingerly, she explained, 'You didn't know it was me. You didn't know I was that soldier on the field. I could've been anyone, yet you still risked your life to save a common soldier.' Harris gave a slow blink, sitting up in his chair. 'You would do that, for anyone, but still. Everything you achieve. Everything you do. You should celebrate with your champions, those you've saved. Instead, you're here, preparing for the next. Seeing the suffering. Now, I *think* I understand a little more about you.'

Harris placed his quill down. He glared towards Branwen, reclining in his chair. 'Still, you don't know everything, Branwen.'

'As a friend, I'm always here to talk,' she offered.

Harris rose and made his way towards her. His strange mood broke. 'I am different,' — he slowly nodded, — 'Lister was here earlier. He told me about your mother's plans. Your mother seems very fond of me.' His brows raised. 'Some may say she's fascinated.'

'Stop building your ego.' Branwen watched him saunter towards her. He had a menacing look. Leaning down and placing his hands on either side of her chair, he locked her in. Branwen held a look of concern. She glanced at his hands on the arms of the chair.

'Harris, what are you doing?'

She gazed into his deep green eyes. His hair, which was usually tied neatly back, fell to the side of his face.

'What your mother plans is no business of mine. What is my business, however, I have had a very rough day. I'm expecting company,' — he blinked, — 'that is one reward I give myself.'

Branwen's heart sank. 'Very well,' she sighed as she stood. Harris stood to allow her up. She stepped to the door. The same feeling of resentment hit her. She spun to face Harris. Her lips separated. A moment of sheer awe in him passed. 'Good night, Commander.'

Harris leered at her. 'I could call her off.' Branwen twisted. 'If you wish.'

Branwen stood, conflicted. She had been sure to make her feelings clear to Harris, but she did not know if he was playing with her or not.

'I would like that, but also, I would like you to be peaceful, in whatever way you feel is right for you.'

He sauntered towards her, taking her hand. She felt a warm tingle run through her blood. He entwined her fingers with his.

Tenderly, he whispered, 'You bring me all the peace I need.' He leant forwards and faintly kissed her lips. He settled back slightly. 'I want to please you; I feel like I've not done that lately.'

Branwen gave a twisted smile. Wrapping his arm around her small waist, he kissed her neck. A fire ignited her body. Burning passion seized her.

Softly, he held her throat and kissed her chest. He untied the top of her flowing lilac gown. Her breasts were deceivingly large. Kissing them, her veins pulsed with excitement.

Harris took a knee and gave her a satisfaction she never believed existed. He remained knelt on the floor. She curled her fingers through his hair. He wrapped his arms around her legs and raised her. While continuing to satisfy her. He laid her on his bed.

She finally got her own way with Harris. Having never known the touch of a man, her chastity was still unbroken. Harris was certainly unique.

As they lay in his bed on the warm Marrion night, they could hear the merriments from the courtyard below. Harris rested his head on his hand and his elbow on his pillow. He gazed down towards her in his bed. Her soft skin blended with the silk sheets. She held them over her.

'I never considered it possible,' she softly whispered. He ran his finger over her creamy skin on her chest.

His eyes met hers. 'Never considered what was possible?'

The mystical gaze he held had her trapped, enchanted. 'I thought none of that would be possible. I am not Xencliff, Harris, I cannot be crude.'

Harris gave a tender smile. 'I didn't fuck you, but you experienced the deep pulse of pleasure. Is that what you mean?' He lifted his brows.

Branwen grinned and buried her face in her hands. She glanced at Harris; her captivating smile remained. 'I struggle to be so crude.'

'I'm Xencliff,' replied Harris. 'It's all we know,' he chuckled. A moment of purity struck him. He fixated on her flawless face. Her skin was bright and warm. Her touch was tempting, but one thing that he could not resist was her warm and enchanting smile. 'Has anyone ever mentioned you have the perfect smile?'

'Never. Has anyone ever mentioned your eyes?'

'Always.'

It would be a night she would never forget. He kissed her velvety skin and stroked her breasts. Again, his head drifted down her youthful body. Kissing every inch of skin on the way down. Her cries of passion were drowned out by the merrymaking that night. Her addiction to the commander would last.

A grey stretch of craggy mountains led Gaius and Daniel to the bleak mountains of Morigah. The untamed north called to them. Settled along the side of a small lake, their break with fifty of Kairne's finest fighters was silent.

'He is serious about this, isn't he?' Gaius squinted at the reflective water of the lake.

'I've never known him to joke,' replied Daniel.

'I was nothing but a warrior, a fighter. Daniel, why me?' Gaius, desperate for answers, came closer, shuffling from one rock to another.

Daniel put the crust of bread he was eating down. He scraped his hands on his trousers. 'I wasn't even a soldier. I've never seen war or battle. The first time I saw any variant of death was only last turn.'

'Then why you?'

'You are just full of questions.' Grinned Daniel. 'I don't like the taverns, but I do like to gamble. I took a place at the guards' table, won half their wage. Little did I know, Kairne was watching. My luck is his now.'

'Superstition? That's why?'

Daniel gave a low nod. 'The Mae Apha have struggled for a foothold for years. Kairne was the first. Pure luck won the island of Crede, from Cronnin. He believes that if a sign is shown, you must take it.'

'He hopes to guide his people, win this war, based on stupid luck?'

Daniel flicked his brows. 'Of course, he will never admit that. His following would decline. His name would fade into history. Kairne sees more than you think. He may get by on superstition, but his power is real.'

'A necromancer, power to raise a corpse for a day,' scoffed Gaius.

'It's more than that. He sees the otherworld where others see nothing. The Mara, when collecting the dead from the fields of battle, he sees them.'

'And?'

'You are clueless, young Gaius. The Mara are neither living nor dead. These creatures are the spirits of the living fae, able to pass through worlds, while their bodies remain in state in the temples. Kairne has a plan, and that plan could see both worlds threatened, both worlds belonging to the Atlanti.'

'Both worlds being torn apart. No peace, even in the otherworld. Is that what you want?'

'For the faeman and the fae, yes, for the Atlanti, what is peace when we have lived in unrest for over a hundred years?'

'And where do the coblyn fit into his plan?'

'Their need to consume, they will do exactly as we say.'

'We are to lure out thousands of these creatures with nothing.'

Daniel peered over his shoulder, where a large cart stood on the beaten road.

'Kairne has equipped us with a plan.'

'And what plan is that?'

'In that cart is a powerful negotiation tool, something which will bring you your new army.'

'My army?' scoffed Gaius.

Daniel shook his head. A wide smile grew. 'You don't expect me to lead them?' he said with a chuckle. 'You survived Marrion. You wandered for an entire turn, from the boiling lands of Cronnin to the frozen depths of Rathen. They made you for this, Gaius. You question the sanity of our leader now, but wait and see, Kairne has a plan for you, and you will not let him down.'

'That sounds fine, but if I don't know what he plans, how can I follow?'

'You'll see.'

Sat in her secret room, Librye watched the council. Their tedious talk of war, tax, and food shortages. The council halls became a dismal mumble. The light faded. She emerged for the evening, dusting herself off in the enormous tower.

'So, this is where you've been hiding,' scolded Maude. It startled Librye as she spun. 'I have spent the entire day searching for you,' she moaned, throwing her hands up.

'Apologies, Maude.' Librye held her head low. Her innocent eyes did not have the same effect on Maude, who remained furious with Librye.

With a sharp tone, Maude replied, 'You worried me out of my mind.' Librye emerged further from the doorway. 'Dinner is ready. Councillor Kailron wishes to dine with you this evening.'

Librye furrowed her brow and tilted her head. 'Kailron?'

Maude leant down towards Librye. 'I suggest you get yourself washed and ready. A dress which is not inhabited by spiders would help.'

Librye washed and changed. A pink silk dress took her fancy that evening. Small pink slippers fit perfectly with her dress. She tied her hair back, making her way from the mezzanine, and waited at the fountain. Kailron strutted from his chambers towards her.

'Child, they have given me the task of dining with you this evening.' Kailron held a noble tone of joy. 'I hope it will be a pleasurable experience for us both.' He made his way towards the fountain.

'I'm Librye,' she responded, as she stepped forwards.

Kailron shook his head. 'I know who you are.'

Librye strolled towards him. Her shoulders pulled back. 'That's strange. I have been here for quite some time now. Although I have spoken to you many times, I am yet to have an answer, or conversation, from you.'

It struck Kailron. He rejected her several times. She was a child; she did not know how to filter her feelings.

'Well, let us take this as an opportunity for us both, then.' He guided her towards a small dining hall in the lower east wing. The room was bland, with green walls surrounding a wooden table, enough to seat a group of six. He took a place at the head of the table. Librye sat directly opposite. Servers set the table with silver dinnerware, a white tablecloth, and white plates.

Librye stared towards Kailron. 'To say they have given you the task of discovering more about me, you're silent.' The sniggering staff were used to Librye being forwards. Kailron was not.

'Apologies. Where were you born?'

Librye began eating. 'I don't know. I was a baby when it happened.'

Kailron gritted his teeth. 'Did you know your parents?'

'No, they died, or so I assume, they found no survivors.'

'Did you know their names?'

Her eyes tightened and head twisted back. 'How could I know that? I was a baby! How many babies do you know of who know their parent's names? The village where they were born, or anything other than how to feed while not drowning?' The staff grappled to hold their laughter.

Kailron grated his teeth further. 'I apologise, Librye. It has been many years since a child lived in the palace, or since I came across one myself.' His tone relaxed. 'I rarely have a task such as this placed with me.'

She relaxed her posture. Kailron was not like the other councillors. His fifty something face was not as wrinkled. Imperfections were not yet showing. His hair was still brown, not the grey the other councillors carried.

'I understand. Let me guide you,' she suggested. 'To begin with, a child is not an animal. I don't bite, often, unless provoked.'

Kailron suspended his hand, stopping Librye. 'I understand.' His eyes lowered to the table. 'Why don't you tell me what you know?'

'As far as I'm aware, a soldier found me in a village in the north. Called Farhope. My parents were both assumed dead. They took me to a war camp, close to the Bourellis borders.'

Her exceptional linguistic skills baffled Kailron. He leant forwards; he had not even started eating yet. His tone filled with mystery, wonder. 'How old are you?'

'They believed I was only a few months when they found me. I like the orange turns, the autumn. I decided I would celebrate my birth in the turns I like the most. By now, I could be six, maybe seven years old.'

'Fascinating,' commented Kailron. 'Let's talk about your abilities.'

'My abilities?'

Kailron sat back, placing his hands firmly beside his plate. 'They tell me you have a gift.' His wonder turned sinister, twisted. 'A gift of power. I know Angus has seen it. Maude also explains she has seen you turn water into an enchanting blue glow, and your ability to read so well at a young age.'

'I'm onto the other wall of Angus's chambers,' she proudly announced. 'I have powers. Mother taught me how to use them.'

Kailron froze. He furrowed his brow and thinned his eyes. 'Mother?'

'Yes.' Her eyes softened and relaxed. She continued to eat her meal. 'A puca in the north, they call her Mother, because that's what she is.'

Kailron relaxed. He placed his hands on his lap and sat back in his chair. 'And what are these powers?'

'I can make things grow. She taught me of nature, and how to wield it. She also taught me a little fae magic, but that is something I can learn from the fae. She also taught me about listening to the stars. Egan was sure to teach me more when he visited. But the one thing she taught me was how not to use them.'

'Why would you not want to use them?' His growing curiosity turned to fascination.

'Because I don't want to kill people.' Her innocent reply sent a shiver through to his soul. 'You might want to eat. It's going cold.'

Librye hid nothing from the council, apart from her secret room.

'You have a gift. That is not something one should waste.'

'I have no plans to waste it,' replied Librye. She sat straight, shifting her weight. 'One thing I know is that if I have a gift, I cannot use it in a world which is tainted by war.'

'Why would you say that?' sniggered Kailron.

'Because of nature's teachings. It is about balance. Nature knows no right or wrong, only balance and imbalance. The gift of magic, when used in war, creates an imbalance. Nature will correct it, and the consequences are often dire.'

'You speak of the Solnox.'

'You have heard of them?'

'Of course I have. This world holds plenty of mystery and magic. Most of it comes from the fae, but the Solnox has often caused issues for the higher councils.'

'Well, if I am a Solnox, I can assure you, I do not wish to cause any issues. I have read about them, and I do not agree with anything they did. A Solnox should use their power to heal nature, not to wield it for their own gain.'

Kailron gave a broad smile. She warmed him. Librye was a fresh set of eyes in a council of dusty old men.

She told him all she could of her secrets. Servers cleared the table.

'Before we take leave,' Kailron stood. 'Your secrets. How do you know they are not just your own mind seeking to guide you?'

It was a valid question, but Librye knew the consequences of such questioning. 'A warning, councillor Kailron.' She stared directly into his eyes; a frosty glare came towards him from the small, formidable child. 'I like you; I think you're nice, stiff, but nice. Never question my secrets. Eternal damnation, in the pits of Tataria, is all that awaits those who question *them*.'

Her warning was clear. It chilled Kailron. As they left the room, he watched Librye skip towards the main hall. Connor awaited Kailron's arrival at the fountain.

'Good evening,' greeted Librye. She skipped past him. He smiled and bowed towards her.

Kailron made his way towards him. His clean black robes brushed the floor.

'Well?' Connor rushed his tone, forcing Kailron to shush him. He did not want Librye to hear.

Kailron watched as Librye disappeared up the stairs and into the east wing. 'The girl is remarkable.' Kailron held a look of kindness towards the disappearing figure of Librye. 'She holds promise.' Looking back at Connor, his look of affection died.

Connor pressed Kailron. 'Is she dangerous?'

'She is a frightened little girl, who will one day become a formidable woman, fear her, yes, but only if you wrong her.'

'And those are the words you wish to attend council with?'

Kailron looked down. He stretched his fingers. 'No, she is hiding nothing. She is an innocent child, but she can become dangerous if not treated correctly.'

'Is that a risk you will take?'

Kailron glanced at the balcony. 'I believe she is where she needs to be. As time passes, we must reassess.'

Connor nodded and began a slow saunter away. The west wing echoed with the footsteps of the councillors. The halls remained silent.

The Duir moon quivered in the ocean's wake. The view from the high turrets was perfect that night. Harris and Branwen stood alone atop the Castle Marrion as the stars lit the sky above them.

'Did you ever think this was possible?' asked Branwen. Harris settled behind her; his arms wrapped around her waist, he kissed her delicate neck.

He spun her to face him. 'Think what possible?' His voice sent a sultry shiver through her.

'Did you ever think that you could spend your life with one woman only?' Her brows raised, awaiting his reply.

Harris drew back. 'It's been less than a turn,' he mocked, 'I can hardly say that is life.'

Branwen glanced down, avoiding his eyes. 'From the way you act out there,' — she flicked her head towards the fields, — 'this is near the end of your life.'

'I have seen worse, Bran,' replied Harris. His tone was low. 'You make it sound as though you are convinced we could one day be together.'

'A woman can dream.' He could see the hurt in her eyes. 'Why would it be so awful?' The frustration in her voice sparked misery in Harris.

Harris let her go. He ambled to the centre of the turret.

'We've spoken of this.' He glimpsed at the cold turret floor. 'We can't. We can be together here, but your mother —'

'Again with this?' she interrupted him; she stepped forwards, holding her hands out, palms up, begging him. 'My mother need never know.'

'I am Xencliff, Bran. I know you don't fully understand, but us,' — he gestured at them both, — 'this,' — he pointed, — 'It can't happen. Even if I was the son of Waron, it would never happen.' His impatience grew. 'We can have our moment here. I've done as I promised. I've kept you untouched. Your chastity is still yours.'

'And if I don't want it?'

'Then find yourself a willing sacrifice. Because I won't take it —'

'Harris, come on!' she scolded. 'I can do as I choose. If I choose you, then my mother will have to accept it.'

'What do you know?' scoffed Harris, walking closer to her. 'I am Xencliff, Branwen. Do you even know how this war began?' He shouted, 'How all of this shit began?'

Branwen stepped back. She shook her head. 'The Atlanti wanted control. My father set to work, ensuring they would not get that.'

'That's it? Is it?' he hissed. 'That's the fairy-tale bullshit they fed you as a child?' he laughed. 'Oh, Branwen, how you have been lied to. Your father, Taranis, acted when it was too late. Xencliff came under attack ten years before he acted, ten years! Ten years of death, rape. Mothers taken to Crede, children left to rot in the wild! And what did your daddy do? Fuck all. Then the moment they breached the border, what a surprise. Daddy decided now it was personal. They can kill all the Xencliff bastards they want, but they touch a blade of grass in Sonnin, and now the world is at fucking war!'

'If you hate the fae so much, why are you here?'

'I don't hate the fae. I hate those who failed us, who left Waron begging for help and didn't listen. Those who burnt my father alive in his bed.' His voice shuddered as he tried to keep his words in. An icy shiver ran through Branwen. 'This isn't just about your mother, Branwen. I love you. You are the greatest friend I could ever ask for, but you are from a family who allowed an entire nation to suffer, and did nothing.'

'My father didn't know, surely?'

'Branwen, you are many things, but you are not stupid. Your father hoped Xencliff could hold them off, fight his fight, but there were too many. Waron has spent years purging Xencliff, he will not invite them back now, and if his stepson had anything to do with the family of Duirwud, he would burn me himself.'

'I didn't know,' she whispered with her head low.

'You could have, but no one sees the suffering until it happens to them.'

'That isn't me, Harris!' she snapped.

'I know. The most painful part of this is, I know your mother would give you all the blessings you want if I were the stepson of someone else. But I'm me, she hates Waron because the moment the Atlanti left Xencliff she called him a deserter, we fought for ten years, with no help, but he is the one in the wrong for not fighting longer, now it's your turn.'

'So why are you here?'

'The day my father died, I could hear his screams. The village nearby, children running into the woods, the boys would be killed where they stood, but the girls, they kept them, they have their uses.' Branwen put her hand over her mouth. 'Right there, that is the problem with Sonnin. Your mother has told you nothing about this war in the hope she will protect you, but all she does is weaken you.'

'I am not weak.'

'Branwen, you know nothing of this world, and that is why I will protect you. The moment I leave Marrion, this will end.'

Branwen watched as Harris hurried through the door and down into the castle. A brisk breeze swept through her.

Rushing through the castle, Harris finally reached his door. Anna sat with her feet up on his desk.

'I am so disappointed in you,' she sneered.

'What do you fucking expect, Anna?' he snapped. 'The perfect fucking gentleman?' He slammed his fists on the desk while yelling. 'I am not like them!'

'Better?' she sardonically asked.

Harris stood straight. 'Better.'

'Harris, you are just like them, conniving, slimy, loathsome at times. Why are you even doing this?'

'Doing what?' He shook his head.

'You're not fucking her, but you are doing something. Even Lister's seen it, the way she walks, the increased confidence. Is this to get one over on Harelda?'

Harris squinted. 'What?' he puffed.

'It is!' gasped Anna. 'This is to fuck with Harelda.'

'No.' Harris lowered his eyes at Anna, raising his brows. 'Branwen makes me hate myself more —'

'Never thought that was possible.'

'But what if it is time? What if Xencliff should join this?'

'That's what the shouting was? About Xencliff?'

'What else could it be?'

'Romance is dead, isn't it?'

'Romance is a concept created by the fae to make Xencliff appear uncivilized —'

'Stop!' moaned Anna, lumping back into the chair. 'We all get it, Harris, but the fae don't look down on you.' Anna stood and walked towards him. 'Xencliff did. Your own mother did. Does that make them responsible for the war? No, because the war, Harris, is not about you. Give Branwen a chance, and I hate myself for saying that.'

'Harelda would have my bollocks.'

'Yes, she would, but surely, if you love someone, it's worth it?'

'Who in the almighty name of fuck mentioned love?'

'Oh, you don't have to say it, Harris. It's in the eyes,' replied Anna with a vast smile.

'I hate you sometimes. Do you know that?'

'There is passion in hate, Harris. You of all people should know that.' Anna turned to leave. 'Let her down gently, Harris. She isn't like us,' she called as she left.

The king's carriage roared over the barbican and into the courtyard. Branwen watched from the balcony. A bundle of clothes in her arms were ready for the laundries. She watched as Angus stepped from his carriage. He thanked his staff. She wanted to meet Angus but was not dressed to meet the king. Her drab clothes did not speak of royalty. She pressed on towards the castle laundry.

Harris stood in his chambers. He heard the rattle approach. He stared at the door and waited. Angus burst inside.

'Ah! Wonderful to see you dressed, Harris,' mocked Angus while stepping inside.

Harris snorted. He dropped the papers he was reading onto his bed. 'What a wonderful surprise.' He stepped towards Angus with a wide smile. 'What has you here?'

'You nearly killed me,' mocked Angus with a low tone. 'I put a lot of work into getting the council to approve your leadership.' Angus stepped further into the chambers with his arms behind his back. 'Then you nearly get yourself killed.'

Harris laughed. 'It was just a scratch.' He strode towards the drink's shelf and poured a glass of moonshine for Angus. 'Surely you aren't here just for that?'

'I said the same,' sneered Afie. She stepped from behind Angus.

'Apologies, Harris, this is my chief adviser, Afie.' Angus stepped to the side, allowing Afie to the front of him.

Afie inspected Harris's form. Her examining of him was uncomfortable for Harris. 'So, this is your commander? I didn't meet you the last time I was here. I was unwell.' Afie stepped closer to Harris. A fresh essence of tea tree hit her.

She made her way behind him. 'The rumours are true.' She nodded towards Angus.

Harris flashed a smile. He glimpsed over his shoulder. 'I could prove it if you like.' He twisted to face Afie. 'Age is nothing but a concept. Would you like a drink, my lady?'

She raised her brows towards him. An instant like for him was clear. 'No, thank you.' Harris took a large drink of his ale. 'I have seen your work. It's impressive. However, you're needed elsewhere now.'

Harris stopped drinking; his eyes widened. 'Pardon?'

Afie strode back towards Angus. 'I am here to deliver your orders. Time is ticking. This turn alone has seen the end of one battle, and the start of three.'

'I can't leave here,' insisted Harris. His body weakened, his hands trembled. 'I'm not ready yet.'

It was the first time Angus had seen any kind of emotion from Harris. 'Harris, your talents would serve the kingdom better in Cronnin. I am here to put things into place before you leave for Cronnin.'

Harris shook his head.

'Leave?'

He heard from the door. Branwen stood. Her face was a picture of loss and dismay.

Harris tried to break the mood. He strolled towards her. 'Branwen,' he greeted, 'I believe you're yet to meet our king.'

Awkwardly, Branwen stepped inside. 'I know that name.' Angus spun. He squinted slightly, peering at her. 'My goodness. You're so much like your mother, such ageless beauty in the face of the fae.'

Branwen curtsied at him. Not wanting to be rude, she spun to Afie. 'My lady,' she bowed.

'Oh please,' smirked Afie, 'we will have none of the formalities.' Her insistence on a relaxed meeting was understandable. Standing on ceremony at the palace was always an awful bore to Afie. This was a chance for her to let go. 'My dear, why are you here?'

Branwen was coy. She sashayed towards Harris. 'I am in my service. I had plans to leave at the last turn; however, duties here have hindered my leaving.'

Harris explained, 'Branwen has been helping your champion heal.' He glanced at Angus. 'She makes the most wonderful nurse. She saved my life.'

With a faint laugh, Branwen replied, 'I didn't save your life.'

'Don't be so modest, my dear.' Angus stepped towards her. 'I must extend my thanks to you. The world needs more nurses, the bravest of the battle.' His brows raised. 'Harris,' he groaned. 'Tell me you have behaved in the company of this young lady.'

'Oh please,' chuckled Branwen. 'My mother would gut him. I am untouched, one of the sacred fae. Harris has no power here.' Harris stared at Branwen with a wrinkle in the centre of his brow as Branwen went on. 'He is neither king nor lord.' She gave a fleeting glance towards Harris, who stared at her with his mouth gaping. 'He has tried, but I am not destined to be the outcast of a Xencliff wife.' Her laugh cut through Harris like a knife.

'Surely, you wouldn't be that foolish. You'd even try?' mocked Angus, glimpsing at Harris.

Harris gave a huff of laughter with a pinched expression.

Afie stepped forwards. 'Who could blame him? The family of Duirwud is well known for their beauty.' Her eyes drifted about Branwen. 'But the family, Bearwood. Must also be known for theirs. If you weren't so young, Harris, I would take that offer.' She saved Harris the embarrassment of the royal scathing.

With the night finally calm. Anna sauntered into Harris's chambers. Crumpled on his bed, Harris sulked.

'Well?'

Harris glared at his boots in front of him.

'Well, what?' he mumbled.

'You're acting like a scorned teen. What did Angus say?'

'I have my orders. I must be in Cronnin before Onmidden.'

'How did Branwen take it?'

Harris rolled his eyes. 'Does it matter?'

'Of course it matters. She's going to be stuck here until the third return, so I'll have to put up with her.'

'She seemed upset, but I said I'll only be in Cronnin.'

'And that's it?'

'Yes, Anna, that's it.' Anna turned to leave. Before she did, Harris called. 'I chose you, Anna.' She slowly turned. 'The next commander, I put your name forwards. As the commander of the Narra army.'

Her mouth moved, but words were vacant. Anna stood, shocked, at the door.

'Thank you.' She struggled.

'I could think of no one better.'

An orange swirling dust chased the king's carriage as it disappeared over the barbican.

'So, that's it then?' asked Anna. She leant on the railing of the mezzanine. Harris stood silently beside her.

'That's it.'

'Did he say how long you have?'

'Until the end of the turn, and I'll have my space in Queensbury palace. My own staff even.'

'You don't sound thrilled about any of that.'

'I thought I wanted it, but I don't know now.'

'We can survive without you, Harris, only just, but we can still survive.'

'Well, the third are on the way. Angus said he passed them on the way here, so they should be a matter of days.'

Anna squinted towards the barbican. Several horsemen led an army towards the castle. 'Or minutes,' she mumbled. She looked at Harris. 'Why didn't you hear them?'

Harris huffed a laugh. 'My mind is elsewhere, Anna. But that's me now, my last piece of advice, keep the third on the borders, have them surround the castle, only use them if it is absolutely dire.'

'Could I ask why?'

'Just trust me, the moment the Atlanti know we have a specialist army, they will be anxious and that makes them more dangerous. They will try anything to hold their ground.'

'It all seems so unreal.' Anna twisted, facing the cold castle walls. 'How long have we been together now?'

'Seven years, seven years of misery, Anna.' Harris turned. 'If there is one thing I would like to take from this, it's you.'

'What do you mean?'

'You deserve to be happy. I thought I could do that once. Freedom, that's what you need. Just get out alive.'

'I don't need freedom. What I do need is a commander who will stop using his past as an excuse, and start looking at what future this world could have.'

'I don't see one,' he murmured.

A quiet knock at Branwen's door startled her. Opening it, she saw Harris. He stood with his arm leaning on the frame. Branwen opened her door for him to enter. He stepped inside; she could think of nothing to say to him.

'Death terrifies me now,' said Harris. 'You speak of children, of husbands and everlasting happiness.' A lingering depression filled his voice. 'That isn't what you'll have with me. You'll have secrets and lies, death as a lonely widow. No one there for you as you grow old, because the man you chose couldn't have you, and you couldn't have him.'

'I understand you're down, but that is going a little too far. We never know what could change when you end this war.'

Harris huffed a laugh. 'You think I can change an entire culture.'

'Surely you have some idea?'

Harris pressed his lips into a tight smile. 'Only the gods know what happens in my head.'

The summer turns carried a bustling array of wildlife to the gardens of the Cronnin palace. Librye released her grip on the east tower to enjoy the gardens more. Her increasing need to learn saw her through thousands of books in Angus's chambers.

Maude stepped onto the patio of the gardens. She had seen Librye leave earlier that day, but saw no trace of her since.

Traipsing along the dust path, Maude turned the corner, where something lay crumpled in the lane. A heap on the ground at first had Maude baffled until she came closer. The wolves in the kennels howled. Their host was away, tending to a matter in the stables at the front of the palace. The sound shook Maude. Librye lay on the dirt road, paralyzed. Running towards her, Maude fell to her knees.

'Librye!' She rolled her over. With her face full of dust and soil, Librye didn't flicker. Maude lifted her and carried her lifeless back towards the palace.

Several guards dashed towards Maude. 'Call for the alchemist.' A calm in her voice sent chills through the guards.

Rushing to Librye's bedchamber, she laid Librye on her bed. Maude paced the room; her hands caught her chin, waiting for the alchemist to enter. The door burst open; the panicked guard, Evan, walked into the chambers with the old alchemist following.

Godfrey was the entrusted palace alchemist, well established in the palace. He was an honourable man, and uncommonly old. His age was a tender reminder that time could be beaten. His frail frame was like an ancient willow tree. A wispy grey beard lay proudly down his front. His aged brows towered past his eyes; he had broken time.

'How long has she been like this?' Godfrey glared at Maude.

Maude shook her head. 'I found her in the meadow's lane. Completely passed out. I don't know how long she's been there.'

His eyes widened, inspecting Librye. Godfrey said in a lofty tone, 'She is still breathing, Maude, but something strange is in this child. Something I cannot explain.' His confusion increased. He pushed her eyes open. Her eyes struck him. It was the quickest he had moved for years. Her eyes were as black as midnight. Not a single trace of white. Within her blackened eyes, a swirling image of stars took over. 'Solnox,' he whispered.

Maude wrapped her arms around her waist. 'What did you say?'

Godfrey's eyes were wide as he spoke. 'The Solnox is a gift, given to those destined to lead. Every Solnox ever to have existed has met a premature end. They are a threat to the Atlanti. We can tell no one of this.' He glanced at Maude. 'Keep her in her room until she wakes, when she does, entertain her in here. Do not let her out.' His panicked state was unusual. The mystery only grew. 'She is to remain here until Harelda arrives.'

'Harelda?' asked Maude. 'Why would Harelda be coming here?'

Godfrey rose as straight as his old bones would allow. 'Because she is fae. They always see the waking of magic in this world. She is coming.'

For three days, Harris lingered deep in his chambers, awaiting the last day of Duir. He would arrive back during the Onmidden festivals. A time of year for grand celebrations. He spent days and nights with Branwen in his arms; he did not want to let her go, but the choice was not his.

The nights of Marrion were as hot as the day. The few gathering in the courtyard watched as Branwen left her room. Heading towards Harris's chambers. They dare not speak ill of The Commander. They knew Harris had an ability to hear. Instead, they averted their eyes. Pretending that they had seen nothing.

'Come in, Bran.' Harris sat up in his bed, anticipating her arrival.

Her thick cotton nightgown always made him smile. Even in his company, she tried to retain her modesty. He patted the side of the bed for her to join him.

'Not long now.' Her excitement baffled him.

'True, like you mentioned though, you will only be in Sonnin, eventually.' His need to touch her irresistible skin took over. He reached towards her and stroked her shoulder.

'I have an idea,' said Branwen. Harris raised his head to listen. 'You once said Angus would make a suitable husband. He seems nice. Pleasant enough. That way I would be in the palace at all times, with you.'

Harris glared at the wall in front of him. 'Possibly. The most irrational thing you've ever said.'

Branwen reached out and touched his chest. She untied the string of his tunic. 'It's an option.' She leant forwards and closed her eyes to kiss him.

His eyes remained open. Sitting back, he stroked her face. 'Angus watched as they removed his mother's head from her shoulders for having an affair with a guard. Her lover was torn to pieces by the Bladu on the island of Offenmoor. We cannot be together after this.' Harris drew back. 'Bran, you should know better than any. If I were to be involved in royal blood, they would drain me of mine.'

'Lister told me of your grandparents, and the island of Crede.'

'And your point?'

'You would've been enough, were it not for the hands of fate.'

'Fate,' scoffed Harris. 'Fate is an excuse used by the incapable and lazy. There was no hand of fate. Kairne seized the island, fairly. He deserved it, he won it, and I am no one to argue.'

Branwen sat straight, moving her head away. 'You support them?'

Harris shook his head. 'Sometimes I forget, you are naïve, you forget, like your mother often does, the Atlanti and the Azorae. They are still just people, but they are different. That doesn't mean we need to eradicate them.'

'Then what should we do? Accept them, their treatments, their need for power? For death?'

'I didn't say that. I have more reasons than most to hate the Atlanti and the entire Mae Apha family, but I have also seen enough blood spilt to fill an ocean. I often wonder, at what point will all of this become too much?'

'I feel it already is for some.' Branwen perched on the edge of the bed. 'You may consider me to be naïve, but I am far from it, Harris. You want to convince these people, your army, you don't want to go, but you're ready. You are ready to leave me and those who you would die for.'

'I suppose I am.'

Branwen held bravery in her voice. She faced Harris and pushed him to lie on the bed.

'Then let us make our memories last.' She stood and allowed her nightgown to float to the floor. Smoothly, she climbed onto the bed.

Harris could feel his desires clash. He wanted Branwen, in every sense imaginable. He knew what this could do to both of them. She straddled him. She could feel him growing beneath her. His breath rushed. Sweat appeared on his brow. He unconvincingly muttered, 'We shouldn't.'

Branwen leant down and kissed his neck. 'I saved myself for the man I love.' She sat up on him. Her irresistible beauty was overwhelming to him. His mouth opened in awe. He felt her chest and breasts. 'I am doing exactly that. I am giving myself to the man I love.' Her nature took over. Harris was wrong. She knew exactly what she was doing.

The passionate writhing from both of their bodies entwined in his sheets and rang in the night. Sweat covered them both in the hot Marrion night.

Branwen wanted to feel every bit of him. Being inside of her only made her want him more. She needed him. The touch of his lips. The taste of his kiss. His smell. His passion. She wanted everything, and she had it all, for one night.

Branwen finally had her wish. She had given her chastity.

'You never even told me of war,' said Branwen, resting her head on his shoulder.

Harris stroked the top of her arm. 'You distracted me.' He looked to the wall in front. An endless moment sat before him. But it was not like the others, she was another forbidden fruit. He had tasted and wanted it for so long, now it was here, reality made his liver tremble.

'There is little you need to know about war. Three simple rules, follow them, and the rest will fall into place. Rule number one, always be known to your enemy, make them believe you are worth more alive than you are dead. Rule number two, make yourself seen, while their eyes are on you, they aren't where they are supposed to be. And rule number three, if you are one step ahead, you are already nine steps behind.'

'It sounds simple enough,' her voice croaked.

'But another rule, one I'll add for you.' His eyes drifted towards the wall as he thought. 'Remember, the truth always has three sides to it, but each side is as complex as a system of roots.'

Branwen slept peacefully that night. Harris remained awake. He made a drastic error. Who she was did not matter to him. As he looked at her sleeping face, the fire flowers in his chambers dulled. He whispered, 'I want to live.' A chill ran through him.

A dull screech filled the mountains as Daniel and Gaius arrived with their small army. Dismounting, Daniel walked towards Gaius and waited.

'What now?' asked Gaius.

'You're pretty pointless, really,' said Daniel, raising his brow. He looked at the mountains, squinting as the snow reflected the dazzling sun. 'While we wait, tell me more of your wife.'

'She is devout, a singer of praise for the Mae Apha family. Marrying a soldier who fought for the name strengthened our bond. I can't help but think she has some hand in this.'

'You believe she is the reason you're here?'

'I do,' said Gaius, nodding. 'She protects me even when she's not here. Whatever has been said, she is the reason I'm here and not back on the ground.'

'War isn't your flavour, then?'

Gaius chuckled. 'I don't believe it's anyone's. So, what next?'

'Next, we bring the bag.' Daniel looked at a soldier, stood beside the cart. 'Cooperation doesn't always mean willing.'

The soldier picked up a sack from the back of the cart. A slight movement showed something living was buried deep inside. A second soldier came to the side of Daniel.

He carried a pitch torch. Handing the torch to Daniel, the other handed the bag to Gaius.

Gaius could feel the panicked movement in the bag.

'Set it down, carefully,' said Daniel as he stepped closer. Gaius did as Daniel asked. 'Now, open the top, slowly.' Again, Gaius began slowly untying the bag. Peering inside, two large black eyes stared towards him. A coating of black blood covered a scaled face. Small bits of uneven hair showed on the creature's body. Long fingers sat on the side of its face, covering its ears.

'This is a coblyn child,' said Gaius, looking at the frightened face of the coblyn.

'It is a creature of death, destined to grow and consume. If we wish to negotiate, we need leverage,' said Daniel. He dropped the pitch torch into the bag, sealing it as fast as he could. Flames enveloped, the poor creature could hardly scream before perishing in the fire.

Gaius did not show the horror he felt. He stood, as the Atlanti had taught him, dead. No emotion, no feeling. The death of the creature stirred the mountain. Screeching turned to screaming. The tunnels which led through to the crevices and caves echoed with the blood chilling sound of grief as the coblyn emerged from their dark caves.

Mouths agape, hundreds of coblyn appeared in the icy mountain pass. Their grey tongues hailed the sound of sorrow and shame as the smouldering bag turned to ashes at the side.

'Coblyn!' called Daniel. 'Your master's call to you!' The coblyn remained calling, their bodies hunched as they lumbered closer. 'He knows what you are, the myth of the coblyn is dead, our lord Kairne sees you, and he calls to you!' The coblyn calls became quiet. A dull hum filled the pass. Daniel looked at Gaius. He smirked as he held his arm out. 'Well, I would like to introduce your new army, inspire them.' Daniel stepped back.

Gaius stood with his mouth gaping. A shock of chilling horror hit him. 'Coblyn!' he called, attempting to remain brave in the face of suffering. 'You quiver in your mountains, fearing those who shunned you, hating those who lied about you. We are not them, but we are your masters now. Follow us, and we will lead you to a future free from fear, free from loathing. Refuse, and you will be eradicated from Cammbour. If you are not with us, you are against us.'

The coblyn, with their limited intellect, remained silent as they looked at each other. Their simple minds and complex society led them to only one option, join the Atlanti, or die.

A gathering began as the mountain emptied. A black mass of coblyn lined the mountain pass. They had no king or leader, no coblyn of higher knowledge to guide them in their decision. What they had was a vision, as the smouldering bag remained at the side of the road. They each saw a future they didn't want. A destiny they never planned, and a fate they wished to change.

'There are no children,' said Gaius, stood beside Daniel.

'Kairne always has a plan,' murmured Daniel.

12

Librye sat in Angus's chambers. Now on the other side of the bookshelves.

'What's today's choice?' inquired Rebecca.

'It's about creatures. It's a treasury of all creatures to exist on Cammbour, from humble elephants to fierce lions.'

'And what is your favourite so far?'

'I cannot have a favourite, but if I had to choose, I would say the coblyn.'

Rebecca scrunched up her mouth. 'Why?' she derisively asked.

'Because they bridge the gap, they live like the wild animals of this world, but they have developed societies. They have baffled experts for years. The coblyn are nothing like the fae, faemen, puca, torb, merrow, or even the ggelf, and they know hardly anything about them. They are wild, but they are gentle.'

'Gentle?' Rebecca scorned. 'Are you reading about the same creature?' she teased.

'Of course,' Librye replied. She glanced at the cover. 'Albus Tarkin wrote it. He was a scholar of the ancient order of the fae.'

'And he says the coblyn are gentle?' Grimaced Rebecca.

'He said they have an order to their society.'

'They devour the flesh of their dead, even the babies.'

'But with good reason,' replied Librye, blinking as she did. 'They are not like us. They don't bury or burn their dead, but that doesn't mean they're wrong. They consume the dead to absorb the spirit, so they can live on through them.'

Rebecca shuddered. 'Disgusting,' she said with a curled lip. 'Well, it isn't something I would call civilised. I'll call you for dinner. Maude is out today, but she has asked me to tend to you. If you need anything, I'll be —'

'I know,' Librye cut off. 'You'll be in the grounds.'

'In the galleries,' Rebecca corrected her with a high attitude. 'All this reading is not appropriate for a child your age. I'll be speaking to Angus when he returns.'

'I'm sure your concern will go unnoticed.'

Rebecca sniggered as she left. She enjoyed the futile banter with Librye. Even those in the gallery didn't offer the entertainment Librye often did.

Harelda sat uncomfortably in her white carriage. Decorated with a gleaming gold trim, over a hundred soldiers rode by her side, swarming the carriage. The short day's ride from Sonnin to Cronnin was one of the safest routes that existed, but Harelda would take no chances. A price was on her head, placed there by those she strove to destroy.

'What do you believe she is?' asked Harelda, sat with Grendel. It had been many years since she had made such a journey. The rocking carriage soothed her fiery temper.

'I believe she is something. As I told you, she holds promise. I could do this alone.' He scowled from the window. Refusing to look at Harelda.

Harelda gave a slow blink. Her usual mystique had faded since leaving the magic of Sonnin. 'They have confined me to Sonnin for thirty years. It is one journey, there and back. I need to know.' Her raised brows sent a warning to Grendel. 'So, your mood ends here.'

'She will require more than the fae to guide her.' The carriage continued to rumble towards Cronnin. The roads were empty. Gentle spring sun kept the roads dry. Green pastures brightened the view. 'A Solnox has not been born for over a hundred years, if she is such then a challenge awaits.'

Harelda snapped, 'She needs testing, Grendel!' She quickly calmed.

'I understand that.' Grendel leant forwards, clasping her hands in his. 'You are a mother, before you are a queen. I know that, even though you hide it well. She is a child, and as a child she needs a mother to guide her, to comfort her, not a queen to tell her what she is or isn't.'

'That reminds me,' said Harelda. She looked at Borvo, sat silently beside Grendel. 'Have a letter written. I wish for Branwen to return after the Third. After the business in Trent, I realise they have become a heavy target. I'll send a small unit to assist her return.'

'That is what Librye needs, someone to think of her welfare.'

'Her welfare is of the utmost importance to me.'

'Then by showing that, Librye will have all she needs.'

A small hand lifted as Borvo shook his hand in the air. Harelda glared at him. 'I don't mean to be a bother, but why so much concern for a child who has such power?'

Harelda gave a tender smile at Borvo. 'The Atlanti destroyed the last Solnox. He destroyed himself. Legends are a bore with such matters, so the truth is he was so obsessed with destroying the patriarchal Atlanti he used his power in war, forces collided, his own hand consumed him. His own strength.'

'How?'

'The island of Offenmoor tells you how, the Bladu, creatures of darkness, emerged the moment he used his power to take a life, his hands were tied by then, he pledged to rid the world of oppression, the council of Cronnin called for his dismissal, things got out of hand and his own army destroyed him when they realised how dangerous he was.'

'That's awful,' said Borvo with a gasp.

'And the very reason Librye will need our protection. If she is one of the Solnox, the council will be on high alert. She will not be safe in the hands of Cronnin.'

'Although that is not our decision to make, Angus will protect her,' said Grendel.

'Angus has other concerns. He is in his prime. He needs a successor.'

'Please do not mention it to him. It will upset him. His council speak of nothing but and I know the very mention of it grinds at Afie.'

'So it should, as his private council, she should know better.'

'He doesn't want a wife,' Borvo mumbled. He saw the two glaring at him. 'At least that's what I've heard,' he stuttered.

'When you're born royal, you get all you want, but you rarely get the freedom to have the things you need.'

'You did,' said Grendel.

'You're right, although being wed to my second cousin had its perks, it also had a downside. Taranis is dead and I'm alive, now, back to the conversation about Librye.'

'There is little else we can say.'

The carriage rumbled through the gates of the Cronnin palace. A Cronnin guard ran inside. Rushing through the door to the council halls, he pelted in, interrupting a session.

'What is the meaning of this?' yelled Ryan, stood in the centre of the floor.

The guard caught his breath. A panicked expression on his face worried them. 'Apologies, my lords. The queen has arrived,' he called.

Uproar began. Blowing from the doors, the councillors piled on the step to greet Harelda. Standing to the side, they took a knee as best they could. Allowing her to pass through the centre of them. She sashayed between them. Holding her flowing lilac gown, she made her way into the palace.

Maude stood on the stairs. The moment she laid eyes on the imposing queen Harelda, she dashed to Librye's room.

Kailron strode in from the porch outside. 'Your highness,' he said, slinking to the side of her. He gave a deep bow towards her. 'Such a luxury to have you here.'

Her posture remained one of strength and influence. 'Where is Angus?'

Kailron struggled to answer. A knot in his stomach churned. 'He is away on business, your highness.'

An expression of disapproval met him. 'That is how you refer to this war? It is not business, his duty is vital, his attempts to end this war far surpass yours —'

'Your majesty, please,' interrupted Kailron. He held a contrived smile.

'Do not try, councillor!' she warned. 'Now, I wish to see the girl.'

Kailron narrowed his eyes. His lip trembled. 'Librye?'

Harelda softened her tone. 'Yes.' She could sense the care from Kailron. 'Perhaps you could take me?'

Kailron guided her and Grendel up the stairs and towards Librye's room.

'Maude?' Kailron entered. His face spread, eyes widened, and mouth gaped. 'What happened?'

Maude sheepishly replied, 'I discovered her in the lane of the meadow. She's been weak since. She's been in the chambers, but not much. Rebecca and I have been caring for her.'

Kailron strode inside. By Librye's bedside sat Godfrey. Harelda stepped in. 'Out, all of you,' she commanded.

Godfrey rose and left. Accompanied by Kailron. Grendel remained outside. A sombre mood swirled in the room.

Maude stood to leave. Harelda twisted. 'Wait.' Maude spun to face her. She remained bent into a bow. 'Stand, my dear.' Maude stood. Her hands shook. She gazed at Harelda. 'You are Maude?' Maude nodded. She was not afraid of Harelda, she was terrified of her. 'Good, then you shall remain. Close the door.'

Maude hurried to the door and closed it. She watched as Harelda ambled to the side of Librye's bed. Her eyes remained fixed on Librye. Harelda sat, her back remained straight.

'She has an ailment, your majesty.' She walked to the other side of the bed and sat.

Harelda glanced at the door, silently. She gazed back at Maude; her eyes narrowed to almost a wink. 'Please, call me Harelda. Only in the company of ourselves, though.' Her power did not wither. She simply appeared kinder to Maude. 'You found her, didn't you?' She inspected the face of the defenceless child. 'You found her in Farhope.'

'I believe I did,' replied Maude. 'She was perfect.' She smiled, gazing at Librye's sleeping face. A flood of memories returned to Maude. 'Farhope was a lifetime ago. I would've taken her there, and then, but I was a soldier. I couldn't care for her then. Without even knowing it, she changed my life.'

Harelda broke her stare with Librye and glanced towards Maude. 'You care for her now.' Her tender side seldom showed, but children always brought out a soft side in Harelda. 'Tell me about her state. Recently and when you found her.'

The perfection of Harelda's accent startled people. Maude remained fixed on Librye. Harelda was just a woman to Maude, just like her. The false rumours of a haughty queen were nothing but cruel rumours.

Her tone was a tender breath of memories. She allowed them to flood back.

'When I found her, it was strange. The village appeared ruined. Nothing left alive. I remember the smell of burning.' — Maude softly brushed Librye's face. — 'And then I heard her cry. The blanket they bound her in was perfect. As if they had placed her there, just for us to find. She was a gift from the gods. She brought so much hope to us all. I took her to the medic. That was when we saw the lumps.'

Harelda's head tilted. 'Grendel mentioned these. Would you show me?' Maude stood. She unfastened the back of Librye's dress and pulled the shoulders down. She rolled her for Harelda to see. Harelda stood. Her eyes widened towards the lumps on Librye's back.

Her slender finger softly ran over the lumps. 'The torbs,' she breathed to herself. She gazed at Maude. 'Tell me when she wakes, care for her, Maude.' Harelda walked towards the door. She placed her hand on the door and twisted. 'The child is vital to this world. As are you. Care for her.'

Maude nodded.

In the southwestern lands of Marrion, rain was scarce. The skies opened, clearing blood from the ground. A distinct smell drifted through the castle. As the dawn broke, a western wind hit, lashing the rain out to sea. Silence occupied the castle. The odd few muddy footsteps squelched through the courtyard as occasional soldiers roamed, waiting for their call to arms.

Wandering from her room, Branwen didn't know what she would find. She reached for the knob of Harris's door. Her legs weakened with every step she took.

Sat at his desk, Harris gathered the last of his belongings.

'I thought you would leave without seeing me,' she said with a smile.

'I wouldn't do that,' Harris replied, glancing at her before looking back at the desk. 'That would be a coward's way out.' His speech slurred.

'I'm surprised you're not out there,' she coyly said, while glancing at the window.

Harris glanced at the window. 'Can't. I have my orders. I am forbade, forbid, forbidden? forbode?'

'Have you been drinking?' asked Branwen, narrowing her eyes towards him.

Harris jerked his head back. 'Of course I have. Fuck all else to do.'

'I would rather hope you have a clear head when heading back —'

'Why?' snorted Harris. 'Have you seen what the roads are like? I would rather be pissed than remember that.' He continued packing.

'Harris, promise me you'll be safe.'

Harris stopped. He looked at Branwen with a distant fog in his eyes. 'I will not promise that, because I'm me, and I,' — he whispered, — 'I rather enjoy a few healthy disputes along the way.'

'How much have you drank?' spat Branwen.

'I had a bottle left, wasn't going to leave it, and I don't plan on glassing anyone on the way.'

'A bottle of what? Bloody moonshine?'

Harris nodded with a tight smile.

Branwen exhaled. 'Perhaps a nap before you leave. At this rate, you won't even get on Svend.'

'Svend's fine.'

'But you aren't!'

'I'm fine, I not as think as you drunk I am.'

Branwen stared at Harris, too stunned to show concern. 'You can't travel like this.'

'You're not my mother,' he softly replied.

'Perhaps not, but I am a nurse.'

'So,' Harris shrugged. 'And if you were my wife, you would gladly let me travel like this.' He winked. 'Trust me.'

Branwen took a deep breath. 'Please, Harris, you can't travel like this. I worry.'

Harris was still going through the papers on his desk. He twisted with lifted brows. 'Worry about what?'

'Not only are you pissed, but, taverns,' she replied, shaking her head.

Harris laughed. He swayed towards her. 'I promise I'll behave.' He held her shoulders and gazed deep into her eyes. 'I will see you in Sonnin.' He gave a heavy sigh. 'I can promise myself to you, until you're ready to accept this.'

Looking down, Harris shook his head. 'I can be loyal, Bran. You can't expect me to live a life of celibacy. I will give you as much time as you need. Just remember, we both have needs.'

She spun and sat on the bed. Holding one of Harris's tunics, she held her head in her palms.

'You need to use the rest of your time here, accepting we cannot be together. I will never feel about anyone the way I feel about you. It crushes me to know that we can never be one. But that is the way of the world. Royals are for royals, commoner for commoner, that is the law,' he enforced. 'I drank too much. I really can't see that well.'

Branwen stood. Her voice was deep. 'We have options, Harris, many options. In a world so broken by war.'

Harris sharply twisted. 'I am needed, Bran!' he snapped at her. 'This world will remain torn if this does not end. I have sacrificed myself daily to get this war to the place it is now!' Her needs no longer mattered to him. The needs of the world did. His voice calmed; compassion showed. 'I never intended to bring you into my world. But now you are here, you must understand something, get out now, there is nothing left for you here.'

He took his bag, gave one last kiss, and left. After several attempts, Harris finally mounted Svend. As they came towards the barbican, silence filled the courtyard, until they heard a rattle and thud.

'I'm fine!' called Harris, laying in a heap on the ground.

'I have to say it's not the healthiest way of dealing with grief,' said Dominic, stood beside Branwen in the courtyard.

Atop the plateau, Anna stood. Her heart raced and blood boiled. She wanted to be there to see Harris leave, but they needed her in battle. His instruments would remain, and Anna would power them.

'Your orders, commander?' Saburo stood beside her.

Anna broke her glare towards the Castle Marrion. She swivelled to Saburo. 'I have a final order from Harris.' Her lips remained parted. The task she had taken on was a vast one. To fill the boots of Harris Bearwood was daunting.

'A farewell to us all here.' Her voice raised, she came towards the one hundred atop the plateau. 'He has ordered we have one last reminder of Harris Bearwood in this waste of a land!' she called. They placed several buckets along the top of the cliff. 'Harris left this for me.' She handed a note to Saburo.

Saburo read the letter. He sank his brows. 'Who begins a letter with fucker?'

Anna grinned. 'Read on.'

'The buckets are one last chance to see a genuine Harris send off, dip your arrows and enjoy!' It confused him. 'Is it fire?'

'It is not fire,' replied Anna. 'People often underestimate Harris.' She marched towards the ballistas. 'His time in Xencliff taught him much. His fascination with nature far outweighs ours. If Kairne thinks he has won, because he has named himself as the new necromancer, he is yet to meet Harris's spider bite.' She raised her brows towards him. 'Just watch.' She spun to the archers. 'Dip your arrows. Do not let the arrow touch your skin or wounds,' she warned. 'For they are tainted.'

She called the loose. The arrows fired. Each arrow which struck but did not kill. Left its victim with an uncomfortable feeling within their nether regions. Before becoming a part of the carpet of death. Which now covered the grounds of the battle.

'Spiders were always his favourite,' said Anna, her smile widened as she watched the chaos spread. 'His spider in the palace in Xencliff, killed several guards before they found her. Harris cared little, though.'

'I never understood him,' said Saburo, as he scowled towards the field.

'That's your first mistake.' Anna turned to face Saburo. 'There's no understanding of the broken. He's like a puzzle, but all the pieces are soggy and half are missing.'

'That actually makes sense.'

'Perhaps, but people who try to understand how Harris works often fall into madness long before he does.'

'I never understood the charm,' said Saburo, shaking his head.

'It isn't charm,' chuckled Anna. 'It's honesty, blatant confidence. He can't help it. I suppose I should've warned Angus, really.'

Saburo looked at the scattering of soldiers below. The Atlanti began retreating before falling into the drudgery. 'What is going on down there?'

'It's something he didn't like to use often. To him, it was unfair to kill so many so easily. He seems to enjoy fairness. What that is, he calls Spider Bite, potent enough to kill. But first it will set a man off course with an uncomfortable erection. Before their inevitable death.'

'A warfare which is frowned upon, vastly,' snared Saburo.

'It is, but it's still fun to watch.' Anna shrugged.

Svend was a spirited horse. Well-equipped for endurance. The war beast served as a companion to Harris for longer than they both cared to think. Their joint loyalty could see them apart for days, but they would reunite like no time had passed. This was not retirement for Svend, but Harris had thought long about the complications of war. Svend's scars served as a painful reminder to Harris. The fae and faemen, even the Atlanti, were not the only creatures afflicted by war.

Many of the bleak roads held rest stops, small stone huts, each contained a small hearth for a fire, and a stone staircase leading to the roof. It was suitable for any lone traveller. The taverns would provide Harris a decent meal and rest, but also temptation.

A good meal called to him from The Bear's Arms, in Nortroma. A regular haunt for Harris would allow him some rest before he made his way to the Grenhilda valley.

Several days of gruelling travel lay before him. The loneliness was a welcome break, but Harris craved something. A need for news.

Paying the stable hand in the small village of Nortroma, Harris made his way into the tavern. A few people muttered quietly in the tavern as Harris stepped in. His eyes drifted through. The clean rafters and flagstone floor were well kempt by the landlords. Even the tables were clean. Harris gave a brief, impressed huff. He strode to the clean bar.

'Afternoon, Harris,' called the barkeep. The heavyset gent knew exactly who had just walked into his tavern.

Harris's mouth formed a wry smile. He thumped his arms onto the bar. 'Afternoon,' he greeted. 'Apologies, but is Salonius here?'

'Retired,' said the barkeep. He crept from the shadows at the back of the bar. Where most of the tankards stacked. 'He told me about you, though.' He raised his brow and lowered his head. 'Said that I should receive a good trade from you.' His smile curved. 'Darnus, sir.' He gave a Xencliff welcome to Harris. Holding his left palm flat vertically. He made a fist with his right hand and placed it on the palm with a slight nod. 'Although,' said Darnus. 'I believed you were in Marrion, battling the dark army?'

Harris leant over the bar. He lifted a tankard from the counter and pulled his own pint from the spigot at the bar. His eyes remained fixed on Darnus as he explained, 'I was. Injury had Angus panicked. So, they have forced me to return.' He reached to his side and took his coin pouch. He placed a coin on the bar.

'Return?' Darnus asked in a high, surprised tone. 'You're appointed to the palace?'

'You sound shocked. It was only a matter of time.' He oozed with pride. 'I'm not the man people assume I am,

Darnus. You've heard of me, but you've not actually met me before. Assumption is your enemy as a tavern owner,' he warned with his brows raised.

'Apologies. Here was me, expecting an angry commander. Thirsty for the pleasures of the flesh,' he said with a chuckle.

'Well, that part I wouldn't leave out. It's close to the truth,' smirked Harris.

Darnus laughed. 'And what are your plans with Cronnin?'

Harris lifted his eyes towards him, a menacing look held in his eyes. 'A lot. The dark army will fall. Following that, I doubt the Atlanti will settle. They will rise again, and when they do, I intend to ensure I have everything in place to see them bow to the power of Cronnin.' He took a large drink from his tankard. 'Is Harlenna still here?'

Darnus gave a brisk nod. 'She is. I can call her if you wish?' he offered. He edged towards the stairs behind the bar.

'No!' — Harris shot from the bar. — 'I would rather keep my stay as quiet as possible. I don't intend to stay for more than a few hours. She would see me here all night.'

'Very well,' replied Darnus. 'A quiet corner, perhaps. I'll bring you something to eat. We have a wonderful meat pie my wife makes.'

'That would be very agreeable.' Harris widened his smile. He stood and sauntered towards a small table beside the window. He took the hood of his leather cloak and pulled it over his head. Almost covering his eyes. He remained in the corner. Well into the night, Harris sat and listened.

'I hear it's killed over two hundred. In less than a turn,' said a ragged-looking man ambling into the bar with his companion. His curly hair showed signs that he once had dark hair. Age had taken its colour. They both showed small red blotches on their faces. As their nights of drinking took its toll on them. 'Rumour has it, they only put the flag up yesterday.'

'The black flag has been up for the whole turn,' said his friend as they stood at the bar to the side. Where Harris had sat for the day.

'I just know that it's killed a lot. Seems to be the men affected the most, though.'

Harris stood and made his way towards the bar. His thundering boots startled them as they both twisted to see Harris barge between the two. He leant on the bar in the middle of them. 'And where exactly might this place be?' he asked with a tight smile.

'You're Harris!' said one man, his mouth gaped as he stared at Harris.

Harris held a satirical tone. 'Well done. Now where can I find this place?'

The man stood to his left, pointed towards the east. 'Other side of the valley, sir, it's an awful place, though.' His brows folded down, concerned. 'Bodies in the streets of a terrible illness.'

Harris gave a twisted smile. He looked at the other. 'Is he always this dramatic?'

'He's right though, I hear they're burning them in the field, but can't keep up. Awful place.'

'Awful places are where I always end up.' Harris left. 'About your business,' he called.

'How did you know it was him?' asked the barkeep.

Simultaneously, they both replied, with different answers.

'Armour,' said one.

'Eyes,' said the other. 'He's got lovely eyes.'

'He also took down a black dragon, gutted it, and made his armour, but you're going with the eyes,' the other man asked.

'Makes sense,' said Darnus. He looked at the more disagreeable of the two. 'What? He has nice eyes, Xencliff green.'

Branwen sat on the edge of Harris's old bed. Anna sat at her desk.

'You're not sulking in here all night,' warned Anna.

'I'm not sulking. I'm just worried,' she replied with a sigh. Branwen sauntered towards the desk. 'He was so drunk.'

Anna placed her quill down, an expression of sympathy filled her eyes. 'Apologies, I didn't know.'

'What?' Branwen asked, screwing up the top of her nose.

Anna exhaled a breath. 'I have known that man longer than I care to think. He was drunk the night he left Xencliff, and the night he left Blodmoor, and Justine, and so many other times.' She shook her head while distantly looking at the wall at the side. 'The point is, Harris only gets drunk when he accepts something is over. It's almost like a cleansing for him, a ritual. If he's pissed, he's moved on.'

'From here? Or something else?' asked Branwen.

'I don't know what happened between you two.' Anna turned on her chair, reaching into the draw at the side. 'Whatever it was, it's not up to me to judge.'

'Of course, you're Xencliff as well, so you're used to the strange goings on.'

'It's not strange to be less judgemental. Something the fae are famous for.'

'I don't judge, Anna, you know that.'

'I do, but perhaps you need to move on as well. Make your own cleansing ritual?'

The soaring tower in Rathen saw many leave. As the evening lingered to midnight, a shiver in the air caught Isradella. The view from Kairne's window displayed the procession of torchlight leaving the town below.

'Why are so many leaving?' she quietly asked, wrapping her arms around her chest.

'You look cold,' said Kairne, having prodded the fire to bring more warmth.

'Not in your company,' she coyly replied.

Kairne grinned. 'You needn't be so amorous. We are already united.'

'Does that mean I cannot show affection?'

'No, of course. But you can be honest with me.'

Isradella froze, glancing at the bruise on her arm, showing where honesty last got her. 'I'm sure I'll warm up.' She looked back out from the window.

Kairne sauntered to her side. Wrapping his arm around her waist. 'They are going to Marrion to clean up.'

'Clean up?' asked Isradella. She did not wish to question further. He had already taken plenty of opportunities to make her feel inferior to him.

'What the faemen cannot realise is that we have a new weapon. They have Harris Bearwood. He has a brilliant mind, that I will admit, but that simply means we need to push harder. Harris will wither and die, just like the rest of them. What we have will last forever.'

'And what do we have?'

'You are just full of questions.' Kairne smirked, turning her to face him. 'Here is a question. Would you like an early night? Crawl into bed with your doting husband?'

Her smile grew. 'I would like that.' Isradella turned, lowering her head. 'Sadly, sleep is all we can do. I caught my bleed this morning.'

Her shyness did not deter Kairne. 'If you bleed, then you do not carry my heir, and you need to carry my heir, regardless of your woman's troubles. You have a duty, as a wife.'

His temper grew, and Isradella could feel it. 'I apologise. I'll clean and be ready.'

'Yes, you will.' Kairne's teeth gritted. He took a blade from his desk and held her arm stretched out. Her arm quivered at the force of his hand. Slicing into her flesh, he held the knife to her throat. 'Let that serve as a reminder,' he hissed. 'For every bleed you have, every turn you do not carry my child, your perfect skin will wither and scar.' He threw her arm down. She pulled it towards her chest, covering the wound with her hand.

'I will see myself right,' she sobbed.

'Yes, you will. You are Atlanti now. You must serve your husband.'

It was not the life she chose, but it was the life she was bound to.

'I didn't know it would be like this,' muttered Isradella. Her maid stood behind her, brushing her long locks of hair, ready for a cold bath.

'Not that bad,' her maid replied. 'Our society is different. Our Lord Kairne grew with an oppressive father. Some of that translates to how he treats people at times, but he is still the rightful heir to Cronnin. A false king sits in his place. The monumental task placed with him is beyond our comprehension.'

Isradella lowered her head. 'Of course.'

'Now, a cold bath should clear you up.'

The sting of the water hit Isradella's skin like a thousand needles. She entered her chambers with an icy grasp of misery following her. The tower was her prison. Although she could escape, she had nowhere to go.

The nights were darker away from the reflective ocean. Surrounded by woodland was key to Harris's peace as he drifted through the midnight woodland. The company of Svend was more than enough for him. His thoughts occupied by Branwen. He missed her smell. The feel of her hair. The touch of her skin. The sound of her sweet voice. Thoughts of war were far in the back of his mind.

As dawn broke, the trees came to life with a sound he had missed. Calling songbirds sang a delicate welcome of morning. Harris rode towards the Grenhilda valley. A cool air blasted through his hair. He would not miss the blistering heat and rancid sweat of Marrion.

The Grenhilda valley sat as a few days' ride from Cronnin city. Stretching from the Sonnin and Cronnin west border, it flowed south. Hitting the borders of Thrasia. The deep cavern served as a spectacle of nature. The beauty of the valleys brought many weary travellers. It was renowned for its enchanting sunsets. The Grenhilda river flowed harmoniously through the narrow gorge. Woodland and grassy patches scattered the incline to either side. Different wildlife would gather. The riverbanks offered a free-flowing refreshing drink.

A village due east offered him something he needed before he could take his place at the side of Angus.

Svend was usually a graceful horse. He was clumsy due to the steep paths in the valley. The roads were weaving gravel and dirt. As it descended into night, the sun beat down on the valley. A haunting orange glow lit the basin below them. The shadows of the night-time creatures gathered on the steep banks on the other side. Harris was used to darkness. He was used to the calling wolves and falcons above. The eerie silence spoke to him. He headed towards a small village just above the valley.

An entire night of travel finally saw him to the small, fortified defences.

Resting by an oak tree, Harris waited for the dawn. A modest brown fence surrounded the cottage houses. The call of farm animals was dull as the sun woke the valley. The silence was eerie. He stepped to the gate with Svend. A black flag fluttered and beat in the wind.

Harris took a moment; he closed his eyes while gripping the reins of Svend. A heartbeat thudded; Harris listened past the call of his companion's chest. A coughing blast hit him. Silent moans called out. He could hear the suffering which was being kept from the outside world.

A long dirt road snaked through the village. A man hobbled by the village gate. Draped in a long brown cloak. He covered his face with a black cloth.

'You may wish to stay back, my lord,' called the man in his gruff voice. A cough struck the man.

Harris stepped forwards. He pointed to the black flag. 'What has you all here?'

The man stepped a little closer. Harris took a step back. 'They believe it's the murk, a black death.' He tried not to get too close. 'They say we're here for the turn. Say we're to keep the flag up.'

'Who says?' Harris reached for the gate.

'The council of Cronnin.' He watched Harris drop his hand from the handle.

Harris thought. He glanced at the floor. 'It has taken how many so far?'

The man peered around the village. A few of the cottages sat empty, having lost entire families.

'About a hundred so far.' He furrowed his brow. He glanced at Harris. 'Why?'

'I'm here on business. This illness has taken many, here and other villages. We're trying to find out what it is.' He glowered at the man. 'But in order to do this, we need samples for the alchemists and sharmas.'

The man stood back. He furrowed his brow and narrowed his eyes. 'Samples?'

Harris gave a slight smile. 'I assume you would like to help?' The man nodded. 'Where is your village chief?'

The man shook his head. 'Don't have one, taken a few days back. When this is over, we will find someone, but for now, we have no one.'

Harris widened his eyes. 'Then I will need you to help.' The man came closer to Harris. He could see that the man appeared well, but he did not want to risk such an illness. 'I need you to take some samples of those affected. Those with clear signs of the murk. Can you do that?' He lowered his head and raised his brow.

Enthusiastic to help, the man spun towards the village and swivelled back. 'How?'

'The spit,' Harris pointed to his mouth. 'In their mouths.'

With his samples collected. Harris made his way back onto the road. The valley bought a wet return. He made his way back to the other side and towards Cronnin.

The beauty of the sunsets and sunrises would keep him company for a few days while he rested there. A quick resolve to the battles already brewing was set deep in his mind. He craved a harmonious world.

Maude spotted a flickering of Librye's eyes. She reached forwards from the chair towards Librye. Brushing her head, she shushed her. She could see the panic in Librye's strange purple eyes. Her eyes remained half closed, her skin was whiter than usual, even her hair appeared to have lost its lustre.

'What happened?' moaned Librye. She clung to Maude's arm and lifted herself up from the bed. Her body still felt weak, her eyes still sought to focus.

'It is becoming more frequent.' Maude calmly tried to explain to her.

'It happened again. So, the dragons, they weren't real?' Her eyes squinted towards Maude. A distorted view of the world had entered Librye's mind, and she did not know how to unravel it.

'Dragons?' Maude sat at the side of Librye's bed. 'They could've been real, Librye. It is not for me to say. Tell me what happened?'

Librye peered off into the room. Her thoughts spun. 'I was at the Draco stretch. Egan was there to greet me. He showed me his island, but he said I wasn't there, he said, I was still in Cronnin. He wanted to teach me all he could.'

Her look of honesty confused Maude. She knew Librye. She was honest. Often, she had been too honest.

'He taught me about the dragons and their stars. He taught me how to use the stars to take my thoughts to him.' Librye broke her stare and glanced at Maude. 'They told me of the Solnox.' Her eyes narrowed. 'He said, I must learn about dark magic before it's too late. I don't want to learn about dark magic, Maude,' said Librye. A chill flashed through the room. The sun outside dulled as Librye spoke. 'He told me so many things I've never known before. But dark magic, I've read about it, and I want no part of it.'

Maude needed to change the subject and quickly. 'Well, one day you may wish to learn more about it. So you can help end its use.' She gazed into Librye's eyes.

'I'll never use it, Maude,' she promised.

'Oh, Librye,' sighed Maude. 'My child.' She held Librye close. 'You have nothing to worry about. I will take my last breath protecting you, no matter what from.' She held Librye back and looked into her eyes. 'While you were off on your adventure, which I believe you were. So much has happened here, Harelda. She is here to see you.'

'That's nice,' Librye laid dejected. Her spirit withered.

'And Angus will soon return. For now, the queen needs to meet you, Librye. She can help you.'

Maude peered from the doorway of the room. She twisted to a guard stood in the corridor. 'Could you alert Harelda, please? Librye has woken.' Evan gave a quick bow to Maude and made his way towards the west wing. Maude went back into the room.

Making her way into the washroom, Maude readied a drink of water for Librye. She took a small glass to her.

'What's she like?' Librye hid her excitement.

Maude took a blanket from the side of Librye's bed. 'Normal. I've heard stories of her being a terrifying, cruel, and bitter woman. She was rather warm. She had pleasant enough conversation.' Maude could think of nothing faulty to say about the queen. She had been more than polite to her. 'Anyway, it matters not now. Relax, you're still looking pale.'

Maude helped Librye lay back. As she did, she noticed a strange discolouring on her back. 'Librye, lean forwards.' It struck Maude with horror. She saw Librye's back. A red and black wilting bruise covered both lumps to her back. Adding to the now yellowing bruise she already had.

'My goodness,' she whispered. Harelda stepped in, alone. 'Harelda,' Maude huffed with relief. 'Please, come see.' Librye remained forwards.

Harelda stepped towards her. She inspected the deep black bruising on her back. Harelda glanced at Maude and nodded with her eyes closed. Maude redressed Librye and helped her lay back.

'Librye.' Harelda slowly seated. 'Who named you, my Librye?' Her eyes narrowed.

Librye watched as Harelda sat. Her voice warmed her. 'I named myself, but Mother helped.'

'The puca?'

It struck Librye with excitement. 'You know her?' Her smile grew.

Harelda gave a slow nod. She placed her hands on her lap. 'Before I came here to Sonnin, I lived in a place far north. My parents insisted I grew within the peaceful temples of Assanin. Mother was usually there to greet me.'

It overwhelmed Librye. 'She helped name me. She was my only friend in the camps.'

'A few turns back, I received a message from Mother.' Her mystique grew with every word she spoke. 'A message to tell me that hope had been found. She believes you hold great promise. She tells me you like to read.'

Her passion caught hold. 'I really do. I've almost finished the chambers.'

Harelda smiled. Her children were now all grown, but she made a wonderful mother to them all. 'And you will read them all again. She also told me of your abilities.' Her voice deepened. Librye lowered her head. Her excitement withered. 'She taught you how not to use them. Now, I would like you to show me, show me what you can do in this room.' Harelda sat up straight.

Maude stepped back. Looking around the room. Librye could think of nothing she could do. She noticed the fire flowers. Hanging gracefully from the ceiling on their delicate vines.

'I don't want to hurt you,' whimpered Librye.

Harelda gave a reassuring, slow blink. 'You will not harm me. It may be in your nature, but it is not in your heart.'

'Can you tell me more about the fae?' asked Librye.

Harelda sighed with disappointment.

'The fae hold many powers in this world. We are the gate keepers of magic.' As Harelda spoke, she failed to notice a vine. It grew from the ceiling and headed towards her. 'In every corner of this world, you will find magic.

From the blossoms on the trees,' — the vine slithered closer, — 'to the grasses that we tread. All the way to the mountains. Magic is a growing force.' — The vine drew closer. — 'But the fae are spiritual in their magic. We travel between worlds.' Instantly, it wrapped around her neck. Harelda froze as the vine tightened. She leapt from her chair. A crackling came from the coiling vine. Librye lifted her hand. The vine retreated. Releasing its grip on Harelda's throat.

Harelda held her neck. She tried to calm her panicked breath. She stared at Librye. At first with an expression of trepidation, and then with a look of pure admiration.

'Like I say, I don't want to hurt you. But if I wanted to, I could.' Librye looked down.

Harelda leant down to Librye. 'Rest child. I will be here when you wake.' Making her way towards the door. She noticed that Maude still stood. Utterly shocked. 'You, too, will need your rest. Her lessons begin tomorrow.'

Harelda left. She made her way to her own quarters. Still shocked and holding a hand to her neck. She composed herself as she hurried through the hall.

Harelda planned for only one night to be spent in the palace of Cronnin. That would change. Librye's lessons began. Harelda would learn that she was a sponge of knowledge. Everything she wanted to know, Harelda taught her. She needed her in Sonnin, to teach her more. It was not up to Harelda to take Librye to Sonnin. That would be for Angus to decide upon his return.

The council of Cronnin remained tense. They feared Harelda. With Cronnin being the supposed superpower. Sonnin was a close sister to the power of Cronnin. Without them, Cronnin would fail.

As the turn crawled to its end, Harelda remained in the palace. Guided by several servers, her time there was pleasant, made so by the majestic innocence of Librye.

Arriving on the palace grounds, Angus finally returned.

'A stop in Roma,' he joked with the stable keep. 'I just can't help myself at times. The people are so giving.'

'I assume your commander follows?' The stable keep asked.

'A few days away, probably. Be ready as well. His horse is a beastly thing, will need a stall to itself.'

Pouring onto the steps of the palace, the council did not greet Angus. Instead, they hampered him. Warning him of Harelda's arrival, Kailron pursued him up the steps and into the palace.

'You've finally returned then,' he barked with irritation.

Angus stopped. He sharply twisted to Kailron. 'What concern is it of yours?'

'The child awaits your return,' Kailron quietly hissed. Angus furrowed his brow. It was the first time he had heard Kailron speak of Librye. Kailron's voice changed completely. 'She needs you.'

Angus did not argue. He headed hastily up the stairs and towards Librye's room. The muffled shouting of Harelda's arrival was what he heard. He did not listen, and he did not care. Librye was all he thought of.

Bursting into her room, Librye was not there. He assumed she would be in his chambers and so he made his way across the mezzanine. Ambling in, he saw Maude, stood by the window, alone.

'I take it she is in the gardens?' Angus held a cheery tone. His guards followed and took their place by his door.

Maude roiled. She had been watching Librye and Harelda strolling through the gardens. Hands shaking, Maude felt a rage within her.

'You selfish, self-centred, callous man!' She leered at him. Angus shrank back. Councillors Ryan, Gurrand and Connor stepped inside his chambers to hear Maude's rant. 'She has been in tatters because of you!' Maude continued to walk towards him. A tear caught in her eye.

His voice was deep. 'I placed her in your care. I must tend to delicate matters, Maude. My priority is with this kingdom.'

'King or not, you tore her from all she knew.' Her voice whimpered. 'She doesn't need an attendant. She needs a parent!'

'This is outrageous!' called Connor. 'Guards! don't just stand there!'

Angus suspended his hand for Connor to quiet. 'She needs you; she needs a father; you are the closest thing she has to that!' Maude calmed. She stopped in front of Angus. 'She has spent her days hidden within the palace walls. Sheltering in books, her need to learn is one thing, but she has a need for family as well. You brought her here to show her that. Then you left. You are as bad as the men who took her parents.'

She glared at Connor. 'Even the council has taken more interest.' Her mouth curled with disgust. 'Some of you, at least. These beastly men you call your council are not worthy of the title.' Her eyes lit with rage towards the councillors. They stood, mouths gaping. 'So, arrest me if you wish. But I can assure you. Before night fall, they will fill this palace with hate for your council who already tread on thin ice.' She twisted to Angus. Her voice steadied. Her eyes softened. 'You are not them, sire. You are more. You are worthy. Do not let them decry you.' Her voice became a whisper. 'You are her father now.' Maude stormed from the room.

Angus spun to face his council.

Connor lowered his head. 'Kailron, he dined with the child several times now. He has grown some affection towards her. He told us she is an extraordinary creature.'

They saw Angus's eyes soften, his anger diminished. 'Speak to no one about this.' Angus swivelled to the door. Pushing Connor, Ryan and Gurrand out. They continued to argue for a session. His guards helped remove the councillors from the room.

As the door slammed, Angus spun to Evan. 'Bring Kailron to me. When you return, stay here. I need to know that all he says is the truth.'

Maude remained shaking on the porch. Watching as Harelda and Librye scampered through the gardens. Several of Harelda's guards followed them.

Kailron strutted into Angus's chambers. 'You called for me, sire?' He joyfully stepped towards Angus's desk.

Angus sat silently, his pyramid fingers caught on his lips. Angus pointed to the chair in front with his fingers before placing his hands on his desk. Kailron sat.

'I hear you've been dining with Librye?'

Kailron gave a nervous laugh. 'Well, yes, I didn't realise this would be an issue, sire.'

'An issue, no.' Angus signalled annoyance in his soft, whispering tone. 'However, I was not told of these meetings.' His tone became high, he grew straight. 'I find it highly inappropriate that my council have to resort to the tactics of interrogating her.'

'I sense you're annoyed by this —'

Angus jumped forwards onto his desk. 'Yes, annoyed is one way of saying it!'

Kailron held his hands out for Angus to calm. 'Please,' he begged, 'I volunteered myself for this.' His explaining did not ease Angus. His voice quivered. He remained fixed in his chair. His arms flailed with every word he said. 'If I am honest, I didn't want the *other members* of the council getting involved. I have not been near a child in, well, ever. I didn't want them frightening her. She is a sweet girl. I simply wanted to find out more about her. The council charged me with the duty. I enjoyed her company. I think she is an extraordinary child, but a child, nonetheless.'

Angus sat. He finally calmed. His voice became a calm sneer. 'What have you told the council of your encounter?'

Kailron struggled. He did not want to reveal his doubt to the one person who could see the end of his career. He needed to be honest. 'I didn't. I told them she is a little girl, yes, I believe she has the ability of the Solnox, but that is just something within her. It isn't who she is.'

'You told them this?' Angus asked with his brows raised.

'I was honest with them, something they often struggle with. How many of them do you trust? *Truly*, *trust*?'

Angus joggled his head. 'I trust enough.'

'Enough is never enough. This is political, Angus, not something which should concern a little girl. They are scared, yes, but I have matters in hand.'

'How in hand are these matters?'

'I have an idea. I would like to run by you.' Angus raised his brows. 'A mentor, someone who can guide her down the correct moral path, someone who will not hide the truth from her, honesty will get her a long way.'

'I fear what honesty can do in this world.' Angus sat back with his hand on his chin.

'For most, honesty can destroy, but for a Solnox, honesty will be the only way of keeping her safe.'

'And this mentor?' asked Angus, 'Do you have anyone in mind?'

Kailron smirked. 'Well, you, of course. Who better to guide her with morals than the man who saved her? Leave the matters of war to your new commander in the west. He returns soon. Your duties belong with Librye now. She needs you.'

'I can be neither a father nor a mentor to her. I gave her a chance simply by bringing her here.'

'She is not a weapon, Angus. She is scared.'

Kailron left. Evan gave a quick nod to Angus. He knew Kailron was telling the truth. Angus's mind journeyed to a dangerous place. He had seen Librye as a weapon to end the war, which was tearing at their world. His own father struggled to end the turmoil. Which led to the war. Even his callous council saw the innocence of Librye. He was finally understanding what his duty would become. His time of travel was ending, but his time of journeying was about to begin.

'*I bring you significant news.*' Wrote Angus, seated at his desk, which was now a mass of papers and parchments. '*Of the Solnox. The puca, Mother, knows her well. She is aware she is safe with me. However, I need your guidance. She has an ailment. I trust that your magnificent alchemists are well practiced in the care and treatment of wings. I hope to hear from you soon. I plan to visit after the turns renew. I wish on you and your kin, a blessed Onmidden. May the lady shine favourably on you always. Respectfully, Angus Oakwood.'*

CHAPTER THIRTEEN

13

Isradella woke to a forbidding room. The covers of her bed ruffled on the floor. Slowly she rose, a pain in her body made her legs tremble. Turning towards the bed, a bloodstain on the sheets and pillow showed the cruelty of her new life. They did not prepare her for her future.

'I can't leave,' she said, sat at her dressing table. A younger maid stood behind her, wiping the wound on her head. A sympathetic glow from her face comforted Isradella.

'It isn't safe for you here,' whispered the maid. 'My father has done nothing so brutal to my mother. They follow him through blind hope that one day the Atlanti will have a proper standing in this world.'

Isradella turned, holding her maid's hand. 'Tell me it won't be like this forever.'

The maid tightened her lips and lowered her head. 'I wish I could. The Mae Apha are the only ones willing to lead their people to a better future. That is why we protect Kairne. Isradella, you do not displease him, but he may need more from you. Give him a child and it will stop.'

Isradella turned back to the mirror, her eyes held blackening underneath, where worry and doubt weighed heavily on her. 'I don't even know if I can have a child.'

'Of course you can. You're a woman now.'

'What I mean, in Arktos, Kairne told me that the people there were corrupted. I don't know how, but I know what he means.'

'And what does he mean?'

'The women have struggled to have children for a while. Our pyres are always lit, ready for the breathless newborn.'

'I hear that the people of Arktos contain madness.'

'Many people say that, but they are not insane.'

The maid became quiet for a moment, gathering the courage to ask. 'Is it true your father built his own pyre and threw himself on?'

'Those in the north were conspiring against him. By killing himself, they would leave Arktos alone.'

'And your mother?' asked the maid. 'How were you born?' She cringed, but hid her feelings.

'The square,' replied Isradella. 'My mother was proud of my birth, as she was my brothers. She wished for all those in Arktos to witness my coming into this world. Thousands saw my birth.'

The maid slunk to the front of Isradella. 'I also hear your brothers would hold parties in that square.'

'They did until they killed each other.' Isradella's blatant honesty set an uneasy atmosphere.

'So, you are the last left?'

'Yes, and when my mother dies, I will take her throne and hand it to my husband.' — She frowned. — 'Wait, do you think that is the only reason he married me?'

The maid smiled, stroking Isradella's soft hair. 'Certainly not, he would not marry a pauper, but you, if you were the daughter of a baker, he would have chosen you. It was meant to be.'

'Perhaps,' muttered Isradella, lowering her head.

'Give him a child, and it will stop.'

'What will?' asked Kairne, stood by the door of Isradella's bedchambers.

'We were speaking about children,' — Isradella joyfully turned. — 'I am trying,' she said with a nod.

'Good,' Kairne carried on towards his room. As he stepped inside, a large soldier waited for him. 'Morning.'

The soldier bowed. 'Sir.'

'You have news?'

The soldier bowed again. 'Gaius and Daniel have sent word with a rider. They have announced their success.' — Kairne ambled towards his desk. — 'They also tell of a treaty, prepared to suit our needs.'

'Go on?' asked Kairne, raising his brows.

'The coblyn do not wish for any harm, so their elders, I suppose you would call them, have journeyed to raise their forces in the south. The coblyn of Grenhilda and Trent have been woken and agreed to join our cause.'

'And do they hope for anything in return?' asked Kairne, tightening his eyes.

'They didn't say, or at least if they did, no one could understand them.'

Kairne nodded. He lowered himself into his chair. 'Their speech will improve with influence.' He smiled tightly. 'A good morning it is then, is that all?'

'Also, we had reports that Harris Bearwood has left Marrion, it's believed he heads towards Cronnin.'

Kairne sat silently, thinking. 'He would've left alone. Are the coblyn in the south informed of their duty?'

'Yes, sir.'

'Good, send a few of our men, gather the coblyn and have them convene here.' The soldier bowed and left.

A hard summer shower pummelled the roads along the Artver river. The nights and days were gratifying for Harris. With only Svend for company.

His devoted horse had seen him through many battles and campaigns. A gift from Waron. Svend's physique was rare. Born of a black stallion and working horse. His size was enormous compared to the nimbler Cronnin horse breeds.

Sat on the porch of a modest rest stop. Harris remained by the side of Svend. He sat watching the rain patter across the road in front.

'Just one more tavern?' Harris glanced at Svend. Svend lowered his head and shook while puffing. 'No, didn't think so. It could mean a decent night, though,' Harris argued. Taking an apple from the side of him. He divided it using one of his daggers from his boot. 'Just one night.' Svend swept his tail along the floor. He clearly disagreed with Harris. 'Fine, but you know,' — his mouth was full as he ate, — 'I can't be with her. I can never be with her.' Svend twisted to Harris. He relaxed his head, placing it in front of him. 'I know,' — Harris stroked his mane. — 'I like her too, love her even. But she is the daughter of Harelda,' he whispered to Svend. 'She would have my bollocks as a new coin purse.' He took another slice and offered the rest to Svend.

Harris continued watching the wet and clamorous wood. The air was warm, the spring rain was a welcome break from the sun. Marrion was still stuck in his mind. He wondered how they were doing without him.

Retiring into the rest stop. Harris did not bother lighting a fire in the crude stone hearth. The night was wet, but it was warm. The pattering of rain on the canopy of the trees broke the rustled noises in the woods surrounding. Watching from the open window. He sat on the sill. Harris glared into the woods. The fluttering shadows in the trees confused the senses. His eyes drifted through the trees. His hearing did not match with what he was seeing. Something was there, but the unseen force remained deep in the shadows of the woods.

The pattering rain slowed. Harris could finally hear the rustling. His eyes narrowed towards the speckled shadows in the woods. The moon that night was absent, consumed by clouds.

'I think I will light that fire,' he drawled to himself, jumping from the sill. His daggers jarred together as he landed on the cold stone floor. He took some kindling, which was piled on the wall at the back. Making a fire. He reached into his quiver, which he left at the side of the door. Taking some arrows and his bow. He took a bag and pulled out a jar filled with tar. He coated his arrows and stepped back towards the window. Lighting the arrows from the fire. He shot them into the trees outside. The rain pattered and hissed as it hit the burning flame. The trees remained safe from the fire. Harris could see the hidden creatures as they inched through the woods.

Ominous shadows prowled along the dense woodland ground. The rustle fired Harris's senses into overdrive; he took his swords. Taking Svend safely into the rest stop, he pelted onto the road and ran to the back of the building. From the bushes bound three snarling coblyn. The creature's skin was black scales. Along their backs, a stiff hair had mutated to spines. Teeth as sharp as knives and claws like daggers. Their eyes filled with animalistic fury as they ricocheted towards him.

Slicing, thrusting, and gashing, he took the three in seconds. Their blood coated the trail. Harris stood restrained in the woods, listening for more. 'Is that it!' His swords dripped with the stench of blood.

His eyes coiled through the woods. The rain slowed, but he could still hear something. A rumble, but not from the sky. A booming of running paws thundered towards him from the west of the woods. Harris pivoted to meet the onrushing cohort of coblyn. He assumed his position. Digging his heels in, he waited. The booming became heavier. The sounds of hard breathing belted towards him.

His sword flowed from his arm and sliced the first few down. He danced in the night-time darkness. Spinning and slicing, jumping, and thrusting. One after another, they tried to get a bite, but he took them down. Over thirty coblyn now trembled battered, beaten, and dead in the woodlands of the Grenhilda valley. It did not impress Harris that they roamed so close to Cronnin. His journey would now become urgent. He needed to return, and fast.

Angus remained in his chambers. The evening broke over the city outside. Librye remained on the mezzanine. Angus gazed towards her. The mood was distinctly one of injured discomfort.

'Heart, I apologise.' He glanced towards the mezzanine. He could only see the top of her golden head.

Sat against a bookcase. Librye did not even have a book in hand. She sat with her arms folded around her knees. 'Why did you go?'

Her cracked voice broke him down more. He wanted to answer as honestly as he could. 'Because the war is still ongoing. I am needed elsewhere. That is what I would say if I believed it. Even I don't believe that anymore.' His day of being shouted at was slowly paying off.

'I know why,' — Librye stood. She strode down the mezzanine and headed towards the stairs — 'You're lonely here. You don't search for adventures, but you do search for change. You can do your work from here. But you also call for freedom.'

Angus stood and walked towards her. 'I truly apologise. I promised to give you a happy life here, but so far, I have not been here enough.'

'I believe that is about to change.' Her gleaming smile warmed him.

Each morning Harelda woke. It was with the excitement of spending more time with Librye. Librye waited on the porch. The gardens remained dull that day. Rain moved towards them from the west.

'Good morning,' greeted Harelda.

'Tell me more about the magic of the fae?' Librye immediately wanted her lessons to begin.

The days of wandering in the palace gardens were indeed pleasing to Harelda.

'I have told you all I can, child. I can tell you about my daughters. They have taken service with the Mara.' Her calm voice lost its power.

'Then tell me of the Mara?' Librye's eyes widened. With a wide smile, Librye took Harelda's hand and made her way to the path. Towards the gardens.

A cool breeze drifted from the west. 'In the world of the dead; the Mara are a chosen few who serve Haridon—'

'The god of the otherworld?' Librye interrupted.

Harelda gave a wide smile and a slow blink. 'That is correct. The duty of the Mara is to ensure that all arrive in the otherworld, just as they should. The Mara are still alive, but they are as spirits to this world.'

It fascinated Librye. 'They serve for ten years in the temples of Tyrone. Do you miss your daughters?'

'Of course I do.' Harelda's laughter covered the worry she had for her children. 'Only one is a Mara. The other is a temple sharma. They care for the vessel left by the Mara. While they do their service. I can do nothing to help them, but the temples are safe. Protected by the gods.'

They came to the lane towards the meadows. 'Everything in this world is connected, like the vines on a tree, the intricate vessels of a leaf. Every blade of grass is vital to the balance of nature. Our ancestors still wander these woods, as spirits of the trees. The puca are the ones who will teach you all you need to know of nature's magic. I know you're already well versed in their teachings, though.' Harelda strolled beside Librye.

'Mother once said I have the powers of the puca, like I showed you.' Her innocent eyes drifted to meet Harelda. 'She also told me of an ancient Solnox.'

'The Solnox is something we will discuss, but you must learn of the beauty in this world first.' Her voice held a tone of wonder, mystery.

'Egan told me of dark magic, and I don't want to learn.'

'You seem sure of that,' said Harelda with a noble smile.

'I've read books, and I don't want to know anymore.'

'Books will only tell you so much, Librye. Experience is necessary to grow.'

'So,' — Librye stopped walking, — 'do you think I should learn it?'

'Eventually,' said Harelda, she continued to walk towards the meadow. 'For now, concern yourself with the greatest gift you have.' Harelda stopped walking. She came to the front of Librye. 'One day, you will no longer be a child. A world's burden will rest on your shoulders. Take every moment you can, Librye, ever second to find the freedom of childhood.'

'You're talking like you're leaving.'

'Well, I must. I have a kingdom to run.' Harelda chuckled. 'Sonnin is not far. I will visit as often as I can, but for now, I believe Angus needs you, just as much as you need him.'

Stepping into Angus's chambers, Maude brought his breakfast in. He had not yet left his desk. Silently, she placed his plate beside him.

'Apologies, Maude,' he murmured. 'You were right.'

'I know.' Maude held a slight smile. 'I am seldom wrong.' Angus remained looking at his papers. He laughed. Maude was honest with Angus. Few would speak to him the way she had. He respected honesty. He respected Maude.

Angus sat alone in his chambers as the afternoon lingered. His eyes twisted from his desk. His constant eyeing over poorly written parchments dragged him further than he already felt.

Having swirled his chair to watch from the window and contemplate his future. He heard the voice of Harelda. 'The gardens are a joy this time of year.'

Startled, Angus stood. 'It is wonderful to have you here.' He greeted with joy, bouncing towards her.

'I've not left Sonnin in so long. It's wonderful to be anywhere for me,' mocked Harelda. Making herself comfortable in the chair at Angus's desk. Angus sat as well.

Having twisted his chair back. 'Librye is remarkable. Although she is just a child.'

'She belongs here, Harelda,' insisted Angus.

Harelda argued, 'She is not your daughter.'

Her derisive tone triggered a fatherly side to Angus. 'Not yet, but eventually, given the approval from the council, she may take the title of Oakwood.'

Harelda shook her head. 'She can never take your title of queen. I know you see her as a wonder. Try seeing her as a daughter. Then your thoughts may change on where she is better placed in this world. Our children are our future. Keeping them at arms-length can do more damage than good.'

'That reminds me,' — Angus sat back, — 'I met Branwen, in Marrion.' Harelda's eyes lit. 'She is well.' He assured with softened eyes. 'Why didn't you tell me she had been tending to my commander?'

Harelda's eyes drifted through the room. Her head followed. 'It will not tempt Branwen,' laughed Harelda. 'Her chastity means more to her than it does me. I simply want her to be well. I also hear that Harris Bearwood is a protector. Who better for my daughter to care for than a man who cares for all?'

'Then if they decide they share an affection?'

'Then I would be sure to add a new eunuch to the temples of Tyrone.' Her warning was clear. 'I destined my children for greatness. Kingdoms are what they will all see, not a bloodied commander who struggles to keep his cock to himself.'

'You approve of everything he does—'

'But not my daughter!' snapped Harelda. 'I can approve of his battle plans. His attempts to rescue this world from the shit storm that's hit us. I did not mean for Branwen to be a part of this. I saw an opportunity, and now you're making me nervous.'

'Harris is an insufferable flirt. He's known in every tavern I've passed so far, but one thing which he stands out for, above all else, he has respect. I am sure he will respect

Branwen.' Angus stood. He wished to change the dark mood which took over the room. 'We need to discuss our plans.'

Harelda reclined back. 'I will set a plan for Librye in place. You must settle into palace life,' — she stood to leave, — 'find yourself a wife. You aren't getting any younger.' Harelda left his chambers.

Angus was being ground down by the persistence of finding a wife. He glanced at the guard at his door.

'Seriously,' he blurted with his brows raised and eyes wide. 'Does your wife have a sister?'

'Sire,' Evan replied, sheepish. 'I know it grinds on you *daily*,' he slowly began. Evan relaxed his arm. His spear dropped slightly. Lifting his arm, he suggested, 'Harelda has many daughters. I'm sure she has seven, including Xania. They say she is the most beautiful creature to grace our lands.'

Angus glared at Evan from under his brow. 'I'm sixty-seven years old, Evan. Hardly suitable for a woman in her thirties.'

'And what of Branwen?' asked Evan, with his eyes wide. 'I know she's younger, but she is very available.' Angus twisted to face Evan. Marching towards him threateningly. 'This kingdom needs a leader, a woman with power, authority, presence. She will provide all three. She isn't one to back down easily. In fact, given the right training, coaching and confidence. She could be better than Harelda.' His brows raised and remained fixed towards Angus.

'I can see your sense, but I can also see a great regret in her. I would not want a wife who lives a life of regret, by the side of a stale old husband.'

'Why not?' laughed Evan. 'Mine does.' Angus gave a sniggering laugh.

The scraping and booming noise of hooves rode towards the western gate. In the dull wake of the early morning darkness, the guards gathered on the rampart towers. The gates were closed. The thundering stallion screamed as he reared at the gate. His rider, Harris, remained fixed to him.

'Call your name!' yelled the guard atop the tower.

'Commander Harris Bearwood and this is Svend!'

Instantly the gate opened, allowing Harris into the vast stone city of Cronnin. He had passed through Cronnin many times, but he never stayed long enough to see the palace. Fearlessly, he rode through the main streets of Cronnin and towards the palace. The early dawn only saw the odd few market stalls as they opened for the day of trade. The fires in the bakeries were starting. Blacksmiths walked through the streets. The quiet city would become a place of bustling trade. His long black cape flailed behind him, speeding towards the palace gates. Again, Svend stopped at the gates, screaming and rearing.

'Call your name and purpose!' shouted a guard at the side of the gate, a long spear in his hand pointed towards Harris.

Svend continued circling. Harris trained him to keep moving frantically to avoid making them both a sitting target. The sight of the spear reddened Harris's face.

'Harris Bearwood, your new fucking commander, remove the pointer or I'll remove your cock!'

The guard straightened his spear. 'Open!'

The gate opened. Harris stopped Svend by the side of the guard. Panicked, Harris asked, 'Do you have dire here?'

The guard shook his head and narrowed his eyes. 'Dire?'

'Wolves, you blithering idiot! Do you hold dire wolves here?'

The guard frantically nodded. 'We do. Why?' His lip curved.

'Out them now!' His voice filled with anger. 'The west of Grenhilda is swarming with rabid coblyn. I took down a few myself. But more are out there, out the wolves. They'll have them by morning.' Svend thundered towards the palace. Harris jumped from the still moving horse. Svend calmed. A stable hand ran towards them.

'Here you go, boy.' Harris brushed Svend's forehead. 'A decent rest for you.' He handed the reins to the stable boy. 'He needs resting, two days, then onto pasture.' — The boy nodded. — 'Following. No one rides, only me. He'll just fuck anybody else up.' Harris watched the boy turn with Svend. Giving one final hard slap to Svend's rear, he trotted away, taking the boy with him. Harris gazed at the imposing palace. His smile grew, and eyes widened. 'It's so clean,' he whispered to himself.

Making his way up the steps, a short man met him. His small size shocked Harris. Greeted by a pale grey and wrinkled hand. Dark silvery hair slicked back. He was the greeter of the Cronnin doors. He hunched over, stepping towards Harris. Coming closer, it surprised Harris the man had not yet tumbled on his long black robes. Which trailed in front of him.

'My lord,' greeted the man. 'I am Balthus. Welcome to Queensbury.'

'Balthus.' Harris smiled, coming closer. 'I have an appointment with Angus.'

It threw Balthus. 'We call him sire here, my lord.'

Harris raised his brows. 'And people call me many things. Harris is the least offensive,' — he removed his thick black riding gloves, — 'people call Angus many things too,' mocked Harris. 'I believe he would be happy with me calling him by his name.'

'Yes, well,' — Balthus averted. — 'We also ask that we leave weapons at the door.'

Harris gave a slow, unimpressed blink. 'I am a weapon. It will not be possible.' Balthus glared at him. Raising his brows. 'Stare all you like, old man. Every blade, every arrow, remains with me. I am here to see the King, not kill him. If you refuse, then very well. I'll find another way in.' His eyes examined the palace.

Balthus struggled to decide. 'What is it you're here to see him regarding?'

'He has appointed me Chief Commander,' replied Harris. His eyes continued hunting.

Balthus relaxed slightly. 'The new appointed title.' — He glanced down and nodded. — 'I am aware of this. However, you must understand. We have rules for a reason. Your need for weapons is pointless —' Balthus paused. The calling of the wolves froze him. The howling madness took over the silence of the morning.

'They're with me always. Always have been, always will be,' — his patience wore thin. — 'Look, are you going to let me in or not?'

Balthus did not want to. His internal quarrel was worsening. 'I want to let you in, but not them.' He glanced at the sword by Harris's side.

Harris gave another slow blink. His annoyance grew. 'Fine, inside, then I will remove them.'

Balthus nodded.

They escorted Harris into the main hall. Balthus took him towards the west wing with four guards and into the small dining room. Harris removed his weapons. The guards and Balthus watched on in shock. Forty-seven bent daggers. One bow. Fourteen arrows. Three swords battered and bent. Two axes were all upon his person. The guards, Balthus and even Harris, looked staggered at the amount.

Harris glared at the guards. His eyes widened. He twisted to Balthus, 'They were rather heavy. They all stay here.'

Leaving the room, Harris twisted to see the guards seal the room behind them and walk back towards the central hall. Harris marched with Balthus to a small guest room at the side of the dining room. A place for Harris to sit and wait while the palace woke. A large white sofa almost filled the room. Harris could not resist. He dropped onto the sofa, face first. His body melted into the comfort of the soft pillows.

'This will do me fine.'

Balthus glared at him. 'I might also add,' — Balthus stood holding his hands to the front of him. Harris clumsily rolled, facing upwards. His lizard skin armour stuck to everything. — 'Our city has some of the finest barbers.'

Harris raised his head. Looking down his torso at Balthus. 'Why would I need a barber?' He lifted his brows to Balthus.

'Well —' struggled Balthus — 'we have a certain standard in Cronnin.' His mouth drew down. 'I don't mean to be rude, but returning soldiers often look as though they've not seen a barber for years. You, my lord, well, as I say.' He tried to redeem himself and avoid Harris's glare. 'We have standards. I'm sure you will journey out when you see fit.' He quickly left the room.

Harris remained glaring at the door. 'Nothing wrong with my hair,' he murmured. He laid his head back and stared towards the ceiling. His eyes drifted around the intricate detailing above. Finally, in the comfort of the Cronnin palace, and for the first time in years. Harris could relax with his legs crossed and resting over the arm of the chair. He entwined his fingers to his front and let his eyes grow heavy.

'Harris.' Angus stood in the room. Watching Harris heaped on the couch, fast asleep.

'I'm awake,' moaned Harris with his face crushed into the sofa. His body had become a crumpled mess. 'I'm resting my eyes,' he mumbled.

With a high-pitched tone and wide eyes, Harelda twisted to Angus. 'He's resting his eyes.'

Her high-pitched tone forced Harris to jump from the sofa. Rubbing his face and trying his best to wake up, he hurriedly stood. His eyes widened. 'Ooh! too fast.' He sat back down frantically, blinking. 'I've had a long journey. Please forgive me,' he begged. He gawped at Harelda. His smile screwed to the side of his mouth.

'I understand. Perhaps later.' She gave a brief wink to Harris before she turned and left.

Harris again stood. His eyes widened. He shook his head and rubbed his face. Regaining focus, he glowered at Angus. 'That was Harelda. Why would you do that?'

Angus's lip curled up. 'Because it's fun.'

'Well, not funny,' Harris replied, annoyed. Angus strutted from the room. 'I want my weapons back,' — he caught up with Angus and marched to the side of him, — 'you need to speak with your guards and Balthus. They did well but shouldn't have let me in at all.'

Angus sighed. He twisted, lowering his head. 'They knew you were coming.'

'Still, no weapons. Throw me in a fucking dungeon for the night, assuming you have them?'

Angus nodded. His smile grew. 'We have them, and there's still time,' he commented, walking from the small room. 'I need to ask, though, why my wolves were sent from the gates in the small hours?' He stopped and twisted to Harris.

Harris sighed. 'A hoard of coblyn ambushed me in the Grenhilda woodland in the dead of night. The dire will sort them. But we need to know what has the coblyn on edge.'

'I have my suspicions.' Angus stopped. His mouth was gaping. 'You were unharmed?'

Harris spun in the hall and replied, 'As I told your doorman, I am a weapon, a few coblyn aren't an issue.'

Angus was without doubt impressed. However, he was also worried. 'Trouble seems to find you, Harris. Let us hope this ends now,' he warned.

Harris made his way to the dining room. The guards unlocked the door where his weapons still lay on the table.

Angus held a derisive tone uttering, 'This is the palace of Cronnin, Harris.' — He glanced at the weapons. — 'You could take out an army with that lot.'

'What did you think I was doing? That's the idea.' Harris replaced his weapons. Three different belts held his swords. He wore thick black bracers on both arms. Each had two small daggers inside. His boots also held room for four daggers each. Finally dressed and feeling whole again. Harris stepped from the room with Angus. He glowered towards Balthus, he made his way through the central hall and towards the mezzanine.

Balthus scurried towards him. 'My lord, please, you must understand. Here you have no need for them, a sword, singularly, perhaps,' he shrugged. 'But all of *those*?'

Harris blinked. 'I arrived in the early hours of the morning, from Marrion.' — He raised his voice towards Balthus. — 'If ever you'd seen war, you would know. You can't travel on the roads now without something to protect you,' — he whirled in the hall with his arms held out, — 'I don't see an army with me!' He glared at Balthus. 'Because I am the army. I am my protection. These are my protection!' Balthus averted his eyes. He could feel Harris's burning rage getting worse. 'Next time, don't let me in. No one passes those doors with so much as a file!' Balthus glowered towards Harris. His mouth curled and gaped with confusion. Harris dropped his anger completely. 'You did alright, old man. Next time, though, just get the guards. Throw them out. No weapons. Stick to your own rules.' He placed a consoling hand on Balthus's shoulder, making him jump.

The many councillors coming and going from the halls to the dining hall watched Harris. He walked up the stairs with Angus. Harris was sure to look back at them and give a wink. Leading Harris towards his chambers, the guards to the side stared at Harris.

'Eyes forwards,' Harris widened his eyes.

Stepping into the chambers, Harris made his way towards Angus's desk. He saw Librye sat on the mezzanine in Angus's chambers.

'Good morning, Harris.'

'Morning, small, child.'

'Are you not taking lessons with Harelda today?' Angus glanced towards Librye.

'Not today. I have plans.' She made her way from the mezzanine. Librye marched directly towards Harris and Angus. Angus sat at his desk. Harris took the chair opposite. He saw the enchanting girl make her way confidently towards another chair at the back of Angus's desk.

Harris gawped at Angus. 'Are you going to introduce me?'

Angus glanced towards Librye and back at Harris. 'Apologies,' Angus gave a smile towards Harris. 'This is Librye. She is my ward,' — Angus sifted through the papers on his desk, — 'as good as my daughter.'

Harris glimpsed at Librye. Her questioning look intrigued him. He remembered being a child in a palace himself. Although where he grew up, the extravagance was not as visible.

'Good morning, Librye,' he greeted. Librye nodded slightly. 'Your name intrigues me.' Harris gazed towards her. He narrowed his eyes. 'The name Librye, saved for the best of the best. Your parents must have exalted you.'

'I didn't know them,' said Librye.

The usual sorrow he would see from orphaned children was lacking in Librye. Her friendly face and bright wide eyes spoke to Harris of a concealed truth. He knew very little about Librye, but it provoked his interest. She sat and listened.

'I apologise. It's awful to hear that,' replied Harris.

'Don't be,' said Librye. 'I cannot mourn for those I didn't know. I'm sure I will someday. But for today, I would rather live, learn, love, and laugh.'

Harris blinked. His mouth was gaping. 'Molgron.' — He had heard those words before. — 'If I remember rightly,' — he placed his fingers on his chin. He glanced towards the window behind Angus's desk. His eyes held a look of reflexion. — 'Today is the day we live, learn, love, and laugh. We mourn with those we leave behind. A day spent in mourning is a day more, that the gods rejoice in the loss of your love. Fore they are the virtuous. The ones who hold their hands and their hearts until you rejoice once more. In the arms of those you love. A wonderful work,' he commented. He glanced at Librye with a twisted smile. He placed his hands on his lap.

Librye was overjoyed. She sat forwards in her chair. 'You know Molgron?'

'Of course,' Harris leant towards her. 'He was once a commander too, but he was never involved with war. I believe a king gave him the title,' — Harris leant back in his chair, — 'who loved his poetry so much, he couldn't help but name him as a commander of the heart.' Harris clearly held more knowledge than Angus gave credit. Angus sat, shocked, in his chair. Harris could see the look of awe Angus held. Harris spun. He widened his eyes. 'I am educated, however, Librye. I apologise, we have work to do,' he urged. He glared at Angus.

'Work,' mumbled Angus. He continued rummaging around the papers on his desk. Trying to find what he was looking for. Scrolls rolled onto the floor.

Librye stood. She rushed towards Angus's desk. Taking several scrolls. She passed certain ones to Harris. His smile widened and eyes lit.

'Here, these are the kingdoms. We map the losses on these. I am sure that one day, Angus will organise.' She blinked towards Angus.

Angus shook his head. 'I don't know what I would do without you,' Angus smiled towards her.

'We would lose you to paperwork. You've also received word from King Iorn. The new prince has been born in Volnot. I believe they've named him Igor. I have already arranged for a gift to be sent.' Her manner staggered Harris.

'So, the coblyn?' asked Harris, blinking his attention away from Librye.

'Harelda warned me that Morigah was silent. The usual business of the mountain faded. This is no coincidence.'

'Of course not, but the coblyn are simple, too stupid to take sides,' commented Harris.

'Are dogs stupid? Or dire? Or horses?' asked Librye.

Confused, Harris replied, 'I wouldn't consider them stupid.'

'Then neither are the coblyn,' — she slowly drifted towards him. — 'A horse cannot choose sides, but they do not mourn for their dead. They don't have the same standards as coblyn society —'

'I apologise. How old are you?' Harris asked with a breath, narrowing his eyes.

'My age doesn't matter. What matters is that I am clearly better educated in coblyn society than you are.'

Holding his hand to his heart, Harris smiled. 'You wounded me.' He pointed at her while looking at Angus. 'Where did you find a Solnox?'

Angus rose from his desk, glaring at Harris. 'How did you know?'

Harris shook his head. He looked into Librye's eyes. 'Your eyes change with the movements of Cammbour, your hair changes with the seasons, your mind is free to wander this world, but I don't believe you have a full grasp on that yet,' — he looked at Angus. — 'I was raised by a man who was so fascinated with magic, he banned its use in his kingdom. It wasn't the fae who did that. It was the threat of a Solnox being born to the Atlanti.'

'That could never happen. But, Harris, I'm confused,' — he drifted from behind his desk, — 'you mean to tell me, a simple look at Librye and you can see it?'

'And hear it,' whispered Harris. 'Thump, thump, triple thump.' He twisted in the silent room, facing Angus. 'Merrow, remember? You must have studied my family. We know the Solnox have a different heartbeat, two thumps and a triple.'

Librye asked, 'Why?'

Harris's grin widened. He realised, at that moment, the child in front of him did not know who or what she was. Her need for knowledge was because she couldn't help it.

'The last Solnox had a strange ailment. They often depicted him as having the legs of a horse, for speed, the heart of a Solnox beats thrice to power whatever creature dwells within.'

'And what creature dwells in me?' she asked, staring into Harris's eyes.

Harris grunted and sat back. 'Only time knows.'

'I believe the torbs know,' said Angus, lowering his brows.

'Torbs? The northern cowards?' Harris casually asked.

'They are not cowards,' argued Angus.

'They sit in their dark caves, drinking themselves into a stupor and refusing to join our cause.'

'Does that make Xencliff cowards?' asked Angus.

Harris's smile died instantly. 'They did their time.'

'And so did Bourellis. Now, we can discuss Librye later. For now, we have pressing concerns.'

Librye spun to sit back in her chair. Councillor Connor trudged directly into the chambers. He did not give any consideration to the meeting that was already taking place. Librye could not stop herself.

'Were you never taught to knock?' Librye scolded with disapproval. Harris sniggered.

Connor continued his course towards the desk, giving a scornful look towards Librye as he did. 'Sire, they have asked me to bring you to our session.'

Angus glared at Connor from under his brow. 'I am sure you can proceed without me for today. I have important matters to tend to.'

Connor stepped closer. 'But, sire, you have been absent for far too long.'

With a stern voice, Harris insisted, 'He said no, Councillor.' He twisted from his seat as he stood. 'The council is capable. We have important matters to tend to. Matters which may ease your duty.' He stepped closer to Connor. His broad frame overpowered Connor's slender and elderly frame.

Connor could not find the strength to argue. Harris escorted him to the door.

Connor stood on the mezzanine. Councillor Ryan awaited him. 'Will he attend?' Ryan strolled with Connor.

Connor sighed. 'His new boy has arrived. The man is dangerous to our cause.' They spun towards the stairs and made their way down. 'A frightful thing to have in the palace. I fear our efforts could be for nothing.'

Ryan spoke low. He feared being overheard. 'I believe our efforts will pay handsomely. The commander will slip up, and when he does. We will be waiting. I know he will make a mistake. However, that mistake could cost us our lives. The man plays with creatures of the darkness. Did you hear what he caused in Marrion as he left?'

Ryan glared at Connor with furrowed brows. 'I've heard nothing.'

Connor whispered. 'His concoctions have caused an uproar in the camps of the dark army. His farewell to his soldiers was crude and immoral —'

'What do you speak of?' Connor's inability to speak openly irritated Ryan.

'He gave them all an erection!' he loudly whispered. His mouth drooped at the sides. 'Each one of them hit by the commander's arrows. Ran from the field with a pole between their legs. Within minutes, they were dead. It was a horrendous way to leave this life.'

Councillor Ryan sniggered. 'What? Surely you see the amusement in that?'

'Our predecessors would've seen him hanged for half the crimes he's committed,' hissed Connor. 'He is a menace. Using such distasteful tactics should be banned.'

'If you feel so strongly, perhaps you should meet with the council and see how they feel about this matter?'

As the door closed, Angus looked at Evan at the door. 'No one enters until I say,' he grumbled. Angus relaxed at his desk. Several others joined the scrolls Harris held. Librye searched through those left.

'I assume I have my work cut out for me?' Harris sat back.

'That you do,' said Angus, an awkward grin wobbled. 'I do, however, wish to know more about you. We could hardly talk in Marrion, and your mother hasn't been forthcoming.'

Harris called, 'Ha!' His smile stretched across his face. 'She fucking hates me, that's why.'

'I doubt that is true,' scoffed Angus.

'You don't know what happened, and I will not be repeating it. The damage is done.'

'That isn't actually true, commander,' said Librye. Looking into Harris's eyes sent a shiver through him. 'And you know it.'

Harris looked back at Angus. Breaking the conversation away from Librye. 'I was in the Xencliff palace. I have no title, but the wives of Waron trained me daily. My mother became a favourite of his.' His eyes drifted to the desk. 'I can't remember a lot of laughter, but it was a lifetime ago. I'm here now, and that's all that matters.'

'What was Waron's standing with the war?' Angus was blatant with his question.

Harris's lips parted; his words softly tumbled out. 'You didn't just bring me here for the war.' His icy glare cut through Angus. 'What is the real reason I'm here?'

Angus sat forwards. He glanced towards Librye. 'Librye, could you give us a moment, please?'

Librye sat back in her chair. 'No, I can't do that. This is far too interesting.'

Angus dropped his head.

'You have nothing to hide from her,' said Harris, memories of being a palace brat himself flooded back.

With a hefty sigh, Angus replied, 'I have brought you here to help end this war. That means more than giving orders to commanders. Although that will be your duty,' — Angus stood from his desk, — 'use your tactics, spread everything you know to every battle we have.' He glided towards Librye. 'The other reason you are here.' Angus paused, taking a moment to read Harris's tense body language. 'Maude is Librye's attendant. She is the one who will look after her basic needs. She does, however, need to learn.' His voice lowered. 'Your arm is what she needs. Teach her to fight, for that will save many lives.'

'What do you mean?' Harris narrowed his eyes.

Angus took a slow blink. 'She was born with an ability. The Solnox, as you must know. Has a power unlike any other. To end someone with a sword would be kinder than what she could do.'

'You're suggesting,' — Harris sat forwards. A cynical smile grew, — 'I teach Librye how to fight, at her age? Lessons never begin before fifteen.' It disgusted Harris. Suggesting that a child so young would take lessons to kill.

'She is practically an adult,' — Angus strolled back towards his chair, — 'she knows Malgron, and everything in the books in this library.' His brows raised and eyes softened. 'Besides, this world needs fighters now, not poets.'

Harris sat back; he was unsure what to say. 'I suppose.' He struggled to think. 'I can teach her some things. But this isn't a quick process. I saw so much in my youth. I don't want to plague Librye with the same.' — Harris stood. He walked around the desk and sat on the edge. 'Look at me.' — He held his arms out. — 'Just look.' His smile twisted. He glared forwards and shook his head. 'I'm not the man to make any mother proud.' His voice was soft. 'The weapons I wear cover up the years of hurt,' — he leant close to Angus, — 'you've heard of the berserker. The commander, the shadow, the wolf. Would you like that for your daughter? The things you've heard said about me. Would you want those same things said about your own daughter? Your Librye?' Harris sat straight. He glanced at Librye, who sat silently. She placed her hands on her lap.

Angus glanced at Harris. Slowly, he stood. 'I would be proud to have a daughter with such a record. Harris Bearwood, you are not a berserker. You are a loyal fighter. You could've joined the Atlanti forces.' — He meandered to the side of the desk to a drink cabinet. — 'They would've paid handsomely for your knowledge, but you chose your kin. You fought, and often nearly died, protecting Cronnin. That is why you're here.' Angus poured two glasses of moonshine and walked back to the desk. He handed one to Harris. 'I can honestly say if Librye has you on her side. To teach her your morals, your life. That is the lesson she needs. It is a lesson we cannot teach.'

Harris drank his entire glass of moonshine. He gazed at the innocent face of Librye. 'My regrets,' — he croaked as the moonshine burnt his throat, — 'is that what you mean?' He narrowed his eyes at Angus.

'I know little of your regrets, Harris. But if those are what have set your moral compass, then very well.' Angus took a sip of his drink. 'The dragons can teach her nothing. The fae can teach her nothing. Even the puca will struggle.'

'Then what am I to teach?' asked Harris with a deflated tone.

'Harris, I know you're well versed in poison. Tactics. Creatures of the shadows.' — He sat back in his chair. — 'You had a pet at the palace of Xencliff. I heard, when you left, she killed fourteen guards before they found her.'

'It was an accident,' Harris stood. He sauntered back to his chair. 'Daru was my only friend in that place, and they just crushed her. They didn't feed her, that was the issue.'

'What was she?' asked Librye, intrigued.

'Daru was a spider. No larger than a coin. A little brown thing which I found among some of the fruit brought from Thrasia.' He explained with compassion, 'She could kill within hours. The skin around the bite would rot. Awful thing to deal with,' — he shuddered. — 'But she was my pet. She never bit me, but that was because I respected her. They killed her. Poor creature never stood a chance.'

Angus was further enthralled with Harris. Leaning forwards, he pointed to Librye. 'She is a unique creature.'

Harris shot to his feet. 'She isn't a fucking creature. Never refer to her as that again.'

Angus drew back. He gazed at Librye. The word creature did not sound cruel to begin with. Seeing Librye with her head low. He realised it bothered her.

Harris walked towards Librye. 'And what about you? Would you be willing to learn what the most broken man in Cammbour offers?'

Librye laughed as she stood. She reached for Harris's hand and held it with both her small delicate hands. 'I think you're less broken than you believe. One day, I hope to help teach you that. For today, though, I would be honoured to learn from The Commander.'

Harris had never been one to show emotion. He struggled to show a tender side when not in the company of a woman or in a tavern. His hardened form melted. He gazed into Librye's eyes. The sweet innocence of her offered him a chance to redeem himself. He did not want to go easy on her. He knew, somehow, he was being given the toughest challenge of his young life so far.

'But that isn't all.' Angus opened his hand upwards towards the seat where Harris had been sitting.

Harris dropped Librye's hands and strolled back towards the seat. He gave a firm look towards Angus. 'I will be busy then,' he commented as he sat.

'The might of Cronnin needs reinforcing. Plans are in place to assist in finding fighters.' — Harris narrowed his eyes towards Angus. — 'However, these plans are in the future. We need fighters now. That is where you come in.'

Harris sat back with his mouth gaping. 'Don't you dare do this, Angus,' he warned in a low, grumbling tone.

'I have to try.' Angus held a cynical look. He sat back. 'We need Xencliff on side, Waron, predominantly.'

Harris replied, 'I'm appalled to even think of what that would do to Waron's already massive ego.' He sat back and caught his hands in front of him. Leaning forwards again, he reached over the desk. He took Angus's drink and drank the lot in one go. 'I took myself away from that place for a reason. I will not go back.'

Angus could see the suppressed fear Harris held. 'What are you so afraid of? Waron will not speak to me. He needs convincing to join this war. I cannot do that. He believes I sit behind a desk. Not understanding the danger that the coast faces. He needs someone he trusts to tell him that.'

Harris sat back, glancing at his hands. 'He already knows the danger they're in,' — he stood, — 'if that is the reason you want me here. The answer is no. Send me back to Marrion now.' He was firm with Angus. His voice quivered as he spoke. 'I will have no part in it.'

Angus narrowed his eyes. 'What happened between you and Waron?'

Harris glimpsed at the door. He glanced at Librye and back at Angus. 'It's not something I wish to speak of.' — He stepped towards the desk, — 'I will do all it takes to ensure the safety of Cronnin, but not that.' He whispered, 'I can't.'

Librye slowly stood. A strange look caught her eyes. As they narrowed, her head tilted towards Harris. 'You will.' — Harris shot around to face her. — 'Not today, certainly not tomorrow. But eventually, you will.'

'How would you know, little one?' he asked with a grin.

'My secrets told me.'

Harris stared towards her with his mouth gaping. Slowly, he shook his head.

'In the darkest of corners. The hottest of fires. The screams of hope will rise.' She quoted Malgron. 'I know you see it. You won't find it until you stop hiding.' Her words wounded Harris.

'How did you know that?' Harris asked with a tear which refused to fall.

'Know what?' asked Angus.

Harris took a hard blink, closing his eyes for a while before he looked back at Angus. 'I can't talk about it.'

Following Maude, Harris made his way towards the lower west corridor. Silence engulfed the halls as dinner was served.

'You'll be pleased to know that we have set the dining hall out for you,' said Maude. Harris remained silent. Her attempts to make small talk failed. Scurrying past the fountain, Harris's eyes searched the halls. 'I've heard you have an acute sense of awareness.'

Harris simply grumbled in response. He glanced towards the galleries. 'What's that way?' He pointed to the corridor to the left of the stairs.

Maude stopped walking. She glanced towards the corridor. A small table with a pot plant was all that adorned the corridor. 'That's the galleries, my lord.'

Harris did not break his stare with the corridor. 'Ha,' he drawled with an open mouth blow. 'Thank you.' Harris broke his glare and glanced back at Maude. 'I hear we're tasked with the same mission.' His smile grew and a strange mood broke.

'Mission?' Maude continued sauntering towards the corridor.

Harris followed, with his hands relaxed on the hilt of his swords. 'Librye, they have given me the task of protecting her and teaching her what I can.'

Maude froze. She twisted to Harris. A wide-eyed look of rage met him. He stepped back slightly. 'Teach her?' she narrowed her eyes.

Harris stepped back. He suspended a hand to her. 'Nothing bad, I can assurc you —'

'Assure away, commander,' she warned.

Harris stepped forwards. 'You know she isn't your usual eight-year-old —'

'She's seven,' snapped Maude.

'Seven then,' replied Harris. Trying to calm her, he stepped closer. 'You know she needs all the help she can get. She's a bloody clever one, I'll give her that. According to Angus, she is vital to this world. If his orders are to teach her to protect herself, then sobeit.'

Maude drifted towards Harris. A malevolent smile twisted from the corner of her mouth. 'It isn't to protect her. It is to protect others from what she can do. She has powers. Soon, you'll know. Never question her secrets she speaks of. Soon, you will see the challenge you have been given. Your duty of war, it pales compared to this.'

Her warning sat heavily in Harris's gut. As they came towards the old, brown wooden door. Harris mentioned to Maude. 'To keep your mind secure.' — She spun to face him. — 'I know she is only a child.' His tender voice comforted her. She, of course, had heard stories of the commander. She could see the appeal.

Maude spun to the last door on the left. Her voice remained angry. Although she calmed slightly.

'This is temporary accommodation.' Taking the key from her pinafore, she unlocked the plain wooden door. 'It's a simple room. But as I say, it won't be for long,' — she opened the door for him to step inside, — 'it appears you've gained favour with Angus. The unused east tower will eventually be your place of work and rest.'

Harris laughed. 'They're the same.' Making his way inside. His few bags had already arrived. 'Thank you.' He twisted to her. Still annoyed. 'Maude, and please, call me Harris. I'm not a lord,' — he flailed his arms, — 'and forget all you've heard about me.' He stepped into the room. The simple room was little, but it was better than a woodland or stone floor. 'I hate nothing more than having to explain away the rumours people have heard,' — he spun to face Maude, — 'I assume you've heard many, being a chief yourself.' His eyes glassed through her.

Maude gave a shallow nod. Her lips parted. 'How—' She struggled to find her words.

'You have all the makings of a chief,' replied Harris. Before Maude could finish. 'Stern, honest, passionate, and shows far too much compassion. Always searching for something, weren't you, Maude?' He faced her. He held his hands behind his back. Sticking his chest out. 'Most chiefs spend all their time searching for what will make them a commander. When all they have to do is to be less kind.'

'Hope—' she softly interrupted Harris. — 'I was searching for hope. Some way of seeing that the war would end. Some way of finding a survivor.' Maude took a fleeting glance towards Harris before walking further into the room. She caught her hands at the front of her and stared towards them. 'I was in the search.' She was embarrassed to call herself a chief because she had never seen a battle. 'I just wanted that one sign. That things would eventually get better.'

Harris leant towards her; she broke her stare into her hands. 'Did you find it?'

'Yes,' — Maude glanced at Harris, — 'when I found Librye. The day I found her. I began my papers. I left the army the following end and came here.'

Harris was gobsmacked. 'You found Librye? It's strange how these things have a way of coming together.' He narrowed his eyes.

Maude stood straight. Her eyes met his. Her lips softened. 'Fate plays a big part in that girl's life. Let's hope you are a part of it.' Maude turned towards the door. She peered at the few bags beside Harris's bed. She smirked at his meagre belongings. 'I assume you wear most of what you would have in those bags.' She glanced at the armour Harris wore. The many daggers and swords. The expensive lizard skin armour. It spoke to her of a man who travelled light. Afraid to settle anywhere. 'I'll see about getting you an advance.' She glimpsed at Harris. 'Settle here, don't hurt her, please,' — she glanced at the bags again, — 'I'll leave you to unpack.' Maude left, pausing by the door. 'Assuming the rumours are but rumours. I'll have a maid appointed to you.'

Harris lifted his brows. 'A maid?'

'The councillors all have their own maids. To fetch and carry. Your task is much greater than theirs. It would be only fair.'

Alone in his room, he peered at the simple structure. A double bed. Simple cotton sheets. A wardrobe to the wall at the foot of the bed, and a small chest of draws to the side would be enough for him. A bedside table and a large trunk at the end of the bed. Beside the wardrobe was a small washroom.

‘Oh, this is boring,’ he sighed, he lumped down on his bed. He studied the poor state of the room. He spread back onto his bed and stared at the stone ceiling above.

The night’s rest was enough to keep Harris well in the palace. With a hot bath and a decent night’s rest. His promise to Branwen remained. He avoided the taverns. He had not even considered exploring the city.

His eyes flickered as a sunbeam crept up his bed. The morning illuminated his drab room. The small window to the side allowed sufficient light for the day. Fire flowers provided a small light at night. He raised himself in his bed. He heard a slight knock at the door.

‘One moment!’

He quickly dressed and opened the door. A lady stood before him. She tied her long brown hair into a spiralling bun on the back of her head. Dark brown eyes glared at him from her aging face. She held a look of aged beauty. She certainly was a handsome woman. In her youth, she would have been staggeringly beautiful.

‘Good morning.’ She burst into the room. Harris slid his arm from the door and rolled his eyes. ‘I’m Maple. Anything you need. Ask.’

Her offer was inviting to Harris. ‘Well, there is one thing.’

Maple continued placing any used clothes into a basket. ‘Not that,’ — she pointed at his armour, — ‘would you like that dealing with?’

Harris flickered his eyes towards his armour. Which remained in a heap on the ground. ‘My armour?’ he stuttered. ‘No one is to touch.’

Maple wandered towards it. ‘It smells like a dead horse and is covered with blood. Get a grip of yourself. You can’t be wearing that!’

‘Is there anyone in this place who doesn’t need to pick fault?’ — he sat at the edge of his bed. — ‘Fine,’ — He flailed his arms. — 'Have it washed, but do not soak it. It's lizard skin. Soaking weakens the fabric.'

'I know that. I'm not new to this.' She continued pattering around the room. 'There's a cart outside. Perhaps some tea would calm you.' — Harris wandered to the door. Stricken with confusion. — 'My husband always used to say tea solves many ailments. A poor attitude being one of them. Now, what are your plans for today?'

Harris stood with his cup. Not wanting to offend Maple, who was far too outspoken for his liking. 'I have no plans. You said used to say? Is your husband no longer with us?'

'Dead. He was the last commander before you took over in Marrion.'

Harris blinked. 'Apologies. It took many good men and women.'

'And still does.' Maple was a well-formed woman. Powerful in her own right. 'That is why I will do whatever is needed to help you end this war. If that means cleaning your armour, then so be it.' She stood proudly in front of Harris. She was a woman on a mission.

His smile widened. 'I like you,' he said with a nod.

'Not for long.' She smirked at him as she left.

Harris walked from his room. All he wore was a black tunic. Black trousers, and long black leather boots. He wore his usual harness strap with several of his daggers and a sword on either side. His footsteps echoed around the corridor. Not a single sign of a councillor was there that morning.

Coming towards the central hall, he turned left. The galleries were a delight to Harris. Several windows surrounded the upper ceiling. Two doors led into the walled garden and back patio of the palace gardens. A large wooden table in the centre of the room surrounded by wooden tables. An entire wall of ovens. The galleries were as hot as a sweat filled Marrion summer. It was the place where all the information from the palace flowed through.

Harris strode in with his arms behind his back.

'So, who knows what?' He peered towards Gethen. Stood in the centre. Covered with flour, and rolling out his bread dough, Gethen glanced up.

Rebecca jumped as she heard him speak. 'Commander!' She instantly bowed to him.

'No need for that!' he laughed, he stepped into the kitchen. 'It's Harris, just Harris.'

The staff slowed what they were doing to get a glimpse of the commander they had heard so much about.

'I believe you've lost your way, sir,' — Gethen dusted his hands on his apron, — 'our king's chambers are up the stairs.'

'Oh! I'm not lost.' He was an instant hit with the ladies there who couldn't help but stare. 'You're the lifeblood of any palace. All I need to know is right here.'

'Then have a seat,' — invited Gethen. He pointed to a stool opposite his table, — 'finally, a commander who knows.'

Long into the afternoon, Gethen spoke of the goings on in the palace. 'Librye is strange, but you'll get used to her,' mentioned Gethen.

'She isn't strange at all.' Insisted Ana, she strode through with a basket. 'It's a pleasure to meet you, my lord,' she gave a short curtsy, smiling at Harris.

'Please, call me Harris,' he insisted. He gave a wink to Ana, as he had been doing for most of his stay there.

Ana leant forwards, still carrying the basket. 'I'll scream it if you like,' she flirtatiously whispered.

Harris burst with approval. His smile grew large. 'Trust me, I'll leave you speechless,' he flirted.

With raised brows, Ana made her way into the laundry on the right. 'One can always dream, I suppose.'

'As I was saying,' — said Gethen. Trying to pin Harris's attention. — 'Librye, she isn't one to be toyed with. It would see you fit to make friends with her. They're calling her a Solnox.'

Harris took a drink. He pondered for a moment. 'What do the council think?'

Rebecca marched in. Harris watched her stop by Gethen's side. 'The council cannot think half the time. Kailron has taken interest in her, some mistake it for affection,' said Rebecca.

'You don't sound convinced,' said Harris.

'The council of Cronnin destroyed the last Solnox, and they will do it again. She isn't safe here,' Rebecca sounded sure. She wrapped her arms around her waist.

Harris narrowed his eyes. 'And where are you from? I recognise the accent, but I cannot place it?'

'I'm from Dorm, south of the banks,' she replied.

'Enderton?' Harris deepened his voice. 'You're from Enderton?'

'That isn't what I said,' argued Rebecca.

'The south banks of Dorm is Enderton.'

'I am not from Enderton. I would never associate with the Azorae.' She blinked as she turned away.

'Do you truly believe the council will harm Librye?'

'They wouldn't dare,' grumbled Gethen. 'Have you met Maude? She would gut every one of them.'

Harris laughed. 'But this, Kailron, who is he?'

'His father was a lord of Enderton,' replied Gethen. Harris glanced at Rebecca. 'Kailron is here as an impartial agent for when the time comes, when the Atlanti surrender, he will lead negotiations.'

Harris snit, 'They think the Atlanti will surrender?'

Gethen nodded. Rebecca, however, screwed up her face.

'They would never do such a thing,' said Harris. 'Would they, Rebecca?'

She shrugged. 'Who knows? They are unpredictable.'

Calven meandered into the galleries. One of the stable hands. He froze upon seeing Harris. As Harris stood to leave. He waited in the shadows by the door. Just out of view of the staff there. The galleries erupted with talk of the new commander, Harris Bearwood. He gave a broad smile as the excitement began in the kitchen. Rebecca's silence was noticed.

Making his way up the stairs. Harris tried to get to grips with the different rooms. Before he could continue. He saw Maple leaving Angus's chambers.

'You look lost,' she mentioned, as she strolled towards him.

'I may look lost, but perhaps I'm found. I'm simply getting acquainted with the palace, that's all.'

Maple continued towards him. 'Maybe the chambers would be a good place to start.' Her brows raised. 'That's where your work starts, Harris.'

Harris gave a twisted smile towards her. He narrowed his eyes. 'I see you'll be working me like a horse here.'

Maple quietly passed him. 'And then some.'

Harris laughed. He strolled into Angus's chambers. 'You certainly have some outspoken staff here.' He burst into the chambers, giving no mind to knock.

'Harris!' proclaimed Librye. She jumped up from the bottom step of the mezzanine. 'I was coming to collect you.' She jovially bounced towards him.

'Collect me?' He glanced at Librye and back at Angus.

'The eastern tower,' mentioned Angus. He remained eyes down at his desk. 'It needs some renovations. I revealed the plans to Librye this morning,' — he lifted his head from the papers, — 'she hasn't stopped talking about it since.' Librye's excessive talking clearly took its toll on Angus.

Stepping through the door of the east tower. Harris followed Librye into the giant space. The stairs spiralled to the top of the tower. Harris and Librye made their way up the winding stairs. To the very top of the tower. The vast room was an awe-inspiring display of grandeur. A small wall separated the large round room. Harris wandered to the back.

'I can have my bedchambers here,' — he ambled to the back of the round tower, — 'we can split this off; I can have a desk by the window.' He paced back to the other side of the small separating room. 'Build this to the ceiling.' He spun to Librye, who stood by the wall to her hidden secret.

'I like my privacy.' He smiled. 'A few maps on the wall here.' He pointed to a wall which was yet to be built. Harris twisted. He held his arms out, pleased with the vast space. 'The rest is all yours.'

'I only want one wall.' Librye stared at her wall. His brows furled, watching Librye's stare.

Harris stepped towards her. He inspected the seemingly ordinary wall. 'You clever little sod!' He felt around the wall, feeling the same crease that Librye had. Harris crouched. His voice was quiet. 'How long?'

'Quite some time.' — It impressed her that Harris had found the room. — 'Would you like to see?' Her smile twisted.

Harris intuitively knew that Librye trusted him. A secret like this she would show to no one. A childlike excitement caught Harris. He removed his swords and left them at the side.

Following Librye into the winding corridors. He struggled to get through. Soon enough, he sat in the rafters above the council halls.

Harris whispered to her, 'You've spent a lot of time up here, haven't you?' He glanced at the books she had left in the rafters. The years of dirt were absent in the area where they sat.

'Every day,' whispered Librye. 'It gets so boring, though. The council seems obsessed with Angus finding a wife. They also seem obsessed with you.'

Harris came forwards and glared into the hall, trying to listen. 'Why are they obsessed with me?' — Before she could reply, he sat straight. — 'Mind you, many people are.'

'Careful, Harris,' warned Librye. 'Your ego is showing.'

Harris laughed. He leant in closer to listen to the council. Upon the table in the centre of the room was a parchment. 'Can you remember any of what they've said?'

'They said that you're dangerous.' — She glanced at the many daggers on Harris's straps and belt. — 'They said you're too self-destructive.'

Harris raised his brows. 'Now, that is quite true, but people keep calling me dangerous. I'm not dangerous.'

'Have those daggers ever killed anyone?'

'Of course they have!'

'Then you're dangerous.' Librye's unchanged look confused Harris. 'They don't like you, Harris, because you represent change. Change isn't what the council wants right now. If the war ends, then so do their added wages.'

Harris sat and thought. He could hear every word being said at the council. From the floods in the north to the waking of the world in the east.

'Come on, we need to get back,' he insisted. He crawled back. Librye followed.

As he wandered through the large round tower. His footsteps on the wooden floorboards echoed. Librye watched him. The strange man who had walked into her life held influence. She hung on his every word.

'What was the palace like where you grew up?'

Harris gazed out of a window, overlooking the Cronnin city. 'It wasn't like this one.' His memory of the kingdom of Xencliff etched in his mind. 'I remember waking each morning to the call of seabirds. The smell of fresh ocean fish and thick skins, covering the bed. The palace of Xencliff differed from this one. It's caves, all carved into the cliffs.' He took a long sigh. Librye strode towards him. 'I'll never forget the feeling of the fresh sea air.' He peered down towards the city. A breeze through the trees appeared to be dancing on the Cronnin streets. 'I used to hate it, but now —'

'Do you miss it?' She stood beside him. Harris stared from the window. A churning melancholy lingered deep in his gut.

It was odd for Harris. He had never seen himself as a person who worked well with children. His life had seen him from tavern to battleground. The only children he came across were the victims of the Atlanti. He had a soft spot for children. Harris missed his own innocence. He did not want the same for Librye.

'Do you think he's in Cronnin yet?' Branwen sat at Anna's desk.

Anna undressed her soiled armour. The dried blood oozed through into her undergarments. 'Come on, Bran,' replied Anna with a sigh. 'Have you not received your papers yet?'

Branwen shook her head slowly. 'They were supposed to arrive today, but I've heard nothing. One of the Atlanti falcons may have taken them. You would expect my mother to send her guards to collect me,' — she glanced up at Anna, — 'do you think he's arrived yet?'

Anna slumped down in the chair at her desk. The odd few papers Harris had left reminded her of a less arduous time.

'I believe he would be there by now. Then again, this is Harris.' Branwen gazed up. Her begging eyes stared into hers. 'Harris is who he is, Branwen.' — Anna shrugged. — 'No one can change him. Trying will just get you hurt.'

Branwen pressed her lips closely together. She gazed down at the desk in front. The warm air brought a misted sweat to her brow. 'I just wish it was real.'

'Oh! it was all real.' Anna's tone of surety brought a slight hope to Branwen. 'It was real with you. With me. With the hundreds of others too, but this is Harris,' — she sat forwards, — 'The commander will never be tamed. He isn't self-destructive in a sense of battle. He will do the stupidest thing possible, to protect himself from happiness.'

It made little sense to Branwen. 'How?'

Anna gazed into her eyes. She sat back. 'Whoever he loves ends up dead.' Branwen furrowed her brow. Her mouth was gaping. She sat back. 'At least that's what he believes. By hurting you, getting you to hate him, he is protecting you.'

Branwen thought for a moment. 'What did he do to you?'

Anna reclined in the chair. She inspected the room as her eyes narrowed. 'He fucked my best friend. I fell for him, and I made the mistake of telling him that. He told me, everyone who loves him, and everyone who he loves. End up dead. He told me to run, get out while I still could. I was completely devoted to him. So, he met my best friend, and saw it as a chance to make me hate him.'

'And do you?' asked Branwen. 'Do you hate him?'

Anna glanced at Branwen. She fiddled with a piece of paper on the desk. 'That's the worst part, I don't.' She gave a tight smile. 'It proves his theory wrong. I still love him, even after what he did, but I'm still alive.' — She held her arms out and sat forwards, — 'If I can give you any advice. Get out while you still can. I know you love him, Branwen, but he will hurt you. Especially you. He knows you could never be together. You're a royal fae, and he is just a commoner. It would be safer for the both of you to just run.'

The worst punishment known paled compared to life without Harris. Her obsession worsened. As the hot days dragged by, she awaited her guards. Every stone. Every brick in the haunting castle of Marrion reminded her of him. His taste. His touch. The feel of his skin. The feel of his everything. Her addiction grew.

CHAPTER FOURTEEN

14

A golden ray sprawled across the grey room where Harris slept. His bed felt warm, but lonely. He was used to being alone, but he no longer wanted it. Branwen possessed every part of his thoughts. Hers was the face he saw each night before he slept and each morning as he woke. The flowing satin curtains reminded him of her delicate hair. The freshness of the air outside drifted in through his window. His senses worked against him. Even the lavender soap reminded him of her.

Angus's chambers filled with smoke from his pipe as Harris made his way in. He dragged his feet drifting sleepily headed towards the desk.

'Morning, Librye.'

'Good morning, Harris.' Librye sat above the stairs with a book in hand. It was something he was gradually becoming used to seeing. The sounds of hammering and banging in the east tower resounded through the halls.

Harris peered around the room. 'Has Angus even ventured in here yet?'

Librye momentarily lifted her head from the book she was reading. 'The council called for him early. Harelda plans to return to Sonnin within the next few days.' Her eyes drifted back to the book.

'So soon?' Harris stood at Angus's desk. He read some letters and notes left there from the early morning curriers. 'I thought she would at least see the end of the turn here; the festivals start soon.'

Librye sat straight, sniggering. 'Harelda doesn't care for such barbaric displays of drunkenness, as she calls them.'

Harris glanced back. 'I love barbaric displays of drunkenness. And as Chief Commander, I feel it imperative to partake in these displays.'

Librye glanced towards Harris. Holding the book down, she laughed. 'You would, you're The Commander. Not only chief, but Harris Bearwood. Infamous throughout the taverns.' She fluttered her head.

'Oi! You shouldn't know about any of that!' Harris disapproved. 'You're far too young.' He went back to scanning the letters on Angus's desk.

'Besides, she hasn't got to the books of the shadow yet.' Harelda stood by the door. She elegantly placed her hands at her front. She stood in a bright satin cream fae gown. The fabric sat perfectly on her frame. The seams were a golden pattern which drifted down her slender frame.

Harris twisted, shocked. He pointed with some papers towards her with his mouth gaping. 'How did you do that?'

Harelda's everlasting grace grew. She drifted forwards. 'Do what?'

'How did you get there without me hearing?' he staggered his words.

'You're gifted.'

Her powerful voice soothed him. 'In more ways than one. Nevertheless,' said Harris.

'I am fae, one of the highest. Even your merrow hearing is no match for the fae.'

Harris replied with a low grumble, 'Your daughter was wonderful at that as well.' — He watched her brows raise. — 'She is well. She said, she hopes to return to Sonnin soon.' He gave a cheerful smile to Harelda.

Making her way to Angus's desk. She sat in Angus's chair. Harris sat opposite. 'Well, finally,' she sighed. '*The Commander.*' Her awe was clear. Harris did not know where the discussion would lead. 'So, tell me of your plans for Cronnin?'

He sat back. 'I have many plans, my queen. First, sort out the shit storm in Belgravia, Tosta and Roe. Following that, I plan to settle the rest that is hitting. Meaning we can push our powers towards the west.'

Harelda softened her eyes. She skimmed the papers on Angus's desk. She was used to a more organised way of life.

'I admit I'm impressed with your work so far. However, you are yet to prove yourself capable of such an undertaking. Your ambition is understandable. Proof is what we need now.' Her reply was harsh, but fair.

He could sense a desperation in Harelda. Her need to end the war plagued her.

'This war will end. Our armies will end it. You'll see it in your lifetime.'

Harelda shook her head. 'I can only hope you're right,' — she raised her head, — 'I wish to see you at the end of Nean, for an update.'

Harris rose as Harelda stood to leave. A smirk of doubt showed. 'I could write to you.'

Harelda spun, her eyes lowered towards him. 'You do not wish to see me again?'

Harris stood back; he gave a laughing smile of embarrassment. 'I apologise, your highness, the end of Nean it is.' She met his agreement with a coquettish smile.

Librye waited for Harelda to leave. 'I think she likes you, Harris,' shc commcntcd.

Harris's eyes remained fixed on the door as she left. 'That's what concerns me.'

Librye frowned, confused by his comment. Harris twisted to give a reassuring smile to Librye.

'Harelda is kind, and gentle,' said Librye.

'Again, that's what concerns me,' mumbled Harris.

'I am just a child; you know that?'

'Are you bollocks,' — Harris twisted back to the desk. — 'You're a Solnox, meaning you have more ability to understand than your average village idiot.'

'Hey!' She stood.

'Apologies, you certainly aren't average.' His smile grew. 'What colour are we going with today?'

Librye made her way towards him. Gawping at him, she watched as he turned. 'Ah, Xencliff green.'

'They change each day, but I don't know why. As does my hair. Harelda told me my eyes change with the days. Every day is different. My hair changes with the seasons. Only, I don't know why.'

Harris twisted. He walked towards her. 'Ha,' he huffed, surprised. 'Normal is boring. You're far from normal, and you're far from boring too. Your hair is seasonal. Yes, most Solnox had seasonal hair, but your eyes are different. They represent your mood, your wants, needs, and innermost desires.'

'Innermost desires?' she grimaced.

Harris grinned. 'You met me only a few days ago, already your eyes have remained the same colour as mine,' — he leant towards her, — 'I wonder what that could mean?'

Librye's smile spread. 'Because I'm excited to learn from the Commander. Someone who likes Malgron as much as me.'

Harris stood straight, powerless to release the smile she had given him.

He spent his day in Angus's chambers, while Angus took council. Having had his workload almost removed, Angus finally found more time to spend with Librye. Their days spent in the gardens brought a distinct youth to him. His brave little Librye did not care about the night-time darkness as it drifted into the woods. The days were longer than the nights, as the height of summer took over the bustling city of Cronnin.

The Onmidden celebrations would be a genuine test of control for Harris. His usual way of celebrating would involve women, alcohol, and brawls.

Harris stood in the galleries beside Gethen.

'The first of five begins today, Harris,' gasped Calven, shocked to see him still there.

'That they do,' replied Harris, taking an apple from the bowl at the side.

'Well, I've heard the stories. I was hoping to see it for myself.' Calven narrowed his eyes.

'Chief Commander, Cal,' snickered Harris. 'I have an example to set. What would they say if their Chief Commander behaved in such a way?'

Calven tightened his teeth. 'Yeay?'

'No, it would unleash disorder.'

Gethen turned. 'Since when have you been a bad influence?' he snarled at Calven.

Calven lifted his hand. 'Oh, come on, we've heard the stories. I just want to see it.'

Harris left. Tapping Calven on the shoulder, almost sending him to the ground. 'Sorry, Cal, those days exist in memories only.'

Harris began the first of five celebrations, writing.

A spare moment for Harris was rare. With Librye busy and Angus in council, he wrote to Branwen. For the first time since arriving in Cronnin.

'*Branwen, I am lost. The palace has provided a place to sleep, a place to sit, but it is not my home. My home was in Marrion. I only hope you're safe and well. I have thought of nothing but returning. Hoping to whisk you away to a far distant land, where rules don't apply. But Xencliff isn't really the place you'd wish to be.*'

Even in his writing, his humour was hard to hide. He wanted to tell her he loved her, but he did not want to give her false hope.

'*I look forwards to seeing you soon, in the palace of Cronnin. For now, rest well, and please, return safe. Ever yours, Harris.*'

Before entering the city to join the festivities. Harris made his way with his piles of letters, towards the west tower. The stone floor rung with his footsteps, making his way towards the pigeon loft. He hesitated. In his right hand, he carried the scroll, addressed to Branwen of Marrion. His eyes peered around the empty corridor. His hand shook. He took the parchment and crushed it in his hand. He tucked it into the pocket of his trousers and continued his way towards the loft.

Back in Angus's chambers, Harris awaited the call of the bells from the south tower. Marking the start of the Onmidden celebrations. He took the parchment from his pocket and placed it to a candle. Throwing it down into the fireplace. He watched his words burn. He wanted to send it, but he knew the misery it could cause, if anyone ever found out.

The city was lit with colourful banners. Cheering began, the palace guard rolled out hundreds of casks of ale. The gift for the people of the city to help them celebrate the coming harvest.

Drunkenness took over the city. Whilst it was a time of celebration, the city guards could not celebrate. Most of their work involved breaking up fights. Harris used to love Onmidden. It was a chance to have an unprovoked brawl. To remove some anger on some unsuspecting drunk who probably deserved it. This year, the celebrations withered. The noise rattled through streets and alleyways. The smell of ale as it filled the streets. All the shouting, laughing, and screaming stopped at Harris.

He had chosen a bar close to the palace. For the entire night, he sat, he drank, he even tried to laugh with the locals. The bar was a dingy place of drunken fun. He easily broke a few fights with the help of the city guard. Harris could not laugh. He felt guilty about having fun. A warm bath and early night were the start of his celebration.

'Have you heard from him at all?' Anna stood in her new chambers of Castle Marrion, having just returned from a two-day battle.

'Not so much as an empty shell.' Branwen sat at the desk. Where Harris would remain for hours at night, considering his move for the next day. She swirled her finger over the raised wood on the desk.

'I know the pigeons often get taken down by falcons, but surely, he would've sent a letter, or note, by falcon, or even a currier?' Her eyes drifted around the desk. The candle wax on the desk had melted into a pool surrounding it, all left by Harris, in his attempt to preserve Marrion.

Removing her armour and chains. Anna wandered the room.

'All I've heard is the order from the council that the third return. Nothing from Harris. It certainly wouldn't be Harris who issued the order. They left a while ago, so you should receive your return soon.' It was a fleeting thought for Anna. She could see the expression of loss Branwen constantly displayed.

Anna stepped towards the desk. Her crude cotton undergarments showed the scars she too carried. They were worse than Harris's. Slowly, Branwen glanced up. Anna sat. She reached across the desk and took a small balm, which Branwen had made for her, to ease muscle aches and pains.

'I feel like we've become close since Harris left,' — she rubbed the balm on her leg, — 'but I feel that is only because you can't leave this room.' She sat up straight. Branwen's eyes drifted about the desk, with the odd few glances towards Anna. 'Branwen, you need to let him go.'

She glared at Anna. 'I can't do this,' she sighed. She stooped forwards, placing her head in her palms. 'How can I do this?' Her words muffled in her hands before she lifted her head. 'I can't go back to Sonnin, knowing what I know now.'

Anna lifted her brows, easing back. 'It's a hard choice,' — she took some more balm, and began rubbing her arms, — 'I can't imagine how it must be for you. I know I've had my time with Harris. He makes a wonderful friend, though, one of the best I've ever had.' She rose. Making her way towards the window, she collected a robe on her way. 'I know, if I ever need anything, he will always be there, like many in this camp.' Anna peered from the window.

Branwen stood and stepped towards her. 'I just think, someone needs to be there for him.'

Anna glanced at Branwen. 'He is Xencliff. Xencliff, believe they need no one. They are hardened. Harris took it one step further and became a walking hard on.'

Anna turned her back to the open window. A gentle breeze fluttered in. 'Perhaps you can love him from a distance. It doesn't take the physical. Be the person who always looks out for him. You can't be together, but friends can love each other.'

Branwen gave a loving smile to Anna. Their talks had been a great comfort to her.

'Anna!' Branwen heard screaming from the mezzanine outside the door. Branwen spun. Anna remained by the window. 'Anna!' They both heard the wailing.

'In here!' Anna stood by the window. 'I swear this place will be my death,' she giggled. Her face turned cold, a look of pain slowly formed, her brow wrinkled in the centre of her forehead.

Branwen stepped forwards, not knowing what was wrong. 'Run!' Anna whispered. Anna's mouth opened. A silent scream refused to leave her body as an arrow passed into her stomach. Another passed through her shoulder. A hail of arrows hit from behind. Darkness fell on the room as one passed through her forehead.

Stood in terror, Branwen's hands shook. She glared at them. Speckled blood spat into her clothes.

With a breath of horror, Branwen doubled over. Her shrieks muted. She rushed to the door. The castle Marrion was squirming with coblyn. The wretched creature tore through the soldiers with their teeth. Nothing but a loin cloth covered them. Coblyn flocked the courtyard. Heavy in numbers, they swarmed through the gates. A black wave of death hit the castle.

Branwen madly searched for a way out. The entire castle swelled with coblyn. She ran towards the bridge to the left of the mezzanine, into the heart of the castle. Her panicked eyes kept darting back. The smell of flames blocked her nose. Howling from the terrifying creature filled the air. She held her hands against her ears. Struggling to drown out the horrifying sounds of hollering and growling, soldiers screaming as their inners were severed from their bodies.

As quick as she could, Branwen flew through the curving passages of the bleak castle. Her feet pounded up the stone stairs towards the huge turrets. Before she reached the turrets, something snagged Branwen around the waist. Her mouth covered by an unknown hand. Screaming and kicking, Branwen could not calm. Screeching as loud as she could, she hit out. A hand caught her wrists, forcing her to turn. The face of Lister glared towards her.

'Follow me,' he whispered.

She gave a gasp of relief and silenced. 'Praise the gods, it's you.' She followed Lister down the winding passage. She followed Lister through the shadowy hall and down towards the galleries. Cries resounded through the castle, following them as they rushed through. As they made their way into the galleries, half the staff lie on the floor. Limbs and heads left ripped from bodies. Guts laid torn open. Every manner of bodily fluid oozed on the floor. She followed Lister to the back of the galleries.

'Where are we going?' she cried, stepping through the gory mayhem.

Lister came to the back storerooms in the galleries. His eyes searched the room. 'It's how Harris got the vitriol into the caves.' He took Branwen by the shoulders, holding her firmly, he warned. 'You follow the caves. Head east. It will bring you to the Una Forest. Keep going east, you'll see an army. They left this morning, heading towards the eastern pass. If you go now, you will see them, go, go!' He demanded, opening a cupboard door he thrust her through. She saw the shadows in the hall towards the galleries. Shrieks became louder as the creatures scurried towards them.

Branwen glanced back. 'Come with me,' she wept.

She could see the look in Lister's eyes. He was not ready to die, but he always needed to be ready to fight.

'You need to tell them what happened here. The Cronnin council called the third off this morning. Tell them what they have done. Tell them they killed me.'

He forced her into the door and instantly closed it. Branwen thudded against the locked door.

Desperately, she begged, 'Come with me!' A thud on the door sent her backwards. She stood in the tunnel's darkness.

Panicked, she followed the cave east. Anna's blood still filled her clothes. Her hair hung ragged and torn from her bun. Sweat covered her brow in the hot tunnels and caves. She grabbed the front of her skirt and ran as far and as fast as she could. The tunnels were dark. Echoes from the chaos outside dulled. Not knowing which way she was going, Branwen fled faster, following the main vein of the tunnel, ignoring the tunnels to the left of her. She kept going east.

A bleak pile of corpses laid quivering in the heat of the Marrion night. The sound of flesh being devoured hushed the flames, which cracked and flickered in the courtyard. A procession headed over the barbican. Gaius and Daniel stood to the side, allowing the flow of their warriors.

'It's only a matter of time,' said Daniel, his eyes twisted up to Gaius. 'As soon as Bearwood finds out, he'll be here.'

'Then we're lucky to be leaving soon,' said Gaius, his eyes remained steady on the army as they poured in.

'Leaving?'

'He can't expect us to stay here. The army will hold Marrion, we move east.'

Daniel tightened his eyes. 'Why east?'

'After seeing what they did, Cronnin is ours for the taking, surely.'

'You attempt to predict his next move?'

'I attempt to predict his ultimate move.'

'He will keep it from us,' — he strode towards the castle, — 'Kairne rarely lets his plans known until the last minute.' Daniel turned to Gaius. 'He's suspicious, remember.'

'Suspicious he may be, but without trust, all his work could fall apart,' said Gaius, as he followed behind.

Daniel stood, he pointed to the left of the castle mezzanine, and then the right. 'I'll take that one,' — he walked towards the old fae quarters, — 'give it a few days. Kairne will send us his orders when he's ready.'

Gaius stood on the mezzanine. A muddy dream sat before him. He looked at the stone wall. Remembering, it was where he first saw Harris. His torturous memory recalled the screams from the dungeons, the stench of rotting flesh.

He wandered further, towards the commander's quarters. Vines of broken fire flowers hung dimly from above the door. He sneered at the extravagance. Stepping inside, the body of Anna lay decaying on the ground. A fresh pool of blood trickled from underneath her.

Lifting her arms, he flipped her over. Her eyes were open, an opaque glow took over her once shimmering green. 'I remember you,' he muttered. Lifting her arms, he dragged her from the room towards the mezzanine.

'Calm now,' her mouth moved, a voice came from her breathless lungs. Gaius dropped her corpse and stepped back. 'Worry not, Gaius, Kairne speaks.' Gaius stared at the animated corpse. 'Convene at the tower. You have done well.' Her lips stopped moving, her lungs were flat.

After a moment, Gaius stepped forwards. He poked her, ensuring she was gone. He threw her body from the balcony.

Stepping back into the commander's chambers, he took a seat at the desk, easing back. He lifted his feet and crossed his legs onto the desk. A hollow victory at first grew into a triumph.

A victory of engineering saw the east tower transform. A separate room at the back now served as Harris's sleeping quarters. His chambers to the front took over the rest of the tower. The windows were still to be replaced. A colour was yet to be added to the walls, and warmth added to the room.

Many noticed his routine. Each morning he would make his way from the tower towards the central hall, being sure to collect Librye on the way. Together, they would venture into the city. Where Harris would collect his daily sweetbread from the bakery.

Upon arriving back. The two would make their way towards their tower. Harris would settle for the day at his desk. Librye would settle for the day above the dusty rafters.

The days were an unending battle for Harris. His time in the palace was laborious. Talks with Angus and his time spent in the galleries with the many staff broke the arduous task of talking to councillors.

Sat quietly at his desk, he watched as Librye emerged from the door. His grin widened.

'I just need some water,' she said with a smile. Wandering towards his desk, she took a glass and his pitcher.

Harris turned to the side, rubbing his knee. Librye took notice. 'What did you do?'

'Old war wound, I have plenty.'

'Do you miss it?' She took a sip of water.

'I miss certain aspects.' His eyes drifted through the room. 'The adrenaline of battle. The slow breath it took for me to face fate. I miss my freedom, away from the politics of the council.'

'You avoid them so well,' said Librye with a smile and a quick blink.

'What news do you have?' He set his quill down to listen.

Librye appeared shaken. 'It was boring,' she moaned.

Harris laughed. 'Come on, you were helping me.'

Librye raised her brow. 'It's worth at least one new dress.'

'Agreed,' replied Harris with a small nod. 'Now, report?'

Maple, who had been clearing clothes from Harris's room, scurried from the door of his bedchambers. 'You're supposed to be teaching her.' She made her way across the intricate parquet floor. 'This isn't teaching, Harris.'

'It's what I used to do, Maple!' called Harris as she left down the stairs.

Librye sighed. 'There seem to be some issues south of Thrasia. Pestilence, I think they said. Also, their obsession with Angus getting a wife has worked with Angus now.'

'Ha, anything else?'

'Bad news. The evening before last, letters to Marrion.' Harris gazed at her; he listened intently. 'They've removed the Sonnin third.' Her voice trembled. She saw Harris's mouth coil down. 'They began their return. They made a mistake. The letter wasn't supposed to be sent, following a vote at the council, but the Sonnin third have left. Marrion is vulnerable.' She saw the look of horror on Harris's face. She could see a slow rage building in him. 'Are you alright, Harris?'

'I'm fine, I'm fine,' he repeated. His look of anger broke. He glowered at Librye. 'What do your secrets say?'

Librye shook her head. 'Please, Harris, don't do this.'

Harris stood. 'Librye, tell me what they say,' he patiently insisted.

'You'll be needed in the hall soon. The castle was taken, the council don't know yet.' Harris shot from around the desk. He ran to the back into his bedchamber. Desperately, he searched, gathering his armour. 'There is nothing you can do.' Librye followed him.

Harris swivelled to her. 'I have to try!' He rushed his lizard skin armour onto his legs. He sat on the bed.

'Harris.' She ambled towards him. She held his hand. He calmed. 'They're gone. The castle is gone,' she insisted. Harris calmed his breath. For the first time, he did not know what to do.

Harris rushed from the chambers and rumbled down the stairs. Librye followed as fast as she could. The staff saw Harris, and they felt his temper as he drove some out of the way. Others followed Harris and his display of fury. Maude followed at the side of Librye. Harris buckled his swords.

Evan stood at Angus's door, he rushed into Angus's chambers. 'We have a problem!' Angus peered up. 'The Commander, I think he's heading towards the council hall.' They heard the doors to the hall slam open with a mighty boom. Evan squinted. He stared at Angus. 'Yep, definitely that,' he nodded.

Angus shot from his desk and rushed towards the halls. Harris thundered in; the end of council was just about to be called. Kailron stood in the centre of the hall. Harris burst in; dust went sailing from areas that had not seen fresh air in years.

Harris strode menacingly in. Kailron remained silent as he stepped back.

'Four thousand, eight hundred and forty-nine,' Harris calmly began. The council glanced at each other, baffled. 'Four thousand, eight hundred, and forty-nine!' He exclaimed spinning in the hall. Council members mumbled to each other. 'That is how many you've killed today!' he yelled. He made his way towards the centre of the hall and jumped with a single leap onto the table. Kailron watched. He stepped back with his mouth gaping.

'Marrion would've been won. The third were the defences outside of the castle, but now, each one of you has killed them!' His voice revealed his fury, his rage spilled into the room, burning the air they breathed. 'Marrion has fallen, the war just got a lot worse, because you can't do your duties. The war was mine!' he screamed, leaning forwards. 'It was mine to deal with, mine to sort, yet you all go behind my back, send your own orders, and have them all executed!'

Angus rushed into the hall to see Harris's display of ferocity.

'Each one of you, who played a part in that letter being sent to call off the third. Should be hanged for your crimes!' He jumped from the table and stormed towards Angus, who remained at the door. Harris glowered at him. 'Are you going to tell her? Or am I?'

Angus furrowed his brow towards Harris. 'Tell who, what?'

Harris turned in the council halls. His flame of contempt towards them grew. 'Branwen is dead. Someone needs to tell Harelda, this council killed her daughter.' His lip curled with hate, he ripped from the hall and out towards the palace stables.

The warm summer air felt icy to Harris. Balthus and Angus followed him. Librye remained with Maude at the top of the stairs. Her terrified hands clung to Maude.

'Come, child, back to your room,' Maude softly led Librye away from the drama in the hall.

The gravel crunched under Angus and Balthus's boots as they tried to follow Harris. 'Harris, please!' called Angus in a deep tone.

'Being hasty will get you killed!' called Balthus.

Harris marched towards the stables to the front of the palace wall. 'It's always served me before!' He thundered towards the end stable.

From the stable, Maple had already braced Svend.

'I got him as soon as I heard. Go quickly, Harris.'

Harris gazed at Maple with his mouth gaping. 'I knew there was a reason I liked you.'

Taking Svend's reins, he mounted and roared from the palace gates. Hoping to see Harelda's carriage somewhere along the Sonnin pass.

Branwen clamoured through the caves, heading east. She toiled through the last set of dense caves. Seeing tangled vines blocking the cave exit. Her hurried breath steadied. She rested on the floor. She did not want to look out for fear of what she might encounter. Curling her arms around her knees, she wept. Blood and clay from the walls of the caves covered her hands. Slight cuts from the stone walls made her hands bleed. Her tattered clothes hung from her. Saturated with the years of dirt which had settled there. She could still see Anna's dried blood. Her stomach was hollow. She silently wept in the cave. The only clean part of her face were the marks of the tears.

She did not have time to rest; knowing the Sonnin third were close. She rose, rubbing her face as she made her way out. The rustle of the vines as she pulled them back horrified her. Anxious that the wrong thing may hear her approach. She ventured from the cave. The ground was muddy below her feet. The early morning dew drifted past her as her eyes searched the scattered woods. She needed the innermost part of her nature to guide her. The trees were silent. As Branwen stood at the cave entrance, she heard them; they told her where the army was.

She continued through the scattered trees. Her footsteps hushed. Her breath calmed. For the entire day, she stalked through the woodlands. Finally, a smell of smoke drifted towards her. She was close.

Harris roared down the pass on Svend. A bolt of black shot past those resting on the late-night road of the Sonnin pass. Finally, Harelda's carriage came into sight.

'Halt!' Harris called to the riders behind. They immediately saw Harris riding ferociously towards them. Dressed in nothing but a black tunic, black trousers, and lizard skin leg guards. With only one sword.

'Halt!' they called forwards.

Harelda sat in her carriage with Grendel. Harris rode to the side. He leant down to the window. 'Harris?' She peered from the carriage. 'What is the meaning of this?' She glanced around, panicked.

Harris held a look of empty fear in his eyes. 'I needed to see you.' He jumped from Svend. Opening the carriage door. Harelda sat back. 'I'm riding west.' A curled mouth showed his fear. 'Marrion.'

Harelda widened her eyes. A hollow sense of loss took hold of her. 'What happened, Harris?'

Her glare chilled him. 'Harelda, my queen. A member of the council took it upon themselves to call the Sonnin third off.' He softly began, his hardened look showed. 'Librye, she has seen the castle fall. I ride west, to save her.' His quivering voice spoke volumes to Harelda.

Her eyes shot about the carriage, trying her best to take everything in. Without showing fear or rage. 'She is alive, Harris.' She gazed towards Harris. A look of desperation filled her eyes. 'Find her. I know she is alive.'

'Commander!' Grendel leant forwards in the carriage. Harris peered around Harelda to see Grendel. 'Tell me you have your kit?'

'Of course I do. As always, a good alchemist never leaves without it.' A twisted smile from the corner of his mouth impressed Grendel. Harris gave a quick nod. He mounted Svend and called, 'On!' He shunted his reins and rode as hard as he could, west.

Harris had survived without armour before. He did not need too many weapons. He just needed Branwen, safe.

Her panicked breaths worried Grendel. He reached out, taking her hand. 'It is something many people do not know about The Commander. He is not just a common commander. Harris has the teachings of Thrasia. He knows alchemy. I would argue he knows more than me. If she has suffered injury, then there is no one better than Harris. He will find her, and he will bring her home.'

Harelda broke. Her mouth curled, her eyes filled with tears, cascading down her face, she silently cried.

Long into the morning, he rode as fast as Svend could bear. It was a true testament to his strength and endurance. Harris knew the only way out of the castle. He rode towards the Una Forest.

Harris rode for days and nights, giving Svend limited breaks. The terrain changed. Dense woodlands and forests faded into grassy plains. Rivers became warm swamps.

Among the scattered redwoods, the thick ferns lay restlessly. The towering trees stood silent in the forest. Harris stood on the borders. The isolated silence helped him listen. He dismounted Svend, who laid down, exhausted.

'Stay here.' He glanced at Svend.

Harris drew his blade. The sword on the leather was silent. He could hear the faint sound of muffled talking.

He made his way towards the noises. Creeping through the trees, he came upon a camp. He wandered through the trees as a guard stepped out.

'Harris?'

'Where is she?' Harris asked, lowering his sword.

Gawping at Harris, the guard sauntered towards him. 'Do you mean Branwen?' His mouth gaped.

'Please tell me she's alive,' Harris begged.

'They only sent the letter this morning; how did you know?'

'I have something better than letters, please. Is she here?'

Immediately, the guard escorted Harris into the camp. The faint whispers did not bother Harris. It shook the army to see him there. Their commander, Lukas, stepped from his tent.

'Lukas!' Harris marched towards him.

'She is safe.' Lukas lifted his hands towards Harris. 'But Marrion has fallen. She told me everything.'

Harris blinked heavily. 'Can I see her?'

Lukas raised his arm, guiding Harris towards his tent. 'She's returning with me,' urged Harris.

Lukas raised the door to the leather fae tent. The magic of the fae provided a large area inside. Sat on a small chair on the left of the room. Branwen remained wrapped in a thick deerskin blanket.

'Thank the gods,' sighed Harris, striding in.

Her smile grew. She stood in disbelief. The blanket dropped as she ran towards him. 'Harris!' She broke down, throwing her arms around him. 'I thought I would never see you again.' Her voice cracked. She stepped back. 'Anna—'

Before she could finish, Harris nodded with softened eyes. 'I know, I know.' He held her head close to his chest as she sobbed. 'How did you find the caves?'

Her voice muffled through Harris's clothes. 'Lister, he saved me.' She broke her hold on him and gazed towards him. Her tears burnt her eyes and face. 'He's dead, Harris, they're all dead, they sent the coblyn, they took everything.' Her tears covered his tunic, still he held her close.

Harris spun to Lukas, who stood beside them. 'I'll need some supplies.' Harris's raised brows towards Lukas spoke volumes. 'She is my friend, Lukas. Nothing more. We leave within the hour. Her mother needs her home. A horse would help as well.'

'We have some spare.' Lukas held a soft voice. He felt for Branwen. She was not used to seeing the horror both he and Harris had seen. She was an innocent lady of the palace. She gave her time to help those who needed it most, and they would both do all they could to ensure her recovery. Just as she had done for countless others.

The ride back to Sonnin was silent. Her mind filled with the screams of that night. Anna's face haunted her dreams. The last words Lister had spoken echoed in her memory. As they made their way into Sonnin, the heat of Marrion faded. The nights were silent. Branwen would not speak of what she had seen. Harris already knew. He was glad she was alive, broken, but alive.

Each morning, Angus still made his way towards the council hall. His throne felt empty. He should have known. The council should have told him. Having received several messages from Harelda, Angus needed to act.

Kailron ambled into the silent hall. His footsteps echoed through the stone structure. Angus glared at him. Kailron felt tiny in the powerful hall.

Kailron glanced around the empty hall. Angus sat alone on his throne.

'You called for me, sire?'

Angus stayed his hand to the guard at the door. The large door closed, sending a boom through the hall.

'I did. I need to know I can trust someone. You know that the role of Chief Commander would see Harris at the forefront of this war. The council was to leave matters of war to him. Tell me, who sent it?'

Kailron gave a heavy sigh, striding towards the throne. He made his way up the steps.

'The council tried to call a meeting when Harris arrived. His absence forced a vote.'

'A vote in a matter removed from their hands.'

'The war has been a council matter for quite some time. Removing their power over this clearly had some of them on edge.'

'So, this was a power play?' asked Angus, resting his hand on his chin.

'We lost three armies. That is not a power play, that is a massacre.'

Angus twisted his head, watching as Kailron lowered himself into the seat beside him.

'That chair has been empty for too long,' — Angus rose from his throne, — 'Where is your loyalty, Kailron?'

Kailron slowly rose, facing the king. 'After the atrocities of Marrion, my loyalty is firmly with you. The Azorae had no hand in this, but the Atlanti, every one of them, their blood will fill the ocean before I give any loyalty to them.'

'Who sent it?' grumbled Angus.

'Connor. The vote was against them. I asked Connor to destroy the letter. He was passionate about voting to remove them. He must have sent it.'

Angus's eyes filled with rage. 'Then bring him.'

It only took a few moments. Angus remained stewing in his rage in the hall. Connor stepped inside. His frail frame shook, scurrying in.

'You have a choice, Connor,' grumbled Angus. 'The only option is the truth. Did you remove the Sonnin third from Marrion?'

Connor waved his head. He scowled at Angus. 'We all did. A few who voted against, they didn't see the real implications. Marrion was as good as won. Even the Chief Commander told us that. Harris himself, he wrote it was as good as won.' His hands shook, he came closer towards the towering throne. 'I was simply following what he had said. I sent the letter, as Marrion no longer needed the third.'

Angus nodded. 'Harelda will not rest until I find someone at fault. You sent the letter; it left your hand. Even though all matters of war were to bc left to the Chief Commander. They placed it into law, Connor, that the Chief Commander would be the only one to deal with matters of war.

'The Sonnin third is the army of Sonnin. Meddling in the affairs of another kingdom is treason.' Angus leant forwards. The calmness of his voice changed to darkness. 'I have heard much about you, Connor. I refused to believe it at first, since a tavern owner is not the most trustworthy we have. The council will suffer for this, but you have another choice.' Angus took a parchment from the side of his chair. Connor enlarged his eyes; he knew what the parchment was. 'Connor Malroy Jenkinson.' Angus officially began. 'Power of the gods places it upon me, to find you guilty of treason, murder, and mass extinction of life. I will now offer you your choice.' Angus leant forwards. Connor quivered as he did. A tear sat in his eyes. 'Offenmoor, or death?'

'The council would see sense.'

'The council is not here. And they do not have authority over treason.'

'I demand a trial!' Connor called. His voice was frail and weak.

'You are in no position to make demands,' — Angus stood, — 'choose, or I will choose your fate for you.' Angus glanced at the guards in the hall.

'I was not alone!'

'Guards,' called Angus, 'have him ready for Offenmoor.'

His deep voice sent a shooting fear through Connor. 'Please! death! I choose death!' — The guards dragged Connor away. He continued to howl. — 'Kill me! Please, just kill me! Death, Angus! Angus!' His calls of anguish echoed through the central hall of the palace. Finally, the calls died. The guards placed him in a cart at the front of the palace and took him to the first quarter to await his fate.

Sat silently in the woodland, Harris lit a fire. Branwen hadn't spoken since leaving. Travelling on the back of the small mare given to them by Lukas. Her soft hair turned to straw. Healing wounds still filled her tender skin. The blood was gone. A soldier gave her a tunic and some trousers. Her skin was clean from the clay of the caves, but the memory of that night sat heavy on her.

The woodlands offered little solace to Branwen. She felt neither hot nor cold as she watched the licking flames.

'Once you're safe in Sonnin, I'll be going back to Cronnin. I need to ensure that this is dealt with accordingly.' Harris sat beside the fire. The flames danced in her glaring eyes. 'Bran.' He tried to get a response from her.

'Smoke,' she uttered. Harris sat back. A look of sympathy caught his eyes. 'I remember smelling smoke.'

'I know,' he whispered.

For the first time, she looked into his eyes. 'I was so scared. I remember thinking how much I needed you there.'

Harris stood and marched towards her. He dropped by her side and held her close. 'I'm here now,' he tenderly said. 'I couldn't think of living, knowing you were gone.'

Branwen narrowed her eyes towards him. 'How?' Her voice quivered. She sniffed her nose and sat back. 'How did you know? Cronnin would only have found out today. How did you know so fast?'

Harris leant back. He held his index finger up. 'That is an interesting question.' He held her hands. 'You once mentioned, Librye, Angus's ward.' He sat beside her and gazed at the flames. 'She's certainly interesting. The moment it happened; she knew. She's a Solnox, but there's something else with her. Her powers are beyond belief.' His words held pride in Librye.

He glanced at Branwen, who hunched over with her elbows resting on her knees. 'I can honestly say, if one person can force me to settle, it's Librye.' His smile broadened. 'She's so small, but so big at the same time. Her mind is a maze of knowledge, and she's only seven,' — he spun to Branwen, — 'you'll meet her, soon.' He sat back with a breath. 'She will love you.'

'Do you think?' Finally, she smiled. 'I can't wait to meet her.' Branwen finally turned, twisting her tired body towards Harris. 'My mother never sent word. She sent no one to bring me home. Why do you think that is?'

Harris narrowed his eyes. 'Your mother didn't want you leaving with the third. They've become a target, so she was planning to have you come back with a small guard. I'm sure she was arranging it.'

Branwen turned back, looking at the flames. Memories danced in her mind. 'Why would they act like that?' — her lips gaped as she spoke — 'the coblyn have never attacked such a place.'

'Your brother,' — his eyes narrowed, — 'before he died, he told me that Kairne will soon gather a new army. He suspected the silence of the torbs, but I knew they wouldn't do such a thing. The coblyn was a genius move by Kairne.'

'Genius?' Scowled Branwen. 'Genius, to manipulate a placid creature. To tear apart an army—'

'I apologise, I didn't mean it like that.' Harris stayed his hands, reaching over, he took her hands in his. 'This is war, Bran. We see things differently. The only thing that concerns me is that for the coblyn to join the Atlanti forces, Kairne must have something massive planned.'

Branwen lifted, sitting straight. She pulled her hands away from him. 'Something more than Marrion?'

Harris nodded. 'This isn't the end, Bran.'

'What do you believe they have planned?'

'That doesn't matter now. I have plans to stop it before it's too late.'

'And what plans are these?' She narrowed her eyes.

'Never you mind,' — he gleamed a smile towards her, — 'in the meantime. I know it's a lousy moment, but I need to mention it. How are you feeling about us?'

'Honestly.' She raised her brows towards him. Her eyes were still red with tears which had now dried. 'Better. Anna, she helped me.' Branwen's smile grew. 'When you left, I stayed in the commander's chambers, helping Anna in whatever way I could. Our talks helped. She knew about us,' — her smile withered as she gazed down, — 'I suppose that doesn't matter now.'

'Anna would tell no one. She was one of the few I trusted. I'll miss her.'

'Either way, I am glad to have you as my friend, Harris. Although, you could've written more,' she scolded.

'I would have, but Librye is demanding, and I was very busy—'

'I will not accept such poor excuses in Sonnin,' she said, her smile gleamed. Relief hit Harris, knowing she would eventually heal. She would never forget that day, but it would not taint her life forever.

The Sonnin woodland lit. Songbirds enlivened the summer forest. An evening rain left a fresh smell drifting through from the long grasses in the far meadows. It was a beautiful relief. Riding in on the white mare, Branwen came through the palace gates. Harris followed on Svend. The guards stood gawping at the sight of them.

Stepping into the palace hall, Harelda shot from a room at the back of the plinth. Her arms widened as she ran towards Branwen.

'My girl!' cried Harelda, embracing Branwen. She twisted to Harris. 'I am indebted to you, Commander.' A dewy tear formed in her hardened eyes.

Harris softly replied, 'It was my pleasure, my queen. I did this for me, as much as you.' Harelda gave a dark look towards Harris. 'Branwen, and I,' he paused, looking down. His voice was soft. 'We have a history in saving each other's lives.' He gave a huff of a laugh before he went on. 'Let's just say, whenever we need each other, we seem to be there.'

His twisted smile towards Branwen caused her to laugh. 'He's very right, we do indeed have a colourful past,' — Branwen twisted to Harris, — 'thank you, commander. For again, saving my life, we are both indebted to you.' Her wide smile grew. 'Please, stay, at least for one night, before returning.'

Harris shook his head. 'My work isn't over.' He glanced at Harelda. 'I need to find the person responsible.'

The slate icy glare from his eyes sent shivers through Harelda. She enjoyed it.

'They already have.' She strutted towards her chambers at the side. 'Connor. They will execute him at the start of Nean.' She stepped into her chamber, Branwen and Harris followed. He touched her soft hand as Harelda's back turned. They both stood in the doorway. 'They believed he sent the letter without consent from the council.' She spun to face Harris. Immediately, he moved his hand and tilted his head towards her. 'I believe more is at play. That will be your task.'

'Wonderful,' — he twisted his smile, — 'because we all know how much I love work.'

Harelda gave a quick blink. 'Harris, I know you have ways of finding out. You and Librye work well together. I'm sure Librye will be more than willing to help. Now, go, you will make it back before nightfall if you leave now.'

Branwen did not want Harris to go, but she did not want to raise her mother's suspicions. She watched from the hall as Harris left towards the stairs. He gave a quick glance back over his shoulder before making his way up the stairs, back towards Cronnin.

With the night lingering, Harris made his way through the Cronnin city. The guards on the turrets offered their respects to those in Marrion. The Cronnin flags were at half-mast. Harris passed through the gates. The soldiers on the streets stood with their spears held horizontal. Their heads bowed low. Harris jumped from Svend. He sauntered through the city. The people, who would usually go about their business, stopped.

They each lined the streets and stood silently with their heads held down. As the commander passed by, whispers were silent. Losing Marrion hung heavily in the air. A few branches tore his tunic as he had thundered towards the Una Forest. Red clay still covered his boots. They did not care about the state of him. He had shown a bravery, none of them had ever before seen. The shadow, the commander, the wolf, earned his title and more.

Walking through the east corridor towards his tower at the end, Harris paused outside Librye's room. He stepped towards the door and listened. Her calm, sleeping breath comforted him. Taking a moment, he left towards his tower.

A dull blue glow from the fire flowers showed someone waited in his chambers. His tired legs thumped up the stairs. Godfrey sat at his desk, patiently waiting.

'I appreciate you being here so late,' said Harris as he approached him.

'The letter sounded rather urgent,' Godfrey shook as he stood. His frail bones could hardly carry him. 'Are you injured?'

'Not at all,' said Harris with a wide grin.

'Then why?' Godfrey lowered himself back down.

'The alchemist's guild,' said Harris. He hurried towards his desk, taking his harness strap off. It clanged as he dropped it at the side of the desk. 'When I was a child, my mother insisted, I learnt all I could. I did well, but there are certain aspects where I need a more experienced hand.'

Godfrey nodded. 'I am sure Grendel could've helped with such a task. You have only just returned from Sonnin.'

'He could, I'm sure, but this matter is far too delicate for an alchemist in the ear of a queen.'

Godfrey sat back. 'I see,' he mumbled. 'Harris, commander. I know you have a stout reputation. They ban alchemists from war for the very reason you clearly took lessons.'

'You disagree with my tactics?'

'I don't know a single alchemist who agrees, however, I note that your reasons lie beyond winning a simple battle,' — he shook his head and sat forwards, — 'whatever you have planned, with the movement of the coblyn, it must see an end to this.'

Harris looked at his desk, a moment of thought passed by. 'If you are in the king's ear, I cannot ask you to help with this. He must remain ignorant.'

'I know why, Harris. The question I have is what?'

'My return from Marrion saw me to a village stricken with a plague. I'd only ever seen it once before, when it took my father. It wasn't the murk; his convulsions differed. I heard them in the village showing the same signs. It was the only time my mother truly protected me by keeping me away from him.'

'And now you plan to unleash this?'

'I plan something, but the less you know, the better it will be for all. The illness is currently in a liquid form. It takes a long time to spread. What I need from you is to—'

'Say no more,' Godfrey hovered his hand up. 'If you have the sample, I will do all I can. When the council knock at my door for answers, what do I tell them?'

'Nature has a strange way of creating balance. This war will end.'

CHAPTER FIFTEEN

15

A chill cascaded through Harris's chambers. A broken window allowed the morning dew to rest on the papers of his desk. The tower still required work. He would toil away, while specialist teams from Elmoor fixed his cracked windows.

Sat at his desk, Harris had not woken Librye that morning. The city streets filled with a torrent of sympathy. He didn't want it. He could not bear sympathy. With Nean only a half turn away, he would enjoy seeing the end of Connor.

Harris sensed her eyes. Looking at him, Librye stood on the other side of Harris's desk. His eyes stayed locked on the papers in front of him.

He stayed motionless. 'Is there something you need, tiny one?'

'Is she alright?' Librye kept giving Harris an intense stare. Her nose barely reached his desk.

He placed his quill down, while giving a weighty sigh, and rubbing his face. 'She will be, eventually.' His brows furrowed towards her. 'Why would you ask?'

'I saw how you left. I saw what you did. Do you love her?'

'I often have to remind myself that you are a child.' His smile grew as he sat straight. 'You could say that. There are many ways of showing love. Empathy, kindness, mercy, forgiveness.' His voice was soft, broken.

'Does that mean those in Marrion, those you let live? Do you love them?' Librye hushed her voice.

Harris's voice was tender. 'We must show love to all, otherwise the world stops turning, misery takes over, and we have nothing left to fight for. Branwen, however, she was my nurse in Marrion.'

'I know it isn't my place, but what was she nursing you for?'

Harris raised his brows and took a deep breath. He sat back and gazed into Librye's questioning eyes. He did not want to frighten her, he wanted to be as honest as he could.

'Would you like to see?' Librye nodded. Harris untucked his tunic and lifted it to reveal the scar on his chest and back. 'Arrow went straight through. It was Branwen who had to push it through to get it out. She nursed me back to health, were it not for her, I would not be here now. Also, caught one in the knee.'

His tender voice spoke volumes to Librye. She felt the scar on his back. 'Did it hurt?'

Harris raised his brows and gave a comical look forwards. 'Like you wouldn't believe.'

As she leant over, he noticed her dress was slightly red. He dropped his tunic and sat. 'Librye, turn around.' Librye did as asked. He saw the strange lumps on her back. Small dots appeared through her dress. 'Librye, you're bleeding.' He swirled her back. 'What happened?'

Librye peered down. Her eyes drifted about the floor. 'They're just bleeding, that's all. The torbs, they will eventually sort them.' Harris furrowed his brow; his mouth gaped. 'My wings, Harris, I have wings, like a torb, but something went wrong.'

Harris raised his brows further. 'Ha,' he grunted. 'When does Angus plan on taking you?'

Librye shook her head. 'I don't know.' Librye softly placed her hand on his injured knee. She could see that his kneecaps did not quite match each side. 'Did you know this is still broken?'

Harris drew back, unsure what to think he leered at her with his head twisted. 'It's not broken, just painful, it'll heal with time.'

Librye shook her head, her lips held tightly together as her tiny hand sat firmly on his knee. Warmth filtered into his knee. He watched in awe as his kneecap sank back to normal. The pain left. Librye's hand remained. He watched, shocked.

'You are not just Solnox,' he muttered. Her eyes lowered. 'Tiny one,' he spoke softly, 'what do you see?'

It would have been a strange question, but not for Librye. 'I see a field, swamped in red. Armour, laying everywhere, spears sticking out of the ground, I see a cliff, and a man at the top.' Her words haunted him. 'You burnt them with the blue sin.' She pulled her hand away and stepped back, waiting for Harris to explain himself. Her head perked up.

For the first time in a long time, Harris felt ashamed. 'Vitriol oil,' he muttered, 'it's war, Librye. It isn't nice, and neither am I.' Harris shot from his desk and tucked his tunic back in. 'Come on, I owe you a dress.'

'Harris, wait!' She remained at the desk. Harris twisted. 'I am supposed to be learning from you.'

'You will, but lessons take time, and I have a war to sort out, so your education can be slowed slightly.'

'I am learning some things, and I know you know a lot of things—'

'Debatable.'

'But killing people like that, how?'

'They aren't really people,' he stuttered. 'Well, they are people, but when you're out there, and swords are flying, people are screaming, and they're all trying to kill you, it makes it easier.'

'Killing should never be easy.'

'Well, when you're older, you'll understand.'

'That's your answer to a lot of things.'

'Yes, it is,' he replied with a sharp nod.

'It doesn't answer the question, though.' Her concern worried him. He paused for a moment and crouched in front of her. His knee felt fine.

'What question, tiny one? Ask me again.'

'How can I kill someone, and it be easy, without using magic?'

'You can't. That is the simple answer. You must learn many things, Librye. I am not here to teach you how to take a life, that will never happen. Your duty is to learn all you can about repairing the world I am trying to break.'

'Break?' She tightened her eyes.

He reached out, putting his hand on her shoulder. 'Ending a war, Librye, it leaves the world confused, broken, as we emerge from the shattered remains of our homes, we realise the colossal mistake we have made, and you will be there to ensure that not only this never happens again but also to make the Atlanti see we can live in harmony.'

'You're not a very harmonious person, though.'

Harris grinned. 'No, but I can be.'

Librye's eyes struck with a moment of thought. 'Harelda once said you have the merrow in you. What did she mean?'

'I have merrow blood. One of few,' — he rose from the ground, — 'why?'

'The stars told me about the merrow. They are a peaceful people.'

'I know they are.'

Librye lowered her head, looking at the ground. 'Because Xencliff people are as well. I suggested that you talk to your mother, but if you involve Xencliff in this, then the merrow will also be forced.'

Harris chuckled. 'The merrow are peaceful, but they are not the kind of peaceful you think. The merrow would help this effort, but I have nothing planned with them yet.'

'And what about Xencliff?' A narrowing of Harris's eyes concerned her. 'The coblyn are innocent in this. The Atlanti disturbed their peace. The quicker it stops, the better it will be for them.'

'Tiny one, the coblyn made their choice. If the Atlanti have some hold over them, they can get a message to us and we will do all we can to help. We don't need Xencliff, or the coblyn, we only need Bourellis to help you. I have enough plans to see us through this war without bringing others into it.'

'Why haven't the stars told me your plans? Or my secrets?' she asked, tightening her eyes.

Harris grinned. 'Because I haven't told the stars, and your secrets clearly don't want you to know. Librye, if your secrets are voices from the gods, then they know meddling in the affairs of man can cause more harm than good. They do not guide you, they are not there to tell you what to do, or how to live your life. They are there to comfort you.

'Librye, your secrets know the challenge which lies ahead. All your secrets can do is talk, and hope you make it through.'

Librye watched Harris walk from the chambers. He knew more than anyone she had spoken to before, and she didn't know how. He knew more about her secrets than she did, he knew more about the Solnox than what she would deem as normal. His mind was a cesspit of knowledge, and it was all knowledge she wanted.

Needing to escape, Harris held Librye's hand through the busy streets of the city. Whispers in doorways grew Harris's grin. Tavern pornes hung from their windows, but their wonder remained, why Harris had not yet visited a single tavern.

Their return from the market was a triumphant one. It saw Librye in a new lime green dress with silver trim.

Stood by her wardrobe, Maude struggled to find space.

'Harris!' she scolded as he walked past towards Angus's chambers. He peered in.

'Why?' she sighed.

Harris stepped inside, holding some parchments. He shrugged, not knowing what the issue was.

'She has enough. Why get her more?'

Harris looked at the parchments he was carrying. 'I live my life vicariously.' He sniggered. Maude was not smiling, nor laughing, and he noticed. 'Look, I had none of those things. I like to treat her. That shouldn't be a problem. We have plenty of rooms she can use. The lords of the land no longer visit because of the danger. We don't need all these rooms.'

Maude softened her face. 'I believed you grew up on the cliffs?'

Harris nodded. 'I did, yes.'

'But you had nothing?' Maude softened her voice further.

'I never deserved it. We give gifts to those who learn, do as they're told and behave. I could do none of those things,' — he widened his smile, — 'I was lucky to have rags.'

'You were a challenge for your mother?'

'And then some.'

'So, it wasn't all her fault?' Librye crept from her washroom.

Harris did not know she was there. He sheepishly replied, 'No, but her punishment was too harsh for a child who wasn't allowed to mourn for his father or' — he looked around the room. — 'Never mind.' Harris left towards Angus's chambers.

The guards at Angus's door stood to the side to let Harris pass.

Stepping into the chambers, a distinct smell of smoke drifted through. 'Someone's having a bad day,' said Harris.

'Is there ever a good day anymore?'

Harris paused. 'I never took you for a cynic.' He continued walking. 'Well, I have some good news that could brighten your evening.'

Angus leant forwards. 'Anything, Harris.'

'I have a final count for Belgravia, Tosta, and Roe. It's not looking good.'

Angus gaped. 'How is that good?'

'Because now we know how truly fucked we are.' Harris's smile gleamed. He sat in the chair in front of the desk.

'Please tell me you have more than that.'

'Of course, I wrote to Egan, bidding our farewell. If the dragons refuse to help our cause they can at least hold some of the guilt.'

'Harris, I must admit, I expected more,' Angus groaned, disappointed.

'Well, that's just stuff I can tell you. Haven't written to my mother, and I won't be writing to her. But one thing I need to add is the less you know, the safer it will be for all.'

'So you have something planned?'

'Always,' snickered Harris.

Angus sat forwards, widening his eyes, and lifting his brows. 'Well?'

Harris shook his head. 'Well, I won't be telling you. You're the king, Angus. The moment the Atlanti accept their fate, everything will be looked at with prying eyes. Your involvement in this war must remain limited.'

'Why?'

'To absolve you of your guilt.'

Angus reached to his draw and took out his pipe. Packing it, he reclined back. The smell never bothered Harris.

'For goodness' sake!' spat Afie. She stormed into the room. 'Harris, remove his pipe!' she commanded.

Harris twisted in his chair. 'I will do no such thing,' he softly replied, turning back to Angus.

Coming towards the desk. Her long, wide black skirt appeared to arrive long before she did. 'Have you written to your mother yet?' A stern frame crept above Harris as he remained seated.

'Certainly not,' Harris calmly replied.

'Harris, commander. You must realise, placing all personal issues aside for the sake of the kingdom will have no one looking down on you.'

'I don't care about that,' sniggered Harris. 'Yes, we need Xencliff but only if my plan doesn't work.'

'And what plan is this?'

'A plan he refuses to reveal,' sneered Angus. Harris grinned wildly.

'Oh Harris, come on, tell him something.'

'My mother is the whore of the king, my father is dead. I care little for ale,' — he looked back at Afie, — 'Is that what you mean?'

'My father was a rather nice man,' groaned Angus. 'I do not know why so many celebrated his passing.'

'Your father was a bastard,' said Afie, glaring at Angus. 'You knew this. You also knew your mother did all she could to escape him, but he poisoned you against her.'

'Afie,' Harris spun towards her. 'I like you more each day.' His smile widened. 'An honest woman, the world needs more of them.'

'You'll only ever get honesty from me.' She glared at Harris. Finally, he realised what she was looking for and leapt from the chair to offer her a seat. 'Thank you.' She lowered herself into the chair. 'Now,' — she folded her hands onto her lap. — 'Are you going to tell us anything?'

'My parents have been a talking point for so long,' said Harris. 'I would rather like to hear more about his?' He looked at Angus.

Angus glared at her. His eyes turned to cold steel. 'If you must.'

'Your mother was a wonderful woman,' she began, slightly lowering her harsh tone. 'However, she was given to your father by King Farrier, of Volnot, as his only daughter. He would not listen to her plight. Your father was horrible to her. She did not wish to have the company of men.' Her tone lowered as she leant forwards. 'She preferred women. You were her everything.' Her voice became soft. 'She hated leaving you behind. But knew that the only way to restore our relations with the dragons. Was to make the people see just how cruel your father was. Even if it meant ending her own life.'

Angus listened to every word she said. 'I loved my mother and my father. But here we are, they're both dead.' He sat forwards and glared at Harris. 'Harris, you can wipe that stupid grin from your face now.'

'Apologies,' smirked Harris. 'I think I would've liked your mother a lot,' he commented.

'Well, so did I, but perhaps you could take this as a chance to repair what is left of your relationship with your mother?'

'No, the ice-cold claws of death could not force me. You certainly won't.'

'Why so hostile?' asked Afie.

'Some things cannot be repaired. I can give my blessings to you to attempt a reconciliation with Xencliff, but I cannot and will not be there.'

'Stubbornness is the sister of regret, Commander,' said Afie.

'Ha,' — he huffed — 'sister, yes. Either way, I will build nothing with Xencliff, throw me in the taverns like she did, lock me in a dungeon, and beat me half to death. Starve me,' — he shrugged — 'she made me this stubborn, and I have my reasons.' Harris wandered from the chambers, his mood twisted from a bright, gleeful cheer to a sombre, melancholy depression.

'A glorious morning.' Kairne stepped into his chambers with his arms held stretched.

Isradella sat on a sofa by the fire. 'It's very cold here,' she mentioned.

Kairne lowered his arms. 'You're displeased?'

'Not at all,' she oddly replied. Many noticed her oddities, from her maids to the soldiers. Her midnight walks into the haunting woodland barefoot, a strange, lost look remained in her eyes.

'Well, we have the first victory of many.' He rushed towards her and kissed her cheek. Isradella stood. A smile widened; her brows lifted. 'The coblyn has succeeded. They have taken Marrion, the south is in anarchy, and they head this way.'

'The coblyn?' sneered Isradella. 'I would rather not see such creatures.'

'Why? They are our army now, part of our people.'

'They are no such thing!' she spat. 'They are disgusting.' Kairne wandered towards his desk. 'The creatures are not welcome in this world,' Isradella hissed.

'You sound like the fae. The Atlanti were never welcome, either.'

'No, the Atlanti are the rulers. It is jealousy. But those creatures.' Her hate for the coblyn confused him. 'I think my time would be best spent with a visit to my mother.'

Kairne smirked. 'How?' Isradella looked at him blankly. 'The war drains us. We have no one to take you. A carriage would cost too much. I cannot spare a single body to take you to Arktos. A ship alone would break us. You pledged your life to me, Isradella, despite that, no child.'

Isradella lowered her head. 'I have been trying.'

'Clearly not hard enough, and now you wish to travel to Arktos. No child can be conceived when my wife journeys to the other side of Cammbour.' His voice rose. Isradella felt her confidence weaken. 'You are going nowhere.'

'My mother may need a vis—'

'You are going nowhere!' he yelled. His voice echoed through the halls.

'Apologies. I understand,' she softly replied.

'Such a glorious morning!' Harelda stood in the hall of the Sonnin palace tree. She made her way into her chambers to the left of the hall. Stepping inside, she saw Branwen sat waiting for her.

'Your plans for today?' Harelda walked around her desk to sit.

Branwen had missed the extravagance of the palace. She sat radiantly in her chair. A long blue fae gown flowed on the floor.

She replied with a sorrowful whisper, 'I would like to think I have plans, but sadly, I have nothing left.'

Harelda's brows dropped. 'You miss it, don't you?'

'Somewhat. I can't deny that feeling needed. At first it was addictive.' She sighed. 'But then, you realise your true worth.'

'I have felt it too. The end of service can often lead to a more fulfilling role, therefore it is insisted upon. To serve your people, at a great time of need, it is not only for them but also for you, Branwen.'

Branwen understood. Even so, it did not make her feel any better. 'I feel empty, Mother.' She sorrowfully sighed. 'I don't know what I have planned today. Or the next day, or days following that.'

Harelda leant forwards. Her deep tone threw Branwen. 'Then you have completed your task, next on your agenda, is to strengthen our kingdoms.' Her suggestion was fair. Branwen knew it would only be a matter of time.

'What if, I have someone in mind?'

Harelda sat back. A look of wonder and concern drenched her face. 'Then I would insist you tell me who?'

Branwen did not know how to reveal her truth, but she knew what she wanted. 'I think you've met him—'

Harelda stood. Her hands slammed to her desk. A dark mood fell on the room. Her deep, booming voice sent a thunderous shiver through Branwen. Her blood ran cold.

'If you say Harris Bearwood, I will have you both!'

'Mother, I—'

'Don't try it girl!' Harelda warned. Her frightening demeanour terrified Branwen. 'I like Harris, he is valuable to me, to this world even, our kingdom will reward him, but not with you!'

Branwen stood, shocked. Harelda had never spoken to her with such anger. Branwen had her answer. 'I was going to suggest Angus.' Branwen saved herself from her mother's bitter warning.

Harelda sat. She took a moment to calm. She thought for a while. 'I like Angus. However, he is too old.'

'Age is but a number,' laughed Branwen. 'Besides, he is faemen, he has less than eighty years left. Which will eventually leave the throne to me. Also, I feel that the council of Cronnin could use a dose of Sonnin culture.'

Her highbrow attitude forced a smile from the corner of Harelda's mouth. 'You can't wed someone you don't know. It may call for some time in Cronnin,' replied Harelda. 'Ready yourself, Librye is a wonder to behold.'

They reserved the first quarter of the Cronnin city for the most iniquitous villains the city offered. The small holding cells were enough to sit, not even lie. A small bucket to relieve themselves. Food would comprise something similar the farmers would feed to the pigs. Sat in his misery, Connor silently reflected on his life. His dirt filled rags stank of the surrounding filth. His fingers were now black with the grime in the small cell. He accepted his fate; anything would be better than Offenmoor.

The rattling of heavy chains kept him awake at night. He would have to wait for his misery to end. With only one per day being led to execution, he had seven in front of him.

The gates to the city bustled with trade. The King's Guard was out in force, as Angus joined Librye and Harris for their morning commute. Maude joined them that morning, being treated to a sweetbread from Harris. She made her way back towards the palace with Librye. Harris and Angus strolled towards the first quarter, over an hour's walk from the palace.

'The city is busy this time of year,' mentioned Harris. He took a bite of his sweetbread.

'It's the trade market's next turn. The back quarter to the northern gate. Will open to trades from around Cammbour, Thrasia, Xencliff, even Qasar and Amerius. They usually begin now. They'll all leave before winter bites us.' He bit into his sweetbread. Harris noticed a small crowd gathering. He could hear calls from the people, bidding them a 'good morning.'

'So, the trades begin soon, so what will this mean for the safety of Cronnin?'

Angus gave a rumbling laugh. 'We see every inch of this city from those walls.' He gazed at the towering white walls which guarded the city. 'They built Cronnin on dipped land, meaning the walls stand on the highest part of the city's foundations. There is nothing the guards don't see. The city is safe.'

They made their way along the busy streets. The market traders rubbed their hands as they saw them coming. Harris liked to spend. They both had an affection for a certain young lady in their lives. The jewellers were a favourite for them both. Emerald necklaces, gold bangles and bracelets. Even a tiny fire flower head diadem Harris just knew she would love.

Spending over four-hundred gold coins and 3 chains. The book seller was well on his way towards an entire turns trade.

They came towards the first quarter. Harris and Angus stepped through the tall gates and into the death arena. A kennel-like structure ran down the side of the high walls.

The yard swarmed with guards. The smell of sweat and bodily fluids burned their eyes.

'You made it then.' The guard came towards Harris.

The guard was a tall black slim man, his eyes were the colour of hard worn slate, he stood proud within his yard of death.

'What's on for today, Theo?' Harris stepped towards him.

Theo peered at the back of him. The cell to the end housed the prisoner for the day. Theo escorted them towards the cell. He hit the cell with his short sword, making the man jump.

'Smile, Keith.' The man glanced up, his hair drenched with filth. Sticky mud dried to his clothes. 'Your king is here to see you.' Keith simply glared towards the filth he sat in; he lost hope in everything. The stench from the cells forced Angus to cover his nose with a small handkerchief from his pocket. 'Keith thought it would be a good idea to take the lives of his wife and four children during Onmidden.' His smile twisted. He glared at Keith. 'In his drunken state, his lover found him sleeping beside them.'

Harris's lip curled with disgust. 'I remember the warrant well.'

Angus wandered on. Theo followed Angus towards a viewing bench at the side of the gallows. They led Keith out of his small cell. The fresh air on his skin and the warm sun in his eyes chilled him. He saw the noose fall from the old wooden crossbar. They forced him up the steps.

'So, the next thing we need to think about is getting an army to Marrion. We need to take it back.' Harris's eyes followed Keith up the steps.

The muffled sound of the executioner sounded dull in the small arena.

'The very thought of it terrifies me.' Angus glanced to Harris and back towards the gallows.

Harris reclined back, using the raised bench at the back to rest his elbows. 'We still need to try.' He watched. Keith had a moment of relapse. Three guards forced him towards the rope as it swung provocatively in the breeze. Muffled sounds of Keith struggling swirled in the air.

'Try as much as you like.' Angus glanced towards Harris. 'We lost Marrion. Now we need to fortify our defences surrounding.'

Keith stood at the gallows. The executioner gave his last order. In a deep voice, he grumbled. 'Keith Dune Duhanon. We hereby find you guilty of the mass extinction of life. You shall be hanged by the neck until dead. May the gods weigh your transgressions.' He stepped to the side and pulled the trapdoor. Keith's legs flailed out, he struggled and spun. Like an un-fallen leaf, he vibrated below the rope.

'Ooh!' called Harris. 'That's going to hurt in the morning.' He sat up straight. 'So, if you think Marrion is a lost cause, can I at least try?' Angus glared at him from under his brow. 'Just try?' His eyes tightened, and nose wrinkled.

'How can I say no?' Harris's vague attempt to be charming took him. 'Very well, but your priority is still with the ongoing battles. Belgravia and Tosta are the first ones you need to sort out. Then work on Roe. Following that, Marrion.'

'I can do that. I need one thing though,' he stood. They made their way back towards the gates. Sat in the end cell close to the gate, Connor watched. 'I need a blind eye,' he softly said to Angus. 'And for you to turn it,' he nodded, wide eyed. 'Remember, ask no questions, get no lies.'

Angus puffed his cheeks slightly. 'What you do is your business. I need no part in it.'

As they left, Harris peered at the end cell. He took his sword from his sheath. Smashing his sword against the bars of the cell, the eyes of Connor glared towards Harris. His face was now caked with dirt and filth, his wrinkles stood out more.

'See you in Nean, the depths of Tataria await your arrival.' Harris glared at him. Connor did not argue. He grabbed the bars, glaring towards Harris. A sorrowful look in his eyes withered and died. His hope left him. Angus had nothing to say to Connor. He walked from the gate with Harris and his guards.

Arriving back at the palace, they were both met with a scornful look from Maude. She stood at the bottom of the stairs.

'There you are!' She thundered towards them. 'You both spoil her far too much!'

Harris and Angus laughed as they meandered towards her. 'I got you something.' Harris immediately stopped Maude. She came towards them. Her brows furrowed as Harris reached into a coin purse on his belt. He took out a small necklace, a single purple fire flower hung as a charm. 'I wouldn't leave you out.'

Maude was beside herself, in awe of the pendent. 'Thank you, Harris.' Angus whirled to Harris. He had failed to get Maude anything. His eyes widened towards him, and lips pressed tightly together. 'Despite that, you both need to stop spoiling her so much. She has hardly any space left in her room.'

Angus retired to his chambers and Harris to his tower. Harris strolled towards the east tower and peered into Librye's open room.

'Did you like it?' His smile was so wide, his eyes almost closed. She sat at her dressing-table, trying on the necklace and diadem Harris had sent back for her.

She shot from her table and bolted towards him. 'Thank you, Harris.' She threw her arms around him.

'You're quite welcome,' laughed Harris. He crouched in front of her and held her hands. 'Now, you stay here. Take the day to do exactly as you please. I have some sensitive matters to tend to,' he insisted. Knowing it was likely she would follow him.

Librye did as asked and remained in her room. She heard Harris make his way towards his tower.

His day of working would be short. He sent his orders to Belgravia and Tosta.

The sweet summer sun warmed his room. The soft breeze crept through, taking the soft curtains with it as they danced in the breeze. All was well in Harris's mind.

The door to the tower below his chambers creaked open. Harris listened, sat at his desk. He heard the slow pounding of footsteps coming up the stairs. He glanced up to see Godfrey. Slowly and exhaustedly, he climbed the stairs.

'I would've come to you myself.' Harris watched Godfrey struggle up the last few stairs. His delicate frame concerned Harris.

'No need,' laughed Godfrey. Astonishingly out of breath, he finally reached the floor of the chambers. 'You've made quite the impact so far.' Godfrey ambled towards Harris's desk. He struggled to lift his head. His neck filled with age. His bones barely supported his weight anymore.

'Impact?' asked Harris. 'It's what I do,' he chuckled. He watched Godfrey make his way towards the desk. He did not offer to help, knowing that at Godfrey's age, dignity was everything. He respected his right to struggle.

Finally, Godfrey reached for his desk. Slowly, he sat in the chair opposite and placed a leather-bound box on the desk.

'I assume you know what you're doing?' Godfrey stared towards Harris. His small eyes struggled to widen through the wrinkles.

Harris reached forwards. He took the box and placed it in front of him. 'You were successful?' He widened his eyes from under his brow towards Godfrey. His hands flattened on the desk, either side of the box.

Godfrey gave a single low nod. 'Very,' his deep tone echoed through the room. 'Pestilence, Harris, it's a dangerous game.'

Harris did not pay any heed to his words of warning. He opened the box. Three separate vials sat inside. They appeared empty.

'I know, the Atlanti pissed off The Commander. The gods will now make them pay.'

'You liken yourself to the gods?' Godfrey sat back in his chair, unable to hold his laughter.

'I play my part in this. If the gods believe I'm wrong, then may they strike me down.'

'A piece of advice from an old man,' — Godfrey rose. — 'Your actions now matter not. Look to your future, your death bed awaits. The Kalanti on the bridge will weigh your guilt.'

Harris had no guilt; his actions were logical. He stood and placed the box into the draw of his desk. He glanced at Godfrey from under his brow with his head lowered.

'Tell me something, Godfrey.' He sat back in his chair; his elbows rested on the arms as his fingers caught in front of him. 'Do you have any guilt, in what you're helping me do?'

Godfrey raised his ageing brows; his eyes grew weary. 'None, Harris. You cannot replace a life by taking another.'

'No, you can't,' Harris leant forwards. He took his quill back in hand. 'But it gives me a lot of satisfaction to try.' He continued his work.

Godfrey stood. He ambled back towards the stairs until a thought came into his mind. He peered towards Harris from over his shoulder. 'Vengeance is a dangerous game. Know who you're dealing with. We live in a world of balance, create an imbalance, and you will suffer for it.'

'Suffering is something I do best,' murmured Harris, his eyes remained on the paper in front. He glanced up at Godfrey. He spun to leave. 'I'm righting a wrong. I am the balance.'

Rain fell on the city of Cronnin. The streets outside Harris's window emptied. The sounds of the city turned to a pattering of rain. The voices silenced. Before he finished his work for the turn, Harris had one last job to do. Making his way from his chambers, he donned a long, black leather cloak. The hood almost reached over his eyes and to his nose, completely covering his face. He wore his braces and boots, concealing the many weapons he carried.

Hurrying past Librye's door, he gave a quick glance, ensuring she was not there. The main hall was still. He reached the fountain. Balthus made his way towards him.

'Off to the barbers?' Balthus asked in a sarcastic tone.

Harris glared at him with his piercing green eyes. 'Don't try me, old man,' he warned with a twisted smile.

Balthus called to him, 'It would help your image!'

Harris shouted, 'My image is fine!' He liked his long locks of barbaric black hair. Leaving the door, he mumbled, 'Nothing wrong with my hair.'

Svend was ready to receive his rider. He waited in the palace's courtyard. Dark black skies poured with rain; it was Harris's favourite weather to ride in. He rode from the palace gates and into the city. Harris rode to the west gate, out of the city and hurried towards the Grenhilda valley. The roads were now dark. He rode towards Roma, a large town west of Cronnin city. The town shared its borders with the Grenhilda forest.

Falling rain dripped on the trees. The road splashed as Svend's hooves thundered by. They came out of the cold black wood and into the town of Roma. The Traveller's Rest was a tavern Harris was familiar with. He was not there for any physical attention.

Harris burst through the doors with his arms open wide. 'Harris!' came a call from the long bright brown bar, as the barkeep, John, widened his smile. 'Who are you here for today then, Commander?' Before Harris could answer, John called, 'Beth! He's back!'

A young blond woman stepped from the back of the bar. Her smile lit her pale face. Her light blue shining eyes widened at the sight of him. She came towards him as quickly as she could. Her slim frame did not have any effect on his solid body. He wrapped his arm around her tiny waist.

'I've missed you,' she whispered with a breath.

'And I you. All of you.' He glanced at the wide-open, busy tavern. 'However, I'm here on business. I'm here to see your father.' She released her grip and pouted her bottom lip. 'I'm sure I'll return soon,' he promised.

He lumped his elbows onto the bar. John glared at him from under his brow. 'Another favour?' John asked with a low grumble, 'how much this time?' He washed some tankers and placed them back on the shelf. Harris reached into his coin purse. He took the heavy leather bag as it rattled on the bar. John stopped what he was doing and spun. He placed his hands on the bar and glared towards Harris. His eyes widened towards the leather bag. 'How much, Harris?'

'There's enough to see the tavern through to next year,' replied Harris. John's eyes widened further. His lips parted towards the bag. 'It's a lot, John, but you know, I wouldn't give a lot unless I was asking a lot.'

'Shit, Harris,' commented John. He lifted the bag. 'What you done this time?'

Harris laughed. He leered at John and explained with a wide smile. 'I've done nothing.' John busied himself by pulling a pint of Command Ale for Harris. He placed it in front of him. 'You heard about Marrion, I assume?' Harris asked in a low tone.

John sucked air in through his tightly pressed lips. 'Nasty business that.' He shook his head.

'What part?' Harris narrowed his eyes at John. He took a drink of his ale as he listened.

'I know nothing much about what happened. That Branwen, she was the only one who lived, but the nasty part,' — John spun to carry on drying tankers. — 'That was your battle. We've all been watching, waiting, for The Commander's revenge.' A darkness in his eyes brought a silence to the busy tavern. The people coming and going passed quickly. Not wanting to get involved, not wanting to bother the commander. 'I can only assume now. That's why you're here?'

'John, you can say no.' Harris's eyes relaxed. He did not want to bring danger to anyone. Especially a family who had helped him so many times in the past.

John replied with a quiet and sincere voice, 'No, I can't.' He stopped his work and twisted back to Harris. 'You've saved this tavern from many problems. The least I can do is keep your secrets.' His trusting eyes forced Harris to take a small bag from the side of him, no larger than a coin purse. 'What's that?' asked John.

Harris glared at John with his intense green eyes. 'This is The Commander's revenge.' Harris's voice broke, knowing what he was about to unleash. 'I need you to take these, three vials, three pigeons, one to Marrion —'

'It wouldn't make it past the falcons,' John interrupted.

'I know, that's the idea.' Harris held a low tone. 'The second is to go to the Atlanti camp, to the east of Tosta. The third is the settlement of Belgravia.' He spelt a warning in his eyes. 'John, I need you to do this. Do not open them, do not let curiosity take over.'

John leant onto the bar; his eyes lit with curiosity. 'What's in them, Harris?' he whispered.

Harris peered over his shoulder. The tavern was busy, but they were all going about their business. He glanced back to John and whispered, 'Death, I am death, John, no one takes from The Commander.' With the first part of his plan done. He knew John would send them that night, and so he had to be fast with the second part.

He rode further west, towards the next village of Coyrome. The tavern there was small. A second traveller's rest called, 'The Old Inn.' Stepping inside, the tavern was empty. The small beams above him covered with years of dust, dirt, and grime. The floor was sticky, and a stench of stale ale hung in the air.

'Arris!' called the barmaid.

'Cally!' called Harris. He gleefully stepped inside.

'What can I get you?' Harris stepped towards the bar. Cally was a well-built woman. Her curled locks of messy orange hair reminded him of the chaotic Tharacka tree in the heat of summer. Her round figure fitted perfectly with her rosy-red cheeks and perfect smile. 'Or you can just have me if you like?' She winked as Harris sat at the bar.

He gave a slight shake of his head. 'Come on, Cally, the last time you nearly killed me. I can honestly say, though, given more time, I would gladly stay.' He lowered his tone. 'I need a favour.'

Harris slammed a coin purse on the bar, along with a letter. The thud of the purse caught Cally's attention. She glared at it. 'Oh! for the sake. What you done this time?'

Harris held his arms out. He replied in a high-pitched tone, 'I've done nothing!'

'Then why, Mr Bearwood, are you offering payment for a favour?' She lowered her brows.

'Cally,' sighed Harris, 'just send the fucking letter,' he moaned, 'don't read it, just send it.'

She narrowed her eyes and leered at him from the corner of her eyes. 'Why do I struggle to say no to you?'

Harris gave a broad smile. 'Because you love me,' he laughed. 'All letters to the taverns have to be marked from the sender. I don't want trouble for you. The letter is to be sent to Enderton, to your cousin, Sam.'

'Apologies, Harris.' Cally's tone of regret only made Harris smile. 'But, me and Sam 'ain't talked in an age. Letters aren't getting through. Everything is being taken by the Atlanti,' she softly explained. Harris gave a burning look of glee towards her. Cally spun, her look of regret twisted. She spotted Harris's cunning plan. 'Unless that's what you want?'

Harris's smile grew. 'Cally, the least you know, the better. I would never put my ladies in danger.'

Cally twisted to place some plates on the shelf behind her. 'Lady,' she laughed, 'that's something I ain't heard in a while,' she commented. As Cally swirled back, Harris left.

The door to the small tavern was slowly closing. 'Bye, Arris.' She lovingly looked towards the door.

His plan complete, Harris headed back towards Cronnin. The midnight moon hid behind gathering storm clouds. An overwhelming feeling of doom followed him through the gates of the city as the guards lifted them. A feeling of danger lingered in the air. He unleashed revenge on the world. Before the end of the turn, the name of The Commander would carry a terrifying curse. He would be known.

The smell of rain drifted in to Librye's window. The early morning mist crept along the floor of the cooling city outside. A knock at the door startled her.

'Come on, Librye, I want my sweetbread,' called Harris from the door.

'One moment!' As fast as she could, Librye rushed about her chambers getting dressed. She removed her nightgown, shocked to see the bloodstain on the back of it. In the night, she had again bled. She rushed to get dressed, hoping that the bleeding had stopped. Harris tapped his foot. He stood impatiently outside. 'I'll be out soon!'

Finally, the door opened, Librye emerged. 'Rough night?' Harris glanced at the state of her hair. 'You become more like me every day,' he sniggered. Librye tried her best to straighten her hair as they hurried towards the main hall.

They came down the stairs towards the hall. Harris dropped his enthusiasm. He saw a tall man stood with Angus, Kailron and Afie in the main hall.

'Ah.' The man called out gleefully seeing Harris approach. His hair was fair. He wore robes of the finest satin and silk. He stretched his title of Lord across every part of his person. 'And this is the man I am to thank?' He spun to Angus.

'Lord Arring,' Angus purred in a low tone upon seeing Harris and Librye approach. Angus was nervous. He knew Harris's opinion on many of the lords of Cronnin and was not sure how he would react. 'This is Harris Bearwood, the new CC to the crown.'

Lord Arring clearly did not see the spite in Harris's eyes. He held his head low. 'Lord Arring,' Harris grumbled as they came to the bottom of the stairs.

Librye remained close to Harris's side. She could see the look on Harris's face, and she did not like it. She reached out and held his hand. Harris broke his glare. 'Be nice,' she softly whispered.

'It's a pleasure.' Harris's mood instantly changed.

Lord Arring stepped closer. At first he was a decent gent, a kind man. He twisted, glaring towards Harris. 'Who would've thought, a commoner taking a rank like that.'

Harris gritted his teeth. He could feel his blood boiling, but he could also feel Librye's tiny hand tightening.

'Why so rude?' Harris raised his brows. He felt odd. The words he spoke did not seem like his.

'I simply point out a fact,' stumbled Lord Arring.

'A fact that needn't be spoken.' Harris's brows curled down. 'I understand you would be grateful. After all, you were vastly unprepared for the attack on Blodmoor.' He stepped closer, Librye's hand remained clutching his. 'Which begs the question. Of what happened to the funds that were released to your lands? To hire the correct defences.' Harris glanced down, unable to think of where the words came from.

'Harris, please,' said Angus.

Before Angus stopped Harris, Ryan, who had been listening to every word, stepped forwards. 'He has a point, my lord.' He came closer. Councillor Adamar, Bart, and Gurrand stepped from the council hall. 'If you wish to explain, then please, we are free to hear your fair explanation.'

Harris stood silently.

'My people were struggling for supplies. We've had to use most of the funds to support those in need.' Lord Arring's story was unconvincing.

'I shall leave this to you, gentlemen.' Harris peered around the hall to the gathering council. 'I have a sweetbread to collect.' Harris and Librye strolled past. He leant towards Afie, his brows raised, and a smile widened. 'Could I get you anything?'

Afie gave a smile to Harris. A sparkle in her eye pleased him. 'You have given me quite enough.' She leered back to the panicked Lord Arring.

As Librye and Harris left through the palace courtyard. Harris leant towards Librye. 'That was the strangest thing ever. Please don't put words in my mouth again.'

'It worked though; I saw.' Harris stopped. He glared at Librye, who twisted to him. 'I saw you wanted to hit him, to kill him possibly.' She ambled towards him. 'It would've got you in to more trouble. I simply saved you the hassle.'

'I don't need you to fight my battles, Librye,' replied Harris in a low tone.

Librye strolled towards him. 'I know you better than you realise, Harris. I have seen the days you wear a smile, but you've hardly slept that night.' Harris parted his lips. She strolled towards him. 'You smile through the pain. Standing upright, refusing to fall. Walking through all the madness of this world.' She raised her brows. 'Even crawling through some. You shouldn't have to do it alone.' Her voice filled with the pain she had seen in him so many times. 'I am here for you, Harris, I am here for us all.'

Harris furrowed his brow towards her. His mouth remained parted. 'They do not sound like your words, Librye.' A quiver in his voice sent shivers through her.

Librye replied, 'Because Aranwa wishes to send you that message.'

Her words crushed him. The goddess, Aranwa, he had not heard for a long time. Harris stepped closer to Librye. He crouched in front of her.

'The gods did not start this war. You can tell her I will end this. I'm never alone, Librye. I have a world on my side.'

CHAPTER SIXTEEN

16

The Dark Forest stretched from the borders of Elmoor to the North of Cronnin. A wide stretch of haunting woodland had taken many weary traveller's lives. For days, the small army, led by Gaius and Daniel, forced their way through the dense forest. Resting north of Enderton, their new army of coblyn remained deep in the shadows of the forest. Conversation with the creatures was scarce.

Sat at a small foldable desk in his tent, Gaius began reading the letters they had received while travelling. The canvas door opened. A broad soldier stepped in.

'Sir, we have a problem,' he sheepishly said.

Gaius rose from the desk, making his way from the tent. He silently followed the soldier and listened.

'We had word this morning of a rider. It was the coblyn who saw him and alerted a chief.'

'But what is the problem?' asked Gaius, wandering by the side of the soldier towards a black tent.

'The man is a messenger. He returns from Marrion to deliver news to Kairne.' His stuttering concerned Gaius. 'Well, see for yourself.' He lifted the door to the tent, handing a cloth to Gaius. 'You will need to cover your mouth.'

Gaius took the crude cloth, bending down as he crept in. He placed the cloth over his nose and mouth. A single bed was in the centre. The man, blue to the lips and eyes, lay motionless.

Gaius stood straight. 'Your name?'

The man turned his head. A rush of blood from his mouth was spat to the floor as he coughed. Gaius stepped back, horrified at the state of him.

'I was well when I arrived,' the man panted.

'Tell me what happened.' Gaius kept his distance.

'The castle, when I arrived, it was empty. The barbican was still. I went in. In every corner was a man dying. The castle moaned,' — the corners of his mouth curled downward, — 'it moaned.'

'The castle moaned?' asked Gaius.

The man exhaustedly nodded. 'It moaned,' he breathed. His eyes closed; his head drifted back.

Gaius stepped out of the tent. He threw the rag to the floor. His eyes twisted to the soldier at the side.

'Where is Daniel?'

'I've sent someone to bring him.'

'No one is to go into that tent. The moment that man dies, you burn it. No coblyn is to enter, not a single soul. Is that understood?'

The soldier nodded. Gaius spotted Daniel on a narrow path, coming towards the camp.

'You can't go in there,' Gaius called out.

Daniel pointed to his right. He marched with the line of tents towards a quiet part of the woodland.

As they arrived, Daniel asked, 'Well?'

'Pestilence,' said Gaius with a low rumble in his throat. 'The castle must have been teaming with it before we took it. It would only have been a matter of time, and it would've taken the fae instead.'

'You don't believe they had a hand in this?' asked Daniel.

Gaius took a moment to think. 'I don't know, but I doubt anyone would be evil enough to set about a plague.'

'This is Bearwood we're talking about.'

'Yes, but he let me live. I have to believe there's something good there.'

'Once again, this is Bearwood.'

'Regardless, Kairne will not be happy with this. We need to get back now.'

'You're working too hard,' Librye made her way from the doorway to Harris's chambers.

'I keep telling him that.' Maple placed another pitcher of water on his desk.

Harris glared towards Maple. 'You're the one keeping me here!' he argued.

Harris gazed at Librye; a wide smile grew. He glanced at the bright sunlight pooling in his window. 'I think you're right. How about a walk in the gardens? I'm yet to see them properly.'

Her smile grew. Harris and Librye made their way from the tower and towards the gardens. The bright sun brought the sweet scent of the lavender and rosemary lining the paths. Rose bushes lined behind.

'I'm still shocked at how clean the whole place is,' Harris commented, making his way with Librye towards the meadow.

'That was my first thought as well! Where would you like to go?' It excited Librye that Harris was finally in the gardens with her. Librye skipped in front of him, turning as she did. 'Where would you like to see?'

'Meadows, the temples perhaps?' asked Harris. Librye ambled in front. Harris strolled with her.

Harris saw two guards returning from the kennels. Both sweated in the summer heat as it beat down on them. As they came close to Harris and Librye, Librye passed them.

However, Harris heard the guard muttering with a snigger, 'The new palace sitter.'

Instantly, the sniggering stopped as Harris removed a front dagger. In the blink of an eye, he swung the guard around with his throat and locked his head with his forearm. Holding his blade close to the guard's neck.

'Hold your fucking tongue,' he warned with a whisper close to the guard's ear.

Librye ran towards them. 'Harris!'

The guard shook. 'Apologies, sir,' he begged, his eyes closed with anguish. Sweat fell from his brow. Harris glanced at Librye; his teeth gritted. 'Please,' whimpered the guard. The guard appeared baffled. 'It was just a comment, sir. Please, I meant no harm.'

Harris released his grip, allowing him to stand. He placed his dagger back in its holder. 'You are fucking lucky, boy,' Harris snarled, 'on your way.' With a vast sigh of relief, the guards left. 'At least I know what they're saying about me now,' he commented with a twisted smile.

Librye stood, horrified. 'Would you have killed that man?'

Her broken voice unhinged Harris.

'No,' he replied, shaking his head. He continued marching towards the lane to the meadow. 'I'm simply asserting my authority.'

'What if I wasn't here?' she wondered aloud.

Harris took a deep breath. 'Fist fight? I would've pelted shit out of them, then carried on, I suppose.'

'But that's not you anymore.'

'What do you mean?' His eyes narrowed towards her.

Librye stopped skipping ahead. She strolled by his side. 'It isn't you now, Harris, you know yourself. They watch you in the gardens. Connor's fate was because of a mistake he made. He thought he was right, it was a single mistake, that is the cost of a mistake here.'

A shiver ran down Harris's spine. His stomach weakened. 'Connor was different. His was not a mistake. It was a choice. He worked with the Atlanti. Besides, I haven't changed, tiny one.' They continued towards the lane. His voice was low, a deep feeling of shame filled his voice.

'Please, Librye, never think you know me, the things I've done, the things I still do—'

'Are for a reason,' she interrupted. 'I know what you did, Harris.' Her haunting tone shook him further.

Harris lowered his eyes. The lane to the meadow no longer felt so inviting. 'One day, they will judge me. I'm willing to take whatever punishment is coming my way, for every mistake I've made.'

Librye continued plodding by his side. She glanced up at the strap on Harris's chest. Although he no longer wore his armour, his harness strap and swords remained with him. 'Why do you have so many?'

Harris glanced down. He looked at the daggers he was still carrying and swords at his side.

'What? These? They all remind me of something.' Librye widened her eyes, waiting for an answer. 'I was told to teach you. Take this as a lesson. When you're me. Around every corner, there is someone wanting to see you dead. Each one of these reminds me. If I travel a dark road, I can only take so many corners, eventually, I'll run out. The world is filled with bad people, tiny one. Trust few, watch everyone, and always carry a lot of protection.'

Librye understood his wit. He was the only one who treated her like an adult. 'I am a weapon.'

'Like I say, you're more like me every day,' he commented as they carried on walking.

'Tell me about Daru?' asked Librye. Harris glared towards her. 'You said it. You need to teach me.' Her brows raised, awaiting his reply.

Harris gave a heavy sigh; he caught his hands behind his back as they drifted down the path.

'Daru was my first love.' His smile grew. 'In Xencliff, the god Haridon, he is widely celebrated. I, of course, took lessons in Haridon, the god of death and creatures. It always fascinated me that something as small as a coin could kill hundreds.'

His eyes widened as he spoke. 'Daru was a brown spider. She lived peacefully in my room until I left and she escaped. It was Daru who sparked my interest. Another, which sparked it, was a spider which often came in on the banana carriers. Bigger than brown spiders, but deadly. However, they had a side effect which led to the most embarrassing death in men.' Looking down towards Librye, he struggled to go on. 'The banana spider. It became a favourite of mine and has been since. I often use the venom in battle.' His voice lowered; a sound of shame spilled from him.

'You've used venom a lot, haven't you?'

Harris sighed. He did not want to reply, but knew he had to. 'I know I have to teach you, Librye, but teaching of poisons, venoms and other iniquitous sides to Haridon. It would only burden your thoughts. It's a lesson you can hold for later. When you're older, perhaps?'

'I have to know, Harris, they charged you with the duty; you need to teach it. Besides, I would rather protect myself using venom. Rather than having to plunge a blade into someone.'

Harris raised his brows, his mouth curled, and head nodded to the side. 'Very true, alright, how about I give you all the books you need? I'll teach you how to use them correctly. In the meantime, the strongest venom can kill in minutes. It's from the waters of Xencliff, called a sea wasp. The difference between venom and poison, you can drink venom, and remain unharmed. Poison, you don't stand a chance against.'

'Have you used it before? Sea wasp venom?'

Her innocent eyes twisted towards Harris. He felt numb. He was doing exactly what he wished never to do. She was learning how to become a weapon.

Harris raised his brows. He gawped down towards her. 'A few years ago, a book was written. I think it was called, 'from the shadows' or something similar. Have you read it yet?'

Librye thought. She could think of no such title. 'I don't believe I have.'

'Good,' he replied in a deep tone. 'Don't!' he warned.

Librye smiled. She menacingly glared up towards him. 'That only makes me want to read it more.'

The woodland was an inviting change for the two of them. It had been a while since Librye had ventured into the meadow. There was a certain place she always longed to be when she was there.

'I thought it was you.' Dane stepped from the side of the kennels. The wolves silently slept. 'Bloody wolves been at it all morning,' — he came towards them and held his hands up, — 'suddenly, poof! Silence, as usual, here you are.' He leant down towards Librye; his smile widened. 'How have you been?'

Librye glanced towards the slumbering beasts. 'I've been well, Dane.' She spun to Harris and introduced. 'This is Harris, the newly appointed Chief Commander.'

Dane gave a customary welcome, bumping his chest with his fist. 'Of course, I've heard of you.' He had indeed heard of Harris; however, he had heard more than most. 'I also hear you, too, have a way with animals?'

Harris laughed. He gazed at the sleeping wolves.

Librye glanced up towards Harris. 'Harris, what is he talking about?'

'The mabeara.' His eyes softened. He crouched and glanced back at the wolves. 'They have a gift to tame bears. Their power over the bears doesn't mean they're better than them, but the bears see them as part of them. Xencliff, they have the same with wolves.'

'You're being modest,' said Dane.

Harris laughed. He stood and glanced at Dane. 'If there's one thing I'm not, it's modest. I know wolves well.'

'And elephants, lions, tigers, some of the biggest beasts we have.' He peered at Librye. 'Harris seems to know them all. His gift reaches further than the ability to tame wolves.'

Harris stepped towards the kennels. He could feel the restful energy from the slumbering beasts. 'My ability with most animals is no ability at all. It's about respect. Show them you mean business, and anything will submit.'

Dane sniggered. 'Hopefully you don't see women the same way.'

Harris raised his brows. 'Actually, I do,' he commented. Dane did not know if he was being serious or not. 'Not about taming or submitting, but it's all about respect.'

Wandering into the meadows, it was not the place Harris wanted to be. The wide-open meadow played with his senses. He could hear the breeze through the long grasses. The smell of poppies, daisies, peas, clover, bush vetch, cornflowers. All mannerisms of long meadow grasses. All beautiful to see, smell and hear, but he was used to a more ordered place of relaxation. Woodlands and forests were usually his chosen retreats.

The woodlands of the Cronnin gardens offered a shelter from the heavy pollens of the meadow. A few butterflies and bees offered Librye a wondrous delight. Harris and Librye sat in the temple of the Cronnin wood. The birds offered a perfect chorus. The outdoors was his home. The palace offered nothing but work and shelter. From the shadows of the Cronnin wood, he peered at the daunting superstructure. He watched as Librye wandered outside. He still was not sure what he was about to teach her. A girl who knew everything was proving to be a serious challenge.

As she wandered through the wood, he watched her picking small stones from the ground, no bigger than coins. She ambled back towards him. Gently, she placed them on the marble semicircle bench where he sat under the pagoda.

'What are those?' He glimpsed at the ordinary stones.

'They are my treasures,' she announced, proud to have found them.

Harris lowered his brow, uninterested. 'They're stones, Librye. Put them back.'

'They aren't just stones.' Her bright blue eyes sparkled at him. A breeze rushed across the floor of the wood. 'Watch.' She took his hand and rolled it palm up. Taking a stone, she placed it in his hand. 'While you teach me, I can still teach you. Sometimes, we see something ordinary.' She flickered her eyes, inviting him to look down. Harris watched. She placed her finger on the top of the stone, a tiny blue spark shot from her finger and hit the stone, breaking it open. 'Whereas what lies beneath. Is extraordinary.' She removed her finger. The stone had broken open. It hid a pink and lilac coloured geode inside. Harris sat with his mouth gaping towards her, astounded.

'Ha,' she huffed, surprised to see the colour she revealed. 'I chose this for you. It's the stone of love and loss.' Her brow crinkled in the centre. 'It's rare you get the two together.' She gazed at him, filled with wonder.

Harris kept his mouth gaping. He mumbled, 'No.' Librye narrowed her eyes. 'I'm not going to tell you.' He dropped his look of amazement. Librye held her stare. 'I'm not saying a word.'

'You think of her daily. She's all you think of. You have changed, Harris.'

'Librye, please stop.' Harris pinched the top of his nose and squinted his eyes.

'You've been absent from the taverns,' she continued. 'That's where you're known. It's part of who you are, or who you used to be.'

'Librye,' warned Harris with a deep tone. He glared at her wide eyed. 'Stop.'

Librye did not stop, her filter was off. 'I see you every day, Harris, you're always in two places—'

'Stop!' Immediately, he spun to Librye. Noticing he had made her jump. 'Apologies,' he begged, as he leant down towards her. 'I didn't mean to frighten you. I just can't do this now. I can never do this.' He placed his hand on her shoulder. Librye's mouth dropped, her eyes widened. She felt it, she felt every drop of his pain, but she was not as hardened as he was. A tear fell from her eye, trailing down her cheek. 'Librye, please,' begged Harris. He held her close. Believing he had frightened her into crying.

'No,' Librye's voice was soft and filled with sympathy, 'I know you love her.' Harris held her shoulders and leant her back to look into her eyes. 'I didn't mean to. Sometimes,

I just feel people, what they feel. I felt it, Harris, it tore you open, the day you had to leave her, that's why you left.'

'It's not something I ever want you to worry about. Librye, this is my burden, it is not for you to bear.'

Librye's eyes filled with sorrow and flooded with tears. 'How do you go on? Knowing what you know?'

Harris dropped his head. He sat back on the marble seat. Librye sat beside him. He gave a heavy sigh.

'Your next lesson, Librye. The world isn't always fair, but we have to work around that.' She could sense his frustration. His anger at everything boiled beyond rage to defeat. 'The world will provide more lessons than we often see fit to take in.' He sat forwards with his elbows resting on his knees and glanced back at her. 'But one that we must always follow is that we don't always get our own way. I love her with every inch of my soul. I can't bear the thought of being without her, but for now I love her as a friend, only.'

'Branwen.'

Harris nodded. She peered directly forwards. 'Yes, Branwen,' he admitted with a broken voice.

'No,' Librye pointed out towards the gardens. 'It's Branwen, over there.' Harris immediately glanced up to see Branwen. Plodding through the gardens and towards the wood. He stood as quickly as he could, his heart raced. 'She's just as beautiful as my secrets said.' Harris still panicked. He spun in the centre of the pagoda, not knowing what to say, not knowing what to do. 'Harris, are you going or not?'

'Yes,' he staggered. 'I'm going, I'm going.' He ran from the pagoda. Librye followed behind and slowed. She came towards the meadow path.

Branwen saw Harris shoot from the woodland. Her smile lit the world as she saw him. Her soft pink dress cascaded around her, shaping her perfectly. A radiant glow to her face shone. She rushed towards him. Every part of him was on fire with a need to reach out to her.

'Harris!' She ran to him, holding her pink silk dress so as not to trip. Meeting him at the end of the path, they both froze. 'I missed you.'

Harris could still feel his heart racing, his hands shook, he stared towards her. 'I've missed you, too. How are you feeling now?'

She could feel how awkward it was for them both. They had been through so much together, yet it was like the first-time meeting. Branwen was blunt with Harris. 'Why is this so awkward?'

Harris shook his head; he widened his eyes and gave a slight laugh. 'I don't know.' His mouth curled down. 'Perhaps because we're different now? Marrion, what it was for us, was a dream. This is reality, as depressing as that may be. I've never been so happy to see someone.' He struggled to catch his breath. He could not hold back any longer. Throwing his arms around her, he pulled her in for a warm embrace.

He held her around the shoulder. Ambling back towards the woodland, where Librye still stood on the path.

'Why are you here?' asked Harris as they came towards the woods.

'My mother, she wants eyes in Cronnin. For now, that will be me. The council has allowed it. For now, I am an honorary member,' — she proudly waved her head, — 'I'll take a seat beside Angus, representing Sonnin.'

It impressed Harris, but he had more important matters for Branwen. 'You remember me telling you about Librye?' Branwen nodded. Harris stopped and stood in front of her. 'I need you to meet her. But one warning.' He held a low, quiet tone. 'Don't speak to her as a child, talk to her as you would me, or Angus or your mother even.'

Branwen twisted her eyes to look behind him where she could see Librye stood on the edge of the lane to the wood.

'I'm sure I'll cope,' replied Branwen.

Harris allowed her to walk on while he trailed behind.

Harris listened to Librye and Branwen talk. They spent the afternoon talking of Marrion. Branwen's work there was something she was proud of, and it showed. Librye told her all she could remember of the camps where she once lived. Of the palace where she now lived.

For hours, they talked about their likes and dislikes. Librye realised that she and Branwen had a lot in common. The one thing that the two clearly shared was their love of Harris. His childlike excitement was obvious. He watched the two most important women in his life enjoying each other's company. As the skies dulled, he knew he would need to return soon, but he had enjoyed the day beyond belief.

The palace galleries filled with life as Harris stepped in from the empty main hall. Gethen was busy preparing for the next day. His under cooks worked as hard as they could. Even the laundry staff worked over-time as the grey skies gathered. A threat of rain would force them to dry their washing indoors.

'I see Branwen has settled in well,' said Rebecca as Harris stepped into the galleries.

'Of course she has,' — Harris's brow crinkled, — 'she's from a palace, not that hard to settle.' He sat on the stool near Gethen's bench.

'Is that why you settled so fast?' asked Leon, a stable hand from the front stables.

'No,' grumbled Harris, 'how's Svend, by the way? I've not been out in too long.'

'Kicking up a storm,' huffed Leon. 'His boy is trying to do what he can. He said that the harp calms him, strange boy.' He walked from the back porch.

'What brings you here?' asked Gethen.

'Curiosity.' Harris took an apple from the table in front. With a dagger from his boot, he sliced it. 'I came here, wondering what the news of today is.'

Gethen continued kneading his dough. 'Same as always, although,' — he twisted and stopped working, — 'I hear talk of a proposal,' he purred in a low tone.

Harris gave a quick furrow of his brow. 'Proposal?'

Gethen turned in closer. 'Branwen,' he whispered, 'I've heard talk that Angus might be on the cards for her. Harelda always has a plan,' he drawled.

'Branwen?' Harris gave a laugh, slicing another piece of apple. 'He's far too old for her. He would never go for it.' His tone of doubt spilt into the kitchen.

'I think he would.' Bethany stopped.

'How did you even hear that?' Harris widened his eyes towards her.

'We hear everything,' she laughed. She came closer to him. 'I heard that Angus wants a young wife, who can continue his work when he is gone. Someone he can trust. Who better than Sonnin?' She shrugged.

'Branwen is a child compared to Angus,' argued Harris. 'It's preposterous.'

'I may sense some jealousy?' said Rebecca.

'I'm jealous of no one,' laughed Harris. His eyes widened towards her, she swirled.

'I hear rumours will get you nowhere in this place,' came the warning rumble of Maude, stood by the door. She sauntered further into the kitchen. 'Harris, you're needed in the chambers.' Maude spun and left towards the main hall.

'Tomorrow then,' smiled Harris, he placed his apple down, 'duty calls.' Gethen watched as he left.

As Harris stepped into the smoke-filled chambers. He could tell something bothered Angus. Sat by his desk, Angus glared at the desk in front, now almost void of papers. Most sat on Harris's desk.

'You called for me?' Harris stepped inside.

He marched to his chair at the front of Angus's desk and lumped down. Angus broke his glare, looking at Harris. His mouth was still gaping.

'I'm going to ask Branwen for her hand. I have no other choice.'

Harris felt every part of his body spike with dread. The very thought sickened him. 'She's half your age. How much have you drank?'

'I haven't drunk,' scoffed Angus. 'I have no other choice, and it was suggested.' Angus lifted his head. He glared directly towards Harris. He gave a slight shake of his head. 'It wasn't my idea.' Harris narrowed the bottom of his eyes. 'It was hers.' A pelt of disappointment hit Harris. He could not show his emotion. 'This afternoon, we sat and talked. She suggested a union. At first I couldn't go ahead with it, but the more I thought, the less I could argue. It makes complete sense.'

'Angus,' Harris stood. He pleaded with him. 'Think about this,' — he raised his arms, — 'for fuck's sake, think about who your mother-in-law would be!' The guards on the doors gave an audible laugh. 'I can't think of anything more awful!'

'Why are you so against this?' asked Angus, startled at Harris's reaction.

'Because you're twice her senior. Plus, it would give Harelda a hand in palace affairs. We all know Sonnin has a power problem.'

'You know Branwen,' sighed Angus. 'Harelda, I have known all my life. She is not one for Cronnin to fear. She wishes to strengthen Cronnin and Sonnin, Harris. I asked you here, not for your blessing, simply to let you know. I know the two of you are friends. Your influence will help in this.' He sat forwards.

'I will not convince her of anything. If it's her idea, then she's made her mind up. Trust me, what that woman wants, that woman gets.' Harris hurried to the drinks cabinet. He poured two glasses. Before he turned, he drank them both and poured them again. He strolled back towards the desk. He thought as quickly as he could, but he could think of no reason they should not be married, apart from his own needs.

'Congratulations.' Harris gave a glass to Angus. 'I feel like this could be quite entertaining.'

'Thank you, Harris,' grumbled Angus, 'besides, I don't look that bad for my age,' he pouted.

Harris laughed. 'You're right there. In fact, I can't see why Branwen wouldn't want to.' His eyes drifted about the room.

Sauntering through the east tower, Branwen made her way towards her room. Having bid Librye good night, the hour was late. She stepped into her chambers and began readying herself for bed. The dark room lit with a dim orange glow from the fire flowers. From behind the door of her room, a shadow emerged as Harris stood in the darkness. Branwen had not yet seen him. She carried on removing her necklace and sat at her dressing table. She took her long locks of caramel hair down, flowing to her waist. There was a shadow in the mirror. Something moved. She twisted to see Harris. She held her pounding heart.

Harris stood silently. 'What are you doing?' she whispered playfully as she stood.

Harris held a look of ire. His chest moved deep with every breath he took. 'I just need to know one thing.'

Branwen stepped closer towards him. 'Harris, what is it?'

'Do you love him?' His eyes filled with a softened rage.

Branwen shook her head. She glanced down. 'I don't know what you want me to say.'

'Just tell me, honestly, do you love him?'

Branwen stepped closer to Harris. She took his hand in hers and entwined their fingers. 'I told you, Harris, I love you. Just because you're incapable of feeling it, I shouldn't be the one to suffer.' Her soft look of love towards him shattered to a look of resentment.

'Incapable?' He narrowed his eyes and gave a spiteful look. Branwen dropped his hands. 'I gave you everything,' he whispered.

'No, Harris, I will always be here for you. I will always be your friend, but I am not one of your Xencliff pornes there to please you when you feel fit. I deserve to be loved.' Branwen spun from him. Her anger grew. 'I know you saved me, and I am grateful for that, but I gave you a chance. I would've done anything for you, gone anywhere.

We could've left, together, from Marrion.' She raised her voice towards him. 'We could've lived out our days wherever we pleased, but no,' she spat. 'You're the great, Harris Bearwood. You aren't happy being loved by one person alone. You need to be loved by all.'

Harris stood, utterly dumbfounded. 'That's not true,' he quietly defended.

'Oh, come on, Harris,' — her tone turned to rage, — 'I wasn't enough, I would never be enough—'

Harris avoided shouting, instead gritted his teeth, 'That's not true! I love you, Branwen. I've never been able to say that about anyone but you.' A tear caught in his eyes; his stubbornness would not let it drop.

'Too little, too late. I gave myself to you, wanting to spend my life in your arms. If I must watch you instead, then so be it,' she calmed.

Harris stepped towards her. 'We can't do this. I risked my life for you so many times, and I would do it again and again and again.' His eyes contorted to a hurt look of anguish. 'But I won't risk yours. Angus's own mother was killed because she fucked a guard. Imagine what they would do to you.' His voice shook with fear.

Branwen stepped towards him. 'Then it's agreed. We watch from afar, knowing we will never have what we had again.'

'That is what I told you, in Marrion.' His eyes twisted around the room. 'I told you we cannot be together. I am nothing, Branwen.' He leant close to her face. 'I am a commoner. I warned you, Branwen, never get too close, don't love me, feel nothing for me.' His teeth gritted. He hated saying it, but he had to. 'I cannot love you. It's a punishment to love you. Please, just hate me.'

His whispers hurt her. She felt cold. 'Anna was right.' Harris stood straight; his brow creased to the centre. 'She said you push people away, afraid to love, afraid to be happy, but the truth, you're afraid to fail.'

Her words punctured his chest. The fractured silence around them was eerie. 'I'm not afraid of anything. I fear nothing but you.'

Her eyes lit the room, she drifted towards him. Her dress fell from her shoulder, giving him a glance at the soft flesh he used to enjoy.

'I have thought so long and hard about Marrion. The things you did, the things you said. Did you save them, to better your numbers? Because you didn't do it for them, did you?'

It was the first time he had seen her cruelty. The first time he had seen just how spiteful a woman could be. Her love fuelled her hate. His voice quivered.

'Ha,' he breathed. 'You know nothing about me. Everyone I saved; I did that to save a life.' His eyes filled with rage, he refused to let her better him. 'The numbers didn't matter to me. What mattered were families. I lost mine because of this war. I wasn't willing to let more lose theirs. Branwen, I saved you because your mother asked me to.'

Like a dagger to her heart, her love for Harris was dwindling. 'Not because you wanted to, but my mother wanted you to?'

'I did what I did to save our kingdoms. To save you and to save your mother's heart. I did what I did because I love you, Branwen. But you cannot love me.' Harris begged. 'I know you say these things to help push me away. I've seen it time and time again. Don't love me, Branwen, hate me.'

Branwen lowered her head, looking at the floor. 'I thought enough time had passed. Those are all the things I have wanted to say.' She sat on her bed, a paused silence floated through the room. 'I was trying to make it easier for you. But I can't be you. Seeing you today, it melted my hate. That is why I suggested it to Angus. I can love you, Harris. That is my choice.' — She stood and stepped closer, — 'Let me love you, we don't have to be close, but I can still have my friend.'

'It's unfair, I know. That is all we can ever be, Bran.'

'I want more, even after days and nights, thinking of every conceivable reason to never look at you again. I still want more.'

He reached out, wiping the tear which flowed down her cheek. 'This will be the last time I say it. I love you, Bran. My duty is to protect you and this kingdom.'

'To be my friend,' she struggled to smile through sobbing eyes.

'I really want to hold you, but I know this place, how quickly rumours spread. Even being in here is dangerous. An arm's length is always best.'

Branwen watched as Harris crept from her room. He stood at the door for a moment, listening for footsteps before he did. She did not hate Harris. She hated what he represented. Despite her own royal heritage, his common status symbolised an unfair world where royalty was left out, yet she still loved him.

The first quarter filled with guards. Harris, and Angus sat silently on the front benches. A smell of freshly fallen rain invited them to the execution that day. The rotten stench of waste and filth again forced Angus to cover his mouth and nose. Harris reclined back onto his elbows. He watched Connor being dragged from his cell. Several of the council members watched.

Harris and Angus stared towards the rope. They held the same bloodthirsty look in their eyes. A look of hatred covered Connor's face. Connor glared at the council. He wanted to retain his dignity. Connor proudly stood and strode towards the gallows. His filth covered tattered rags hung on his frame, as if someone had pulled them from a corpse.

As a councillor, they gave him the right to speak; he stood at the foot of the gallows stairs and spun. His dirt filled face showed no horror or trepidation, he showed no remorse.

Connor glared towards Harris. 'Your words, councillor,' ordered Theo, stood beside him.

Connor's glare remained with Harris. 'Your day is coming,' Connor croaked towards Harris.

'And yours is already here!' Harris was unphased by Connor's warning. He watched as his feet stood heavy on each step. 'Short drop and a quick stop!' Harris shouted. Connor twisted, giving a snarling look towards him.

Angus remained plain faced. He watched the rope fall around Connor's neck.

'We have word from Marrion,' Angus casually mentioned, turning to see Harris, still leaning back.

Harris sat forwards, his eyes widened, and lips parted. He held a finger towards Angus.

'One minute,' Harris whispered, waiting for the noose to tighten. The door thudded open. Connor dropped, instantly his neck snapped. His body swung with no kicking.

'Oh, boring,' sighed Harris. 'I prefer to see them kick for a bit,' he groaned. The two stood and made their way back. The councillors mostly remained in the yard. Paying their last respects to the body of Connor as it swung from the rope. 'You were saying about Marrion?'

Angus strolled by his side. 'Yes, I was. I received word this morning from some of our scouts. They say that the castle appears abandoned.' Angus stopped walking. Turning to Harris, he explained, 'There appears to be nothing but bodies. Something terrible seems to have happened there.' He glared at Harris from under his brow.

'So much for that blind eye.' Harris widened his grin.

'Say no more,' agreed Angus. 'Just promise me we won't have any repercussions?'

'Never make a promise you may not keep, even with the slightest doubt.'

'Ask no questions, get no lies, is more like it,' he groaned.

Harris laughed. 'You know me too well.' He opened the gate for them to leave.

The streets were busy. Many of the people of the city had got used to seeing Harris and Angus on their quarterly commute to the first quarter.

A crowd gathered in Small Street, blocking their path back to the palace.

'Wait here.' Harris left Angus with his guards and marched forwards.

Harris came towards the back of the crowd, believing it was some drunken brawl. Barging his way through, he came to the front to see Branwen. She crouched on the ground, talking to a small child as he passed her a bouquet. Her radiant smile lit the streets. She glanced up to see Harris. A soft breeze caught her shining caramel blond hair. Her shining blue eyes lightened by the bright sun. Harris made his way towards her. Several of the palace guards escorted her through.

Branwen joined Harris. 'You've been to the gallows.' The two strode through the street back towards Angus.

Harris's love for Branwen would forever lock him in a world of punishment.

'How did you know?' he asked with a jilted smile.

'A small part of you. It seemed to have disappeared when you left Marrion. I see it again now.' Harris stopped and gazed towards her. 'Death, Harris, it seems to wake something in you, a need to experience it.'

'I don't need to see it to feel myself.' Harris raised his voice slightly. He did not want people to hear, but in such a narrow street, he had to be quiet. 'What he did, to you, to Marrion. He needed to suffer.'

Her eyes shone with something Harris had never seen in her. Bloodlust. 'Did he? Did he suffer, Harris?'

Harris nodded. 'He did. He created his own suffering.' He continued walking towards Angus. 'Just as you're doing.' He noticed the glances from the people in the streets. Whispers carried towards him of what a wonderful couple Harris and Branwen made. Whispers he did not want to hear.

'What do you mean by that?' asked Branwen. Harris held his hands behind his back as they wandered down the street. Branwen collected another bouquet from a small girl who skipped towards her.

'Thank you,' Branwen leant down. Her smile lit the child's face. The child quickly escaped; she rarely saw such celebrity.

'So come on, Harris, how am I creating my suffering?'

The gesture from the child could not have come at a worse time for Harris. The people there clearly liked Branwen. Her short time at the palace had created an impact so far.

'All I'm saying is you need to be sure, Bran. You're my friend, the most important person in my life. I can't stand to see you unhappy.' He would not force Branwen's hand. She made her choice. All he could do was turn to his nature and help her grow into the powerful woman he knew she could be.

'Afternoon,' greeted Angus. He saw Branwen coming closer. 'I see you're in favour with Cronnin.' He smiled upon seeing the flowers she was holding.

Branwen laughed. 'The people here are wonderful. I feel so welcome here.'

'That's because you are.' Angus held his arm out to escort Branwen back.

Branwen declined his offer. She stepped back while holding her smile. 'I have plans for today. The council has decided that there will be no meetings today. I've decided to spend my day exploring the vines.'

Angus widened his eyes. 'The children's camps?' He showed concern. 'Just be careful. They're not as innocent as they may seem.'

Branwen smiled, passing them. Harris counted the guards, ensuring enough was there to protect her.

Angus and Harris ambled back towards the palace. A light rain misted along the streets.

'Harris, she is remarkable,' he mentioned as the two strolled along Fort Street.

'I know she is.' Harris blew a regretful sigh. 'Can I tell you something?' He gauged Angus's reaction.

Angus replied, with a low tone and wide smile. 'You can tell me anything, Harris, within reason.'

Harris gazed at the palace in front. 'Growing up in Xencliff, it wasn't all that bad.' The gates to the palace screeched open. 'The one regret I had. I wasn't born there. There was a girl I remember, Lauren.' His eyes filled with a sorrowful reminiscence. 'She was the daughter of Waron's sister. We were the same age, but she was born a royal. I was nothing.'

'You aren't nothing, Harris,' commented Angus. He had a lot of affection for Harris. He appreciated he had history. Doubt was something he had never seen in Harris.

'But I wasn't enough,' Harris ambled towards the palace doors. 'My mother retained her title of Lady, but me, I am nothing. I've always tried to be more, maybe, that's what makes me who I am. It's the same with Branwen. If I were born of royal blood, you wouldn't have a look in,' he laughed.

'Well, you weren't,' laughed Angus, 'but she needs you as a friend, Harris. We both do.'

It was the first time Angus had referred to Harris as a friend. It was a warm feeling to Harris. Angus, who showed a strange need to have him there, made his slow settling into the palace easier.

'It's good of you to say,' replied Harris. They stepped onto the palace steps, Balthus came towards them. 'Afternoon,' greeted Harris.

Balthus sarcastically commented, 'No barbers open, I see?'

Angus laughed, making his way inside. 'No amount of badgering is going to make me change my hair,' insisted Harris. He followed behind Angus.

'What about a vote?' Balthus twisted to see them leaving.

Harris spun; his eyes narrowed towards Balthus. 'What have you done?'

Balthus pulled out a small parchment from his robe pocket. 'Three hundred and twenty-four staff in the palace. The majority voted for a haircut.' Balthus smiled, handing the parchment to Harris. Harris stood with his mouth gaping at the parchment. 'The guards still haven't got their vote back to me. With over a thousand guards, it may take some time.' His eyes widened. He glanced at Harris. His face was a picture of utter trepidation. 'It was a lot of effort,' he commented.

'I can see that, Balthus!' Harris stormed back into the palace, flailing the parchment. 'Fine! I'll get a bloody hair cut!' He spun to Balthus and continued trudging backwards. 'If the guards reflect the same!' He pointed to Balthus. 'Well played, old man, well played!' Turning, he walked back inside.

The hall fell to silence. The council sulked about the halls. Losing one of their own hung heavy in the stale air. The only councillor who appeared remotely happy that day was Kailron. Harris greeted him, coming towards the fountain in the hall. Kailron was walking towards his chambers.

'One minute!' called Harris. Kailron stopped as Harris searched the parchment.

'You voted.' His finger trailed down the parchment. His eyes widened, glaring at Kailron. 'You voted for me to cut it!' He held no anger in his shouting, 'Why?'

Kailron laughed, 'Your reputation has already proven fact. Your work is without doubt some of the best we've ever seen, but your hair, Harris, we struggle to take you seriously.'

'Ha,' sighed Harris. He shot up the stairs and into Angus's chambers. He glared at the guards on the door who had also voted. 'You as well!' Harris stepped into Angus's chambers. Angus stood by his desk, giving a grumbling laugh. 'I expected better from you.'

'Come on, Harris, you could nest wild birds in there!' he laughed as Harris came towards him.

Harris glanced at the stairs. Librye's name was missing from his vote. 'Where's Librye?' Harris dropped his humour. His eyes searched the room.

'I thought you would've known.' Angus's tone held a spark of wonder. They both left the chambers towards her room.

Harris gave a knock on her door. Maude peered out. 'She isn't well.'

'Is it her back?' asked Angus as Maude stepped to the side. Harris and Angus walked into the room to see Librye shivering in her bed.

Godfrey sat by her side. 'Godfrey, what is it?'

Harris hurried to her bedside. He sat on the edge and held her hand. Her eyes drifted towards him. 'What is it, tiny one?' Before she could reply, she sat up and threw up down his front.

'Oh! That is horrid!' Panicked Harris. He hurried to the washroom, where he listened to Angus and Godfrey.

'Well, she isn't fevering,' said Godfrey, 'which is a relief, however, her illnesses seem to come in waves.'

'What does that mean, Godfrey?' Angus took Harris's place and sat by her bedside.

Godfrey leant towards Angus. 'In all honesty, I'm not sure. Her symptoms always have something to do with the outing of her wings.' Angus's eyes drifted towards Godfrey, a look of doubt stuck in his eyes. 'We know what they are, sire. We cannot deny them.' Godfrey stood as straight as he could. 'My work here is done. I can no longer help her. She should be with the torbs now, sire. They can help.' His raised brows spoke to Angus.

Harris continued listening as he tried his best to remove the sticky vomit. Bushwell had yet to reply to Angus, who was looking at Librye in her slumber and realising that they were lost without her.

'I can take her.' Harris stepped from the washroom, holding a towel. He continued cleaning his tunic. Angus twisted. 'I can take her.' Harris repeated with his eyes wide. 'Bushwell will be pleased to see us, I'm sure.'

'Not yet,' Angus spun back. 'We will await his reply.' He softly stroked her forehead.

The night brought a pattering of rain from Librye's window outside.

'You go,' whispered Harris. He sat with Maude beside Librye's bedside. She had spent the entire day in her room.

'It's my duty, Harris. I can cope fine. You have more work than me. Get some sleep,' Maude argued.

Harris rubbed his eyes. 'Maude, go now, please,' he begged. 'I've gone for half a turn without sleep before. One night will not be my end.'

Maude stood. 'Only if you're sure.'

Harris widened his eyes. 'Go.' He brushed his hand towards the door. Maude left, taking Harris's armour with her.

Harris spent the night hunched onto the side of Librye's bed. He still sat on the chair and rested his head on her bed.

Librye woke. The darkness of the room took over. She slowly opened her eyes. She saw Harris laying his head on her bed.

'I'm just resting my eyes,' he mumbled.

Librye sat up. 'What's wrong with me, Harris?' she moaned.

Harris sat up straight. He gazed at her, his eyes filled with a wondrous sympathy. 'There's nothing wrong with you. What makes you say that?'

Her eyes still wearied. She sat forwards. 'Harris, it hurts so bad.'

He had not seen it before. He had only ever seen a slight dotting on her clothes. He looked in horror as he leant her forwards. Blood covered her sheet and back. The sticky red covered his hands. He tried to see where it was coming from.

'Guard,' — shock took his voice, — 'guards!'

The guard stepped inside. 'Again, with this, Librye?'

Harris thundered towards him. 'Don't just stand there. Get the fucking alchemist!' he shouted in a deep, grumbling voice.

'It happens a lot, commander.' The guard tried to assure. But Harris would not calm. He frantically searched the room, trying his best to gather some towels. Leaning Librye forwards, the pouring blood would not stop. 'Harris, it's pointless,' said the guard, 'it'll stop soon.'

Harris frantically carried on; he pressed the towels into her back.

'Harris,' whispered Librye, 'it'll stop soon.' He peered at her, his eyes widened and panicked. 'Please, Harris, just stop,' she softly begged.

Harris would not listen; he needed the bleeding to stop. He untied her nightgown and pulled the back down. The strange lumps had again grown. Raw bone protruded from her back. Small thick bones stuck out from her back by a couple of inches.

'What the fuc—' whispered Harris.

'What did you expect, Harris? Things like this don't happen over-night.'

Harris glanced at Librye. He took some towels and placed them on the bed. He softly laid her back.

'Librye,' his voice quivered. Words were hard for him to find. 'You could bleed to death.' His mouth curled down with horror.

'She could.' Angus stepped into the room. Branwen was by his side. She ran towards Librye. The attentive nurse Harris remembered so well was back.

'Hence the reason we need the torbs,' said Angus. He came towards the bed. 'Librye, how are you feeling?'

Librye swayed her head, her exhausted eyes swirled around the room.

'She isn't well, Angus. She needs help,' insisted Harris.

'The torbs can do that for her.' Angus sat beside the bed. 'She is going through a fast process. The torbs need to slow it down. They are the ones with the potions and magic. Even the fae's magic doesn't compare.'

'The point is, if this happens again, it might be the last,' Harris warned. He peered at the blood covered bed. 'She needs to go now.'

Angus shook his head. 'Bushwell will do something. He has already received the letters I've sent. I know he will do something.'

'Harris, your boots,' Branwen insisted. She remained inspecting Librye's back. Harris gazed at her wide eyed. 'I'm not playing, Harris, I need your boots.'

She knew Harris well. He took his boots off. Using a small dagger; she unscrewed the bottom of his boot, revealing his alchemist kit.

'Impressive.' Commented Angus.

'I spent far too long waiting for him to wake, after that, I spent every waking hour waiting on him. I know the commander's secrets,' said Branwen. 'Well, some of them at least.'

Branwen took a small bag of white powder. She placed some on the end of the wounds. The bleeding slowed to a stop. 'There, now, if you need anything else, call me,' her voice carried a warning. She looked at Harris and Angus. Harris replaced the screws and his boots. 'I shall leave you to rest.'

'Harris, you are full of surprises,' commented Angus, his tone remained impressed.

'I'm not an alchemist. I'm not even good at it. But I know enough, and I have enough to save a life if needed.'

Wandering back to his chambers, Angus stopped by the door. Evan stood statuesque at the side.

Angus froze and turned to him. 'What kind of life must one have led, to always need to save their life?'

'A pretty dim one, I would say, sir.'

'Yes,' he muttered.

'If you speak of Harris, then it would spin your head to think of the reasons. But there is a reason he will not speak to his mother.'

Left with a painful thought of Harris's past, Angus retired to his bedchambers.

Harris rested his head on Librye's bed. Another day had passed and still Librye remained unwell. A captivating scent woke him. His eyes opened. Harris lifted his head to see Maple sneaking into the room.

'Good morning,' greeted Harris.

'If that's what it is.' Maple came close to the bed. She was holding a large plate draped with a white cloth. Her grin was wide. She placed the plate down for Harris.

'I made you something.' She removed the cloth to reveal a small loaf of bread. The scent of lavender and rosemary took over his senses. He peered at the delicious-looking bread. Beside it were two sweetbreads.

'I know you must miss your journeys, so I had the sweetbread brought in for you. The other is of my making.'

Her formidable voice captivated Harris. He took a piece of the delightful bread. He fell back in his chair.

'Oh! Maple,' he sighed with a wondrous tone of utter enchantment, 'you know how to make a man happy.'

Maple laughed. She folded some sheets beside Librye's bed, saving a job for Maude.

'You sound like my husband.' Her smile softened as a sparkle of reminiscence hit her eyes. 'He always used to say my bread could revive an army.'

Harris listened. He gazed at her, feeling slightly guilty that he did not know the man that well. 'What was he like?'

Maple stopped folding. She took the seat at the side of Librye. 'He was a wonder.' She gave a sorrowful sigh. 'I always said he was meant for the temples, not a commander. He always wanted to make people proud. Always pushing himself further. No matter how much I told him, he still wouldn't listen. I was so proud of that man, everything he did, everything he witnessed. His work never felt good enough for him.'

Harris leant forwards. 'They were big boots for me to fill. When I arrived in Marrion, I had been there for only a few days. A stray arrow took him amidst the chaos.' Harris heavily swallowed his bread. 'Were you told what happened?'

Maple shook her head. 'No,' she whispered, 'it was far too chaotic for details to be sent.'

Harris glanced towards her. He remembered what happened, and he knew he could bring some comfort to Maple. 'The village where you're from, Shawhope.' Maple sat upright to listen. 'That's where I sent the letter, hoping you would receive it.' His head lowered. Sitting back in his chair, he cleared his teeth with his tongue. 'I wrote in that the details of his death.'

Her voice quivered. 'I never received the letter.'

'Very well,' Harris's tone changed. He sat forwards. 'Then I can tell you. He did not die without cause, he died to save several others from death. He fell to a barrage of arrows, using himself as a shield. I was there.' His eyes drifted down. 'I brought him to the camp, atop Svend. We tried for hours to save him. I took his last command, before he succumb to shock.'

'What was his last command?' A tear in her eye graced her cheek.

He struggled to talk, but he needed to tell her directly. 'He told me I was to end Marrion, end it, he said, don't let the bastards take it.' Harris looked at Maple. Her face was now wet with tears. 'He asked me to tell his Holly that he loves her.' Maple broke, her tears fell freely from her eyes. 'I never understood why I was writing to a Maple, but he called you Holly?'

'He would call me Holly, saying I was filled with unbreakable spines, but with a soft centre. We always wanted children. When Marrion ended, we were to live out our days in a village to the east of Shawhope. Organa, a beautiful place, untouched by Atlanti hands. We will never have that now.' Maple stood. She swirled to leave, peering back at Harris. 'You did though, you ended Marrion, Harris.' She gave a soft, tight smile. 'Thank you,' she whispered.

'Marrion fell, Maple.'

Maple spun, a glow in her eyes spoke of secret knowledge. 'You say that.' She noticed his eyes narrow. 'Even though Marrion fell, you didn't let the bastards have it.'

The palace had been talking. The gallery was alive with rumours of Marrion. Many lie dead in Castle Marrion, an invisible killer had taken them all. Harris did not allow them to take Marrion.

Lounging on her bed, Isradella read. A rustle in the corner of her chambers kept her company as her maid tidied her bookcase.

'I would rather like to go out in the daytime,' said Isradella, raising her eyes from the book.

'Our lord has insisted you remain in during the day,' the stern maid replied. 'Your night-time walks will do for now.'

'But what if I'm not happy?'

'Then you need to speak with your husband.'

'He's aware,' said Kairne, stood on the other side of the door. He looked at the maid, who promptly left.

'I gave you everything, and still, you ask for more.' He walked towards the bed. 'All I ask for is a child, Isradella, it isn't a lot to ask.'

'I have been trying, my darling,' — she turned on the bed, — 'I only hope my mother's mistakes have not impacted our —'

'You blame your mother?' — he rushed towards her, — 'I will no longer give you a choice. I gave you freedom, you throw that in my face.' He stormed towards the door. 'From now on, you remain in this room until you give me what I need.' The door slammed, Isradella didn't move, she laid back on the bed, staring at the stone ceiling.

Stood in the corridor, Kairne narrowed his eyes. A swirling feeling deep within plagued him. He hurried to his chambers. Thudding into the chair at his desk, he leant forwards with his head in his hands. Unable to understand the sinking feeling within.

'Guard!' he called. A tall soldier stepped inside. 'Any word on Daniel or Gaius yet?'

'No, sir, nothing.'

Kairne looked at the grey wall of his chambers. 'Something is wrong,' he muttered. 'Death is abundant, it fills the west, and I don't know why.'

'Sir, perhaps you could see why?' asked the guard. 'You are gifted. Surely you can use that to your advantage?'

'I am gifted.' He grinned. 'I see through the eyes of the dead, but I cannot move the bodies of the decomposed. All I see are fractions of darkness, silence. Marrion is silent.'

'Perhaps you raise one?' asked the guard.

'You don't understand. I will only raise them to carry a deadly message. We must all have our rules.'

'Then perhaps your gift has spoken?'

A cawing of crows was silent. The usual sound of seabirds died in the warm Marrion sun. The only sound which echoed through the halls was the sound of the ocean, as it crashed along the high cliffs. Moans had died long ago, even the crows remained away from the cursed land. The battleground still shone with glints of bent steel. The castle fell to silence.

CHAPTER SEVENTEEN

17

For days, Harris could not leave Librye's side. His desk piled with letters. The galleries remained quiet as Harris's visits dwindled and stopped. Librye remained in her bed. The Greendia moon approached. Harris would need to catch up on his work soon. He was requested in Sonnin. Leaving her bedside was an ultimate challenge for him. The only time he had left was to change his clothes and bring her food from the galleries. Even Branwen no longer possessed his thoughts.

Maude thought it best to give Harris a break, to allow him to catch up on his work. On his way up the stairs to the east tower, Harris could hear her, the faint footsteps of Branwen, as she paced his room. He came to the top of the stairs and remained silent. Her glare towards him held concern.

'How is she?'

Harris threw his sword and belt to the side of his desk. He made his way in. 'She'll live, for now,' he sat, letting out an exasperated breath, pondering the work on his desk. Sitting in his chair, he read.

'I remember this,' Branwen lowered herself into the chair opposite. 'The days and nights, sat at your desk, watching you work.'

Harris glanced up from under his brow. His hair trailed down his face. Taking some papers, he threw them towards Branwen. 'You can help if you like.' He continued reading.

'I'm needed in Sonnin in the next few days. Your mother has ordered me there for an update.'

Branwen lifted her head. 'I could come with you,' she excitedly suggested.

Harris gave a grumbling laugh. 'You made your feelings abundantly clear.' His tone was rational. Her words still hurt him. 'Stay here. Librye and Angus will need all the help they can get.'

She was not the type to enjoy people's misery. But knowing that Harris felt so strongly woke something in her. She was passionate. She did not know it before meeting Harris, but her mother's manipulation clearly ran in her.

The chambers fell to silence as the two worked. Branwen came across a letter which caught her attention.

'Harris,' she gasped, 'Tosta.' She passed the letter to him. 'The army is requesting to return.' She handed the letter to Harris.

Harris widened his eyes; his smile grew as he read on. 'The Atlanti's numbers have dwindled over-night, this gave us a chance to take the battle. The Atlanti surrendered the field indefinitely.' Harris shot up. He frantically searched his desk, looking for a certain letter.

'A blue seal!' He flustered, searching the papers. 'Branwen, help, a blue seal!' Branwen searched the desk. She saw an unsuspecting letter, a blue seal on the back, forced her to throw herself to pick it up. Harris snatched the letter from her. He held his hand up to apologise.

'They gave the field. Our army has asked to return.' His smile grew further.

'What did you do?' A shock of excitement filled her.

'I'm going to make your mother the happiest woman alive,' smiled Harris. His mouth curled down, and lips pressed tightly together. His plan had worked.

'Coming from anyone else, I would be happy. Coming from you, Harris Bearwood, I'm not sure how to take that.' Harris nodded his head to the side, agreeing with Branwen. 'But how?'

'I would say it's my secret, but soon enough, you'll know.' His smile of hidden mystery grew. 'Come on.' He flung his head to the side for her to follow. 'I'm sure the council would love to hear about this.'

His boots pounded into the council halls; Councillor Ryan stood back from the table.

'Gentlemen,' greeted Harris, stepping in. Angus sat forwards on his throne. 'May I take the floor?' He bowed towards Ryan while holding a joyous smile.

Councillor Ryan held his hand forwards. 'Please.' He offered for Harris to step forwards. Harris jumped to the table with one leap. 'Tosta and Belgravia are ours. The battle has ended, the Atlanti has retreated!' He celebrated, holding his arms out. The council halls erupted with cheers. Only a few remained seated, Kailron being one of them.

Angus stepped down from his throne. Harris leered at Angus. 'See what happens when the eye is turned?' Angus nodded his head. 'Today, gentlemen! We celebrate!'

Harris and Angus left the hall with Branwen. The chambers filled with the sound of clanking glasses. They toasted to Harris's success. Angus sat at his desk. Their thoughts remained with Librye.

'It feels odd.' Harris poured another glass of moonshine for himself. 'I don't like how empty it feels in here without her.'

Angus grumbled with agreement. His eyes were heavy with a drunken stupor. 'It's been a strange end to the turn. Let's hope that Greendia brings us good fortune,' he toasted. 'What are your plans for Sonnin?'

Branwen remained in the chair. A sweet elderwine was enough for her, she liked to keep a steady head. Especially with Harris getting blind drunk.

'I'm certainly going to enjoy it now,' Harris replied with a wide smile. 'I made a promise to your mother,' — he walked by Branwen's chair and towards the desk. — 'A promise she would see the end of this war in her lifetime. Something I can now see following through.' He slurred his words.

'And what of Roe? It is yet to see an end.'

'Always one to bring it down,' laughed Harris. 'Two battles aren't enough for this one.' He glanced at Angus. 'All or nothing,' he huffed. Angus laughed, taking another drink. 'Roe will end soon. Roe is a test for me, you'll see, eventually.'

'You keep saying that, Harris. What does the commander have planned?' She stood. Angus had clearly drunk too much. Leaning back in his chair, his head dropped back.

Harris strode over to her; she pushed her chest towards him. 'Come on, Bran, you know me. I never reveal it until the very end.'

Branwen stepped back. She was far too close to Harris. The guards at the door were still sober. Angus was still awake. 'I'm sure my mother will be pleased. When do you leave?'

'I leave in the morning.' He gazed at her. She was unfeeling. It was a sobering image for Harris. 'So, bed for me, the night is drawing close, and I need to see Librye before I go.' Harris ambled towards the door. He twisted to give one final farewell to Branwen. 'I'll see you when I return, Bran.'

Her lips parted. 'Commander,' she softly bid him farewell.

Harris left to Librye's room; the cold room sent a shiver through him. 'You need a fire in here Maude,' he shivered as he roamed in.

'Librye is fine, she doesn't feel cold, or warm.' Maude sat by Librye's bed reading. She glanced up from the pages and inspected Harris. 'You're drunk.' She watched him wobble into the room.

'No such thing with me,' he defended. He came close to the bed. 'How has she been?'

Librye still slept peacefully. Her back had not bled for a while, although she was still in terrible pain. Maude placed her book on her lap. She gazed at Librye.

'No change. What was all the cheering earlier? I've seen no one all day since I replaced you.'

Harris stepped forwards. Pride oozed from every pore of his skin. 'Tosta and Belgravia. They're requesting extraction from the area, following a complete victory.' He slurred his speech, glaring towards Maude. 'From this angle, Maude, you look very fetching,' he commented.

'Don't!' she warned. 'I know you're pissed, Harris. I can smell you from here. Well done on your victory.'

'It isn't my victory,' — he smirked, — 'it was the army who did it. I just helped.'

Maude stood. She saw his ego melt into a humble abyss. He was not willing to take credit for anything if he was not there. 'So, what now, Commander?'

'Sonnin calls. I leave in the morning. I'll only be gone a day or two.' He gazed at Librye, still fast asleep in her bed. 'Hopefully, I'll be back before she knows I'm gone.'

'She will know the second you leave the gates.' Maude raised her brow. 'Have fun, Harris. Take your time, you deserve it.' She sat. 'You've worked hard enough to afford yourself some form of pleasure.' She gave a twisted smile.

Harris softened his eyes. He left the room and headed towards the stairs to his tower. As he reached his chambers. He noticed that the fire flowers surrounding dimmed. Stepping inside, they lit. Someone was there. The fire flowers could sense it.

He reached the top of the stairs. Branwen sat in his chair. 'It's a heavy burden to bear.' She glanced at Harris at the top of the stairs.

Harris's heart fluttered, frustrated. 'Are you going to stop this?' He ambled towards the desk.

'Stop what, Harris?'

Harris gave a heavy sigh. He shook his head. 'The more time we spend alone together, the more at risk we put ourselves.'

A silence fell on the chambers as they stared at each other. Harris stood at the front of the desk. Branwen remained seated at the back. As the moments passed, neither wanted to talk. Until Harris broke. He lifted his arm to his forehead.

'This isn't fair,' burst Harris. She crinkled her brow, glaring at him. 'I just want us, I want you, and having you here, it's killing me, Bran.' His eyes investigated hers.

'I just want us to be what we were, but we will never be us from Marrion, Harris. Harris, I value you so much as a friend. I can't be away from you.' She stood and walked around the desk. 'Everything I do makes me think of you. Everything I say. Every move I make, I just think of you.' Her lips parted. She came closer to him. 'I want us too, Harris, but you were the one who made it clear. You were the one who broke me first. How does it feel, Harris?' She narrowed her eyes.

Harris sighed. 'You wanted this. I told you it wouldn't work. Bran, there was no chance we could ever be together. I love you. If that is what you want to hear, you've broken me.' He came close to her face, he whispered, 'You win.'

'It has never been about winning, Harris. I knew what this was. We had so many chances, you had so many chances, to leave your life as it was, and have one with me.' She took his hands and entwined their fingers, her eyes softened. She gazed at him. 'I understand, Harris, the world was more important to you.'

Harris lowered his head, ashamed. 'Knowing what I know now, I have no regrets.' Harris dropped her hands. 'The only good part to come from this, as painful as it may be. I get to love you from a distance.'

He slept that night in an empty bed. His mind filled with a victory he felt was not his. He was yet to see his plan fulfilled. His name was becoming known throughout the Atlanti camps. Enderton had seen many Atlanti come and go. It was now a vast network of Atlanti settlements. Spreading along the borders of Elmoor and Sonnin.

'Sir,' Claire walked into a small room of the commander's hut. A large hut on the side of the settlements where the commanders would commute during battles. Gaius sat silently, his head rested in his hands. 'I have a letter for you,' her voice shook, her hands stiffened.

Claire stepped towards him. His large hand reached over the desk and took the letter from her shaking hand. Gaius's eyes examined the letter.

'My dearest Sam, I hope you're keeping well. This will be the fifth letter I've sent you in over a turn. I hope you are receiving them as I need to warn you. Of a deadly force coming your way.' His lips curled. His eyes narrowed. *'The Commander, he has cursed the lands. His hand in Marrion was forced. He did not wish to leave it. The day he did, it was with a premonition of the Gods. The Commander, with the help from the Gods has cursed Marrion, and all Atlanti fighting blood. Those who are cursed are said to fall to a terrible illness. The Commander has turned to dark magic. He has swayed the gods in his favour. The Commander is safe, he is well, he has not fallen to magic, the gods have favoured him. My dear Sam, I do hope you are well. Please stay strong, stay safe, and keep away from the passing Atlanti. The illness, the curse, it frightens me so, to know it is close to you. Please write as soon as you can. Your loving cousin, Cally.'*

'What is this?' He flailed the letter in the air.

Claire shook. 'They delivered it to the edge of the village this morning.' Her deep tone spoke of the danger they were in. 'Marrion fell to a mystery illness shortly after we took it back. The Commander, he has cursed our lands.'

Gaius took a moment to think. 'Who sent it?' He reached for his cloak.

Claire thought for a moment. 'They sent it from a tavern, close to the Cronnin city borders. That's all I know, my lord.'

'Is Kairne aware of this?' His soft voice confused her. He had not once insulted her. She was used to a different commander.

'No, sir, but I can reach Rathen in less than a day.'

'That would be most helpful.' Irrationally, he thought hard. 'Also, tell him our army will not be convening in Rathen. In response to this, our war will now be in the hands of the gods. We move south.'

'What does that mean?'

'Please, don't worry, he will know.' Gaius hurried out into the busy corridor of the makeshift pub. He turned to the side of him where a guard stood. 'Find Daniel, we leave now.'

'Sir.' The guard nodded.

Rumours slowly took hold. The gods favoured the Commander, or at least the Atlanti thought. The battle of Roe was yet to be won.

His head was still heavy from the night's drinking. A rolling mist darkened the path to Sonnin as it rolled through the haunting wood. The thin, cold mist swirled and danced as Svend and Harris rode through.

The Harelda road was a long slim road, leading towards the forest city of Sonnin. Each tree home was visible by a small door and trodden path leading towards it. The Commander woke the world of the forest. He thundered by on Svend. The streets lit by the light of the misty moon. The fingers of the wind brushed a haunting hiss through the trees above.

A small wooden house, the only house which stood in the forest, welcomed travellers on the main road of the Taranis pass. The ordinary shack was a strange sight in a place of such mystery and wonder. Especially because the owner was the most powerful man in the forest. Grendel stood on his small, rotten wooden porch. He waved to Harris as he stood smoking his morning pipe. His son, Marcus, stood by his side.

Svend slowed as they came towards the palace gate. The guards at the gate stepped forwards.

'You know we have to ask,' sighed the guard. They differed from the guards of Cronnin. They wore full bodied golden armour. A golden barbute shaped helmet and gold spear. Harris sighed, seeing them stood by the gate. He dismounted Svend.

'Come on, Harris,' said the guard. 'If we take you to the tree, we can have a cart brought in for the weapons.'

'Hilarious,' smirked Harris. 'Take this.' He passed Svend's reins to the other guard. 'Rest him today, out tomorrow and back by the morning.'

Harris followed the other guard towards the side of the tree. A small wooden hut served as a weapon store. Allowing him to keep one sword, his arm and leg braces. They placed the rest in safe keeping. The palace was a wonder to Harris. He had seen the palace only once before. Another beauty distracted his eyes that day. Now, he took in the full wonder of the Sonnin palace.

The early morning chorus was in full bloom as he stepped inside. The sounds of the forest echoed through the hall. Harelda stepped from the back room to her throne.

'You bring me good news.' Her voice echoed through the haunting hall. She stepped towards him.

Harris bowed to her. He took her hand, kissing the back. 'As promised, my queen. Your daughter is well.' He stood straight. The guards to the side stood statuesque. 'I hear that she and Angus are getting along wonderfully.'

'That is pleasing to hear.' She walked to the side and into her chambers. Harris followed. Her chambers were as perfect as he remembered. 'I am, however, concerned.' She took a seat. A small man sat at the side of the desk, his quill was ready in his hand, a small board and parchment sat in the other. 'Please, sit, Commander,' she invited. Harris kept glancing towards Borvo. 'Please, Commander, this is Borvo, my scribe. He records everything that is said here.'

Harris laughed. 'Might be a good time for Borvo to take a break.'

Harelda twisted her eyes towards Harris. Her glare did not break. 'I think he may be right. Take a moment, Borvo. I will call you if needed.'

'Your majesty?' questioned Borvo with a shaking voice. Her eyes widened and twisted towards him with a threatening glare. Borvo left.

Sat silently, Harelda leant her arms on the desk. Her fingers tightly tangled into a ball. 'So, tell me, Harris, how did you do it?'

Harris leant back; he placed his lower leg over his lap. 'I enjoy creating mystery and wonder, but you are fae. It would be pointless to even try.' Her eyes lowered in agreement. 'You will hate me for this, though.' His eyes narrowed.

'I don't believe there is anything you could do that would make me dislike you at all, Harris,' she assured.

Harris did not think, 'What about your daughter?' Instantly, his eyes widened. His mouth gaped with regret. Harelda's eyes became a look of dark anger. 'Apologies, I truly apologise.' Harris laughed. Making things worse for himself. 'I did nothing. I simply forget my place.' He held his palms to her. 'Apologies.' His smile and laughter remained.

'Don't even joke, Harris. I have had guards, lords and ladies constantly asking about this,' she moaned. She sat back in her chair.

Harris crinkled his nose. 'Really?' His tone was lofty, shocked. 'I mean, I know I have a reputation, but that keeps me being who I am. I value my balls.' Harelda rolled her eyes towards him. 'I mean it. I'm bloody terrified of you.'

He breathed with a struggling breath. 'I don't mean to sound rude, but you're a frightening woman.' With each word he said, her smile twisted and grew.

'Back to the issue at hand before my bollocks join the acorns of your tree.' He twisted his head. 'When I left Marrion, it took me through the Grenhilda valley. There is a village on the other side of the valley, stricken with illness. I took it as a sign. I rode to the village; I collected samples of the illness. Someone helped me, but I will never say who.'

Her eyes turned to disgust. 'You released pestilence on the Atlanti?' Her eyes widened towards him.

'Not only that.' He saw her disgust turn to anger. 'I sent a letter to Enderton. I knew letters were being intercepted by the Atlanti on the northern pass. The letter spoke of a curse. It connects me to a curse. The Atlanti are superstitious, they will believe I am favoured by the gods. The battle of Roe will end.'

'Have you even taken the time to think about this?' — She stood. — 'The Atlanti are indeed superstitious, but my goodness, Harris. They will wreak havoc on these lands if they ever found it to be untrue.'

Harris stood; he paced the room. 'I did what I had to do,' he defended. 'I don't care if the gods strike me down for this. Two battles are over. The villages surrounding are safe. Our armies can come home,' he announced with a breath of hope. He leant over and placed his hands on the desk. 'I have proven myself; my loyalty speaks for itself.'

Harelda slowly sat. She peered around her empty desk. 'And if they retaliate?'

'Where?' asked Harris with a spiteful tone.

'Anywhere, Harris.'

Harris sat, he leant towards her. 'Then I will be there. On blackest day. On darkest night. I will come from the shadows, I will be there,' he quoted.

'The world is not a tavern, Harris.' She glared at him.

'The world is my tavern,' he insisted with a darkness in his eyes. 'I will win this. One day, I will march into the villages of the Atlanti. To unite us and tame the bastards.'

'What gave you this idea?'

Harris sat back with his mouth gaping. Before he could reply, Harelda sat forwards.

'Ah,' she softly sighed. 'Your father.' Harris widened his eyes; he shook his head. 'Xencliff is a wonderful place. Our king Waron, he is quite willing to tell me all he could about you. Your father, he was ill with the black. But the Atlanti took your home before he had the chance to die.'

She could see the look of rage in his eyes soften to a look of sorrow. 'If he has been so forthcoming, please tell the rest.' He lifted his head towards her. He was mocking her knowledge of him.

'You mean your sisters?' Harris sat back; he tapped his leg, listening to what Harelda knew. 'How old were you, Harris? When they forced you to watch, as they raped and burned your sisters alive? When you had to leave your father behind?'

His eye fluttered with a tear. He had tried so hard to forget. He had lied for so long about what happened that night. Trying his best to change the story, but it only ever made it worse.

'So, you know,' — he nodded his head to the side. — 'I wonder what else you can tell me of my life, Harelda?'

The room succumbed to a darkness. A strange magic filled the room, as he sat, cold.

'Your mother speaks of you with great pride.'

Harris shot from the chair and swirled in the room. 'No! I will not do this!' His eyes widened with rage. 'I came here to update you. You have your update.' Harris headed towards the door.

'Sit!' Her voice of overwhelming rage shook Harris. 'I still have room on my tree.' Harelda sat forwards, her hands caught at the front of her on the desk. Harris stood by the door. 'I will say it, only once. Sit!'

Harris sauntered to the chair and sat; his eyes glared towards her. 'Don't speak of her, ever,' he pleaded.

'What she did, Harris, you will one day have to forgive.' Her powerful voice of solace came from Harelda as a mother. 'What they forced her to do. She will never forgive herself. There was no right or wrong choice. She did what she had to do, to save you and your brother.'

'Do you even know?' He bolted forwards. 'Do you even know what she did?' He gritted his teeth.

Slowly, Harelda nodded. 'She sacrificed her girls, her daughters, to save her sons. Knowing that you had more chance of escaping. If the Atlanti barbarians who took your home were busy with your sisters. It gave you a chance to escape. She also hoped they would take the girls to Crede. She was wrong. It was a choice she had to make.'

'It should've been her,' he whimpered. He held his hand to his face, wiping a falling tear. 'For years, that woman plagued me. She left my father, my sisters to die, in that place. Then she marries a fucking king. Who already had eight wives? Why would he need another? And then the moment I step out of line, I'm beaten and starved, in a dungeon!'

'Because your mother was desperate,' snapped Harelda. 'She did what any mother in her position would do. She had to choose to see her children, her babies, die, so she could save the youngest two. Your sisters sacrificed themselves for you and your brother.'

'She didn't need to do that!' He threw himself from the chair. Pacing the room, his hands shook. 'She starved me. Were it not for Lauren, I would have!'

'Who do you think helped her?' drawled Harelda. 'She would never let you starve, Harris. She was trying to teach you, while running a kingdom and having a wild child who had never seen order. You had to be changed.'

'She killed my sisters, she killed my brother, for her own chance at a kingdom. Nothing is worth that sacrifice.'

Harelda lifted her brows. 'I beg to differ. She saw she could build a life for you. All she needed from you was order, you brought her chaos.'

'Adella and Allie,' Harris whispered. 'I oddly remember them, stood at the top of the cliff close to the farm. Every so often, on good days, I still hear them calling me to come and play. I was eight. No one knows the truth. I remember me and Odalis camping in the woods with my mother. She sheltered us under the Tharacka trees to keep us safe. The next village was a day's ride.

'My father enjoyed being secluded, away from the big villages and towns.' His eyes filled with a soft reminiscence. He glared at the desk and fiddled with his fingers in front of him.

Slowly, he sat. 'The day I arrived at the palace was the last time I spoke to her. I was nine.' He lifted his head to Harelda. 'It's been over twenty years since I last spoke to her.' His voice broke. 'It will be twenty more before I speak to her again.' He sat back.

'When Odalis left for war, do you know what she said to him?' His eyes narrowed towards Harelda. She remained silently sitting, listening. 'Go,' he whispered. 'She told him to go. He was twenty, I was twelve, I had eight years to wait before I could find him. I believed that when I did, he would already be dead.'

'But he was alive, and you killed the black beast. Harris, your life, it reads like so many others.' She reached forwards, placing her open hands on the desk. She turned them over, placing his hands in hers. 'That is all I needed to know. I can forgive you for your recklessness. You remind me of Taranis, no matter what they threw his way, anger, rage, that would guide him. Ultimately, it was the black that took his life as well.' Her eyes filled with sorrow, she thought of her husband. 'Your plan has worked so far.' She held his hands tighter. 'Well played, commander.'

Her lustful eyes confused Harris. He sat back, releasing her hands. 'Well.' He gazed into her eyes for far too long. 'I have given my update, and more. Is anything else needed of me, my queen?'

'Please, call me Harelda, when not in the company of others. Your time here will be short.' Her whispering breath was confusing to Harris. He could sense a passion from her. 'I only wish to make it as enjoyable as possible.'

She stood. Making her way to the door, she opened it for Harris to leave. Once into the hall, he gave a breath of relief. Glancing back at Harelda. She stood at the door, inspecting his figure. He left towards the palace grounds. She bit her lip and watched him leave up the stairs.

Borvo scurried towards her. 'Anything to report?'

'In, Borvo!' she spat. Having blocked her view of the commander leaving, her mood suddenly changed.

Kairne sat at his desk, his chin rested on his fist.

'Did they give any other indication why they would go south?' he asked the shivering guard.

'No, sir, just that they will head south in response to the letter, that our war will now be in the hands of the gods.'

Kairne's eyes drifted through the room. 'Very well, have someone sent, see if they can intercept them.'

'Sir.' The guard nodded and left.

Sauntering from his chambers, a dull pain hit his stomach. Kairne remained on the other side of Isradella's door. Listing to anything she might say, silence sliced through the room.

He continued to the end of the tower, taking the stairs all the way to the bottom. He walked to the end of the corridor. Three guards stood on the side of a large, heavy wooden door.

'Open it,' he said, widening his eyes.

'Sir, we have not fed them yet,' said one guard.

'I didn't ask that, I said to open it, your only reply should be, certainly, my lord,' he scolded.

'Certainly, my lord.' The guard held his head low as he unlocked the cell door.

A network of open cells held the small creatures. A stench drifted through, rotting flesh and excrement. Kairne pulled out a handkerchief from his pocket and covered his nose and mouth.

The eyes of hundreds of coblyn young stared at him, cowering in corners, scurrying to escape the shadow which entered their cell.

'Speak!' he shouted. A shudder of fear came from the black masses in the corners. 'One of you speaks, and I will spare you all.' Silence met him. 'I need one of you to travel south, to find your parent, and deliver a message.' Again, silence met him.

As Kairne left, a small coblyn crept from the corner. 'One's days, one's days,' it whispered.

Alone in her chambers, Isradella laid on her bed. Her broken and bruised body was seen by no one. She no longer believed in kindness. A tear trickled down, landing on her damp pillow. Her own husband, as wise as she once saw him, would be proud of his work. For days and nights, her body was his, everything he wanted, she gave to him. He broke her youth and tainted her mind. Is this what men do? She wondered in the darkness of her chambers. Will it ever change? Or will my life be nothing but pain?

The bright forests of Sonnin offered Harris nothing. The soft breeze felt dull on his skin. His stomach was twisted and empty. Losing his family left a hole and now he was feeling it more than ever. Harris walked from the palace gates. He needed a place of tranquillity. The forest offered enough areas of peaceful contemplation. But they were not fit for Harris.

He left from the east of the palace tree and towards the stables. Taking Svend, he rode towards the Eastern ridge. The lands darkened with an overcasting of rain. A daunting temple took over the landscape. He left Svend outside, on the edge of the woodland. Sharma's wandered through the temple in their white robes. Druids, the highest of the temple keepers, swarmed the temples inside. Silently, they went about their day. Serving those unable to care for themselves and those without family.

Harris stepped inside. A woman dressed in white robes sauntered towards him. Her long white sleeves covered her hands.

'Sir, weapons are not allowed in the temple.' Her voice remained with her. The large hall offered no echoes. 'I see you are not from this area.' Her smile held. Her grey hair covered with a large white hood from her robes. A small silver tie around her waist held a small silver coin purse. 'What brings you here?' Her voice was deep. A haunting tone of peace shook Harris.

'My past.' His deep voice rumbled through the temple. He removed his belt, placing it on the pews at the side. He strolled down the temple aisle and towards the altar.

'I feel as though you're in the right place.' Again, her soft voice offered no echo. Harris's footsteps were the only ones that could be heard.

To the front of the temple was a long altar, which held a large metal votive candle display. Thousands of candles lit the walls of the altar. A soft orange glow hit her face. She gazed at Harris, holding the same peaceful smile.

'My name is Lorena,' — she spun to the altar, — 'I am the high Druid here.'

'Harris Bearwood,' Harris introduced. He glanced at the candles.

'The Commander.' Her smile grew. 'I assume you will leave your title at the door?'

Harris smiled. His eyes lightened by the burning candles. Their tender flickering flames hummed as they burned. 'Of course, also, my reputation,' he mocked.

'Reputation is welcome here,' she assured, she spun to the side and took a taper for Harris.

As she handed it to him, his lips parted. He glared at the taper. 'I don't need that, thank you.'

She looked distressed. Her voice deepened. 'You did not morn them?'

'Who?' Harris raised his brows.

She gave a slight laugh. His misunderstanding was sweet to her. 'Those who you've lost.'

'There aren't enough candles on Cammbour.' His eyes spun to the candles. He felt their warm glow against his face. 'Besides, it wouldn't bring them back.' Harris twisted. He headed towards the front pews. Lorena followed behind him.

Lorena held a tone of wonder. 'You are here for comfort, but you refuse to embrace it?' She took a seat beside Harris as he sat. 'Why is that?'

Harris leant down. He caught his hands in front of him and rested his elbows on his lap. 'I don't come here for comfort. I come here to remember.' He twisted his head to her. 'My sisters, they wanted to serve in the temples, in Xencliff. My father was so proud when he found out, it was just before—' Harris stopped. He could no longer speak of it.

'I assume their candles are yet to be lit?' Her tender voice brought comfort to Harris. He did not feel angry, he felt lost. 'You have carried this burden for far too long, Harris.' She placed her hand on his shoulder. 'It is no longer your burden to bear.'

'It will always be my burden,' his voice broke. 'My life has led me here. To this temple. So much has happened in such a brief space of time. I just need to straighten out, that's all.'

His comment confused Lorena. Her usual knowledge of the world did not provide her an answer. 'I can only offer you this.' She shook her head, not knowing what else to say. 'As long as you feel pain, you are still alive, and as long as you keep trying, there is still hope. The birds sing strongest, after a storm, to let everyone know they're still alive.'

Her words forced Harris to sit straight. 'My storm is far from over.' He raised his brows.

'Then you must end one storm, before another can begin.' Her soft way with words spoke to Harris. He knew she was right, but it was not how he worked.

'You are a wonder of this world, Harris. Your past has brought you to this moment now. If there is something you need to change, you must first let go of it before you can change your future.' Lorena stood.

Silently she ambled back towards the altar. Her flowing white dress was impossible to see past as she swirled. She strolled back towards Harris, handing him a taper.

'It doesn't mean you're letting go. You are Xencliff, Harris, you hold grudges, not your past.' Lorena left Harris in the temple of silent contemplation.

He spent his day with the image of his sisters, standing on the cliff, calling his name. The barn, as the Atlanti entered, giving his mother the choice of whom to save. They taunted her. They were cruel, calculating. He could still hear their screams reaching into the trees. The candles in his deep green eyes reminded him of the flames from the barn that night.

As he sat in the temple. For the first time in over twenty years, he felt pity for his mother. She faced the impossible, and he blamed her for that. He rarely took the chance to reflect on such things, but as the stars covered the skies, he was ready. He wanted to let go of his past. His sister's pain and terror. He realised his revenge many times since. Now he wanted to focus on the next phase of his life. Becoming the commander he needed to be.

As he stood, he took the taper; he lit four candles, and left. Lorena stood at the door. 'May I ask,' — she stepped towards him, — 'who were they for?'

Harris glanced towards the candles. 'My father, Eric, my sisters Adella and Allie.'

'And the fourth?'

Harris glanced back again. 'As I say, there aren't enough candles. The fourth is for the rest. I can tell you their names, but that would take a turn.'

She stood back. Harris had seen more death and destruction than most. His time as The Commander was only beginning.

The beds in Sonnin were far more comfortable than the hard beds of Cronnin. Their use of the soft woods around them and soft wool provided a refreshing rest for Harris. He did not plan to stay in Sonnin for long.

The guest quarters of the palace were at the back of the hall. Past the large round room which stood in the centre of the hall.

His night of rest was disturbed upon hearing footsteps outside of his door. Harris lifted himself up off the bed. The fire flowers in the room lit, a dim blue surrounded the room, the door opened.

'Who's there?' Harris asked. His deep, rumbling voice sent a shock-wave through her. She stepped inside. 'Harelda?' She stepped into his room.

With nothing but a thin gown covering her slender frame, she softly stepped in. 'Good evening,' she greeted with a tender voice, closing the door behind her.

'Why are you here?' He allowed a smile to grow. The very sight of her woke something in him. He forgot that his reputation.

Harelda glided towards him. Her caramel locks of soft, flowing hair hung by her side and waved down her back. Her eyes shone in the light of the blue room. He could now admit that she was stunningly beautiful.

'Harris, let me make one thing very clear.' She strolled towards him. 'I find you irresistible.' Her eyes shone with lust. 'I have waited a long time to meet you and have you alone.' She sat on the edge of the bed.

Her wavy hair drifted towards the bed sheets, blending with the silk. She reached down and undid the ties to her gown. 'I will wait no longer, commander, take me or reject me. The choice is yours.' She dropped her gown.

Harris's eyes drifted about her body. He could not fight his nature. Her skin was as soft as a fresh peach. Her hair was like the softest silk. He knelt on the bed behind her. Kissing her neck and shoulders. His hands reached around to feel her breasts.

She had carried several children, but it did not show in her magical fae body. Her skin was still young and firm. His hands drifted down her stomach. Towards the place where he knew how to give his queen the most pleasure she'd ever felt. Not only did he want to please her, he wanted to impress her.

His Xencliff teachings would show that night. His tongue was his most powerful weapon. He pleased her in ways she had never experienced before.

Harris rode from Sonnin, fresh. But not for any good reason. He came to terms with the hate for his mother. As he rode down the rain drenched roads, his head spun. His stomach twisted, full of guilt. The roads darkened as storm clouds loomed overhead.

'She's obsessed,' he said to himself, riding on Svend. Svend twisted his eyes but continued cantering. 'How am I going to tell her? She will find out. You're not helping here, Svend.,' — Svend slowed to a trot, — 'she's going to kill me, and I mean, actually fucking kill me!'

Luckily, the road was empty, otherwise he would appear insane. Harris held his head. He sat up straight on Svend. 'Ah! What have I done?' His eyes filled with more fear. 'She is marrying Angus. She can't expect me to just go without for the rest of my life. Despite that, she is her mother. I could marry Harelda? Nope, that would be weird. I just won't tell her. Simple. I'll say nothing, and if she ever finds out, I can deny it completely.' He nodded.

He held Svend's reins. Svend gave a shake to his head as his trot became a slow walk. 'I don't think she'll believe me either.' He became silent. His own argument defeated him. He lifted his head and sighed. 'It was only supposed to be a quick stop.'

Never a man to be ashamed of his actions, he thought of every regrettable decision he had ever made. Nothing compared to his night of passion with Harelda Duirwud.

ᚲᚺᚨᛈᛏᛖᚱ ᛖᛁᚷᚺᛏᛖᛖᚾ

18

Isradella laid in the chambers of the tower midwife. An older lady, who had seen many travel by her chambers. She watched in terror as the lady pressed on her lower stomach.

Standing straight, the lady replaced Isradella's garments. 'Congratulations,' she said, widening her smile.

Isradella sat up. Her tears flowed down her cheeks.

'You are not pleased?' the lady asked.

Isradella sniffed up, taking a deep breath in. 'I am pleased. My husband will be most humbled by this.'

'You may wish to tell him soon. Plenty of fresh water. Keep yourself warm and rested. It is not an illness, but your young age can cause certain complications.'

'What complications?' asked Isradella, struggling to stand at the thought of the news.

The lady busied herself, washing her hands. 'Death is the most ultimate complication of childbirth. Of course, there are others. We have a woman in the town who became a cripple, some who simply struggle to recover from a broken mind. Childbirth is not something one can take lightly.' She turned, facing Isradella. Her smile tightened. 'Although, I'm sure you will be fine. We have the best midwives here to assist you.'

'Assist?'

'Well yes, my dear, —' she stepped closer to her. — 'You will not be alone.'

'You will stay with me?'

'Well, of course,' chuckled the lady.

Walking from the chambers, Isradella felt the cold stones of the floor seeping through her silk slippers. Every corridor shed more darkness. A bleak future awaited her.

'I read the book,' Librye whispered. Stood opposite Harris's desk. The early morning sun was still dull in the room. He wrapped his head in his arms. He sat, resting his head on the desk. 'Harris,' she whispered, trying to wake him slowly. 'It's called from the shadows.'

'I'm just resting my eyes,' he mumbled. He had not moved since returning amidst the early morning chorus. The mist of rain seeped into his leather cloak. His arm braces and leg braces were still upon his person. His swords still hung by his side. He didn't even bother to take his cloak off.

Her voice quivered with a sound of sadness. 'I read the book, Harris. Is it true?'

Harris raised his head from the desk, as if it weighed far heavier than it did when he left Cronnin.

'Which book?' A mumbled tiredness dwelled deep in his throat. He reached for a glass at the side of his desk. Having left a glass of water before he left for Sonnin. It would not be the best, but it would quench his thirst. He glared at Librye with his brows furrowed. 'You're looking better, at least.'

'I'm feeling much better. The pain is still there, but it isn't as bad now.' Her voice of anguish snapped Harris from his strange mood. 'Maude doesn't know I'm here.' She glanced down. She stepped back from the desk that her chin only just reached. To reveal she was still wearing her cotton nightgown.

Harris raised his brows. He disapproved of Librye sneaking out. 'What's this book you speak of?'

Librye tutted. 'From the shadows. Is it true?'

Harris gave a twisted smile; he had read the book. 'Artistic licence. Some of it is true.' His eyes twisted to a quick open glare towards the desk. 'Most of it is true.' He gazed back at Librye and softened his eyes. 'I told you not to read it. Why did you?'

Librye thought for a moment, her innocent smile twisted to the side. She leered at him from the corner of her eyes. 'You fascinate me.'

Harris sat back; his brow furrowed. 'Not another one,' he whined.

Librye broke her look, her brow pulled in. 'What do you mean?'

Harris shook his head. He sat forwards, placing his hands on the desk. 'Never mind. Let's just say some of the book carries certain exaggerations.'

'What part?' She stepped forwards. Her excited eyes glared at him.

Harris rolled his eyes and puffed out his cheeks. 'I can't say exactly, but a writer would call it artistic licence.' His smile grew as he sat back.

'Certainly, they would need your permission first?'

Harris gave a slow sigh. He rested back in his chair, placing his hands at the back of his head. 'She had my permission. Her name is Cally, she's a tavern owner. She witnessed most of the things I did in that book, but like I say, some of it is a gross exaggeration.'

Librye stepped further forwards. Her eyes examined his, wondering what parts of the book were true. 'You once hung a man from a bar?'

Harris gave a low nod. 'Sort of.' He was as vague as he could be. 'That one is true.'

'You hit a man so hard he was dead before he hit the floor?'

Harris stood from his chair; his face was a comical unchanged look of hidden pride. 'I don't want to play this game.' He made his way towards his bedchambers at the back.

'It isn't a game, Harris!' Librye pursued him. 'Is it true?' She stood by the door to his room.

Harris twisted; he spun his finger for Librye to turn, so he could change. He sat on the edge of his bed. 'Why are you so interested, tiny one?'

Librye twisted slightly. 'You're supposed to be teaching me. So far, I have very little to go on,' she complained.

Harris gave a heavy sigh of defeat. He stood, placing his armour on the mannequin in the room. 'Very well, yes, that is sort of true. However, no one can confirm if he was dead before he hit the floor or not.'

Librye thought for a moment. 'Is it true you once took on thirty Atlanti and won?'

Harris changed his tunic from one black tunic into another. 'That is true.'

'How?' She spun. Excited to find out more.

He again swirled his finger, mid-air, for Librye to turn. 'I was returning from Rathen. They have a creature there, in the swamps, a frog. Its poison is so potent it can kill a thousand men in seconds. I coated my blades and had some fun.'

Librye was astonished. His honesty was what she needed, even if it made her feel slightly ill.

'What about the Atlanti camp? Even in the book, it says you came across a camp in the dead of night. By the morning, they were all dead?'

Harris laughed. It confused Librye. 'It was an easy one, turn back.' As Librye spun, Harris was buckling his trousers. 'The Atlanti tents are much like ours. The side of them is easy to get under, but I didn't go under. I learnt a lot in Xencliff. We have salt mines. In the mines. It made a horrid smelling chemical, Chlora. Along with the crystals, which come from the running of the mill wheels. Mix the two and add to water. However, I added it to vinegar. The gas killed them all overnight.' His knowledge of such things far outweighed hers. It was the first time Librye felt like a child.

She ambled towards him. Her mouth was gaping, her footsteps slowed. 'You poisoned them?' Her mouth curled down; trepidation filled her eyes.

'They were a party searching for—' Harris paused. He gazed into her innocent eyes. 'Librye, all the people I killed, all those men. They were evil men.' He nodded with his eyes wide. 'The world is filled with the beauty you see, tiny one, but it is also filled with the shit I see.'

'What were they looking for, Harris?'

Harris sat up. He did not know how to reply, but knew he had to. 'I keep having to tell myself you're a child, secretly I know, you're so much more than that.' His face turned to a lost look of sorrow. 'They were looking for women, Librye, young women, to take. They force them to have their children. The Atlanti are much larger than fae and faemen, but the children of these women are as nimble as we are. Only they are larger, better built, and stronger.'

Librye could not reply. She wanted to forget all what Harris said, but knew she could not. Her mind would not allow her to.

'You need to stop that,' she said. Harris furrowed his brow. 'You use terrible language all the time.' It was clear she disagreed with Harris's swearing. 'But you are the smartest person I know.'

Her words shocked Harris. He sat back and laughed. 'I'm not smart, Librye. In fact, I'm very fucking stupid,' he huffed, having flashbacks of his time in Sonnin.

Librye did not know what he was talking about, but what she saw was Harris's modesty. 'I think you're more intelligent than you often let on.'

'You have to be in this business. From a young age, I struggled to understand the world. It was as if I was born with it all,' he laughed. He took his boots and began putting them back on. 'What else did you read?' He sat up straight.

'The man whose throat you crushed.' She widened her eyes.

Her excitement worried Harris, but he still wanted to be honest with Librye. 'True.'

Librye stood back. She lifted her arms. 'Then what part of this is exaggerated?'

Harris thought for a moment. He placed his hand on his chin. 'It says in the book, The Commander told Cally, the author, of his travels.' He grabbed his other boot and put it on. 'That isn't true, most of them she witnessed. I only gave her small snippets of my travels. The rest were from other taverns.'

Her voice softened; her eyes drooped. 'How many have you killed, Harris?'

Harris sat up; his pride withered. 'I couldn't tell you. All I know is that everyone was Atlanti fighting blood. Did they deserve it? Perhaps, did I save lives by ending theirs, most definitely.'

His past was clear to Librye. Regardless of how he wanted to see it, he was a cold killer. Harris, however, was still her guardian, her protector, and her friend. She would have it no other way.

'They never charged me with a crime. No crime can be committed against those who fight the common enemy of the crown,' he quoted. Harris sat forwards. He gazed deep into Librye's eyes. 'What it doesn't mention in that book are those I saved. The village I turned the Atlanti from, killing no one. The Atlanti village I was in, I saved three women there.' His eyes shone with a rarely seen hint of pride. 'The hundreds I have saved should outweigh those I've killed.' Harris stood; he made his way towards the door. 'A bit of advice you may wish to keep close to your heart, Librye.' He twisted to face her. 'You can do a thousand things right, save countless lives. But make one mistake, and that is what people will remember.'

His words shook her. From that moment, she knew he felt forsaken. Those who spoke of The Shadow, spoke of those he killed, not the thousands he saved.

'Harris, can I tell you a secret?' She drifted towards him. Harris stopped. He closed the door and stood ready to listen. 'When I was in the camps, there was a boy. A lot of them were mean to me, but he would hurt us. Some of the other girls there, he touched them in places.'

Harris saw the look of pain in her eyes. He could see she witnessed some atrocities, just like he had.

'There was one girl. She ran to the woods after he touched her. We never saw her again.' Her voice broke. 'He tried to touch me again. I stopped him and the camp keeper discovered him, so they beat him. I struggled.'

Harris crouched in front of her. 'Whatever you did, I am sure it was for the best,' he said, trying to comfort her.

'No,' she lifted her eyes. Her voice remained a broken softness. 'I felt nothing,' she whispered. 'Every scream I heard from him, I enjoyed it, knowing he caused so much pain.'

Harris rose, seeing the hate in her crushed him.

'Every lashing he took, I never wanted it to end, I wanted him, not only dead, but suffering.'

Harris parted his lips, shocked to hear such words filled with hate from a child.

'I know he suffered. But sometimes, I feel like he just didn't suffer enough. He should be dead.'

'Librye, forgiveness starts with the end of the breath,' again he quoted Malgron. 'Failure to forgive is drinking the poison of your enemies. One day, you will learn that you must forgive, in order to continue.'

'Do you?' She stepped towards him. Reaching out, she took his hand. Her haunting orange eyes gazed at him. 'Do you forgive, Harris?'

He took a moment to think. Her eyes frightened him that day. It was a colour he had never seen. 'I do. I forgave my mother, and I will forgive myself for my misguided hate. One day, even the Atlanti, the Azorae, they will be forgiven too.'

'We can only hope,' she whispered.

Harris brought happiness to the lives of many. His eccentric tactics were brutal, but Librye knew now she was just like him. He would rather end a life fast, rather than see the suffering he could bring. He had been a killer for so long, but now, Librye saw him as a saviour.

The palace was busy with the usual hustle and bustle. He marched from the tower and down the east corridor. Stepping into Librye's chambers, he helped her back into bed before Maude finally appeared.

'Oh!' she jumped as she saw him by Librye's bed with his hands in his pockets. 'You're back then?'

'I am, Maude, and I can assure you, it will be for a while,' he promised.

'I only hope you had some form of relaxation.' She raised her brows as she walked to the other side of Librye's bed.

'I don't know if I could call it that, but I'm back now, and I'm off to see Gethen.'

Watching him leave, Maude looked at Librye. 'They say so much about him, and I hate myself for listening.'

'What have you heard?'

Maude shook her head. 'Too many things, all of them lies. He's a gentleman, really.'

'Or perhaps he is both?' said Librye.

'What's he been telling you?' asked Maude, narrowing her eyes.

'Nothing much. I like to keep his secrets with my own,' she replied with a grin.

The galleries were quiet as he entered. Gethen was absent that day. Muffled voices came from the gardens. As he reached the patio, the voices stopped. Rebecca turned and silenced upon seeing him.

'A victory indeed, commander,' she said with a wide smile as she came towards him.

Harris stood relaxed, with his hands behind his back. 'Victory, yes. We can only hope now for a reform.'

'Reform?' she asked as she came closer.

'Well, this is the way with war. For centuries, the Atlanti have tried to rise. We have waited a long time for someone of moderate intelligence to take the seat of power, so they can better guide their people.'

'You speak of integration,' said Rebecca.

'Of course, we cannot make an entire race of people extinct. But they must bow to Angus, as their true king.'

'Do you believe they will?'

'I believe this is the beginning.'

'Of what?'

'You ask a lot of questions,' he said with laughter. 'It is the beginning of something new, whether that is good or bad, I'm yet to understand.'

She came closer to him. 'But what do you really believe?'

'If Kairne has an ounce of intelligent thought, this could see our nations join, were he an idiot. A new war is brewing, much more brutal than the last.' She raised her brows, waiting for a proper answer. 'I don't know him, so I cannot rate his capability.' He turned, but before he left, he looked over his shoulder. 'What do you believe he will do?'

'I wouldn't know,' she softly replied.

'No, didn't think so,' he muttered as he left.

Angus's chambers were empty as Harris entered. Sauntering in, he looked at Evan still stood at the door.

'Do we know where our attentive king is this morning?'

'He came in earlier, but ran off to see Poppy,' replied Evan.

'Poppy?'

'She's a scribe. She squirrels away in the palace archives. Librye mentioned something to Angus yesterday, while you were in Sonnin. How was it, by the way?' he sheepishly asked.

'Uneventful, completely and utterly, nothing happened at all. In fact, it was so boring, I would rather have been back in Marrion.'

Narrowing his eyes, Evan asked, 'That bad?'

'Like you wouldn't fucking believe,' sighed Harris.

'Will this need Xencliff ears?' asked Evan.

'What time do you finish?' whispered Harris.

'You're my commander. It could be now if you're completely desperate.'

'Well then, off we fuck,' said Harris, smiling at Helen on the other side.

'That is completely unfair,' complained Helen.

'You'll get your turn,' said Harris with a wink.

'Married, commander.'

'Good for you. You'll still get your turn,' he said, pushing Evan from the door.

It had been a while since Harris had sat in a busy bar. The bustling city coming and going from the grime covered windows. The city guard watched cloaked figures closely as they wandered the streets.

'It can't be that bad,' said Evan, reaching for the tankard of ale Harris returned with.

'It's worse than bad. I dislike myself because of it.' He sat opposite him. Evan sat with a blank look on his face. 'I could chop my cock off and it could only make me happy.'

'No,' gasped Evan, he sat forwards and whispered, 'Harelda?'

'Shush!' hissed Harris, waving his finger in front of his lips. 'No one can know about this.'

'What about Branwen?'

'Especially not Branwen,' panicked Harris.

'Rumours spread quicker than fires here. I know that stories of me and Branwen must have reached here.'

'Not until you arrived back. To be honest, we didn't get much from Marrion. It was your show to the council which gave it away for us,' said Evan with a smirk. 'So, how true is it?'

'She started it,' said Harris, glancing repeatedly at Evan.

'She just,' — he shook his head — 'jumped you?'

Harris waved his head with a nod. 'Practically.'

Evan chuckled, putting his head back. 'They warned you, Harris, this reputation would bite you—'

'Well, it turns out it did, but now, the moment Branwen speaks to her mother, if she tells her what happened.'

Evan held his hand up for Harris to stop. 'Either you castrate yourself, of let one or them do it,' his sniggering didn't help.

'I'm Xencliff.' Harris shrugged.

'So am I, but I don't stick my cock in everything with a pulse.'

'Who said it needs a pulse?' said Harris with a grin.

'Come on, Harris, it's just a mistake. If what you're saying is right, you didn't really have much choice. Men are weak—'

'So weak,' said Harris, wide eyed.

'And we have very little self-control in that area.'

'I never have.'

'Exactly, so, if they find out, you tell them you are a weak man, a very weak man, who came across two stunning beauties, and you had no choice.'

'Is this before or after the tiny axe comes out to take my cock?'

'Tiny?' asked Evan, his grin grew.

'After today, I don't think I'll ever find it again.'

'Probably for the best,' said Evan with an ever-growing grin.

Madness fell on the Rathen tower. Spinning in her chambers, the morning light slowly brightened the dull walls. The stone floors froze her feet. The air outside was bitter. Isradella pulled at her hair, pacing, tears streamed down her face as her maid tried to calm her.

'Please, miss!' screeched her maid.

'I can't be this! I can't do this!' Isradella panicked through wet tears as she spun. She froze, glaring at the maid. She made a fist. Swinging her arm high, she spun it back with as much force as she could, thudding herself in the stomach. Again and again, she beat herself repeatedly.

Rushing into the chambers, three guards followed Kairne. He ran towards her, holding her hands.

'What have you done?' he hissed. His hands shook, his black hair waved as he tried to still his shaking heart.

'I can't die!' she screamed in his face. He threw her into the arms of his guards.

'Take her to the second tower, tie her down, do not let her out of your sight,' he commanded as he stormed from the room.

A drip of blood trickled down her leg as she left. The maid leant down, seeing the blood. As she rose from the ground, Kairne stood with his hands on the doorframe, glaring at the drip.

'Do not let her out of your sight. Get the midwife,' he demanded.

Harris struggled back towards the palace. Evan made his way home for the day, a small house just outside the palace grounds.

Meeting Harris in the hall, Branwen strode towards him. He buried his hands deep in his pockets.

'What are your plans for today?'

Harris peered around the hall. 'I have work to do, Bran. My duty here is to ensure the safety of the people of this city. I can do that better if I'm there.' His voice was a quivering mess of unrequited terror. 'Besides, now we have Tosta and Belgravia. It won't be long, and negotiations will begin. I need to prepare myself.'

'You are leading them?' Branwen shook, surprised Angus would allow such a thing.

'Xencliff, merrow, mabeara, Cronnin and Azorae. It all runs through my veins. Who better to lead than a man who has everything?' He gazed into her eyes.

Branwen gave a fleeting glance. 'I did not know you were Azorae.' Her voice filled with fear, a dread took over her eyes.

'Come on, Bran,' smirked Harris. 'Many of us contain all. What makes me different is merrow, not Atlanti. I am still Xencliff, to the deepest core of my bones.' It was an odd feeling. Harris turned in the hall, and she watched as he left.

She felt differently about him now. She did not care for his linage. Her admiration for him grew once more. She felt hope.

The streets were seeing the cold onset of Autumn. The Greendia moon was yet to complete its course through the skies. As Harris made his way through the streets, the bitter winds raged at him. It surprised the people of the city to see him out alone. As the commander, he did not need protecting; he was the protection they had.

A small tavern on the corner of Small Street caught his eye. Beside it, a barber shop stood empty. Harris stepped inside. A young man peered back towards him. His hands shook, looking at Harris.

'Better stop shaking, boy,' Harris warned as he stepped further in. The daggers on his boots rattled like chains as he came towards the young man. Towering over him, he peered down. Harris pointed to his hair. 'What can you do with this?'

The young man's face lit. Like a new festival hit him in the face, he inspected the long black locks of hair. 'So much.'

Harris sat in the low chair. He decided. He would become the man Cronnin clearly wanted him to be.

'Tell me, commander,' said the young man, as he began cutting, 'What made you do this?'

Harris took a slow blink. He hated the idea of changing his image. So much happened in such a short time. He needed to become someone different.

'My blood is Xencliff. I hate the Cronnin style. The little shit on the door to the palace is hounding me constantly. They even voted. Can you believe that? An entire palace, voting on the state of my hair?'

The young man continued cutting. 'It sounds like they care about you.' Harris glared at him through the mirror in front. 'Anyone who cares that much about someone's hair. Must care about the person it belongs to.'

Harris nodded slightly in agreement. Relaxing back, he mentioned, 'Just keep some Xencliff.' His voice spilt desperation; it had been years since he had cut it. The barber struggled, as his hair was so thick, but he knew exactly what he needed to do. He kept his hair long. Taking away the thick dreadlocks which had formed in the middle. A simple trim was all he needed, thinning it out with a razor. Harris could still tie his hair, but it would not be so untamed. Cronnin tamed Harris and his wild, barbaric hair.

A bitter cold swept his head as Harris headed back towards the palace. The eyes of the city were on him, or so he thought.

The palace gates were oddly quiet. He came towards them. A woman stood dressed in dark brown trousers, black boots, and a red cape. She stood at the side of the gates carrying a large brown leather bag, waiting for a guard to approach. Harris saw her waiting.

'Can I help you?'

'No, I'll await the guard.'

She inspected Harris up and down; he found it rather odd that she was so abrupt. He investigated her, noticing her cloak. It carried the emblem of a dove, a currier. 'Where are you arriving from?'

She peered through the gates to see the guard approach. 'Bourellis.' She dropped her uptight attitude as she stepped towards him.

Harris widened his eyes. 'Sent by Bushwell Oris?'

'That's King Bushwell Oris, and yes.' Her raised brows dropped. 'How did you know that?'

'Harris,' he introduced, giving a custom welcome. She, too, gave a customary welcome. 'Harris Bearwood, Chief Commander to King, Angus Oakwood. I'm also the one who will ultimately receive the package.'

A guard stepped towards the gate. 'Oh, Harris,' gasped the guard. She stepped closer. 'Much better.' Her smile widened. Harris's smile lit. 'For a moment there, I was thinking you were trying to look like the arse end of Svend.'

Stepping into the gate. He twisted to the currier and took the leather bag.

The chambers were thick with Angus's pipe smoke. Harris lumped the bag on his desk. Angus was nowhere to be seen. He glanced at the guard at the door. 'Where exactly is our attentive king?'

'Librye,' she awkwardly replied. Harris grabbed the bag and ran to her chambers.

Librye was in the throes of another episode. Passed out in her bed. She was wet with sweat. Her skin was a pale blue. Her lips turned the colour of an unripe plum.

Harris placed the bag on the bed. He glanced at Angus, sat holding Librye's hand. He pulled a letter from the bag, his eyes frantically searched the letter.

'Fuck, Angus.' He dropped the letter down. He held his hand to his head. 'It say's in this if we don't slow it, she will die.' Angus stood and snatched the letter from him to confirm. Harris searched the bag. Several vials of blue liquid were in there. He took one and tried his best to pour it into her mouth.

'What are you doing?' Angus felt a heavy sweat on his brow.

'It says on there, this should slow it down. We have a few turns to get her to Bourellis. She needs to be there, Angus.' Harris stood straight. He could see the look of doubt Angus held. Angus glared at him, a rage filled his eyes. 'Don't, Angus, I'm warning you. Don't be selfish. She needs to be with the torbs. There is nothing we can do here.

Holding onto her will only make this worse.' His voice softened. He stepped around the bed. 'I know this is frightening. It is for me, too. But we cannot let her sink further.'

Angus melted as Harris came closer. 'I like your hair,' he pouted. 'I know you're right, Harris.' He walked closer to him. 'You always seem to be right. I should listen more, but we will take her, both of us. We will both take our girl to Bourellis. There we can cure her of her burden.' His words spelt of mistrust in the torbs. He knew of their dark magic, and his Librye was not some experiment for them.

His chambers were dark as Harris stepped in. Fire flowers slowly lit his way. Something was off. His senses were a maze of awareness. His bed was not empty. He took his belt off and placed it at the side of his desk. Slowly, he made his way into his bedroom, wondering, fearing who could be there.

'Marriage, Harris,' Branwen sat on the side of the bed; a bright blue fae gown barely covered her.

'You having second thoughts?'

'Not really, it's just when I am married, then I can never touch another man. Until then, I suppose I'm still free.'

'It doesn't work that way. You are promised to him—'

'Who says?'

'Well, tradition says,' replied Harris.

'Tradition is not law.'

Harris relaxed. He removed his gloves and placed them on a dresser at the side of him. 'No. You promised yourself to Angus. That is a promise you must keep.' He walked towards her. 'We must remain loyal to him, Bran.' He tenderly stroked her hair; she tilted her head for her face to meet the palm of his hand. 'As much as I just want to have you right now, we can't.'

'I can break my bond with Angus.' She stood. 'But I can't with you.' She pressed herself against him. Sliding her hand down, she cupped his manhood.

'No.' He drew back, moving her hand away. He could see her mother in her eyes. Her soft caramel hair, just like Harelda's. 'We can't, Bran.'

'Please, Harris,' she begged, forcing herself towards him. She reached up to him and kissed his lips.

Eyes wide open, Harris gladly received the kiss. He was far too easily swayed by women. She again reached down and took him in her hand. He could not stop himself. He lay her on his bed. She finally got her own way again.

Along the rolling cliffs of Xencliff, the calls of seabirds filled the skies. The smell of freshly caught fish and salty sea air filled the noses of the noise loving people, who dwelled upon the cliffs.

The booming waves crashed on the shores of the kingdom of Xencliff. The cliffs were a honeycomb of walkways. Built into the long cliffs, the palace of Xencliff was invisible to the land. Ships coming and going had the perfect view of the palace cliff. A carved colossal structure overlooking the mighty ocean.

The throne of Waron Chen Lu sat back in the mighty central cave. Protected by land and sea, the palace was impenetrable. The mighty halls within the palace echoed with the thundering ocean. Stood in her chambers, Riah Chen Lu awaited her husband's return.

She was his last wife, his favoured wife. Time had been kind to her. Her long black hair platted down her back past her waist. Wearing a green wrap dress, tied perfectly, showing her slim figure, broad shoulders and wide hips. She had the figure of a woman upon the seat of power. Her ecru skin shone in the light of her chambers.

A knock at her door startled her. Slowly, she opened the door to a palace messenger. She took the letter and closed the door. Her deep green eyes read the letter she hoped to receive for over twenty years.

'I begin by asking you not to burn this. Please, read, and give me a chance. I know it's been a while. This may be hard for you to read. I have not gone completely insane. Although, sometimes I wish I would. I struggle to say I apologise, I struggle to forget or remember. We've both suffered enough. You are all I have left, and I miss my family. I need to know you now. I need to know my family. Please reply. I look forwards to hearing from you. Your son, Harris Bearwood.'

Riah dropped to her knees. 'Guard!' she called out.

Three guards burst through the doors to her bedchamber.

'Bring my husband, now.' Her panicked voice sent them flying through the hall.

A small child wandered through into Riah's bedchambers, seeing her on the floor sent the child running towards her. 'Mama?'

'Kiva,' Riah reached towards her. 'Your brother, he's coming home.' A tear dropped from her eye.

'Harris?' asked Kiva.

Riah nodded, holding Kiva close to her chest.

Harris sat at his desk, awaiting a reply from his mother. His work dwindled. Council meetings became dull. They invited him into the halls of the council. Although he tried not to attend.

Sat silently in his chambers, Harris read the letters placed there that morning. The smell of rain drifted in on the breeze from outside. The mid-afternoon brought a heavy rain, battering the city of Cronnin.

Harris lifted his head. Hearing someone walking through the east corridor. The door below opened. Harris sat back, placing his quill down. He waited to see who was paying him a visit.

Pounding up the stairs, Gethen appeared. 'What are you doing here?' Harris noticed the wide smile on Gethen's face. He carried some secret knowledge.

He placed a bowl of soup on Harris's desk, along with a lump of fresh bread. 'Nice to see you too, Harris.'

Harris's eyes lit. He was not expecting such a visit, but he appreciated it. 'It's just odd. You've never been here before. Why now?' He narrowed his eyes.

Gethen sat. He pushed the bowl towards Harris. Still, he kept his smile. 'I just came for a visit.'

Harris's eyes thinned further. He said with a deep tone of warning, 'Gethen.'

Gethen's smile grew further. He leant forwards. 'Harelda?'

Harris's eyes turned to a look of trepidation. He struggled to hold it in. 'What?'

'Staff from Sonnin, they often bring messages to Cronnin. They said you, and Harelda—' He raised a single brow.

Harris stood. His eyes swirled, filled with horror. With one hand on his hip and the other across his mouth, he took his hand from his mouth and pointed at Gethen.

'Silence them,' he ordered. His teeth gritted. 'You need to silence them now.'

'So, it's true?' asked Gethen awkwardly.

Harris widened his eyes towards Gethen. Filled with threat, he ordered, 'Silence them now!'

Gethen stood, he pointed at Harris as he said from under his brow, 'You owe me for this.' Gethen left back towards the galleries.

Harris remained pacing behind his desk, his brow dripped with a heavy sweat. 'Why?' He placed his hands on his head. 'Why am I so stupid?' he loudly asked, he pointed to his crotch. 'This is your fault,' he whispered.

'I don't think you're stupid at all.' Branwen stood at the top of the stairs.

Harris jumped, giving an audible yell. 'I didn't see you there.'

She came towards his desk, a long, flowing dress followed behind her. 'They have asked me to return to Sonnin, only for a few days,' — she came towards the desk, — 'I only came to let you know.' Her voice was soft, a sadness followed her.

'Very well.' Harris stood frozen at the back of his desk. 'I hope you have a pleasant trip.'

Branwen could see the look of panic he showed in his eyes. She frowned at him. 'What is the matter?'

He frantically shook his head. 'Nothing,' he nervously laughed. 'Nothing wrong with me at all.' He walked to the side of his desk. 'Why would you ask that?'

'Harris?' She watched him walk from one side of the desk to the other. 'Something is clearly bothering you.'

Harris spun. 'I'm absolutely fine.' An idea blasted into his head. 'I've sent a letter, that's all. I'm awaiting a reply,' — he twisted to his desk. — 'But, no reply today, so I'm off out.' He took his black hooded cloak from a hook on the wall to the right of the chambers. 'Enjoy Sonnin.'

Branwen blinked. Her mouth gaped, shocked at Harris's hurried behaviour. 'I was thinking you could come with me?'

He left down the stairs. 'Nope!' He made his way down the stairs. 'That's a terrible idea!' The door to the tower slammed shut. Branwen stood, confused and concerned, alone in Harris's tower.

Librye sat alone in her chambers. The windows cried with rain. She remained in her bed. Whatever Bushwell sent, helped. Although she knew she needed more. She loved the thought of what her future would bring. She slowly hated being different.

Slowly, she rose from her bed and made her way towards her balcony. She didn't notice the puddle on the floor of the balcony. The wind whistled and whispered around the building. The world was talking to her, but she did not know what it was saying.

A call from the streets caught her attention. She could only just see over the stone railing of the balcony. She peered towards the city. The gigantic wall blocked her view of the people there. She wanted to see more that day; she had a strange need within her to see the people. Her chambers offered her nothing but loneliness.

Maude sat with her for the night and took the day to get some rest. With the skies dulling in the wake of a wet evening, Librye left her chambers.

'Librye,' grumbled Helen with a tone of warning. 'Maude said you are to stay in your room. You aren't well.' She crouched towards her.

Librye glared at her. 'I need to get out. I need some air,' she softly pleaded.

She tightly pressed her lips; it was a poor idea. 'Open the balcony.'

'I've been standing there for most of the day,' she complained. 'They can't keep me locked in like a wolf in a kennel, Helen. I need to get out.'

Helen stood, she glanced at the other guard stood with her. 'What do you say? Only to the gardens and back?'

'I agree,' smiled the guard. She took Librye's hand, and they made their way down the stairs.

'Can we go to the front of the palace, please?' Librye peered up at the two guards escorting her down.

The guards glanced at each other. Helen gazed down at Librye. 'Why the front? There's nothing to see at the front.'

Librye's eyes widened. 'The people, I want to see people.' Her innocent reply confused them both. They did as Librye wished. Passing Balthus. They strolled towards the front of the palace and out the large door. Staying close behind, they watched her walk towards the enormous gates. The guards on the gates followed her closely with their eyes. She held the bars on the gate and gazed out into the vast city of Cronnin. Mothers with their children. Fathers, running past to meet them as they finished their work for the day.

Her need for a family had never been clear before. The guards all watched her at the palace gates. Longing filled the air. She did not know her parents. She did not understand who she was or where she was from. She did not even fathom what she was. The reality for Librye was slowly sinking in. She was a creature. Not known on Cammbour, she was different.

The children on the grounds close to the palace ignored she was there. She could hear their whispers. 'Leave her alone.' As her strange turquoise eyes glared towards them. Her mouth gaped. She watched the people of the city, leading normal lives. She was not normal. At first, it was what she liked most about herself, but now it was the one thing she was slowly hating.

'Evening,' greeted Harris, as he hurried towards the palace gates. 'Shouldn't you be resting?'

Librye gazed at him. Tears filled her eyes and ran down her cheek. 'I don't want rest.'

A shock of sadness hit Harris. He saw her tears. He knelt in front of her. The gravel on his knees made him wince as he did.

'What is it?' He reached out and dried her tears with his gloves.

Librye held her head down. She twisted back to the gate. 'I just want to be like that. All that I know, I wish I didn't. I can bear not knowing my family. My past, but what am I, Harris, what kind of creature am I?'

It filled her with a longing to know. She refused to accept the graphic reality of how her family was destroyed. She did not care about Farhope's history where she was found. She simply wanted to know what she was to call herself.

Harris took a deep sigh. He remained on his knees; she twisted back to face him.

'Librye,' he sighed. 'So many times, each day. I have to remind myself you're only a child.' He gazed into her eyes, filled with sadness.

'I'll tell you what you are, Librye. You are not a creature. Never call yourself that.' Harris stood. He was firm with her. He placed his hand on Librye's shoulder and rolled her towards the gate. 'You are this, Librye.'

She glanced at the children playing. 'You are just as extraordinary as all of those children. No one is better than anyone. No one is greater than anyone. They are just as beautiful, just as brave, just as intelligent. They are just like you. The only difference is, you are, Librye, but that makes them different too.' He crouched by her side. 'Librye, what you are, it doesn't matter. You could be fae, torb, Atlanti, faeman, puca. It doesn't matter, what matters is the choices you make. that makes us.'

Harris peered at the children in the grounds, playing. He thought he really should listen to his own advice.

'Can we go out there?' asked Librye.

'Of course, you're not a prisoner, tiny one.' Harris took her hand and guided her into the city.

A few days spent out in the city with Librye helped her feel less secluded. Regardless of what Harris, Maude, and Angus told her, she was different, and she still did not like it.

Waiting for Angus, Harris rested in Angus's chair. Two glasses sat on the desk in front. The end of council came, Harris could hear the outpouring of councillors as they left the hall for the evening. As the door opened, Harris remained with his head resting back.

'It isn't often I allow people to rest there.'

'I received a letter this morning, from the Sonnin border. It appears negotiations will be delayed,' said Harris. He rose from the chair, taking his own seat in the chair opposite.

'What makes you so sure?'

'Many things. I have a list if you'd care to join me.'

'I hope you have a solution to these many things.'

'Always,' replied Harris. 'First, I've directed the new Narra army south to intercept a large number of coblyn. We don't know where they're planning on going and dread to think what will happen when they get there. So far, they've passed twelve villages unharmed.'

'They could simply be travelling?'

'How naïve are you?' chuckled Harris.

'No, there is more. A Gaius Thorpe, a name I know well, leads them.'

'Who is he?'

'Gaius was one of the few I let live in Marrion. He doesn't know it, but I chose him. I believed he was one of the few I came across who could see sense of peace. Clearly, I was wrong. He now has an entire coblyn hoard at his disposal.'

Angus slowly sat. A glare caught his eye. 'What else?'

'Librye.' A depression hit the room. 'As her condition worsens, we need to make a serious plan. You may need to wait to marry Branwen, or bring it forwards. Leave her to take charge here while we go to Bourellis.' It tore him open to suggest such a thing.

'Librye is doing fine with what they sent.'

'For now, yes, but even Bushwell knows she hasn't long without serious help.'

'We will discuss this after we have decided the way this war is going. We cannot leave the council and Branwen to control an entire war effort alone.'

'No, but we cannot lose Librye.'

'What else?'

'Arktos, there has been talk of a marriage, Isradella, the daughter of Queen Fagora Fel Maya. She went missing, and it's believed that she has married Kairne. If this is true, he has rights to the throne of Arktos if Isradella's life is at risk, or if she has his child.'

'They are a kingdom to themselves,' — Angus reclined back — 'I remain away from Arktos. Madness surrounds the lands. I will not get involved and neither will we.'

'She was fourteen. She would be fifteen now.'

'Nobody actually knows how old she is. Harris, as I say, madness has taken that land. I know you would like to help, but have they asked for it?'

Harris shook his head. 'No.'

'They we do not get involved.'

'It's quiet in here, without Branwen.'

'I will use that silence to reflect. I suggest you do the same,' said Angus with a wide smile.

'I am still waiting to hear from Roe. Hopefully, any day now.'

A pattering rain kept Harris awake most of the night. The morning chorus remained silent in the woods. A lingering air outside was thick with the smell of leafy decay.

Staring at the ceiling, Harris did not want to get out of bed, sank into his pillow he remained plain faced. The thought of what Harelda was telling Branwen plagued him. Although he almost ended the war. He made the move to contact his mother. His life changed beyond compare. From dark and dusty ale-soaked taverns. To a lavish and comfortable palace.

Wandering from his bedchambers, Harris stepped directly into his chambers. Still with no boots on. He sat by his desk and plucked through the letters which the early morning carriers left. He reached over towards one which caught his attention, a green wax seal with the emblem of an eagle.

'Horace!' He excitedly grabbed the letter. He shot from his desk and pounded down the stairs. Running to Angus's chambers, he burst in. Flailing the letter in the air, he wore a wide smile.

'We have it!' he exclaimed. 'Roe is officially ours.' He slammed the letter onto Angus's desk.

Angus's wide smile grew. He gazed towards Harris. 'Harris, you never fail to please me,' his voice broke with excitement. 'I can't wait to tell Branwen. She's mentioned it a few times. She returns today.'

Harris dropped his excitement. He swayed by the desk, unable to settle. 'Well, anyway,' — he wobbled his head, — 'the war is over, now we await the official letter of surrender.'

Angus's eyes twisted. 'Let's just hope they send it.'

Harris made his way towards the galleries. Taking the letter with him. It had been a while since he had visited.

'The war is over!' He made his way through the hall. 'Roe is ours!' The council left their rooms towards the council hall. They glared at him. Whispers and talk of the victory filled the hall. They mixed hope with talk of concern.

The galleries were as lively as ever. Harris stepped in with his arms out to his side.

'They did it. Roe is officially ours.' He glanced at Gethen, stood at his bench, chopping carrots.

'Did they send a surrender?' He spun to see Harris. 'Where are your shoes?'

Harris walked towards him; the flagstone floor was cold but comfortable. 'I don't care,' — he laughed, —— 'they haven't sent it yet, but now it's a matter of days.'

'So, you've proven your worth.' Rebecca sauntered past with a basket of mushrooms. 'What now, commander? Are you still needed here?'

'I'm always needed,' replied Harris. 'Many people need me, but usually not the right ones.'

'Well, may I be one of the first to congratulate you on your victory, Commander?' Gethen's smile widened as he came towards Harris.

'I didn't win it. It isn't my victory. I simply tried. It was the victory of Commander Horace, and his army, not me,' he insisted.

Making his way from the kitchen, Harris bounced, stepping through the hall. The fountain felt more welcoming that day. The hall brighter, the world grew kinder. Walking through the palace hall. Branwen returned from Sonnin. Harris forgot himself. He marched towards her, but she thundered towards him. Her face was a picture of fury.

'How could you?' she screamed.

She gave a harsh slap around his face, forcing an audible, 'Ooh!' from several of the guards.

'My mother, Harris!' she screamed.

'You're causing a scene,' Harris whispered. 'Whilst I know you're angry, I deserve everything you need to throw at me. Here is not the place.' He widened his deep green eyes. Her face melted. Her eyes glared around the room. A few of the councillors froze at the door, having seen the harsh slap to his face. 'My tower.'

He led the way through the east corridor. The silence between them left an ice-cold trail as she followed him into his chambers. Harris twisted in his chambers to face her. He gave a look of sadness.

'Apologies.'

'That is all you have to say?' She could not catch her breath through anger.

'It's all I can say. She came into my room while I slept, and I'm weak.' He shrugged his shoulders and tried to defend himself.

Her mouth curled down, and eyes widened. Her voice was deep and low. 'A weak man would've said no, even to a queen.'

'I am weaker than weak then!' He flailed his arm up and twisted to his desk. 'On the bright side, Roe is ours again.'

'I couldn't give a shit, Harris. She is my mother!' Her eyes widened more, following him towards the desk. 'You asked me once if I love Angus.' She came closer to him. Harris twisted. He placed his hands on the desk at the back of him. 'I'll ask you the same. Do you love her?'

'Of course not!' blasted Harris. He twisted his head away.

'Come on, Bran, you're just like her. I tried to say no to you, but you wouldn't take that. I couldn't say no to her. She's a queen. You're more alike than you realise.'

'My mother, Harris, you could've said no.'

'To a queen? Yes, maybe I could, maybe I should have, but I didn't. We can never be us. What happened then and what happened here? It's gone, Bran. Accept it and move on. She's a grown woman, she can make her own mistakes, me being one of them.'

Maple crept from Harris's bedchambers, having collected some laundry. 'You realise that if someone says no, that is breaking the law if you go ahead with it?'

Branwen stopped, giving a few fast breaths. 'Your secrets are safe with me, but I can warn you both. If this gets out, and anything happens to Harris, I will be there to give my side.' She sauntered towards Branwen. 'Men are weak, if a man says no that is the only strength they have, they have no power over their bodies after that, what you did, Branwen, what your mother did, could see you both in Offenmoor, with my account.'

'Maple, I appreciate you, but that won't be needed,' said Harris, calming his anger.

'Apologies, Maple,' whispered Branwen. 'I am simply defending my mother.'

'Were your mother someone else, I would be stupid enough to believe you. Your mother does not need defending.'

Branwen watched as Maple left towards the stairs. She turned to Harris. 'I loved you once, Harris,' she whispered. 'I gave myself to the man I love, but he is dead to me now.'

His role fulfilled, but his life broken. He awaited the letter of surrender, which never arrived.

The tower was turning to a place of cold reminders. It had been less than a year since arriving in Cronnin. In less than a year, he ended all battles across Cammbour. His pride was in tatters. Rumours died within the palace. All talk of Harris and Harelda lasted less than a turn, but to Branwen, their relations ruined her.

With the palace settled, Branwen and Harris remained apart. Angus had not noticed the downfall of his friends.

Harris settled at his desk. Searching through papers. He woke well before the dawn. A chirping of birds softly began permeating his windows. Looking at the fresh light blue and cream paint on his walls, his eyes drifted towards Librye's secret door.

A blood shuddering scream woke the rest of the early morning palace. Angus shot from his desk. Harris pounded down the stairs. Branwen hurried from her chambers. Maude and Maple pelted from the galleries. Librye continued screaming.

Harris was the first to arrive at Librye's door. He burst into the chambers. Two guards stood by Librye's bed, trying to calm her. Harris ran to the bed. She clung to his arm. Panicked, he glared at Angus and Branwen as they thundered through the door.

'What happened?' Harris held Librye back.

Librye's lip trembled. Terrified of the secret she had been told. Her eyes poured with tears. Angus and Branwen stood by the foot of the bed. Slowly, Librye glanced up to Harris, clinging to his arm. Her nails marked his skin. She glared forwards.

'They took them all,' she whispered. Librye closed her eyes. 'I did this once for Angus,' — her eyes opened, she stared into Harris's frightened eyes, — 'Forgive me.'

Harris furrowed his brow. A flash of white took him off his feet. Falling by the side of the bed, Harris saw a completely different scene.

A dark night settled over the sleepy temple town of Ossenlaw. The sacred land dedicated to serving the gods. The sharmas and priests, alchemist and druids continued their night of serving.

'Librye, where are we?' panicked Harris as he looked to the side of him.

'I need you to see this,' she sobbed, clinging to his hand. 'I need you to see what you've done.'

Her soft voice made his spine shiver. As he looked to the distant, misty mountains. A mist drifted towards them from the south. The sound of heavy rumbling followed.

Screaming from Tyrone echoed through the mountains.

Harris spun in the temple town. The skies rumbled as he struggled to make sense of it all.

'Librye, where are we?' he yelled.

'Tyrone is just over those mountains. They took that this morning.'

Her ghostly reply sent a shock of ice through his blood. 'Ossenlaw?' He narrowed his eyes as he looked at her for answers. Her arm raised, a single finger pointed towards the mountains. A pouring of grey spilt down the side.

Mere moments passed. The coblyn hoard came in their fury.

Gaius led them. Spinning to face Gaius, Harris stood, sickened.

'They want war. We'll give them war,' groaned Gaius. Screams echoed around the fields. The temples rang with blood-chilling screeching.

'Why?' whispered Harris. He came close to Gaius, realising he couldn't even see him. 'Why?' he screamed!

Daniel stood by the side of Gaius. 'I can honestly say this will impress him. Even Kairne doesn't have the bollocks for this.'

They watched, grimacing, as three coblyn dragged a woman from a temple. Still screaming, they dragged her down the path to the temple. She held her innards in her hands.

'You bastard,' Harris whimpered. 'Bastard!' He fell to his knees.

Librye stepped to the side of him, placing her hand on his shoulder.

'I did this for Angus, to stop him from making a mistake. If only I knew before, I could've shown you.'

Harris lifted his tear-filled face. He opened his mouth, but winced as the screams took over.

'At least this gets a message across. If Bearwood wants to involve the gods, I will kill them as well.'

'Harris, I have to tell you, they are taking some to Crede.' Harris fell further forwards, wounded by her words.

He slowly turned to face the temple town. Still on the ground, a river of blood took over the drains on the side of the path. The screams deafened him. Coblyn feasted on the flesh of the dead and still dying.

Raging fires from the temples turned day into night. Harris knew that the Atlanti fury caught the temple daughters of Harelda, Sirrona, Olwen, Sulis and Brighid.

'They took them all, and this is my fault,' said Harris, his voice hushed in the calming temple town, as chaos rushed by him.

'What now?' Librye reached out, holding his hand.

He shook his head. Looking into her eyes gave him the only peace he needed. She did not hate him, and that mattered more than the hate he had for himself.

'Don't know.'

'You didn't do this, Harris, you need to know you didn't make that decision for Gaius. You tried to make it easy for everyone, but the easy way out, it's never the best way.'

Harris looked at the chaos of the field as it slowly died to a dull wisp of suffering. Shadows of the coblyn crept around empty corners. Librye remained at his side.

'The Atlanti took them, Harris, not you, your hand did not do this.'

Harris stood in the dark gloom of a temple. A storm overhead brewed, casting a menacing shadow on his face.

'No, but it can destroy those who did.'

It is not the end.

Buir
Nean
Greendia
Aenlic
Wic
Scooer
Saed
Bara
Bieredh
Fruma

BOUND BY BLOOD SERIES

Legend of the Shadows
Into the Shadows
The Brotherhood
The Promised King
Annihilation
The Age of Oakwood
Dawn of Ages

www.aejohnson.online

Twitter - @duchessgrim
Facebook @duchessgrimdark
TikTok @duchessgrimdark
Instagram @duchessgrimdark

Follow for many more updates.

ACKNOWLEDGEMENTS

A noble lady once said, 'Don't hold that one back. She'll be a writer one day.' She directed those words towards a six-year-old. Words of wisdom, indeed.

In a world surrounded by such support, how could I ever feel alone. My deepest gratitude to Malcolm Burton and Kath Barber, who, despite having all the reasons to, never gave up on me. Pushing me to my very limit while allowing me to become the wild child many know me as today.

My dedicated husband, Phill, to whom I owe everything. Thanking you would seem like a drop in the ocean for the years of support you have shown me.

My children, meh, thank you for not allowing me to complete this 5 years ago, I guess.

My ever-growing community of supporters, as well as the customers who I call friends. Thank you for your encouragement and support.

Feed an author, leave a review.

I've often referred to reviews as authors crack, they really are that addictive without the obvious side affects, or effects, whatever, give an author some crack, and please leave a review. We need that shit.

Printed in Great Britain
by Amazon

28414988R00240